Immortal Born

LYNSAY SANDS

First published in Great Britain in 2019 by Gollancz
an imprint of the Orion Publishing Group Ltd
Carmelite House, 50 Victoria Embankment
London EC4Y 0DZ

An Hachette UK Company

1 3 5 7 9 10 8 6 4 2

A CIP catalogue record for this book is
available from the British Library.

ISBN (Mass Market Paperback) 978 1 473 22536 7
ISBN (ebook) 978 1 473 22537 4

Printed and bound in Great Britain by Clays Ltd, Elcograf S.p.A.

www.lynsaysands.net
www.orionbooks.co.uk

Prologue

Allie was curled up on the couch in front of a rerun of *The Big Bang Theory*, slurping down a late dinner of ramen noodles, when the knock sounded at her front door. Her lips immediately slid into a smile. It was nearly midnight and there was only one person she knew who was likely to be up this late. Stella, her neighbor from across the street, was a night owl like herself, but she was also a new mother.

Setting her noodles on the coffee table, Allie scooted off the couch and hurried to the door. It was mid-February, had been snowing most of the day, and was freezing cold outside. Too cold to be standing on a doorstep with a month-old baby.

"Oh, good, you're still up!" the petite brunette greeted her cheerfully when Allie opened the door.

"As usual," Allie said with amusement, automatically

backing up when Stella started forward. "I'm nearly done with the project, so knocked off early."

"And probably want to relax now," Stella said with an apologetic smile as she shifted a bundled-up baby Liam to cradle him in one arm so she could push the door shut behind her. "Well, I won't bother you long." Gesturing to the bag dangling from the wrist of the arm holding Liam, she added, "I just realized that I forgot to drop this off earlier today and thought you might like—" Her cheerful chatter and smile died the moment the door thunked shut. Expression suddenly grim, she whipped the receiving blanket off of little Liam and held him out. "You have to take him."

Allie's eyes widened, but she took the baby and pressed him to her own chest. The moment she did, Stella tugged a doll out of the bag and began to wrap the receiving blanket around it as Liam had been wrapped in it just moments ago. Allie watched her with concern, but before she could ask what was going on, Stella announced, "They've found me."

Allie's arms tightened protectively around Liam, her concern turning to all-out fear. "What happened?"

"Nothing . . . Yet," she added quietly. "I spotted them following me on my way home from the coffee shop."

"So you came here."

"Just to leave Liam with you," Stella assured her. "Now I'm going to lead them away to keep you both safe." Finished with the wrappings, she set the doll on Allie's hall table and reached up to remove the heart-shaped locket she always wore. She met Allie's gaze and asked solemnly, "You'll keep your promise and take care of him?"

"Yes, of course."

"Thank you," Stella breathed, and then quickly moved around behind her to put the necklace over her head. "This has a picture of Liam's father and me. Someday, when he's old enough to understand, show him the picture and explain. Tell him I loved him more than anything. Don't let him forget me."

"No, of course I won't," Allie murmured, peering down at the locket where it rested against her breast next to Liam's small, warm body. Frowning, she glanced up to see that Stella had reclaimed the swaddled doll and was settling it against her chest much as she had held Liam on arriving. Biting her lip, Allie eyed her friend with concern. "Stella—"

"I'm sure everything will be fine. This is just in case," Stella interrupted her, and then managed a smile. "Thank you . . . for being my friend and for loving Liam."

"I—" Allie's mouth closed on the words she'd wanted to say. Stella was already gone. Allie stared at the closed door briefly, startled anew at the incredible speed the woman sometimes displayed. She shifted Liam to cradle him in one arm as she moved to the door and tugged the edge of the blind aside just enough to peek out. She noted Stella cooing to the "baby" as she laid it in Liam's waiting carriage on the sidewalk in front of her porch, but then she scanned the street, searching for someone out of place or watching Stella. She didn't see anyone, but it was dark. An army of men could be hiding out there among the row of town houses and she probably wouldn't see them.

Biting her lip, Allie shifted her gaze back to Stella as the woman finished settling the "baby" and started pushing the carriage down the snow-covered sidewalk.

"I should have cleaned the walk again when I finished work," Allie muttered to herself with self-recrimination. She had pulled out the snow blower and cleaned the sidewalk that afternoon, but it had continued to snow after that and there were a couple of inches of the white stuff out there. Not a crazy amount, but enough to make pushing a baby carriage a bit of a trial. Not that Stella appeared to be having trouble, Allie noted. But Stella was a lot stronger than the average woman.

Despite the hour and lack of traffic, Stella paused to check both ways before crossing the road and making her way to her own town house. Stella then scooped up the "baby" and mounted the steps to her small porch. Allie watched her unlock the door and step inside. The door was just starting to swing shut behind her when the explosion happened.

The sound was deafening, and Allie felt the floor vibrate under her feet as the building across the street shuddered. Its windows shattered, glass flying as flames roared out of them with a stunning fury before receding back inside.

"Don't worry. I'm sure she got out the back with that crazy speed of hers," Allie whispered when Liam began to fuss in her arms as if he had seen and understood what had just happened. The words had barely left her lips when Stella reappeared in the still-open door of the burning town house. The fake Liam was still clutched to her chest and her body was cloaked in fire. Stella stood there briefly, obscured by the flames shrouding her, and then turned back into the house and collapsed into the blaze.

Allie stared at the burning entrance to the woman's house for a long time. She had no idea what she was waiting for. Perhaps for Stella to reappear and wave to let her know everything was all right. But that didn't happen, and finally, she made herself release the edge of the blind so it blocked the burning house from view.

Swallowing thickly, Allie looked down at the baby in her arms. The promise Stella had mentioned was to raise and keep Liam safe if anything happened to her. Stella hadn't been specific on what that something might be, but dying in a fiery explosion would fall into that category.

"Dear God," Allie breathed, staring down at the little orphan in her arms. She now had a baby to care for and keep safe. Her, Allison Chambers—a thirty-year-old single woman with no children of her own, or any likelihood of ever having them—was now a . . . mother? Foster mother? Adoptive mother? She didn't know what she was except that she was responsible for the child in her arms . . . And she didn't know a thing about babies. She knew even less about raising vampire babies. What the hell was she supposed to do?

One

Magnus stepped out of the plane and stopped abruptly on the steps, his fingers tightening around the handle of his suitcase as a frigid north wind blasted over him. It was cold enough to steal his breath away and had him briefly wishing he could turn around, reseat himself on the plane, and demand to be taken home to the UK. Then he spotted the SUV pulling onto the private landing strip.

Straightening his shoulders, Magnus ducked his head and quickly descended the stairs to the tarmac, leaning into the frigid, roaring wind to do so. He was resolved to staying. He hadn't flown all the way here from England just to turn tail at the first chill breeze and fly back home without collecting the woman he'd come for.

"What did you do? Check the weather forecast for

the coldest time of year to arrive and book the flight for then?"

Magnus lifted his head at that shouted comment to see that the SUV had pulled to a halt just a few feet in front of him, and a young dark-haired male had got out on the driver's side to rush around to him.

"Tybo," he greeted mildly, giving up his suitcase when the younger man reached for it. "It is a bit brisk."

"Brisk, my ass. It's freezing." Tybo shouted to be heard over the wind as he stowed the suitcase in the back of the SUV. Closing the door then, he hurried around to the driver's side, adding, "I'll be surprised if the pilot can take off now he's here. His wings probably have ice on them already."

Magnus merely grunted and slid into the front passenger seat, eager to enjoy the waiting warmth.

"How was the flight?" Tybo asked, fiddling with buttons and knobs to adjust the heat.

"Uneventful. I slept most of the way," Magnus admitted as the younger man put the heat on full blast, sending a rush of warm air over him.

"Good. You're all rested up, then, and ready to go," Tybo muttered as he shifted the vehicle into gear and pulled a U-turn on the landing strip.

"To go?" Magnus asked, eyes narrowing. "The only place I am going is to Marguerite Argeneau Notte's. I was told you would take me there."

"Well, as it turns out, Marguerite came to collect you herself," Tybo informed him.

"Then why are you driving past the house toward the gates?" Magnus asked, turning his head to stare at the Enforcer house as they passed it.

"Well, see, as I said, Marguerite came over to get you, and while waiting, she happened to be chatting to myself and Sam about your life mate—"

"Possible life mate," Magnus corrected, mostly for his own benefit. He was trying to keep from getting too excited until he knew things would work out. He'd lived a long time and for most of that time had longed for a mate. Getting his hopes up only to have them be crushed would be unbearable. It was better he hold on to a "wait and see" attitude.

Tybo grunted, but continued. "Mortimer came into the kitchen where we were talking, just in time to hear her name was Allison Chambers."

"Allie," Magnus corrected. "Marguerite says she prefers Allie."

"Right. Allie. Anyway, it seems he'd just heard on the police radio that an Allison Chambers had been arrested for robbing a blood bank and he was going to send—"

"What?" Magnus interrupted with horror. "My Allie robbed a blood bank?"

"Yes. Well, we're quite sure it was your Allie. It's the blood bank where she works. Mortimer was going to send Valerian and me to the hospital to see if this robbery was immortal related or not, but once he realized she was your life mate—"

"She robbed a blood bank?" Magnus repeated, still stuck on the fact that she'd robbed anything. Then

Tybo's latest words sank in and he asked with alarm, "Why the hospital? Was she hurt?"

"Mortimer wasn't sure why the police took her to the hospital. You know that officers only radio in the bare basics."

Magnus scowled at the lack of information, now worried that his possible life mate might be injured, or even dying. That would be just his luck. Find a life mate just as she died.

"So, we're going to the hospital to find out what's what," Tybo finished solemnly.

Magnus nodded and then shook his head. "Why the devil would she rob a blood bank? Marguerite said she was mortal."

Tybo shrugged. "That's something Mortimer wants us to find out. If she was actually robbing the place," he added meaningfully. "I mean, she works there, after all. Maybe the police made a mistake."

"So you're saying this was all a big mistake?"

Allie ignored the dry skepticism in the older police officer's tone and focused her attention on the much more sympathetic younger officer as she answered, "Well, it is if you think I was breaking and entering the blood bank. I didn't break in. I have keys," she pointed out. "I work there."

"And you just went there to move some product. At eleven o'clock at night?" the older officer asked dubiously.

Allie nodded firmly. "I needed to move some blood pegged for the hospital to the proper refrigerator. I forgot to do it before I left earlier today."

"And you thought this was a good idea at *eleven o'clock at night*?"

Allie shrugged. "That's when I left the party and thought of it." Offering a wry smile, she added, "Mind you, I'd been drinking, so my judgment might have been off. Still, I didn't want my boss to have to do it in the morning. She's older and her arthritis has been acting up."

She paused to eye both men to see how they were accepting what she'd said. "Besides, what would I steal from the blood bank? There's no money or drugs or anything there. All there is in the place is blood. Who would steal blood?"

Much to her relief, that seemed to be a convincing argument since the younger officer nodded as if what she'd said made sense, and the skepticism on the older officer's face eased considerably. Then the older one asked, "And your outfit?"

Allie glanced down at the black jeans and black blouse she was wearing, but knew it was really the black cat mask that they were talking about. Fortunately, at the last minute she'd thought to add it just in case something unexpected happened and she got caught. Thank goodness, since she'd fainted midway through the ordeal, and cracked her head on the hard tile floor when she fell. She'd apparently been found by one of the cleaners when they arrived at midnight. Which is how she'd found herself waking up here in the emergency department of the hospital with a doctor and these two officers staring down at her, full of questions.

"It was a costume party," she said now, giving the excuse she'd come up with ahead of time. "I went as a cat . . . not a cat burglar." She added that last bit with a quirky smile and silently prayed they'd buy her excuse. Noting the way the younger officer's lips twitched, Allie felt sure she was convincing them. "I must have left my ears at the party. They were on a headband and it was kind of tight. Started to give me a headache as the night went on. Or maybe that was the booze," she added, although she hadn't had a single drink tonight. It was better they think she was a tipsy idiot than a blood-stealing fiend. She simply couldn't go to jail. Who would watch Liam?

Allie fretted about that as she waited for the policemen to make up their minds about her. What would happen to her son if she went to jail?

"All right."

Allie glanced up quickly at those words from the older officer.

"This is obviously a case of . . ." He grimaced and shook his head. "I'm not even sure what you'd call it besides bad judgment under the influence. In future, ma'am, when going to parties where you intend to drink, leave your work keys at home. Hopefully that will prevent something like this from happening again."

"*If* she's allowed to keep her work keys," the younger officer commented, and gave her a sympathetic look as he explained, "We had to call your supervisor and

tell her what happened. She was on her way to the
blood bank to check out the situation and calm the
cleaning staff."

"Yeah," the older man grunted. "Finding you unconscious on the floor in that get-up and surrounded by
a pool of blood gave the cleaning crew quite a scare."

"Oh, no! Some of the blood bags burst?" Allie
asked, dismayed at the thought of the waste. Blood
banks were always struggling to keep up with the
need for blood by hospitals and such.

"No. The bags were fine. The blood was from your
head wound," the old guy said grimly. "You took quite
a knock as you fell."

"Oh," Allie sighed, and instinctively reached up
to touch her head, encountering cloth there she supposed was bandages. She'd fainted in the middle
of the robbery. Her dizziness had come on quickly.
She'd been a little weak, but fine up until then, but
as she was carrying a box of the bags of blood across
the room everything had suddenly started to spin
and then the floor had come up to meet her. Apparently, she'd hit her head as she fell. Great. She'd lost
more blood.

"Well." The older officer shifted and closed the
notepad he'd been jotting in since she woke up. "We'll
head out and let them get you settled in a room."

"A room?" she asked with alarm.

"The doctor said they want to keep you twenty-four
hours for observation," the younger officer said gently.
"You really took a bad blow when your head hit the
floor. Skull meeting hard tile is dangerous. They want

to make sure all is well. No swelling on the brain or anything."

"But we'll expect you down at the police station when they release you tomorrow," the older officer said sternly. "You'll need to sign the paperwork this little jaunt of yours has caused."

"Yes, of course," Allie murmured, but knew she really couldn't stay. Liam was special. He couldn't be left alone for long.

"Officer Mannly?"

The older patrolman turned at that soft enquiry and smiled at the young nurse who had appeared at the opening in the curtain. "Yes?"

"There are two detectives talking to Dr. Whitehead. I think they're here about Ms. Chambers, so I thought I'd give you a heads-up."

"Detectives, huh?" Mannly said with disgust. "Thanks. We'll go head them off and tell them they wasted a trip."

When the nurse nodded and slipped away, he turned back to smile crookedly at Allie. "Get some rest. But don't forget to come to the station tomorrow. And maybe without the cat costume."

"Yes." Allie managed a smile and murmured, "Thank you," as the men slid through the opening in the curtain and out of sight, but her mind was on how to get out of there. Surely the hospital couldn't hold her if she wanted to leave? She wasn't under arrest. Thank God.

Deciding to just slip out to avoid any hassle, Allie slid off the gurney she'd awoken on, and then had to stop and grab at it to steady herself when the world wobbled around her. It was a full minute before the floor stopped moving, and then she released a small sigh and shuffled to the opening in the curtain. She was in bad shape, worse than she'd ever been. Allie loved Liam to bits, but that love was killing her.

Pushing that thought away for now, she paused and peered out. There were several doctors and nurses bustling around, moving from one curtained-off area to another. There were also two tall men all in black talking to the doctor who had treated her. One of the men was dressed in black leather pants, a black T-shirt, and a heavy black leather coat. The other was in a black suit and long coat. The detectives, Allie supposed as she watched Officer Mannly and his partner approach them.

Allie started to shift her attention away when a flash of silver caught her eye. It wasn't from a wristwatch, or a ring one of the two detectives was wearing, but from their eyes. Her blood ran cold when she saw the metallic glitter in their depths. When one of the two new men then looked her way, she quickly ducked behind the curtain, her heart racing and the world wobbling again.

Allie forced herself to take a couple of deep breaths to steady herself. She was seriously low on blood at the moment. If she were a car they'd say she was running on fumes. At least, that's how it felt. It was what had precipitated this risky and ridiculous venture of robbing the blood bank. It was also going to slow her down. But she needed to get out of there. And without those two "detectives" seeing her.

Allie considered her options and then crossed the small curtained-off room to the opposite side. There, she dropped to her knees and peered under the curtains. Not spotting any feet moving around in the next curtained-off area, she crawled quickly under. There was someone on the gurney here, but they were curled up on their side, clutching their stomach with their eyes squeezed closed in pain.

Thinking that was fortuitous, Allie quickly scrambled around the gurney to the opposite side. Still on all fours, she paused to check this new area. Here, there were feet and legs in white shoes and pants. Fortunately, even as she spotted them, they turned from the gurney and moved out of the curtained area. The moment they did, Allie crawled under the curtain here too and scrambled toward the opposite side.

"Hello?" The question was part surprise and part dismay from the gurney. The voice sounded like an old woman's, but Allie didn't glance around to see if her guess was right. She merely muttered, "Hello, sorry," and scrambled out the other side of the curtained area where she climbed carefully to her feet. It was the end of the examination rooms, if you could call curtained-off areas that. This was a small alcove with cupboards and a sink right next to a door that she suspected led to the rest of the hospital and other exits. She moved to the end of the uncurtained alcove and risked a peek out.

The doctor had moved away from the two detectives

and they were now talking to the police officers. The detectives' expressions were oddly concentrated. The sight merely made her more determined than ever to leave as quickly as she could. She needed to get home, grab Liam and the Go bags she always kept packed, and get the hell out of Toronto. She'd hoped the city would allow them to stay lost longer, and it had seemed to work. They'd managed to stay here for four months instead of the usual two or three, but they'd been found again and it was time to move.

The very idea was a depressing one to Allie. She was exhausted in body, heart, and mind and just wanted to curl up and sleep for a week . . . or maybe a year. But she didn't have that option. She just had to suck it up and keep moving. For Liam.

"So, we have handled the police and the doctors," Magnus murmured as the police officers moved away, their memories of the events surrounding Allie Chambers removed.

"Yeah." Tybo scanned the emergency area, no doubt checking the minds and memories of the nurses and doctors present to be sure they hadn't missed anyone. "Mortimer will have to send someone to erase any physical evidence. The 911 call and so on."

"Is that necessary? I didn't even think it was necessary to remove the events from the minds of the doctors and police. They all seemed to think it was just a mistake. That she was there for innocent purposes."

"But she's a possible life mate to you, Magnus, so that's a connection to us and we need to remove anything that connects to us."

"Of course," Magnus said quietly, knowing that was true. He should have realized that at once, but he was a little distracted at the prospect of meeting his life mate. A possible life mate, he reminded himself. Just because she might suit him didn't mean she would agree to become his life mate. Sighing, he straightened his shoulders. "So? We approach her now and get her out of here?"

"No."

Magnus turned on him sharply. "No?"

"I mean, we can't approach her," Tybo said with a grimace. "At least, not here. She left while we were dealing with the police officers."

"What?" Magnus asked with dismay. "What do you mean she left? Why did you not stop her?"

"Because I didn't want her causing a ruckus here after we'd worked so hard to erase everyone's memories," Tybo said soothingly. "But it's fine. We have her address. We'll just go to her home and you can . . ." He shrugged. "I don't know. Introduce yourself or something. Speaking of which, how did you plan to handle things?"

"I—" Magnus scowled. "Well, not like this. A seemingly accidental encounter, maybe. Something that appears random or natural, and then I would woo her."

"Woo?" Tybo grinned.

"What?" Magnus asked, his eyes narrowing.

"Nothing," the younger man said at once, but his

grin widened. "You're just showing your age. Wooing is kind of old school."

"The word or the activity?" Magnus asked with irritation.

"Both," Tybo decided, and then clapped a hand on his shoulder and used the hold to urge him toward the exit. "I'm afraid the accidental encounter thing is out. We need to find out what she was really up to tonight."

"We know what she was up to," Magnus pointed out as they exited the emergency area. "She was moving some blood she forgot to take care of before leaving work that day and—"

"Maybe," Tybo interrupted. "But we need to find out for sure."

"Of course we do," Magnus agreed wearily, but wasn't happy with the knowledge. He'd hoped to have a more natural introduction into her life. This was not going to be natural and could make things harder. But even hard was better than not having the chance. He'd waited a long time to meet his life mate. "So, we are going to her place?"

"Yeah," Tybo said, and then they both fell silent as they left the building and headed for the SUV. Neither of them actually spoke again until Tybo pulled into the parking lot of an apartment building some twenty minutes later. Turning off the engine, he then turned to Magnus. "How do you want to play this? I mean, I don't want to make this any harder for you than it has to be. You could wait in the car and I could go in alone, read her mind, and if everything is aboveboard, and she wasn't stealing blood, just leave and let you do your whole accidental encounter and wooing later."

"You would do that?" he asked with surprise.

"Sure," Tybo said, and then pointed out, "It's not like you'd be much help anyway. If she's a possible life mate you can't read or control her. So, really, if she wasn't stealing blood, it makes more sense for you to wait here so you can approach her without complications later."

Magnus nodded, but his attention had caught on two men moving through the darkness along the front of the building, half-hidden by the bushes that ran along it. He tensed when he noted the way their eyes glowed in the dark.

"So, I'll leave the car on and—"

"Allie lives on the first floor, does she not?" Magnus interrupted.

"Yes," Tybo said, sounding bewildered by the question.

"The front of the building?" Magnus asked.

"I don't know. I just know her apartment is 107."

"I am pretty sure she probably lives in the front," Magnus said grimly, reaching for his door handle.

"Why?"

"Because there are two immortals presently breaking into a ground-floor apartment," Magnus said grimly as he got out of the car.

Cursing, Tybo turned off the engine and followed.

Two

"Mommy!"

Allie pushed the door closed and forced a smile as she turned to watch her little boy race up the hall toward her. His dark hair was sleep-tousled and his Spider-Man pajamas rumpled.

"Liam," she breathed. Relieved to see he was alive and well and that at least one of her worries had been for nothing, she bent to hug him when he threw himself against her. "You should be napping."

"I woke up and you were gone," the boy complained, raising his head to glare at her accusingly.

"I know. I'm sorry. I didn't mean to be gone so long," she said apologetically, her eyes moving past him and up the hall. She needed to get their Go bags and get him out of there. Allie didn't know how long she had, but having vampires show up at the hospital looking into her wasn't a good thing. All the way home in the taxi she'd been terrified she'd arrive to find Liam gone and vampires waiting to kill or take her.

"What is this?"

She felt him plucking at the bandage around her head and shifted her attention to the boy. "Nothing," she assured him. "Now you need to go get your teddy bear while I grab our Go bags," she said, easing him away. "We need to leave."

"We're moving again?" the boy asked unhappily.

"Yes, honey. Right now. So go get your teddy or we'll have to leave him," she added firmly, giving him a push up the hall. She didn't miss the way his shoulders sagged at the news, or how miserable it obviously made him, but his safety was her first priority and they weren't safe here anymore.

Sighing, she stood and moved to the hall closet. Allie had just grabbed their Go bags and swung them over her shoulder when she heard Liam cry out in fear from his room. Panic seizing her, Allie rushed up the hall and through the living room, headed for the bedroom door. She never made it. She'd barely stepped into the living room when she was grabbed and restrained. The speed of her attacker told her she was dealing with a vampire. His strength backed it up, and then a second man strode out of the bedroom holding a limp Liam, his eyes aglow with golden fire.

"Why haven't you taken control of her?" Liam's captor asked with a scowl when he saw Allie struggling uselessly against the man holding her.

"I like it when they fight," the man holding her said with a laugh, and then stiffened, a gurgling sound coming from his throat. Allie hardly noticed that, though, or the fact that she was suddenly free. Her wide-eyed gaze was fixed on the man who had suddenly appeared behind Liam's captor and caught him around the neck. Liam was immediately dropped as the grubby man who had grabbed him turned to confront his own attacker.

"Liam!" Allie rushed to his side and helped the bewildered, but unharmed, boy up and out of the way of the battling men. She then urged him around her own captor and the man he was struggling with and toward the door.

Allie recognized their rescuers as the "detectives" from the hospital, but had no idea what was going on. She'd assumed on first seeing them that they were members of the vampire group that had been hunting her and Liam. But if that was the case, who were the two men who had just tried to grab them? And just how many damned vampires were out there? Allie had assumed, or at least hoped, that there was just the one group—the head vampire who had turned Stella and his minions. But obviously that wasn't the case. The problem was she had no idea what the case was. She wasn't willing to stop and ask questions, however. Her main concern was getting Liam out of there and to safety.

Tightly gripping the boy's hand, Allie hustled him out of the apartment and rushed him up the hall as fast as she could. At her strongest, Liam could have outrun her easily. Weak as she presently was, and weighed down by the Go bags, she was just holding him back, but there was nothing she could do about it. She was moving as quickly as she could.

They had just turned the corner out of the hallway and into the foyer when Allie was grabbed from behind again and dragged back around the corner they'd just rounded. This time she was caught around the waist and held more gently, her mouth covered so she couldn't scream. Even so, her panic was enough that she nearly didn't hear the man holding her whisper, "Their friends are out there. Look."

Blinking as his words registered, Allie peered around the corner, surprised when he allowed it. She stared silently at the three vehicles that had pulled up in front of her building. Men were piling out of them and moving toward the entry doors. They all looked grubby and most had long hair like the men who had first grabbed her and Liam in her apartment. She also noticed that their eyes were glowing slightly in the night as if reflecting the light like a cat's.

"Is there a back door in this building?"

Allie's attention was forced away from the men approaching the doors when the man holding her eased her back against his chest and turned with her toward the man who had asked the question. The man in black jeans was holding Liam like an affectionate uncle rather than a kidnapper, the boy settled on his hip and one arm around him to keep him from tumbling, but not really restraining him. Still, Allie hesitated. As far as she knew, all vampires were bad. Well, accept for Liam, of course, and his mom had been good too in the end.

"I'm Tybo and the guy behind you is Magnus," the vampire holding Liam announced. "We're the good guys. We hunt rogues like the two men in your apartment and the ones out front, but there are too many of them, so we need to slip you out of here as quickly and quietly as possible, and preferably unseen. Is there a back door to the building?"

Allie hesitated briefly, unsure whether to believe and trust these two vampires or not. But they *had* saved them from the first two in her apartment, and they did appear to want to get them away from the men even now probably trying the entry door, so she took a chance and pointed back the way they'd come. Allie found herself immediately scooped up by the man named Magnus.

They nearly flew down the hall. Allie wanted to protest at being carried like a child, but knew she couldn't move as fast as them, so forced herself to remain still in the arms of Magnus, the "detective" in the black suit and long coat. Who smelled ridiculously good, she noted, and immediately felt bad for noticing.

They'd nearly reached the end of the hall when Allie heard the crash of glass breaking behind them. Then Tybo pushed the emergency exit open and carried her precious boy outside. The door didn't even start to close before Magnus was passing through as well with her.

"We won't be able to get back to the SUV unseen." Tybo's voice was hushed as he paused to peer along the small paved laneway they'd come out on. It was just a track paved to allow the garbage trucks to come empty the building's big bins. Otherwise it was usually empty as it was now. They were standing between the back of the apartment building and a high fence that blocked it off from the business plaza beyond.

"Over the fence," Magnus ordered, and Allie watched with amazement as the man carrying Liam did just that. He took two running steps toward the eight-foot-high fence and then simply jumped over it like some Superman without the cape. He'd barely dropped out of sight on the other side of the fence with Liam when Magnus started forward.

Allie clutched at his shoulders, squeezed her eyes shut, and prayed as they suddenly launched into the air. She stayed like that until they landed on the other side of the fence with a jolt that rippled from his body to hers. When Magnus started running again, she opened her eyes to look around.

They were behind the plaza where deliveries were made to the individual stores, but the men were heading toward the end of it. She thought they'd run around the corner to the front of the stores. There were a couple of restaurants there where they could have sought haven, but instead they went to the back door of the last store with something or other Pizza on the sign. Allie wasn't sure what it read. She never had spare money for fast food anymore so had never paid attention to the name of the nearby pizza joint, and the men were moving too quickly for her to read it properly before the door was open and they were inside with warm air rushing over them.

"I'll see about getting us a ride," Tybo announced.

When the man holding her grunted in what she assumed was agreement, Tybo carried Liam off up the hall toward the noise and delicious smells of the kitchen.

"The boy is safe with Tybo."

Allie tore her concerned gaze away from the pair to peer at the man holding her. She quickly looked away again, though. Holding her as he was, his face was just inches from hers, his breath feathering her lips and cheeks when she'd faced him.

"You can put me down now," she said quietly, and after a small hesitation, Magnus bent slightly to set her on her feet.

"Thank you," Allie said, trying not to sound as relieved as she felt.

"You are welcome."

Allie glanced at him out of the corner of her eye and then turned toward where she could see Tybo talking to an aproned man in the entry to the kitchen. Her eyes slid anxiously to what she could see of Liam. Her son was leaning into Tybo with his little arms around his neck as if it were the most natural thing in the world. Allie frowned at the sight. Liam usually didn't take to strangers. Not that he met a lot of them, she supposed as she became aware that the Go bags were slipping and hefted them to a more secure position higher up her shoulder.

"Can I carry those for you?"

Glancing around to see Magnus's hand reaching for the straps of the Go bags, Allie instinctively jerked back a step and slapped his hand away. "No."

His eyes widened, but he let the matter go, and instead asked, "Who were those men in your apartment?"

The question brought surprise flashing over her face. "You tell me. They're vampires like you."

For some reason her words made him stiffen up like a soldier at attention. His words were just as stiff when he said, "I am an immortal. Not a vampire. And those men we stopped were nothing like me and Tybo. They are obviously rogues."

Allie frowned at this explanation and was going to ask what he meant when Tybo returned with Liam.

"Time to go," Tybo announced. "We're catching a ride with one of the delivery boys. He's pulling up out front. This way."

"Just a minute," Allie said with dismay, hurrying forward to grab the man's arm and drag Liam from him. Holding the boy tightly, she peered from one man to the other and then shook her head. "Thank you for your help, but we aren't going with you. Liam and I—"

"Will not survive more than ten minutes on your own," Magnus interrupted firmly. "We are your best bet, Allie. Tybo and I can get you to a safe house where you will be protected until we can find out what is happening and take care of this situation."

Allie scowled. "And I'm supposed to just take that on faith? I don't know you any better than the first two men who broke into my apartment."

"Magnus," Tybo said quietly. "We don't have time for this. I'm hoping those men will search the apartment building first. But there are enough of them that they can do that and still send a couple over to check the plaza. We need to move."

Allie eyed Tybo suspiciously. It sounded to her like he was asking for permission to do something.

She was sure she was right about that when Magnus gave a short, reluctant nod. When Tybo immediately turned a concentrated gaze on to her, Allie found herself turning and carrying Liam toward the front of the restaurant. It wasn't a choice. At least, not *her* choice, and she should have been panicked and horrified that she was doing something she didn't intend or want to do, but she was oddly calm and unaffected by it.

As if she'd been drugged was the unconcerned thought that floated through her head, but that didn't seem quite right. It was more as if her anxiety and worries were being veiled somehow so that she couldn't connect to them, and a sense of calm and serenity was being pumped through her in their place. Whatever the case, Allie carried Liam straight through the kitchen, and then the bright dining area with its white floors and plastic orange seats to the door and out to the car waiting there.

She got into the back seat, sliding along its length until she was crowded up against a stack of pizza warmers. Allie then settled Liam more comfortably in her lap while Magnus squeezed in next to her and Tybo got into the front passenger seat.

Allie was aware of Tybo pulling out a phone and talking to someone named Mortimer, but her own attention was on the parking lot around them, her eyes searching it for the men who had pulled up in front of her building. Much to her relief, she didn't see anyone before they were wheeling out of the plaza parking lot and onto the road.

"Mortimer's expecting us and is having Sam ready a room for Allie and Liam, as well as one for yourself, Magnus," Tybo announced.

Magnus tore his gaze away from Allie to peer at the younger immortal as he tucked his phone into a pocket of his jacket. Tybo had turned sideways in the front seat to talk to him, and now added, "He's also sending men to round up the rogues at the apartment if they're still there when they arrive. If not, they'll simply take care of the apartment and any video footage from the entry camera, if there is one, then collect our SUV."

Magnus grunted, his attention slipping back to Allie and Liam. The boy had curled up on her lap and fallen asleep with his head on her chest and she had dozed off with her head against the warming bags stacked next to her. While the boy had probably dozed off on his own, Magnus was quite sure Tybo was responsible for Allie's sleep. This situation certainly wouldn't normally put a woman to sleep, he was sure.

"She's extremely pale," Tybo commented from the front seat.

Magnus nodded, his eyes sliding over her classic features and pale skin. Her eyes were closed now, but he'd noticed they were hazel. Her hair was long and light brown, and while most would have said she was just pretty enough, she was the most beautiful woman in the world to him. His life mate, he thought, and then pointed out, "According to the officers who answered the 911 call, she had fallen and hit her head."

"She didn't fall," Tybo announced grimly. "She fainted . . . from lack of blood."

Magnus glanced at him sharply. "What?"

"She's been feeding the boy with her own blood for a good four years," Tybo announced, his concentrated gaze on her face as he found the information he was passing along. "She was trying to rob the blood bank out of desperation. Feeding the boy is killing her, literally. And she knows it. She was hoping to get him blood from the blood bank to give her system a chance to recover, and got a job there to make the theft easier."

Magnus turned his attention back to Allie, wishing he could read her thoughts so that Tybo didn't have to. He didn't like the other man poking through her head like this.

"Unfortunately," Tybo continued, "she passed out during the attempt . . . hitting her head and losing even more precious blood." Tybo shook his head. "At this point, she probably needs a blood transfusion herself. She's very weak, Magnus. Even asleep her heart rate is elevated and her breathing rapid and shallow."

Magnus frowned at this news and reached out to brush away a strand of hair that had fallen across her face. "Feeding a child as young as Liam should not be this detrimental to her health."

"No," Tybo murmured, and was silent for a moment, his gaze still on her, and then he said, "I think she's been letting him overfeed."

Magnus's eyebrows rose. Overfeeding the boy would mean that his system would use up a lot of blood trying to remove the extra blood from his system, which would just mean a need for more blood. It would be a vicious circle—the boy always hungry, always needing more blood. Unfortunately, more blood than one mortal could safely supply. If she'd continued like this much longer, it would have killed her. As it was, Allie was lucky she hadn't already suffered a heart attack or simply died from the blood loss. In effect, the boy was bleeding her to death.

"Who is the boy?" Magnus asked now. "How did she end up the mother to an immortal?"

Tybo was silent for so long that Magnus turned to look at him. The other man's expression was even more concentrated now as he sought an answer to that question, but it was another moment before he murmured, "Stella."

"Stella?" Magnus asked. "Is that the boy's mother?"

"I . . ." Tybo lost the concentrated look and rubbed his forehead with his thumb and fingers as if trying to ward off a headache as he murmured apologetically, "Her thoughts are very confused and almost veiled. It's as if she's so used to trying not to think about this stuff that even in sleep she's protecting her thoughts. All I could get was the name Stella."

"Blood loss can cause confusion," Magnus murmured, turning his gaze back to Allie. He stared at her silently, wishing she was awake to answer the questions he had, but knowing it was better to leave her sleeping until they got to the house. He suspected she would fight them about going to the house if they gave her the choice. It was better to get her there, reassure her that she was safe, and then ask the questions buzzing through his head.

Three

Allie was exhausted when she woke up. But that was normal for her lately. No matter how much she slept, it was never enough. She was always feeling tired and rung out. It was the blood loss, she knew. Liam needed too much of it and her body couldn't keep up. That was why she'd risked robbing the blood bank, a despicable action to her mind. Blood banks were always desperately in short supply and needing more. Even considering stealing some of the precious blood they needed so badly had made her feel lower than low. But Liam needed the blood and she couldn't supply what he needed. She was willing to die for the boy if necessary, but that would just leave him alone in a world that wouldn't be friendly to a child vampire. She had no doubt they'd kill him, or at the very least lock him up and perform examinations and tests on him that would make what little life he had a misery.

These thoughts had Allie pushing herself up to sit in the bed and swing her legs off of it. She needed to see what he was up to and—

Allie's thoughts fled, replaced with alarm as she realized she wasn't in her own bed in the apartment she'd sublet four months ago. Her gaze slid around the cool blue room revealed by the sunlight splashing through the windows, memories suddenly rushing into her mind. She remembered everything that had happened right up until they'd squealed out of the plaza parking lot in the pizza delivery car at what must have been nearly one o'clock in the morning. Everything was blank after that.

She'd probably fainted again, Allie decided grimly. That was the most likely scenario. She'd fainted from lack of blood. She certainly didn't think she could have just fallen asleep, not in the situation she'd been in. Fleeing one group of vampires in the company of another pair of them was hardly a sleep-inducing event. Being around vampires at all wasn't. As far as Allie knew, all vampires were bad. Although, frankly, she'd never imagined there was more than one group. Learning otherwise was more than a little alarming. Especially when Liam was no longer with her.

Mouth tightening, Allie started to rise, but settled back to sit on the side of the bed again when the room began to spin. Damn, this weakness was a nuisance. Especially right now, when she needed to find Liam and figure out where they were and what to do next. Then she spotted the Go bags next to the bed.

Hooking her foot through the straps of the larger

one, she dragged it closer and then bent carefully to pick it up. The damned thing felt ridiculously heavy, but Allie knew that was more to do with the shape she was in than with its actual weight. The thought made her mouth flatten with displeasure. Mostly because she used to be strong. Allie used to have a gym membership and a personal trainer who had put her through a strenuous routine of exercises that included lifting weights. She'd been lean and strong then. Now she was just scrawny and weak and she didn't like it. She needed to rebuild her strength. The problem was, she couldn't do that until she found a way to feed Liam that didn't include bleeding herself dry.

Pushing those thoughts aside for now, Allie unzipped the side flap of the Go bag and retrieved the hairspray and lighter she kept tucked there. The lighter went into the front pocket of her black jeans, the can of hairspray was tucked up the baggy sleeve of her black blouse, and then she set the bag aside, took a deep breath, and got slowly to her feet.

Much to her relief, this time the room didn't spin around her. Still, Allie waited a moment and took a couple more deep breaths before starting to walk toward the door, opposite the window, the one she suspected led out of the room.

She was right and it opened to a long hall painted a warm beige. A really long hall, Allie thought grimly as she stepped out and pulled the door closed. At least, at that moment, weak as she was and knowing she had to traverse it and then the stairs that she suspected the rail ahead protected . . . yeah, it looked miles long in that moment.

She headed toward the stairs, bracing one hand on the wall to steady herself just in case. Her legs were shaking by the time she reached the top of the stairs, but it didn't slow her much. She needed to get to Liam and see that he was all right.

Leaning heavily on the stair rail, Allie managed to stumble down the steps without falling or passing out, but once safely at the bottom, she had to pause again to catch her breath. She was panting as if she'd just run a marathon, and her heart was racing like crazy. It felt like it was going to burst. Actually, the state she was in was more than a little alarming, and for one moment, Allie was afraid it really would burst, or that she'd at least have a heart attack or something.

Grasping the cap of the newel post with one hand, she pressed the heel of her other hand to her chest as if that could stop the attack from happening, and just stood like that as she waited for her heart rate to slow. She didn't realize she was holding her breath until her heartbeat began to slow and she let the air escape her lungs in a long, slow sigh.

Raising her head then, Allie took in her surroundings. She was in an entry. Through the glass window in the door ahead of her she could see several vehicles parked on the driveway that ran along the front of the building, and a snowy yard beyond that. To her right she could see into what looked like an empty living room. To her left a doorway revealed a dining table and chairs and the end of white upper and lower cupboards. The kitchen was her guess. From where she stood, it looked as empty as the living room. Rather than waste the energy to verify both rooms were empty, Allie turned to peer along the hall that ran back past the stairs.

There were more doors this way. The end one on the right was open, and now that she wasn't breathing so hard, she could hear the murmur of voices coming from it, so released the newel cap and headed that way. The voices grew clearer with each step she took and Allie found herself stopping just short of the door as she listened to what was being said.

"By the time the men got to the apartment, it was empty," Mortimer announced, and Magnus tore his gaze away from the idyllic snowy scene out the window to look over his shoulder at the head of the North American Enforcers. Mortimer was seated at his desk, running his hands wearily through his hair. While Magnus had laid down to sleep after arriving at the house and setting Allie in the guest room, he knew the other man had been up all night, overseeing operations. It showed.

"I'm not surprised," Tybo said, sitting up in the seat he'd claimed on entering, one of two that faced Mortimer's desk. "The rogues were breaking into the front of the building as we carried Allie and Liam out the back. It wouldn't have taken them more than a minute to get to the apartment, find their comrades, see that Allison and Liam were gone, and move on to searching the surrounding area." Tybo shook his head as he thought on it. "The plaza with the pizza joint at the back of the apartment building was a stroke of good luck for us. There was no way we could have got to our SUV or even Allie's car without being spotted."

Magnus glanced to Tybo with surprise at that comment. "Her car was in the parking lot?"

"Yeah," Tybo answered, and then quirked his eyebrows in question. "Where else would it be?"

"I just assumed it would still be at the blood bank," Magnus admitted. "I mean, she went there to break in, was found unconscious, and taken to the hospital by the police or an ambulance."

"She didn't take her car to the blood bank. She took a taxi there, and then another one to get home from the hospital," Tybo informed him.

"What?" Magnus asked on a disbelieving laugh. "She took a taxi to a B and E?"

"Well, she had it drop her off down the street from the blood bank, not at the building itself," Tybo said, and explained, "There are cameras in the parking lot of the blood bank. The last thing she wanted was a visual record of her visit when they discovered the blood missing."

"Oh," Magnus said, but then shook his head. "Still, taking a taxi to break in to the blood bank? Did she plan to take one back home after? And how would she explain the blood she was carrying?"

"I presume she had a backpack or box she planned

to carry it in," Tybo said dryly. "And I doubt she'd have it marked 'stolen blood.'"

"Right," Magnus murmured, but was still amazed at the thought of taking a taxi to commit a felony. The woman had balls, that was certain.

"We probably got away in the pizza delivery car just moments or even seconds ahead of the rogues searching the plaza for us," Tybo commented now, his expression solemn.

They were all silent for a moment, pondering how close a call it had been. Magnus was an experienced soldier and could handle himself in a battle, but wasn't arrogant enough to think he could take on a dozen rogues with the help of just Tybo and come out unscathed. Especially when he would have been distracted with the need to keep Allie and Liam safe.

The silence in the room was pierced by the buzz of Mortimer's phone. The man glanced at it briefly and then announced, "Dani's left the hospital and is on her way."

Magnus nodded, knowing he was referring to Decker Argeneau Pimms's wife, Dani, who was a doctor. She'd been at the hospital handling an emergency when they'd called her last night. It seemed the emergency was finally resolved and she could now come examine Allie and be sure that she was all right.

"I will also have her take a look at the boy to be sure he's all right," Mortimer decided.

"The boy is fine." Magnus turned back to the window again to watch the trio playing in the snow outside.

"The *boy* is Liam. My son. Where is he?"

Magnus turned sharply at those words, his eyes widening as he found Allie standing in the office doorway. She looked a little better than she had when he'd laid her in the bed upstairs last night, but was still incredibly pale. She was also swaying slightly on her feet, he noted with concern.

"Where is my son?" Allie repeated grimly, her eyes sliding anxiously from man to man. "What have you done with him?"

Magnus was the first to recover from his shock, or perhaps Tybo and Mortimer were merely leaving him to deal with Allie since she was his possible life mate, but whatever the case, he was the first to speak.

"Liam is fine." Magnus crossed quickly to her side, intent on reaching her before she fainted or passed out again. The woman's lips already had a slightly blue tinge denoting a lack of oxygen, a sure sign that her blood levels were low. "He is safe and well. You are both safe now. No one can get to you here."

"But where is he?" she growled with frustration.

"He's outside playing with—"

"Outside?" The word was a bare breath of horror.

"Yes," Magnus said, confused by her upset.

"But he can't be outside. It's daytime," she protested, and whirled to leave the room, only to stagger as the swift movement set her off balance.

Magnus caught her at once, sweeping her off her feet to keep her from falling. He then carried her quickly to the window and set her down in front of it.

"Look. He is fine," he said, pointing out the window.

Allie stared out the window, her eyes widening as she took in the scene playing out before her. Liam—in his secondhand, gray, and slightly grubby coat—and another boy who looked to be about the same age, but in a bright red obviously new coat, were trudging through the snow side by side, pushing a large boulder of snow ahead of them as a blonde woman in a white winter coat and a white knitted hat cheered them on. The woman was smiling as she watched the boys laugh and chatter as they moved across the yard one way and then another so that their boulder of snow stayed round as it grew in size, but finally they rolled it to a second, even larger boulder of snow and worked together to lift the new ball on top of the first. The boulder was easily the size of the boys themselves. She was sure it would have taken two normal adults to lift it, but the two little boys raised it like it weighed nothing and it was simply the awkward size that forced them to work together.

Once they had it settled on the larger boulder, they began to pack snow around where the boulders met to ensure it didn't fall off.

"A snowman," Allie breathed. Liam and the other boy were making a snowman. The first one he'd ever made, she realized, and felt her heart squeeze with regret. They didn't lead a life where Liam could enjoy the things a normal child did. There had been no friends for him or even any real playing. Their life the last four years had been endless running, moving from town to town, city to city, one new address after another, usually having to leave everything behind and start anew each time. Liam had never complained at losing his toys or favorite blanket with each move.

Of course, he'd been a baby at first, and then a toddler, but he was growing fast. Really, he'd been a wonderful son, but much too solemn and quiet, she realized now. She had never seen Liam like this. He was positively beaming with pleasure, and he was laughing, his face glowing with joy. His life should have been like this every day, Allie thought, and suddenly felt like she'd failed Stella horribly.

But she'd done the best she could, Allie argued with her guilt. She'd fed him, clothed him, protected him. And how could she allow him to play? She'd lived with the constant fear of his being taken. Besides, vampires couldn't go out in the sun. The thought made her frown and she asked, "How can he be outside?"

Magnus peered down at her blankly when she turned on him with the question. After a moment, he shrugged helplessly. "It is what children do. They play outside."

"Yes, but it's daytime. The sun is up," she pointed out, and peered worriedly back to Liam, searching his face for any hint that he might be about to burst into flames. That was what happened to vampires in all the movies when they were touched by sunlight. But other than a nose gone a bit red from the cold, Liam seemed fine.

"He will not burst into flames under the sun. The boy is an immortal, not one of your mythical vampires."

Those words came from behind them and Allie turned to peer at the man who had spoken. Standing in the doorway of the room was a tall stranger with hair so fair it was almost white, and ice-blue eyes as cold as she imagined the snow outside must be.

While Magnus still appeared relaxed at her side, the other two men in the room were now sitting up as if at attention. She supposed that meant the newcomer was someone important. Not that he seemed to notice their reactions. His attention was focused wholly on her. In fact, he was peering at her with a concentration that irritated her, and a displeasure that seemed to suggest she'd said something to offend him. She didn't particularly care. There were more important issues here than this stranger's feelings.

"But he's a vampire," she said now. "I thought the sun hurt vampires." Much to her surprise, that made irritation flicker across the man's face.

"The sun can harm an *immortal*," he said grudgingly, and then added, "But only as much as it harms a mortal. The difference is that while your skin will carry that damage and simply tan and age, our bodies will work to repair our bodies . . . and use extra blood to do so."

That last comment made Allie go cold. To her what he said suggested Liam would need to be fed when he came inside and she just didn't think she had it in her to feed him at the moment.

"You have been feeding that boy with your own blood?"

Allie stiffened at his sharp words. He made it

sound as if she'd been doing something perverted, or at least wrong. Lifting her chin, she snapped, "*That boy* is my son, Liam, and since my conscience wouldn't allow me to run around kidnapping people for him to feed off of, yes, I have been feeding him myself."

"He's not your son," the man said in a distracted tone, his expression concentrated again as he peered at her.

"The hell he's not," Allie snapped, anger roaring through her at the very suggestion that Liam wasn't hers.

"A mortal cannot give birth to an immortal. He is not your biological child and you obviously have no idea how to raise him if you've been allowing him to feed off of you." The man's voice was still distracted, as if the subject was of no importance whatsoever, and that just infuriated her. It also terrified her. Liam was the most important thing in her life. He *was* her life. Keeping him safe, healthy, and happy was her whole purpose now, yet this man seemed to be suggesting she had no business doing it. As if Liam would be better off with one of his own kind.

Would they try to take him from her? She worried suddenly, and then lifted her chin and thought grimly, *Over my dead body*.

Voice cold, Allie said, "I may not have given birth to Liam, but he *is* my son. I've raised him, fed him, loved him, and kept him safe since he was a month old. I'm the only mother he knows, and if you try to take him away from me, you'll have a fight on your hands."

She had slid her right hand into her pocket to re-trieve the lighter she'd tucked there as she spoke. Now she let the can of aerosol hairspray slip out from her left sleeve and raised both. With the lighter in front of the can and her finger on the spray nozzle, she glared at the arrogant ass in the doorway and said, "Now, I may have been wrong about sunlight, but I *know* fire kills you people, so unless you want me to roast your ass, I suggest one of you bring me my son. We're leaving."

Four

"We really need to work on your social skills, Lucian," Magnus said with irritation, but he was watching Allie with something like fascination. Her lips were still blue, but anger had put color in her cheeks, and her eyes were flashing with fury and determination as she held out her makeshift flamethrower.

The woman was a mama bear protecting her cub. She was also his life mate. Magnus had no doubt about that. He'd tried to read her several times since rescuing her from the men in her apartment—first in the pizza joint as they'd waited for Tybo to arrange a ride, then in the delivery car on their way here, and again before leaving her in the guest room upstairs—and all to no avail. He could not read or control her, a sure sign Marguerite was right. Allie was his life mate . . . and she was magnificent.

A little foolish, perhaps, he acknowledged. After

all, she was attempting to take on four immortal men on her own, but she was courageous and beautiful and he just wanted to fold her in his arms and assure her everything would be all right now.

"I am not the one who needs to work on communication," Lucian said abruptly, drawing his attention reluctantly away from Allie. "She has been here most of the night. Why have you three not explained things to this child? She has no clue who or even what we are, or why she and the boy are here."

"I'm a woman, not a child," Allie growled, and Magnus found himself smiling at the way she mirrored Lucian's scowl. Magnificent, he thought.

"Miss Chambers was unconscious when she arrived, Lucian," Mortimer said now, drawing Magnus's gaze reluctantly from Allie. "She only woke up moments ago. We have not had the chance to explain things to her."

Lucian grunted at this and then glanced to Magnus. "She's your woman, Bjarnesen. Explain things to her so we can get down to the business of finding out what she knows about these rogues chasing her."

"I'm not his woman," Allie protested at once, apparently not at all appreciative that she'd at least moved up from child to woman. She also turned to cast that angry scowl at him now, and Magnus couldn't resist smiling in return. She was just so wonderfully brave and fiery.

Even as he thought that, Allie blinked in surprise and her scowl faded as her eyes grew wide. It made him wonder what she was thinking, or seeing.

Allie was thinking he was quite the handsomest man she'd ever encountered. It was an odd thing to notice when she had no idea who these people were or why she and Liam had been brought here. On top of that, the mean blond man's comments about her not being Liam's mother had made her afraid they might try to take her son from her. Which just made her want to grab Liam and flee, hence the reason she'd pulled her makeshift flamethrower.

Not that she knew how exactly she could get herself and Liam away once out of the house. She'd have to steal a vehicle, she supposed. But where could they go? How was she to continue to hide them both from these men as well as the other group of vampires? Last night's attack had ensured they couldn't safely return to the apartment, not even to collect her car. So they were now homeless, and carless. On top of that, after four years of running and hiding, she was pretty much broke. She was also mentally exhausted and physically spent. In truth, Allie just wanted to go back upstairs and sleep for a week. But she couldn't afford to. She had Liam to worry about.

Those had been the thoughts chasing around inside her head before she'd been distracted by the man beside her. Magnus, she recalled. He could have modeled for a living with that face, she decided as her gaze slid over his features. He had a straight nose, high forehead, and an angular jaw presently sporting a trim beard somewhere just beyond a six o'clock shadow that he either kept trimmed close or was just starting to grow. He also had a mouth made up of a thin upper lip, but a full, almost pouty, and very sexy lower lip.

All of that together put him in what she was sure was the top five percent of gorgeous men on the planet, but his eyes pushed him all the way to the top of that list. Large and pale blue with a rim of dark blue or almost black around the outside, and surrounded by naturally long lashes . . . They were beautiful. Exquisite even. Allie could have stared into them for hours, but curiosity made her turn her attention to the rest of him.

Magnus wasn't just beautiful, he was big and built. He'd been wearing a full suit and a winter coat when she'd first encountered him and Tybo, but today he was wearing jeans and a white T-shirt that stretched lovingly over his wide chest and looked ridiculously sexy on the man. He was tall, towering over her by a head, and his shoulders were huge. They had to be at least twice as wide as her own, but probably more, she guessed.

He had big hands too, Allie noted as her eyes slid down his chest to where his hands rested on his hips. Somehow the pose just emphasized his slender hips, and she allowed her gaze to drop lower.

"Please do not point your hairspray there."

Allie blinked and raised her eyes quickly to Magnus's face at those husky words. He was smiling crookedly. She unthinkingly smiled back before he reached down and gently nudged her hand holding the hairspray up and away from his groin.

"Just in case you accidentally press the button," he explained gently. "I would rather not have a wet spot there."

Allie wasn't sure whether to be upset that he didn't seem worried about her weapon doing more than give him a wet spot, or embarrassed that her hand had moved with her eyes, making it obvious what she'd been looking at. In the end, she settled for exasperated with the bunch of them, and raised her hairspray and lighter again but turned it out toward the others as she scowled around the room. "So who are you people and why are Liam and I here?"

Rather than answer her, the room fell silent and then a cluck of irritation sounded from the doorway, drawing her gaze to the small blonde pushing irritably past the man named Lucian. It was the woman who had been outside with the boys, Allie realized. The white hat was missing now, but she was still wearing the white coat, though it was undone and hanging open as she crossed the room toward her with a look that was half exasperated and half welcoming.

"For heaven's sake. I know men aren't the best at communication, but I thought that between the four of them they could manage to explain things and reassure you so that you knew you were safe and among friends." Pausing before her, the woman smiled widely and held out her hand. "Hi. I'm Katricia Argeneau Brunswick, but you can call me Tricia. I'm the wife of Teddy Brunswick, the police chief of Port Henry. I'm also a law officer myself, and mother of Teddy Jr., who your son helped make his first snowman just now. And you, of course, are Liam's lovely mother, Allison." Expression becoming more serious, she added, "You have done a brilliant job with him, by the way. He's a wonderful boy, so sweet and polite."

"I . . . Thank you," Allie said finally and, after the briefest hesitation, slid the lighter into her pocket so that she could shake the hand Tricia was still holding out. "It's nice to meet you."

Tricia beamed at her as if she'd done something particularly clever in putting the lighter away. "The boys are waiting for me in the kitchen. I promised them cookies and hot chocolate to warm up. Care to join us so I can answer all those questions these primates haven't?"

Allie noted the irritated expressions creeping over the men's faces, and had the situation been different, she might have laughed. Instead, she merely murmured politely, "That sounds nice."

"Good." Tricia slid an arm through hers and urged her toward the door saying, "Come along, then. You'll love Sam's kitchen. It's big and gorgeous. Makes me jealous every time I see it. I'm working on talking Teddy into enlarging and renovating ours. Teddy senior, not junior," she added, and then confided, "I think it's working."

Allie found herself relaxing under the woman's cheerful chatter. She knew it was purely to put her at ease, but it was working, she acknowledged as Lucian moved aside to let them out of the room.

Walking her up the hall at a meandering pace, Tricia grinned at the hairspray still in Allie's hand and said, "I use that brand too. It's good. Holds the curl well and makes the best flames too."

"You use it as a makeshift flamethrower too?" Allie asked dubiously.

"Not so much anymore now that I walk the beat in Port Henry. It's pretty quiet there. But I used to be an enforcer in New York and hairspray and a lighter are lightweight and came in handy when we were cleaning out nests of rogues," she said cheerfully.

The woman was smiling so widely Allie couldn't help smiling as well, but said, "Everyone keeps mentioning rogues. What are they?"

"Good Lord, they didn't tell you anything at all, did they?" Tricia said with a disgusted shake of the head. "Rogues are basically immortal criminals, ones who have broken our laws and need tending."

"With death by makeshift flamethrower?" Allie asked. She knew vampires, or immortals as these people seemed to want to be called, were incredibly flammable. Stella had passed on that tidbit in the months before she died. Of course, Allie had seen the proof of it herself when Stella died. She'd gone up like gasoline-doused tinder when the house exploded and Allie was sure one blast of a flamethrower would be a death sentence to an immortal.

"Only when cleaning out nests of rogues," Tricia assured her solemnly. "In those cases the head rogue is usually a very old immortal who has gone mad and turned a bunch of innocent unsuspecting mortals. Unfortunately, they usually aren't kind about it, and then they make the new turns do things that drive them mad as well." She shrugged. "Often it ends up that the whole nest has to be cleaned out."

"'Cleaned out' meaning put down like rabid dogs," Allie suggested quietly.

"It's pretty much what they are in such cases," Tricia said with an unapologetic shrug, and then drew her to a halt as they reached the kitchen doorway. Eyeing her expectantly then, she asked, "Is it not glorious?"

Allie started to look around, but stilled as a shriek drew her gaze to the boys by the sink. In the next moment, Liam was streaking toward her down the length of the long white kitchen. The boy was still several feet away when he leapt at her, flying through the air so that she had to drop the hairspray to catch him. She was aware of, and grateful for, the bracing hand Katricia put on her back as Liam crashed against her chest, otherwise she might have toppled over. This leaping jump was something he only did when he was very happy, and not something a mortal child could have done. It always took her a little aback, but now she was relieved to see it. It reassured her that he was okay.

"Mom, you're up! I have so much to tell you. I drank blood from a bag, and Teddy's mom made us pancakes and— Are you feeling better?" he stopped his rapid fire chatter to ask with wide concerned eyes. "Teddy's mom said you were over the weather and we should let you sleep in this morning. Are you off the weather now?"

Allie stared at the child in her arms, her heart just melting with love. He was such a beautiful, precious little boy she just wanted to squeeze him silly. Which she did now, pressing him to her chest and turning from side to side a little.

"Yes, my sweet, I'm feeling much better now," she assured him, pressing a quick kiss to his forehead, before leaning back to look over the color on his rosy cheeks. "Did you have fun outside?"

Guilt immediately flashed across Liam's face, followed by worry as he said, "Yes. I told them I wasn't allowed to go outside. But they said it would be okay. It was safe here and you wouldn't be upset. Are you upset?"

"No," she assured him solemnly. "I'm glad you got a chance to have fun."

"It *was* fun," he said, his smile returning to full wattage. "We built a snowman, and made snow angels, and now we're going to have hot chocolate . . . if that's okay?" he added with concern, and then blurted, "Teddy says hot chocolate is the best. I can have some, can't I?"

"Of course you can." The words had barely left her lips before Liam was squirming out of her arms and dropping to the floor. Whirling away from her, he rushed back to his new friend, squealing an exuberant, "Yay! We can have hot chocolate."

Allie smiled faintly, but guilt was niggling at her as she watched his excitement. Liam had never had hot chocolate. It was a luxury, and there wasn't a lot of money for luxuries in the life they'd been forced to lead.

"Well," Tricia said with amusement as she bent to pick up the hairspray can and set it on the counter next to them. "A mere kitchen can hardly compete with that kind of greeting. He loves you a great deal."

"And I love him," Allie said softly, looking him

over one more time before turning her attention to the large white kitchen. And it was large. She would have guessed it was nearly thirty feet long with an island in the middle and cupboards running almost the entire length on both sides except for the last eight feet by her and Tricia. There, it had been left open for a large round table and eight chairs to be set up in front of windows looking out over the yard. There were also two doors where the cupboards ended; one was the doorway they were standing in. But across from it was a solid door that Allie guessed either led to a garage or a pantry or something.

"It's pretty amazing," she said finally, her attention returning to Liam and his new friend. Teddy Argeneau Brunswick Jr. was a handsome little guy, with dark hair like her son's and a smile equally as charming, but while Liam had green eyes with a silver glow to them, Teddy's were blue and silver. Both boys would grow up to be good-looking men, though, she decided.

"Liam mentioned that you two move a lot."

Allie tore her gaze from the boys to see that Katricia, or Tricia as she'd said to call her, had moved to the stove to grab a teakettle off one of the burners. She watched her carry it to the sink and then moved to lean against the counter next to the stove as she admitted, "Yes. Unfortunately. But it's been by necessity," she added to ensure the woman didn't think she was just bohemian in nature. "We usually end up moving every month or two."

"Because of the rogues Magnus and Tybo found attacking you?" Tricia asked, keeping her voice low enough that the boys couldn't hear. Teddy and Liam had climbed up onto the chairs at the table at the other end of the room and were now running mini racing cars over its surface and making *vroom-vroom* sounds as they did.

"Yes," Allie said unhappily.

Tricia nodded and, apparently deciding the kettle now had enough water, turned off the tap and carried the kettle back to the stove. She set it down, turned a knob on the range until flames burst out of the burner, set them to high, and then turned to lean against the counter on the other side of the range top to watch the boys before she asked, "Who are they?"

"I'm not sure," Allie said slowly, and frowned because that was true. She knew very little about the pack of vampires she'd spent the last four years running from. Just that they were other victims of the same vampire who had turned Stella and her husband, and that they would do whatever their "sire," as Stella had called him, demanded. Stella had feared nothing more than that man getting his hands on her son. She'd been terrified he would turn Liam into a ravening, blood-sucking fiend like the people he'd turned, and she'd been determined to save her son from that. So much so that Stella had given her life to try to keep Liam safe.

Allie had done her best since then to uphold her promise and keep Liam safe as well. She'd given up her previous life, one that had been successful and stable and safe, for a life on the run. Although she doubted Stella had expected that. She'd probably thought that sacrificing her own life would convince her hunters that both she and Liam were dead, leaving Allie to raise him in relative peace and safety. It was what Allie had expected the night that Stella had died. But things hadn't worked out that way.

"You really are safe here," Katricia said suddenly, drawing Allie's gaze. "Really. We would never harm you or Liam and want only to help."

"Why?" The question was out before Allie had given it much thought, but it was the question that had been on her mind since she'd woken up here. Why were they here? Why had Tybo and Magnus helped them? What did they want from them? Allie hadn't had a lot of help over the last four years. Any, really. She and Liam had been on their own.

Katricia was silent for a moment, considering her, and then she shrugged and said simply, "It's what we do. We are responsible for keeping mortals safe from immortals and immortals safe from discovery."

"So you saved us from those rogue immortals last night, and now . . ." Her mouth tightened and she got to her main worry. "That man said I was a bad mother. Will they try to take Liam from me?"

"He said what?" Katricia asked with shock.

"I said no such thing."

Allie and Katricia both turned toward the door at those annoyed words. Lucian was leading the men into the room, a scowl on his face as he approached. "I said he is not your biological child and that you obviously have no idea how to raise him if you've been allowing him to feed off of you."

"Oh, Uncle Lucian," Katricia said with an exasperated sigh. "It is no wonder Allie pulled the hairspray on you. What were you thinking saying something like that?"

"The truth," he growled, walking past them to open the fridge. "She needs to be educated in our people, our abilities, and our laws to be an effective mother to Liam or she could unintentionally raise him to be rogue. And no one wants that."

Allie felt some of the fear unclench from around her heart at those words. He didn't think Liam should be taken from her, but that she should learn more to raise him properly. She couldn't disagree with that. There were books on raising mortal children, but nothing out there about special children like Liam. All she'd had to go on were movies and fictional books, none of which had said vampires could eat, and yet Liam ate food. She'd fed him a solid diet of blood as a baby, until the first time he'd grabbed a handful of mashed potatoes off her plate, stuffed it in his mouth, and made happy sounds as he ate it. She'd been terrified he'd just throw it back up, that his system wouldn't take the food, but when he'd kept it down she'd started offering him baby food in the hopes that he'd need less blood if he ate. She'd also kept him out of the sun for fear he'd burst into flame. What else was she doing wrong?

Allie's thoughts were replaced by shock when Lucian turned from the refrigerator with a bag of blood in hand that he abruptly swung up and slapped his own face with. At least, that's what it looked like he was doing, self-flagellation with a blood bag. But he didn't then lower it or slap himself again. Instead, the bag stayed at his mouth, covering part of his face . . . and then she realized it was starting to shrink like he'd attached it to a vacuum hose.

"He was slapping the bag to his fangs," Katricia explained gently. "A quick popping motion works best to avoid tearing the bag and making a mess."

"Oh," Allie said weakly, and deduced that his fangs were now drawing the blood out of the bag, which was why it was shrinking. They certainly sucked it up quickly, she noted with a slight frown.

"This is how we feed now since the advent of blood banks," Magnus said quietly, and Allie tore her eyes away from Lucian to find that the very big, very handsome man now stood beside her. He was close enough that their arms would brush if she shifted the smallest amount and the realization made her arm tingle slightly, as if in anticipation of the touch. That hadn't happened before and they'd been closer than this. He'd actually carried her in his arms and she hadn't reacted like this to him.

Allie blamed it on his scent. She couldn't really sort out what it was except that there was a hint of citrus and something spicy to it. He smelled delicious and she was surprised she hadn't noticed that earlier, but supposed she'd been too upset by the events taking place at the time to be aware of it.

"It is how Liam will feed from now on too," Magnus added, distracting her from his scent.

Allie met his gaze, her eyes widening slightly as she did. Dear God, he had beautiful eyes. She had noticed that before, but it took her breath away anew as she peered into their pale blue depths. Except they weren't just pale blue, she noted. There were sparks of silver in them, and they seemed to be growing in number, the silver filling his iris and blotting out the blue. She watched with fascination as it happened and then gave a start when the teakettle started to whistle next to them.

"Can you grab that?" Tricia asked as she moved away.

"Yes." The word was a breathy sound. Embarrassed, Allie cleared her throat and added in a more composed voice, "Of course," as she turned away from Magnus to stand in front of the stove. She turned off the flames and shifted the kettle to a cool burner.

"Here we are." Tricia returned to her side with a tray holding four mugs and a can of powdered hot chocolate. She set down the tray, grabbed up the hot chocolate, began to scoop some into each of the four mugs she'd collected, and then glanced toward her uncle. "Grab the cream from the fridge for me, please, Uncle Lucian," she requested, and then added, "And a mug if you want some too. There should be enough water for everyone."

Much to Allie's surprise, all the men moved to get cups and followed Lucian to the counter where Tricia was working. When the first four mugs of hot chocolate were ready, Allie carried them to the table and sat down at the table with the boys to get out of the way. She wasn't surprised when the others joined her there moments later, each of them settling in one of the eight chairs surrounding the table as their own drinks were ready. She'd thought it was a huge table when she'd first seen it, but with the men crowded around it, it suddenly seemed much smaller, Allie thought, and then smiled at Tricia when the woman joined them with a plate of chocolate chip cookies and a stack of napkins.

"Did Sam make those cookies?" Magnus asked, eyeing the plate suspiciously.

"Yeah, but she's stopped making things with weird stuff," Tybo assured him with amusement as he took several cookies. "They're safe to eat. Good too."

"Mortimer's wife, Sam, was on a health food kick for a while," Katricia explained to Allie with a grin.

Tybo snorted at the words. "You mean she was on a mission to torture us all. The woman was making wheat germ shakes and chocolate chip cookies with tahini and coconut sugar or some damned thing. Made us all wonder what Mortimer had done to piss her off."

"Made me wonder too," the man she assumed was Mortimer said glumly.

"The worst part was, while she was forcing that garbage on us, she was slipping out for burgers and shakes," Tybo said with disgust, and when a surprised laugh slipped from Allie, he smiled slightly and said, "Sure, laugh at our pain."

"Mom, can Liam and I take our cookies to the living room and watch cartoons?" Teddy piped up suddenly, drawing everyone's attention.

"No. You will get crumbs everywhere," Tricia said at once. "Eat your cookies first and then you can go watch cartoons."

The boys looked at each other and then, as one,

shoved their cookies in their mouths. They were large cookies and the boys' cheeks were bulging when they finished.

"Liam," Allie said in a reprimanding tone. "You'll choke yourself on . . ."

Her words trailed away as the boy quickly chewed and swallowed the cookie, then grabbed his mug and downed the last of his hot chocolate even as Teddy did. Setting the mug down, he beamed at her as if he'd done something clever and announced, "All done."

"Can we go watch cartoons now?" Teddy asked eagerly.

"If Liam's mother says it is okay," Tricia said solemnly.

Allie found herself the focus of two pairs of hopeful eyes and Liam said, "Please, Mom?"

Allie hesitated, part of her wanting to keep him close. She had spent every moment of every day with the boy since he'd been passed into her arms nearly four years ago. At least until she'd started the job at the blood bank. But she'd worked days while he'd slept, and while it had been night when she'd gone to rob the blood bank, she'd waited until Liam was down for his nap, fully expecting to be back before he woke. She hadn't been surprised to return and find him awake and upset that she'd left him. He seemed eager to leave her now, though, to play with his friend and she felt a little wounded at the knowledge. But she knew it was healthy for him to make friends. It was also convenient, because she had some questions for Katricia and the others that she didn't think Liam should hear, so Allie forced a smile and nodded. "Sure."

"Thank you, Mom." Liam beamed at her and slid off his seat to follow his new friend from the room.

"They will be fine," Tricia assured her.

Allie nodded, sure that was true.

"Now that the boys are out of earshot," Lucian said, drawing all eyes his way, including Allie's, who grew wary when she noted his determined expression. Before she could worry too much, he ordered, "Explain things, Katricia. She seems to trust you."

Tricia rolled her eyes, but then turned to her with a wry smile and explained, "As I mentioned earlier, we are Enforcers. The police for our people, basically. We hunt immortals who break our laws, such as the ones who attacked you and Liam."

Allie nodded in understanding, but was mentally substituting "vampire" for "immortal."

"One of the ways we do that is by listening in on the police scanner for reports of any crimes that might be immortal related," she continued. "Last night, Mortimer heard that the blood bank had been broken into and the perpetrator taken to the hospital."

"And assumed it was vampire related. Because who else would rob a blood bank, right?" Allie guessed, and didn't miss the winces that went around the table at her use of the word *vampire*.

"Basically, yes," Tricia said. "And because of that, Tybo and Magnus were sent to the hospital to investigate."

Allie nodded, supposing her attempted theft *was*

vampire, or immortal, related. She'd been stealing the blood to feed Liam, who was apparently an immortal, not a vampire. Actually, she preferred the word *immortal*. At least in regards to Liam . . . and Tricia and Teddy, and maybe even Tybo and Magnus, she decided. She wasn't sure about Mortimer yet, but Lucian . . . Yeah, she'd call him a vampire with all his growling and glaring.

A snort of laughter from Tybo caught her attention and he bit his lip, and then cleared his throat and said solemnly, "You should have made the attempt much sooner. You were too weak for such an undertaking by the time you tried it."

Allie could hardly argue with that. Fainting halfway through the job pretty much proved that she'd been too weak. Sighing, she explained, "I got the job there three months ago, intending to find a way to get blood for Liam. I came up with the plan pretty quickly and earned my boss's trust enough to be given keys more than a month ago, but . . ." She grimaced and admitted, "It took a while to convince myself to actually do it."

"That is understandable," Magnus murmured, shifting in the seat he'd chosen next to her. "I'm sure fear would make most people hesitate to commit a felony."

"It wasn't fear that made me hesitate so long," she assured him. "I mean, I was afraid, sure, but I was more afraid of dying if I didn't find another source of blood for Liam."

"Then why did you wait so long to try to rob it?" Tricia asked with curiosity.

"Guilt," she said bluntly. "I'd never thought much about blood banks before Liam came along, but working there I learned how desperate they are for blood. They're constantly struggling to keep enough on hand to keep up with the hospitals' needs and here I was planning to steal some."

"To keep your son alive without killing yourself," Tricia said firmly. "You should not feel guilty about what you tried to do."

Allie glanced around the people at the table. She was kind of glad it had all happened because now she might be able to purchase blood from these people and not have to steal. "Where do you get your blood?"

"We have our own blood banks," Tricia said reassuringly. "We pay donors for it just as the blood bank you worked for does."

Allie nodded, but then frowned as she realized Tricia had used the past tense, as if she wouldn't be working there anymore.

"I—" she began, but Lucian cut her off.

"Your life will be different now," he said heavily. "Your old life is gone."

Allie narrowed her eyes in irritation at his high-handed attitude, but then glanced to Magnus when he ran a finger lightly over the back of her hand where it rested on the table.

Having claimed her attention with the light touch, he explained gently, "We need to teach you the things you should know as Liam's mother. Things like the fact that, with a little caution, he can go out in sunlight."

Allie relaxed and nodded. "Yes," she acknowledged

solemnly. "And I will be happy to learn those things, but—"

"We also need to keep you safe from the rogues who attacked you," he interrupted gently. "At least until they can be rounded up and are no longer a threat."

Allie was just feeling relief at those words when Lucian announced, "To that end, you will be moved to Port Henry."

Allie's relief fled, replaced with irritation again. She had no idea where Port Henry was, but had never taken well to being ordered about.

"Really, Uncle," Tricia said with exasperated amusement before Allie could blow her top at the man. "You cannot *make* her go anywhere." Turning to Allie, she added, "But it would probably be for the best if you agreed to go to Port Henry. It's really a very nice little town, and I think I mentioned my husband is the police chief there. We can keep you safe without keeping you in a fenced-in compound with the dogs and guards they have here."

"There are dogs and guards here?" Allie asked with surprise. All she'd seen when she looked out the back window was a large backyard and a huge building with a lot of garage doors in it.

"Yes," Tricia said solemnly, "Dogs, guards, and a huge electric fence."

Allie's eyebrows rose. "And Port Henry is safer?"

"Perhaps not safer in that way, but it's a small town where strangers are noticed pretty quickly," she assured her. "And there are several immortal families there with children. Aside from the parents offering added protection, it means Liam would have a lot of playmates. It also means there would be several people who can tell you all you need to know about raising an immortal boy."

That sounded pretty good to Allie. At least, it did if Lucian wouldn't be there. The man just rubbed her the wrong way.

"Staying there would give you a chance to regain your strength too, while Lucian and Mortimer worked here to find and capture the rogues who attacked you," Tricia added, eliminating the concern of Lucian being in Port Henry.

"When do we leave?" Allie asked with a wry smile.

Tricia beamed at her, but it was Lucian who answered the question. "The helicopter that brought Katricia and Teddy here is waiting out on the airstrip to take you all back. The six of you can leave as soon as you tell us everything you know about this nest of rogues that attacked you."

"The six of us?" Allie asked with confusion.

"Magnus and Tybo will be accompanying you for added protection," Lucian announced. "It hopefully will not be necessary since it is doubtful the rogues could follow the helicopter to Port Henry, but it is better not to take chances."

"Oh." Allie's gaze slid to Magnus and then quickly away when she saw he was looking at her.

"So . . ." Lucian arched an eyebrow and ordered, "Tell us what you know of these rogues."

Five

Magnus watched Allie struggle with her irritation at Lucian's high-handed manner, but after a moment she seemed to let go of it on a sigh and shook her head before saying apologetically, "Not much, I'm afraid."

He noted the concentration on the faces of Lucian and the others and knew they were reading her thoughts for the information they sought. Unfortunately, he couldn't do that so suggested, "Just tell us what you do know."

Allie nodded and glanced down at her hands briefly, but then nodded again. "One of them is Liam's father."

Magnus frowned at this news. "How did you end up with Liam?"

"His mother, Stella," Allie answered, smiling softly. "I met her about a month after buying my first home, a town house in Calgary. It was summertime, August, and one night some rude idiot decided to mow their lawn," she said with remembered irritation. "I'd put up with the noise of a dozen lawn mowers all day and evening. It's expected in the summer, that's why I worked nights. It was quiet then and I could concentrate. Usually, but not that night. It was around ten thirty—the kids were all inside getting ready for bed if not there already, the rest of the street had finally settled down to quiet, and then *vroom*. Ugh." Allie shook her head. "I wanted to throttle whoever it was, but I tried to ignore it and kept working. When the engine cut out, I was relieved and thought it was done, but then they tried to restart it, and failed, and tried again and again, their machine making the most god-awful coughing sounds. Finally I couldn't take it anymore and went outside ready to tear into the thoughtless prick making all that racket at that hour."

Allie grinned crookedly. "That's when I first saw her. A petite little brunette with an obvious baby bump, looking exhausted and about as frustrated as me and yanking on the lawn mower cord over and over."

Magnus smiled at her description, almost able to see it in his mind.

"Instead of bawling her out for her choice of time for doing lawn maintenance, I ended up helping. I mean, she was nearly done anyway, so I figured a few more minutes of racket and it would be done and I could get back to work. Right?"

When Allie rolled her eyes, Magnus found himself smiling, and asked, "I am guessing it did not work out that way?"

"No," she admitted on a sigh. "I must have spent an

hour checking her lawn mower. I went over the spark plug wire, the spark plug itself, the brake cable, the oil level . . ." Allie grimaced. "Of course, we were chatting while I did it, which slowed me down. It wouldn't normally have taken me that long."

Magnus nodded solemnly at her earnest assurance, but he was biting his tongue to keep from grinning. The fact that she knew how to do what she'd mentioned was impressive to him no matter how long it took. He wasn't mechanically minded himself and wouldn't have known what to check.

"Did you find the problem?" Tricia asked.

"Oh, yeah," she said dryly, and then admitted with disgust, "It was out of gas."

That startled a laugh from everyone but Lucian. Allie didn't appear offended, though, and laughed with them before saying, "I know. That's the first thing I should have checked." She shook her head at her mistake. "Anyway, it was after eleven thirty by then. Stella decided to leave it for the next day to finish, so I wished her good night and went back home to return to work."

She paused briefly, her eyes looking off into the distant memories, and then said, "I don't think it was more than an hour later that there was a knock at the door. I considered ignoring it, but twelve thirty is an odd time for visitors and it might be an emergency so I answered it in the end. And there stood Stella with a bright smile and a pan of freshly baked brownies in her hands to thank me," Allie explained, and Magnus nodded encouragingly.

"I should have said, 'Thank you but no, I have a

deadline and need to work.' Unfortunately, I'm something of a chocoholic and she looked so . . ." Allie frowned as she tried to find the words to explain, and then said, "I don't know . . . lonely, maybe, but hopeful. I didn't have the heart to send her away. It would have been like kicking a puppy." She shrugged. "So I invited her in and made tea."

Kind, Magnus thought. She was kind as well as brave.

"Stella told me later that she'd intended on feeding on me when she came over and the brownies were just a way to get in the door. But we got talking while I puttered around fetching plates and making tea, and by the time we sat down, she liked me too much to bite me."

Magnus frowned at this news, suspecting that Stella's feeding on her would have been a death sentence. The woman had obviously been a rogue if she was biting mortals and not feeding on blood bags as immortals were supposed to do. Rogues didn't often concern themselves with the well-being of their chosen dinner.

"I never did end up getting back to work that night," Allie continued. "We sat and chatted over brownies and tea until nearly dawn. She told me at that time that she was on her own, and admitted she was pregnant and scared. She said she was from Vancouver where she used to be an office manager. But she'd given up her home and job and moved to Calgary to get a fresh start after her husband died. She didn't tell me then how he died. She didn't seem to want to talk about it and I didn't push her. Instead, we talked about other things."

Solemn now, Allie admitted, "It was a good night. We had a lot in common and laughed a great deal. By the time the sun was creeping over the horizon and she hurried home, we were firm friends."

Allie took a sip of hot chocolate. "Stella was at my place a lot after that. I'd often see her leave in her car after the sun set. When that happened, I'd keep an eye out for her return to make sure she got back okay. Women alone have to look out for each other," she added, glancing at Magnus, and he nodded in understanding. The world was a dangerous place, especially for young mortal women.

"Anyway," Allie continued, "she usually returned at midnight or one o'clock in the morning, and often carrying groceries. I'd watch until she got them safely inside if she only had a few, or go out to help her unload if she had a lot of them. Then I'd go back to work. But then she'd show up at my place around three or four in the morning with snacks or a full meal and we'd sit and talk for hours. Stella usually headed home before the sun rose, but on the days she left it too late she'd sleep on the couch and then wouldn't leave until night fell again."

Allie shook her head. "I didn't think anything of it. The fact that she avoided the sun and spent so much time with me. I just thought she was lonely, or worried about having the baby. I didn't even pick up at first that with all the food she brought over, she never ate."

"She did not eat?" Magnus asked with a frown. A woman, whether mortal or immortal, should definitely eat when pregnant. Making a baby took a lot of nourishment.

"No," Allie said on a sigh. "She'd fix herself a plate

and push the food around on it, but I never saw her actually put anything in her mouth. When I commented on it, she claimed she had morning sickness that lasted all day and night and then changed the subject."

"She probably didn't think she could eat anymore," Tricia said with a frown.

Magnus nodded, and when Allie raised an eyebrow, he explained, "It is doubtful her sire told her she could eat. The mythical vampires do not eat and he would want her to believe that was what she was."

"Why?" Allie asked with bewilderment.

"That can be explained later," Lucian said before Magnus could answer. "All the questions you no doubt have can be answered after. Just skip the *Laverne and Shirley* narrative of bonding with the woman and tell us what you know about Stella's sire."

Magnus watched the way Allie narrowed her eyes on Lucian and expected a show of temper, but instead she asked sweetly, "Who are Laverne and Shirley?"

"That *is* a bit before her time, Uncle," Tricia said with amusement when he began to scowl.

"Yeah," Tybo agreed, and then leaned forward in his chair to meet Allie's gaze as he suggested, "Think *Thelma and Louise*, but funny and without ending with driving off a cliff."

Allie nodded, but then tilted her head and asked, "Who are Thelma and Louise?"

"Oh." Tybo frowned. "That movie came out in 1991 when you were probably— Were you born yet?"

"Oh, for God's sake," Lucian snarled. "Just tell us about her sire."

When Allie cast an irritated scowl at the man and growled a sarcastic, "Yes, master," Magnus had to bow his head to hide his expression. He was both amused and proud of her. Most people quailed in Lucian's presence, but not his Allie.

He had just caught the fact that he'd thought of her as his and begun to remonstrate with himself about jumping the gun emotionally when Allie started speaking again. Still, he felt his pride increase when she ignored Lucian's directive and continued in her own way.

"Anyway, the next few months were nice. We had late-night barbecues, attended movies together once the sun started setting earlier, and became best friends," Allie said, her voice deliberate, and gaze meeting Lucian's in quite the most beautiful silent *fuck you* Magnus had ever seen.

When Lucian growled low in his throat in response, she beamed a smile at him and said, "We had great fun when I wasn't working." Her smile faded slightly as she added, "And then that night in early December came."

"That night?" Magnus asked with concern.

Allie nodded. "We'd gone to the movies and then a late dinner. We were walking back to my car when Stella suddenly grabbed my arm and began to move more quickly. It was a moment after that before I heard the footsteps behind us and understood what had her agitated. Or thought I did."

Glancing at him, Allie apparently noted the confusion on his face, and explained, "The movie had been over for more than an hour by then, and the parking lot was nearly empty. There was only one other car at the back of the lot besides ours, so footsteps at that point were a bit . . ."

"Anxiety inducing?" Tricia suggested with understanding.

"Yes," she sighed, and then said, "I had barely registered the sound and experienced that anxiety when I was suddenly hanging over Stella's shoulder, my head banging against the back of her coat as we flew the rest of the way to the car. And believe me," she said solemnly, "in that moment it did seem as if we flew. I mean, she was *really* moving. It couldn't have been more than a matter of seconds before we reached the car."

Dropping back in her seat, she said dryly, "All I can say is it's a good thing I forgot to lock the doors, because I really think she would have just ripped the door off. She damned near did anyway and it wasn't locked." Allie shook her head at the memory. "Anyway, she tossed me in like a Raggedy Ann doll, and then climbed in after me. She had the door slammed and locked in about a half a second, and immediately started to feel up my pockets, shrieking, 'Where are the keys? We have to go! Give me the keys!'"

Allie blew out a breath as if she still couldn't believe what had happened. "And then there was a knock at the car window. We both froze and then slowly turned to look out. A young couple were standing uncertainly on the pavement next to the car. They couldn't have been more then seventeen or eighteen. When Stella just stared, I got out on my side of the car to talk to them. They were the source of the footsteps we'd heard, and while they didn't appear to have seen Stella carting me around like Godzilla, they had heard her shrieking once we'd got in the car, and had hurried forward to make sure someone wasn't being attacked. I assured them everything was fine and said Stella was pregnant with her first baby and a little hysterical about what was coming, is all. They looked in at her and relaxed at once. Stella was very pregnant at that point," she added dryly. "I mean, she was *huge*. I'm sure her carting me across the parking lot over her shoulder with her big belly leading the way would have been a ridiculous sight if anyone had seen it."

Magnus smiled faintly, able to envision it.

"Anyway, to reassure them, I opened the car door so they could see that Stella was all right and told her the nice young couple were concerned for our well-being. Fortunately, she pulled herself together enough to tell them everything was fine—she was just suffering a little pregnancy madness. Her hormones were all over the place and making her a bit crazy. Then we thanked them nicely for their concern, wished them good night, and I got back in the car.

"Stella apologized all the way home, saying she'd thought it was 'them,' that they'd caught up to her and would try to drag her back so they could take her baby." Allie sighed sadly. "I had no idea what she was talking about, but I was a bit freaked out by what had happened. Her strength and speed hadn't been normal," she pointed out, peering at Magnus with big eyes.

When he nodded in understanding, and took her

hand to squeeze her fingers reassuringly, she flushed slightly, but continued. "Anyway, I was upset and confused, but just kept saying it was fine, we'd talk when we got home. But when we got back to my place, she muttered that she was very tired and rushed across the street to her town house. I thought, fine, we'd talk the next night."

"I am guessing there was no talk the next night," Magnus said quietly when she paused unhappily.

"No," Allie admitted. "Or the night after. Stella pulled a disappearing act. She didn't come over, wouldn't answer the door, and wouldn't answer my phone calls or texts. I don't think I ever would have seen her again if I hadn't staked out her place."

"Staked out her place?" Magnus asked, unsure what that would entail in this case.

Allie nodded. "I plunked myself down by my front window and watched for her to leave, intending to rush out and talk to her if she did. I did that for two and a half nights with no results before I lost my patience. When there was no sign of her by three A.M. on the third night, I took the house key she'd given me—" She stopped her narrative to explain. "I talked her into giving me a house key just the week before this all happened. She only had a month and a half to her due date, but she was so big I was afraid the date was off. I was worried she'd go into labor and not be able to negotiate the stairs to the main floor safely on her own. I told her if she started having contractions, she was to call me and I'd go over, use the key to get in, then help her down to the car and drive her to the hospital."

When he nodded in understanding, she returned to the original subject. "Anyway, at three o'clock that third night, I took the key and went over, determined to make her talk to me. We were friends. I'd helped her pick her unborn baby's name, promised to be a free babysitter and help her with him or her. Besides, I had a ton of questions."

"Was she there?" Tricia asked with curiosity.

"No," Allie said with disgust. "Her car was there in the garage, but the house was empty. She'd dug a path through the snow from her back door to the fence and had apparently jumped it and used the footpath through the woods to go Lord knows where." Anger tightening her lips, she added grimly, "On foot. In November in Calgary. November twenty-fifth to be exact. It was *minus 17 degrees Celsius that night,*" Allie told them with a combination of dismay and outrage. "I mean, how irresponsible is that? She was pregnant, for heaven's sake. What if she'd gone into labor while strutting through the snow? Liam would have frozen to death before he hit the ground."

"Liam would have been fine," Tricia said soothingly. "Immortals do not freeze as easily as mortals."

"Well, I didn't know that, did I?" Allie said dryly, and then sighed. "She showed up at a little after four in the morning. I was sitting in the dark so that she wouldn't see the light and avoid coming home. A bad idea as it turned out. She mistook me for a robber and damned near killed me before she realized it was me. Of course, then she alternated between feeling horrible for throwing me across the living room, and being angry that I had been sitting in wait. And of course I was a confusion of anger at her for avoiding me, and apologetic about using the key when I knew she wouldn't have wanted me to."

Allie shrugged philosophically. "We were both emotional, and there was a lot of back-and-forth. One minute she was crying, and then yelling, while I was alternately apologizing and then demanding we talk. But finally we both settled down. She still wouldn't talk at first. Not until I said I considered her the best friend I'd ever had, like a sister, really, the only family I had, and I didn't want to lose her friendship. Besides, I reminded her, I was going to be little Liam or Sunita's godmother. She *had* to talk to me."

"Liam would have been Sunita if he'd been born a girl?" Tricia asked with a grin.

"Yes," Allie answered, and then tilted her head slightly and asked, "Why?"

"That's Elvi and Victor's daughter's name," Katricia said with a smile, and then explained, "They are good friends who live in Port Henry. Our children play together. They have a bed and breakfast and that's where you will be staying in Port Henry." She shook her head. "What a coincidence they picked the same name as you and Stella did for a girl baby. I mean, Sunita isn't that popular a name."

"That's part of the reason we picked it. It's beautiful and unusual. And we could have called her Sunny for short."

"That's Sunita's nickname!" Tricia said with delight.

"Yes, yes," Lucian said with exasperation. "Sunita is

a beautiful name and I am sure Elvi and Victor's calling their daughter that and it being chosen as the name
Liam did not get is some kind of mystical miracle or
an omen that you were meant to go to Port Henry.
Now, can we finally get to what Stella told you about
her sire?"

Allie and Tricia both turned to peer at the man,
narrow-eyed, and then Allie asked, "Is he always this
grumpy?"

"I fear so," Tricia said apologetically.

"Hmm," Allie muttered, and then still staring at
Lucian asked, "Tricia, do you think I could have
some water or something? All this talking is leaving
me dry-mouthed."

"Oh, yes, of course," Tricia said, getting up at once.
"I could do with some water myself."

Allie immediately stopped glaring at Lucian and
stood quickly to follow the other woman, saying, "You
don't have to fetch it for me."

"They are deliberately trying to provoke me," Lucian growled, and Magnus turned an amused glance
to the man to see that he was scowling fiercely after
Allie and Tricia.

"One would think that after all these years married
to Leigh, you would have a better grasp of how to handle women," he said mildly.

Lucian turned his scowl on him, opened his mouth,
no doubt to blast him with his temper, but then paused
to reach for his phone as it began to sing what sounded
to Magnus like "I Touch Myself."

"Obviously not," Mortimer said with amusement as

Lucian struggled to unhook his phone from its holder while it continued to sing "I touch myself," over and over. Just those three words. It seemed obvious it was part of a song, but it wasn't one Magnus recognized.

"Hmm," Tybo murmured in agreement, and in dry tones asked, "What did you do to piss off Leigh this time?"

"Shut up," Lucian snarled, finally wrenching the phone free. Hitting the button to answer it, he slapped it to his ear and barked, "What?"

They all waited as he listened briefly, his face flushing with a deepening anger, and then he growled, "No, I am not interested in a free cruise. Stop calling me." Pushing the button to end the call, he then started to work at getting the phone back in its holder, which he seemed to have as much difficulty with as getting it out, and grumbled, "Bloody telemarketers. I get at least twenty calls a day now from the bastards."

"Maybe Leigh put you on a call list so you get to listen to her ringtone choice over and over," Tybo suggested with a grin.

"What?" Lucian's head shot up, his expression one of dismay. Spearing the younger immortal with his eyes, he asked, "Could she do that?"

"I don't know," Tybo said with a shrug. "But if there's a way to do it, Leigh's smart enough to find it."

"Yes. She is," Lucian agreed, and then suddenly relaxed, smiled, and said, "God, she's magnificent."

"I will tell her you said so the next time I see her," Tricia offered brightly as she led Allie back to the table. "Maybe that will get you out of trouble."

Tricia was carrying a large pitcher of ice water, while Allie followed with a tray of glasses. Noting her pallor, Magnus stood quickly to take the tray and set it on the table for her.

"Thank you," she said a little breathlessly as she sat back down. "We thought the rest of you might want some water too."

"Water sounds good," he said, trying to hide his concern behind a smile as he settled back in his seat. The color that anger had painted in her cheeks earlier was gone, and she was pale and shaky after her short sojourn for glasses and it made him wonder when Dani would arrive. Surely, she should have been here by now?

"Water?" Allie asked, and Magnus blinked his thoughts away and managed a smile and nod.

"Yes, please," he murmured, and then glanced to Lucian. Much to his surprise, the man appeared to be holding on to his patience as he waited for the water to be poured and passed around, but Magnus suspected it took some effort. He'd known Lucian Argeneau more than a millennium and the man had never been known for his patience. Fortunately, Allie wasn't foolish enough to push it too far with the man and started talking the moment everyone had a glass of the icy liquid.

"So, when Stella finally started talking, she began by telling me about the night her husband died," she said abruptly. "She said they were walking home from dinner when they were attacked by a large group of men. She'd heard their footsteps for a while before they attacked, but hadn't thought anything of it. Her husband was a good-sized man and she always felt safe with him. She said hearing those footsteps in the parking lot while returning to the car from dinner . . . She thought it was them, coming to get her again, and just panicked."

"Not surprising," Tricia murmured.

"No," Allie agreed. "Her memory of the attack in Vancouver was a bit blurry, but she remembered being terrified and that she'd been dragged away from her husband, or he from her. She remembered their attackers laughing and taunting them, and then one of them sprouted fangs and began gnawing on her arm and she passed out either from blood loss or fear."

Allie's expression was solemn as she admitted, "That business about sprouting fangs made me wonder if she wasn't really suffering some pregnancy-induced psychosis, but I kept that opinion to myself and let her talk. Stella told me that she woke up in a dark, dank basement somewhere. It was some kind of abandoned building, but she didn't know that yet. At first she couldn't see or hear anything and thought she was dead, but then she heard her husband, Stephen, moan. Stella tried to crawl to him, but she didn't have much strength and she was in terrible pain. Everything seemed to hurt and she was wondering just how many wounds she'd sustained and how bad they were when the door suddenly opened and a light was switched on.

"Stella said it was blinding after the utter darkness before it and she couldn't make out much more than blurry figures, but a man said, 'Ah, there are my pets.

I've brought you a special treat to salve that hunger you must be feeling.'

"Apparently, a whimpering figure was then pushed forward and the speaker slashed at them with something, then tossed them into the room and the door closed."

Allie paused for another drink, her voice grim when she said, "Stella was still having trouble seeing, but she could smell blood and the person was weeping and she managed to get to her hands and knees to move to them. She wanted to help them, wanted to see if she could stanch their wounds or something, but the smell of the blood was overwhelming and her body was cramping. She said the next thing she knew she was licking up the blood rather than trying to stanch it, and then Stephen was beside her licking at one of the other wounds and they both went a little crazy trying to get more and everything became blurry in her memory again except she recalls the sudden onset of pain. Terrible, screaming agony that left her writhing on the ground and shrieking."

"She was probably telling the truth and didn't recall much clearly," Tricia said quietly when Allie fell silent. "It was probably just nightmarish flashes in her memory. The turning can make a person . . ."

When Tricia paused, looking like she wasn't sure how to say what she was trying to explain, Magnus said, "During a turn, the turnee becomes desperate to get blood, but once they get it, the nanos set to work on the body in earnest and it is apparently unbearably painful. Turnees have been known to do themselves great harm trying to bring an end to that pain."

"Yeah," Tybo murmured. "I've even heard of them clawing out their own eyes if not restrained."

Allie stared at them all blankly, and then asked, "Nanos?"

"Explanations later," Lucian said coldly. "Continue with what Stella told you."

For a moment, Magnus thought Allie would rebel and demand answers, but in the end she seemed to decide she'd made him wait long enough and continued.

"Stella didn't know how long she was in that basement. But the same thing kept happening over and over. She'd wake up in terrible pain in that dark room, either just moments before, or to the sound of, the door opening. The blinding light would come on, a voice would taunt them, and then another poor person would be sliced up and thrown in to them like raw meat tossed to dogs. And every time, she and Stephen would fall on the person in search of their blood and then end up writhing on the ground in agony."

Allie peered down at her glass and slowly began to rotate it on the tabletop. "Stella was ashamed of what she could remember. And shocked and horrified that she was capable of what she'd done." Glancing up, she added, "I was rather shocked myself. It just didn't fit with the woman I'd come to know. Stella was sweet, and funny and kind. This all had to be fantasy, I was sure."

Lowering her gaze to her glass again, she sighed.

"Anyway, Stella said eventually she woke up one night and didn't hurt everywhere. In fact, she felt amazing. So when the door opened, the light came on, and a bloodied person was tossed in, she felt sure she could resist."

"But she could not," Magnus guessed quietly, knowing that while the worst of the turning must have been over at that point, it was still happening, and Stella and her husband would have yet needed a lot of blood. They just wouldn't have realized it until the scent hit them.

"No. Neither of them could. But this time there was no screaming agony to follow and help them forget. Instead, they were left sated, no longer light blind, and were able to see the charnel house they had made of the room. The decomposing bodies of their victims were all still there, the walls spattered with their blood, and now she could smell the rot. The combination was enough to make her throw up half the blood she'd just consumed, and left her so weak Stephen had to carry her out when this time their captors returned for them.

"Stella said they were taken to another larger room full of people crowding around the edges while a man sat on the only chair in the middle of an open space, like a king on his throne."

"Did she describe him?" Lucian asked at once. "Tell you his name?"

Allie bit her lip and looked thoughtful for a moment, before saying, "She told me his name. It was strange. Something I've never heard before, but . . ."

She shook her head. "I'll remember it eventually. I just can't recall it right now. I think she said he had dark hair, though. And I remember her saying you wouldn't think him a monster to look at him. He just appeared normal . . . and if you'd put him in a suit he could have been mistaken for an accountant. She said that somehow made him more terrifying. That he was so average-looking, but so horrible and soulless."

Lucian frowned at her words, but nodded and sat back, apparently willing to wait to see if the name returned to her.

"Anyway, he welcomed them and explained that through his generosity they had been turned into vampires rather than merely becoming food for the group like the pathetic creatures they had fed on. But now they could not return to their former lives. They were his. He was their sire. They quite simply could not survive without him, and as the room they'd woken in was their grave, they must return to it before dawn every day, and must never leave it before the sun set or they would perish."

"What?" Mortimer asked with disbelief.

When Allie merely nodded, Tybo grimaced and said, "Some of the tales and movies about vampires suggest they have to return to their coffin when the sun rises and remain until it sets or they will die. A lot also have a thing about keeping dirt from their grave in it if they want to move around and not remain in the graveyard." He shrugged mildly. "Obviously this rogue was using a variation on that to control his turns. They wouldn't run away while he was sleeping if they didn't think they could leave the room where they were turned."

When Mortimer grunted with disgust at that and then turned back to Allie expectantly, she raised her eyebrows. "So you don't have to stay in coffins or something from sunrise to sunset."

"It is morning right now," Magnus pointed out gently, and she glanced out the window to the front yard with surprise.

"Oh. Right. I forgot," she muttered.

"We do not sleep in coffins anymore, and would not have perished if we got out of them during daytime when we did," Magnus assured her.

"So you did sleep in coffins at one time?" she asked with dismay.

"Only because it was safer," Magnus assured her, and then noticing the way Lucian was shifting impatiently, he smiled wryly at her. "But I shall explain about that later."

"Right," she said, eyeing Lucian now herself. "Okay. So, I guess their sire lauded on quite a bit about how lucky they were he had chosen to turn them, and then he gave them a lot of . . . well, sort of rules."

"What kind of rules?" Katricia asked with curiosity.

Allie thought briefly and then said, "He told them food was now off-limits. It would do them no good and they would just vomit it back up along with the blood they did need. He promised he'd kill them rather than put up with subjects wasting blood that way." She tilted her head and added, "Which obviously isn't true since Liam can eat and you guys all had the cookies and hot chocolate and aren't getting sick."

Magnus blinked at her words, realizing only then that he too had eaten a cookie, which wouldn't be remarkable except that he hadn't felt hunger for food for centuries. If he'd doubted that Allie might be a possible life mate, his sudden indulgence in food eliminated it. That was another sign of having met a life mate, a return of desire for food . . . and sex. Magnus didn't yet know if he had the desire for sex. He found Allie attractive, but hadn't suddenly become a slavering animal, wanting to rip her clothes off.

"Huh," Tybo said dryly, drawing his attention back to the subject at hand. "That would have saved him money on food. No doubt it would have got expensive feeding a large crowd of rogues. He saved himself a pretty penny with that line."

"Yes," Mortimer agreed, sounding weary, although Magnus suspected it wasn't a physical exhaustion. It was hard to see the worst of mankind day in and day out and not grow weary of soul.

"What other rules did he have?" Tricia asked quietly.

Allie thought briefly and then said, "They couldn't wear jewelry. Stella said her earrings were lying on the floor and her pierced ears had closed up when she woke. Her sire said it was because metal wounded their bodies or something, and demanded they hand over all their jewelry for him to dispose of, which really upset her. She didn't care about the earrings but he took her engagement and wedding ring too, and a heart pendant with a picture of her and Stephen in it that she never took off."

"We can wear jewelry," Tybo assured her, and then suggested, "He probably wanted the jewelry to pawn it."

"That's what Stella thought too," Allie said slowly. "She wanted to take her rings and the pendant when she left, but the pendant was the only thing remaining. She did wear that with no problems, and thinks it was only still there because it wasn't very valuable, at least not monetarily." She paused briefly and then added, "Apparently, they were ordered to remove the jewelry of their victims and give it to him too, and he had a special group of men who committed various crimes to get more money."

"You mean aside from kidnapping, and turning or killing unsuspecting mortals?" Tybo asked dryly.

"Who's been kidnapping and killing mortals?"

Magnus glanced over his shoulder at that question to see Mortimer's wife, Sam, eyeing them with alarm from the open door to the garage. She was a slim woman, with dark hair and large eyes, her arms presently loaded down with grocery bags.

As he and the other men stood and hurried to help with the groceries, Magnus heard Lucian say, "We will have to finish this after we get Sam settled," and was surprised at the man's show of patience. Perhaps Leigh was having an effect on him, after all, Magnus thought. That or the man was hungry for something more substantial than cookies.

Six

"**W**ell, now that I've satisfied your stomachs, perhaps one of you could tell me who is kidnapping and killing mortals?"

Allie had just popped the last of her bacon, lettuce, and tomato sandwich into her mouth when Sam said that. She glanced to the woman with amusement, unsurprised at the demand. Sam seemed a rather take-charge woman. She had certainly taken charge of the men when they'd started pulling out groceries with hungry mutterings at some of the contents.

Noting that it was close to noon—something that had shocked Allie, who hadn't realized how late it had gotten—Sam had suggested bacon, lettuce, and tomato sandwiches for lunch. When everyone, even Lucian, had reacted positively to the suggestion, she'd immediately moved to start making coffee while giving each of the rest of them tasks. Mortimer had cooked the bacon,

Tybo made toast, Katricia had cleaned the lettuce, and Allie had sat at the island at Magnus's insistence and sliced the tomatoes. Meanwhile Magnus and Lucian had set the table.

The first two sandwiches had gone to Teddy and Liam, who had been pulled away from their cartoons to eat at the table. By the time the boys had finished and run back to the television, the coffees were poured, three large stacks of sandwiches were ready, and everybody was drooling in anticipation. There had been a stampede to the table and silence had reigned as they ate. Now that silence was over, Allie thought as Tybo answered Sam's question.

"The rogues we saved Allie and Liam from," he told her, and gave her a brief rundown of what Allie had already told them as they all stood to carry their dishes to the sink for a quick rinse before setting them in the dishwasher. By the time the dishwasher was loaded and turned on and the group returned to the table, Mortimer's wife was caught up enough to ask, "I am guessing Liam is the reason Stella left her sire and the others?"

"Yes," Allie said solemnly. "To her, his existence seemed a miracle from God."

"All babies are a miracle from God," Tricia said softly, her gaze sliding to the door and the sounds coming from the television in the room across the hall.

Allie supposed that was true. Every baby seemed a miracle to those around them, but that wasn't what she was talking about, so explained, "Yes, but it was different for Stella. You have to understand she thought she was dead. That she had died in that room and risen a vampire. By that reasoning, she couldn't have become pregnant after the turn, but must have been pregnant when she was killed and turned. Yet her baby still lived and grew inside her dead body."

"A baby would not have survived inside the mother during a turn," Lucian said into the brief silence that followed.

"No, it would not have," Magnus agreed. "Stella probably got pregnant in the first days or weeks after the worst of the turn finished." Glancing to Allie, he explained, "Immortal females need to take in a lot of blood to prevent losing a pregnancy, and new turns need a lot of blood for the first while after they are turned. From what you said, it sounds as if Stella's sire was ensuring she and her husband had a lot of blood after the turn. That would have allowed a fetus to grow without the nanos attacking it."

Nanos again, Allie thought, but didn't ask what those were. Lucian would just grump that she could ask her questions later.

"But Stella would have had to continue to consume copious amounts of blood throughout the pregnancy to ensure she kept the baby and carried it to term," Sam pointed out now.

"Her sire told her that when he told her she was pregnant," Allie said. "He apparently was the one who realized it first and revealed to Stella that she was with child. She had no idea until then. In fact, she didn't really believe him when he first said it."

"I am guessing he wanted to terminate the pregnancy and that is why she fled?" Magnus suggested.

"No. He was delighted and hoping for a boy he could mentor," Allie said grimly, as horrified at the thought as Stella had been. Mouth tightening, she added, "Apparently, a girl baby would have been undesirable and, according to him, 'best torn apart by the group before it could take more than a breath.' I gather he considered females quite useless. Stella said there were very few women among the group. A handful, all members of couples that were taken. Never women who were found on their own. They were used to feed the group and never turned."

"So, she was afraid he would kill the baby if it was a girl," Magnus said, looking angry at the thought.

"Yes. But she was also terrified of his mentoring the baby if it was a boy. That he'd turn it into a monster like he was. She didn't want that."

"That would have scared me silly too," Tricia admitted.

Allie nodded. "I think it did more than that, though. I think finding out she was carrying a child saved Stella. It brought her out of whatever madness had beset her when she was attacked and turned. Stella says until then she was wandering around in a kind of fog, doing whatever she was told without conscience, feeding on the people she was given, and even luring men to the others when ordered to. But learning she was with child snapped her out of that. She was ashamed of what she'd let herself be cowed into doing, and wanted to be better for her son or daughter. To do that, and to keep her baby safe, she had to leave."

"I can see that," Magnus said now. "But if her sire had them all convinced that they could not be away from their room between sunrise and sunset and survive, how did Stella get away and move into the town house across from yours? Calgary, Alberta, is a long way from Vancouver, British Columbia, and she could not take the room with her."

"Actually, she kind of did," Allie said, unsurprised by the confusion that caused.

"How?" Tybo demanded.

"She watched the same movies you did," Allie said with a small smile. "Stella remembered that in the movies, taking dirt from their grave allowed vampires to travel. Since the room they'd been given was both where they died and the closest thing to a grave they had, she gambled on the possibility that taking a bit of the concrete floor would allow her to move around at night and stay somewhere else in daylight without weakening or perishing."

"Ah," Tricia said with a grin, and then assured her, "It wasn't true. She could have left at any time without the concrete, but it was clever of her to think of that anyway."

"She *was* clever," Allie assured her, and then admitted, "Stella said she wasn't sure it would work, but if it didn't and she and the baby died, then she felt it was a better ending than they would have suffered with the group."

"So she took a block of concrete with her?" Tybo asked with disbelief. "How the hell did she break it up?"

"Not a block, just a bit of concrete powder she managed to scratch out of the floor," Allie explained. "No more than a couple of spoons' worth that she kept in a baggie. Stella showed it to me once. She kept it in her pocket at all times."

"What happened to her husband?" Magnus asked. "You do not mention him being in Calgary."

"No." Allie frowned at the thought of Stella's husband and then sighed and told them, "Stephen decided to go with her when they started planning, but the night they were to leave he said it wouldn't work if they both went. He said he'd stay behind to delay anyone realizing she was gone and give her a better chance. He wanted her to get as far away as possible before they realized anything was up and pursued her. He also said that by remaining behind and pretending to be loyal, he might be able to throw them off her scent if they were getting too close to her. He said this was the best way he could think of to protect her and the baby. But later, after the baby was born, he'd find and join her. In the meantime they should both think of a way to make it appear as if the three of them had died."

She let that sink in, and then said, "And then he gave her this."

Allie reached for the chain that held the locket Stella had given her that last night, and that she always wore around her neck so that she wouldn't lose it before Liam was old enough to have it. She tugged it out from under her blouse where the long chain allowed it to rest by her heart, and then lifted it off over her head and stretched her arm out so that it dangled above the center of the table for all of them to see. She thought it was beautiful. The locket was a heart with the front made up of detailed wings. She let them look for a moment, and then pulled her arm back and opened the wings covering the front of the locket. They were tiny doors that, when opened, revealed a picture inside.

Allie stared briefly at the happy young couple in the tiny picture. It was a wedding photo of a dark-haired man with a wide grin, and his arm around a petite brunette who was beaming at the camera. They looked incredibly happy. It was hard to look at when you knew the horrors that had awaited them, she thought, and then sighed and held it out again so that the others could see the photo too.

"Stephen gave this to Stella on their first anniversary, but it was taken away along with all the other jewelry when they finished turning," Allie said quietly. "Stephen said he found it while searching around for things they should take with them while everyone was distracted with some of their victims one day. He'd hoped then to give it to her on their escape, but he now hoped it would reassure her of his love until they could be together again."

Allie pulled the necklace back, closed the wings over the picture, and then slipped it back over her neck as she said, "Stella argued with him, begging him to leave with her, but he was determined to stay behind, he said to protect her as best he could. In the end, she had to go without him."

She tucked the necklace back under her blouse. "They had gathered a little money over the few weeks before the escape, keeping some of the cash from their victims when they could. Stella used it to buy a bus ticket to Kelowna, hoping it was far enough away and big enough to hide in."

"How far is Kelowna from Vancouver?" Tybo asked with a frown.

"About four and a half hours," Lucian answered, which was probably good because Allie had no idea herself.

"But it is not very big," Mortimer said quietly.

"It has over a hundred thousand people," Tricia pointed out. "Not exactly a small town."

"Calgary has over a million and would only have been another six hours on the bus," Lucian responded. "She would have done better to go there right away."

"Yes, she should have," Allie agreed. "Stella wasn't in Kelowna more than a couple days before she spotted one of the rogues from Vancouver."

"Oh, no," Sam said unhappily. "Did they catch her?"

Allie smiled slightly at the woman, appreciating her concern for her friend. "No. Fortunately, Stella spotted them in the market before they spotted her. She managed to slip away unseen. But it scared her. They'd tracked her from Vancouver somehow, and the only way she could think they'd managed that was because she took the bus. Stella had used cash for her ticket, and suspected that they'd questioned the people at the ticket counter, and the ticket seller had remembered her and told them her destination."

"That is more than possible," Magnus murmured when she paused. "Stella was a pretty woman."

Much to her surprise, Allie felt a jolt of jealousy slide through her at his words. Which was ridiculous. She hardly knew the man. And Stella was dead, for heaven's sake. Pushing away emotions she didn't understand, Allie continued. "Stella had started to make a home for herself and the baby there in Kelowna, but after the scare in the market, she was afraid to return to it. So, she left everything behind and hitchhiked to Calgary."

"And moved in across the street from you," Magnus said thoughtfully. "How did she end up there?"

Allie hesitated, struggling with what to tell them. But finally she simply told them what she'd been told. "Stella said the last driver she hitched a ride with was the owner of the town house. She said he was a sweet grandfatherly type and they talked a lot during the hours she rode with him, and then as they neared Calgary he started asking where he should drop her off and she admitted she didn't have anywhere to stay yet. Since it was late at night, he kindly offered to let her use his spare bedroom for the night and promised to help her find more permanent lodgings the next day. Stella accepted the offer and was extremely grateful right up until they got to the house and he turned, as she put it, into a dirty old bastard who expected her to blow him for the use of the bed."

"Man," Tybo groaned. "She couldn't catch a break, could she?"

"It would seem not," Tricia said sadly.

Allie didn't comment on that. "Stella said once she set him straight, he changed his tune. She said she thought he even felt guilty for his behavior because he admitted that he actually lived in a house across the city and the town house was a rental property that was presently without tenants. He offered it to her as a temporary solution until she could find a job and apartment of her own."

"Well, that was lucky," Tricia said, brightening.

"Yes. Lucky . . . and a total lie," Allie said grimly, and then allowed, "Well, probably not a total lie. I suspect the dirty old bastard part was true. Stella's voice was pretty bitter when she said it. But I'm thinking he didn't suddenly turn over a new leaf and become the kindly old benefactor offering her a home like she said."

"What makes you think that?" Magnus asked, and she was surprised by how gentle his voice was. It made her suspect some of her own confused emotions were showing.

Sighing, she admitted, "Because after the town house burned down, the owner's body was found in a freezer in the basement." She shook her head. "I don't know if he attacked her and Stella killed him in self-defense, or what. I hope that's what happened. But whatever the case, he ended up dead in the freezer and she just moved in and lived there with his corpse."

Realizing how strident she had sounded there at the end, Allie forced herself to take several deep breaths to calm herself.

There was silence for a moment, and then Magnus asked, "How did the fire start?"

"Hang on," Sam protested. "We've skipped a bunch here. We know Stella ran from the rogues to Kelowna, then had to flee there for Calgary where you two became friends. But what happened when she told you all this stuff? I mean, did you believe her?"

Allie snorted at the question. "I thought she was crackers . . . until she showed me her fangs." She grimaced at the memory. "That was a shocker. And terrifying. Being forced to acknowledge that vampires existed was bad enough, but learning that my best friend was one?" She shook her head. "It rocked my world, and this time I was the one who rushed off. Stella begged me to stay, but I said I needed to think and fled like the hounds of hell were on my heels. I mean, she was a vampire, for heaven's sake."

Considering she was sitting at a table with a bunch of vampires, Allie wasn't surprised when they all glanced at each other rather than her. Sighing, she paused and sipped at the remains of her cold coffee to wet her mouth, before continuing. "Stella gave me the exact same amount of time to myself that I'd given her. She showed up at about four in the morning on the third night. Suspecting I wouldn't open the door, she used my key as I had done at her place. I had given her one when she gave me hers," she explained, and then shrugged. "It seemed the thing to do. Besides, I didn't have close family or anyone to worry about me. It was reassuring to know someone could get in if I suddenly collapsed or something."

The women nodded. The men peered back at her solemnly, so Allie continued. "She was upset. Somehow instead of it being about my distress at what I'd learned, this talk became about her horror and shame. She said I was the best friend she'd ever had. That she loved me like a sister, and that I was the only one she trusted or believed might give a shit about her and her baby."

"What about Stephen?" Sam asked with a frown.

"Stella didn't trust him. She said their sire had seemed to have some strange hold over Stephen. That they'd spent a lot of time together. Not at first. At first Stephen had avoided him like the plague, and when he was forced to be in his presence, he always came back acting strangely manic and stressed. She said he'd usually pace and fret and then make love to her, but it was different than it used to be, almost desperate. But then one night one of the men came to fetch him. Their sire wanted to see him. She said he was gone all night, not even returning at dawn. It was the next evening before she saw him again and he wouldn't talk about what had happened.

"Stella said Stephen was distracted after that, and cold. She said he started going out on raiding parties with the other men, and staying away from her. He even started tormenting their victims like the others. They'd both been a little crazy after the turn, but learning she was pregnant had seemed to snap them both out of it, at least briefly, but he was changing, becoming as cruel and heartless as the others, and it scared her. It made her glad they were leaving. She felt sure he'd be all right again once they were away from the others. Only he didn't leave with her, and she didn't really believe the excuses he gave for why. She said he was no longer the man he'd been before he died and became a vampire. Stella didn't trust him anymore."

There was silence for a minute, and then Tybo suggested, "Their sire could have read their minds, realized they were planning an escape, and decided he liked the idea of Stella gone. You did say he didn't like women much. Maybe he told Stephen he'd let Stella go if he remained."

"Wait. What? Read their minds?" Allie asked with disbelief.

"Reading the minds of mortals is one of the abilities immortals have," Magnus said almost apologetically. "An older immortal can also read a younger one as a rule."

Allie sagged back in her seat with disbelief and gaped at the six people around the table. Then she snapped her mouth shut and asked sharply, "Then why the hell did I have to relive all of this for you? You could have just read my mind."

"Magnus cannot read you at all, and the rest of us can only read your surface memories," Lucian said mildly, and then for clarification, added, "Things you are thinking about."

Allie stared at him briefly and then glanced to

Magnus and back. "Why can't Magnus read me? Is he not a full vampire or something?"

"Immortal," Lucian corrected her tightly. "And yes, of course he is a full immortal, but as your—"

"Explanations later, you said," Magnus interrupted sharply, looking stressed, and Allie presumed that whatever the reason that he couldn't read her it must be embarrassing.

"Yes. Of course," Lucian agreed.

Allie frowned from one man to the other, really wanting to learn why Magnus was the only one who couldn't read her, but knowing she would have to wait for that explanation. She wasn't willing to wait for the answer to another question, though. "Does that mean Liam can read me too?"

"No," Tricia assured her. "Teddy and Liam are too young to be able to read minds yet."

Allie was just relaxing at that reassurance when the woman added, "Immortal children do not start to pick that up until the age of five or six."

"What?" she asked with dismay. Dear God, her little boy might be reading her mind in another year.

"There have been a few who have picked up the skill a little earlier," Lucian countered. "Although I have never heard of one mastering mind control before five."

Allie's alarm immediately increased and she squawked, "Mind control?"

As soon as the words left her mouth, she recalled the sense she'd had the night before of not being in control when she'd walked out of the pizza joint and got in the car. Her eyes immediately shot to Magnus. "Oh, my God, you controlled me last night and made me get in the car."

"No," Lucian said with certainty. "That must have been Tybo. Magnus can no more control you than he can read you."

"Sorry," Tybo said when her gaze shot to him. "But we needed to leave quickly and you weren't cooperating."

When Allie opened her mouth to respond, Sam piped up with, "Explanations later. I want to know what happened with Stella. She was saying you were the only person she trusted, and then . . . ?"

Allie stared at her blankly for a minute, and then sagged in her seat and tried to find the thread of what she'd been telling. She didn't know why, though, if they could just read it from her mind.

"Because we can only read it if you are thinking of it," Sam reminded her. "And right now you're freaking out about what we can and can't do and not thinking about Stella."

"Right," Allie muttered, and then glanced at the other woman sharply as she realized Sam must have read her mind to know she was wondering about that.

"Sorry," Sam said with a shrug, and then prompted, "Stella had no one to trust but you . . . ?"

Allie scowled at her, but forced herself back to the subject. "Right, so after telling me her concerns about Stephen . . . Well, I didn't know what to say to that. I'd found it kind of funky that he hadn't gone with her either, so I could hardly reassure her. And I didn't know about the whole mind-reading thing, so didn't even consider that their sire might have read theirs, realized what they were up to, and used the knowledge to force Stephen to stay," she added in a steely voice, but then frowned and admitted, "I wish I had. The thought that Stephen might have become like the others was crushing to Stella." She sighed at the memory of Stella weeping.

"Anyway, after a few moments where neither of us said anything, Stella said she knew the things she'd done since being turned were unforgiveable, and that she was a dead soulless monster now, but that she used to be a good person and was trying to be one again for her baby. She swore she'd never ever hurt me, and said she needed me in her life. And so did her baby. I was the godmother, the only person she would trust her baby to if anything happened to her.

"It was a lot to take in," Allie admitted quietly. "My feelings were very confused. But Stella had never harmed me. In fact, she'd been a wonderful friend— fun, generous, sweet. She just didn't seem like a monster."

"She was not a monster," Magnus assured her solemnly. "She was just thrown into a nightmare situation and doing her best to survive it and keep her baby safe."

Allie nodded, but the words made her feel better. Actually, all of this was making her feel better. It was a great relief to actually be able to talk about this stuff to someone. Allie had spent the last four years entirely alone, unable to discuss her life or Liam with anyone. This was helping to ease the very heavy burden she'd been feeling crushed under for all that time. Accepting that for what it was, Allie smiled crookedly and said, "In the end, I assured Stella I could handle the situation and we were still friends. And things pretty much went back to the way they had been, except I had a lot of questions."

"I would be surprised if you did not," Magnus said dryly.

She smiled at him, but couldn't help wondering why he was the only one who couldn't read her. Pushing that aside for now, she continued. "I made her show me her fangs several times, and asked where she was getting her blood. She admitted that she was picking up men in bars on the nights she went out, going home with them, and biting them. She said she was careful now not to take too much blood, and other than a couple of false starts when she first got to Calgary, she'd left her meals alive and well."

"Maybe the town house owner was one of those false starts," Sam suggested.

"Maybe," Allie agreed. "It was a couple weeks after New Year's that she went into labor. I had just finished a big project and—"

"Wait a minute," Sam interrupted. "No one told me what you do. What project?"

"She works at the blood bank," Tybo said.

"I've only worked at the blood bank the last couple of months as a temporary part-time gig. Really I'm a web designer," Allie corrected.

Tybo's eyebrows rose. "What websites have you designed? Anything I might have seen? What are you working on now?"

Allie smiled with amusement at the quick-fire questions. He reminded her of Liam when he got excited about something. Before she could answer, though, Lucian said, "She can tell you that later. Let's finish this business with Stella first."

"Of course," she said calmly, unsurprised by it now.

"You were talking about Stella's going into labor," Sam said helpfully. "You were just finishing a big project and . . . ?"

"Right. Thank you," Allie said. "So I was working in my office upstairs, and Stella was downstairs baking something. She had started to spend a lot of time at my place as it got closer to her time," she explained. "I guess it was about midnight when I heard this crash. I rushed downstairs to find Stella on her hands and knees in the kitchen surrounded by liquid and glass. Her water had broken as she was making whatever she was going to bake, and she, for some reason, panicked about the mess on the floor, snatched for paper towels to clean it up, and knocked over a glass. Now she was trying to clean up both of them."

"Oh, dear," Sam said with wide eyes. "What was she thinking?"

"I have no idea," Allie said dryly. "I've never had a baby, so have no idea how a woman's mind works during labor. But Stella's didn't seem to be too clear in that moment. She was determined to clean up the mess. *Seriously* determined," Allie stressed. "I ended up having to sweep up the glass while she mopped up the liquid before I could get her up off the floor. But when I tried to urge her to get her coat on so we could go to the hospital, she balked. She wasn't going to the hospital. They'd know she was a vampire and lock her and the baby in a cage somewhere and do experiments on them."

Allie shook her head. "I think I just stood there staring at her for a full two minutes when she said that. It had never occurred to me that she couldn't go to the hospital. I mean, when I talked about getting a bag ready for the hospital and such before she admitted what she was to me, she'd nodded and agreed and assured me she'd handle it. Turns out she just did that because she couldn't say she wasn't going without explaining why. And we hadn't talked about the trip to the hospital since the revelation because I was too busy asking stupid questions."

Allie pushed the hair back from her face at the memory. "Liam was born in my living room on a mattress I dragged down from the guest bedroom. It was the scariest, most disgusting, most painful yet most beautiful experience of my life."

"Painful?" Magnus asked uncertainly. "You mean for Stella?"

"Hell, no," Allie said on a laugh. "I mean, sure, she was in terrible pain, but at one point, in that pain, she gouged grooves of skin out of my arms and I can't count the number of times I had to warn her to let go of my hand or wrist because she was about to break the bone." She shook her head at the memory. "I should have read up on childbirth. I had no idea it could be so gross. I mean, it wasn't just the baby that came out, and when the pain was at its worst she started vomiting blood."

Tricia was smiling wryly at this news, but Sam paled and whispered, "Oh, my."

It made Allie suspect the woman hadn't had children yet and she completely understood her distress. That experience had been enough to make her kind of glad she hadn't had children herself and that she had Liam. Not that she still couldn't have them, physically, but constantly being on the run with Liam wasn't likely to lead to her meeting anyone she might want to have children of her own with.

"Liam was the most beautiful baby I'd ever seen when he finally showed up." Allie smiled. "I insisted Stella stay with me for a while so that I could help look after him while she healed from the birth. She was seriously exhausted and pale by the time it was over. She was also incredibly cranky and basically ordered me to take the baby and leave her alone. I just thought that was the crankiness until she said I smelled like dinner to her and unless that's what I wanted to be I should leave at once." She grimaced at the memory. "Since her fangs were out, I took her at her word, scooped up little Liam, and hurried upstairs and then just paced around rocking him. It was probably fifteen minutes later that I heard the front door open and close. It was Stella leaving. I couldn't believe she was up and about already, but she obviously needed blood, so I just continued to rock Liam. Stella returned a couple hours later and, I swear, looking at her, you wouldn't believe she'd just been through what she had. She looked completely fine, her old self. Well, except that her stomach was completely flat again, and I know that wouldn't happen with a mortal," she added wryly.

"Immortals heal much more quickly than mortals," Magnus explained solemnly.

Allie merely nodded. "Stella stayed with me for the next week, and then returned to the town house across the street so that I could work without Liam's crying to distract me, which I appreciated. We still spent a lot of time together, and I watched Liam for her while she went out in search of a blood donor most nights, but by the start of the second week of February I was in a crunch with work. I had two deadlines for the fifteenth and was stressed out, so she insisted on taking Liam with her on her nightly outings for the next week, which I thought was just crazy. You can't take a baby to a bar," she pointed out. "But she said she'd go to one of the coffee shops that were open all night or something and insisted it would be fine and I could look after Liam for her again once I finished my projects."

Allie fell silent briefly then, stealing herself against what she had to recall next. But finally, she said, "It was the fourteenth of February. I had finished one of the projects, which removed a lot of pressure, and I was nearly done the second, so I decided to give myself a break and stop early that night and finish up the next. Well, early for me," she added wryly. "It was around eleven thirty when I shut down the computer and went downstairs to grab something for dinner. It was maybe midnight when Stella showed up at the door. She'd obviously just returned from town. She said they'd found her, removed Liam's receiving blanket, passed him off to me, and pulled out a doll that she wrapped the blanket around instead. She also gave me her necklace—" Allie touched her chest where the locket was now hidden under her blouse "—and reminded me of my promise to look after Liam if anything happened to her, and then she was gone.

"I peeked through the blinds and watched her walk across the street to her town house pushing Liam's carriage, and then she went in, and before the door was quite closed, the town house exploded and burst into flames." Allie paused to clear her throat and blinked a couple times to try to shift the liquid gathering in her eyes. "At first I thought maybe it was a trick to make the vampires think she was dead. That she'd somehow caused the explosion that quickly. I mean, she could move so fast when she wanted to. Scary fast," she recalled with a disbelieving shake of the head.

Stella had hidden that speed from her at first, but once Allie knew about her, she hadn't bothered to hide it anymore and she was always stunned at the speed she could manage. Sighing, Allie continued. "I thought, or at least hoped, that she'd rushed out the back door to escape it. But the door hadn't quite closed, and swung back open after the explosion. Stella stumbled to the entrance in flames, the doll still clutched to her chest.

She stood there for maybe two or three seconds and then turned and just collapsed into the flames."

"The rogues blew up her house?" Sam gasped with horror. "But I thought the sire wanted the baby if it was a boy? Why would he kill both of them that way?"

"Liam was not killed," Tricia reminded her. "The baby Stella carried was a doll."

"But they couldn't know Stella would leave Liam with Allie," Tybo pointed out. "They could have killed both of them with that explosion."

"Which is why I don't think the vampires caused the explosion," Allie said now.

Everyone at the table turned to her and everyone but Magnus's expression became concentrated on her forehead. She wasn't surprised when Tricia exclaimed, "You think Stella set up the house to explode when she walked in. You think she sacrificed herself in the hopes of saving Liam."

Seven

Allie read the disbelief on the faces of the people around the table and pointed out, "She had a doll to substitute for Liam, gave me her child, and reminded me of my promise to take care of him if anything happened to her. She then gave me the necklace she never took off, to give to him when he was older. She knew she was going to die," Allie said with certainty, and then told them what she'd decided after years of pondering it. "Stella must have set up something long ago to make the house blow up. Maybe even when she first moved in. She probably planned to be going out the back door with her baby as the house blew up, and maybe even hoped to catch some of the vampires in the explosion."

"You think her friendship with you changed her plans," Tricia murmured, her gaze concentrated on her forehead. "That she decided Liam would have a better chance at a halfway normal life if the vampires actually saw her and what they would have thought was him die."

"Yes," Allie sighed. "But . . . I think she was suffering a bad case of postpartum depression too. I mean, before Liam was born, Stella used to struggle with the things she'd done when she was first turned. But after he was born . . ." Allie shook her head. "Stella loved him so much. She called him her little angel, but she started saying things like he'd probably be better off without having a monster like her for a mother."

"As an immortal she couldn't have been suffering postpartum depression," Sam said quietly. "It was just her conscience and her belief that she was now a vampire that was tormenting her. The sad thing is if we'd known about her we could have told her what she really was and helped her deal with it."

"She had killed mortals," Lucian reminded Sam. "If we had known about her, she would have been put down as a rogue."

"Oh. Yes, of course," Sam said, but frowned at the realization as he turned to spear Allie with a look.

"Did you see the vam—" Lucian began, but stopped abruptly as he started to say *vampires*. Shock and then disgust crossed his face before he said, "Did you see the rogues she said had found her?"

"No," Allie said apologetically. "I did look around to try to spot them, but it was very dark and there was no one on the streets."

"But you have seen them since," he said with certainty, and she supposed the fact that she was no longer living in Calgary probably gave that away.

"About a week after Stella died, I heard a noise in the backyard and looked out to see a man creeping toward the house. He was just a darker shape in the night, but then the moonlight, or maybe the lights from the neighboring houses, reflected off his eyes. Seeing that, I knew at once that he was one of the vampires Stella was so terrified of. Her eyes glowed like that in the night, and she had said it was the easiest way to identify one. So when I saw that, I just freaked. I immediately gathered up Liam, rushed to the garage, jumped in the car, and fled." Allie grimaced and then finished with, "And we've been running ever since. The first stop was Edmonton, but there have been countless cities and towns between then and now. Toronto is just the latest in a long line of them."

"They keep tracking you down?" Magnus asked with a frown.

Allie nodded and said with frustration, "I don't know how. I left everything behind. I didn't even take clothes other than what Liam and I were wearing. I had to replace them in Edmonton when I got there. I also got rid of my cell phone, and stopped using credit cards. Hell, I even drive hours from where I'm living when I have to go to the bank, just in case they can track my banking activity, but they keep finding me."

There was silence for a minute, and then Magnus asked, "Did you keep the same car throughout?"

"Yes," Allie admitted, glancing at him with surprise. "You think they've been tracking the car?"

He hesitated, but then said, "It is a possibility. It sounds like that is the only thing that has gone with you from place to place, except for Liam."

"Well, that won't be a problem this time," Tybo pointed out. "Your car is still in the parking lot of your apartment building, and we're taking a helicopter to Port Henry. They won't be able to follow."

Allie hoped he was right. It would be nice not to be looking over her shoulder for a change. It would be nice too not to have to give up blood to Liam, and even just to be able to talk about this stuff with someone. Those things were making Port Henry seem as attractive as a luxury resort in a tropical locale, she thought, and then glanced to Lucian with curiosity and asked, "Why haven't you asked me to describe the rogues I've spotted over the last four years, or if I recall the head guy's name yet?"

"Because I can read the descriptions from your mind and that you have not recalled the name," he said simply.

"Oh. Right." She felt her face heat up at the idea that he was reading her thoughts, and started running back through them, trying to see if she'd thought anything she needed to be embarrassed about.

"Maybe it would help you remember his name if you thought back to when you first heard it," Magnus suggested. "Do you remember when Stella told you his name?"

"Not really," Allie admitted apologetically, even as she tried to search out the memory. Distracted by the task, she muttered, "I mean, it's been four years since she told me the truth."

"A hectic four years too, from the sounds of it," Tricia said, her voice sympathetic.

"Yes," Allie acknowledged absently, her mind on when she'd heard the name of Stella's sire. It must have been when she'd first told her the story, of course. She made herself remember the room they'd been sitting in, and tried to imagine she was back there with Stella telling her what had happened to her. After a moment, she frowned and muttered, "I remember his name started with an *A* like mine and it was strange. I'd never heard it before. It sounded like *amazon*, but wasn't *amazon*. It was Ackermon, or Addabon or—"

"Abaddon," Lucian growled.

Allie's eyes popped open. "That's it!"

"Dear God," Mortimer said quietly, and then glanced to Lucian. "Basha and Marcus are in San Francisco following up on a report of a possible sighting of him there."

"Call them back to Toronto," Lucian said grimly. "Basha needs to be here."

Nodding, Mortimer started to rise, but Lucian waved him back to his seat. "After we finish here." Turning to Allie then, he asked, "Stella lived in British Columbia when she was attacked?"

"Yes." Allie nodded firmly. "Vancouver."

"When she arrived on your doorstep the night she died, did she specify who had found her? Did she mentioned seeing Abaddon himself there in Calgary?"

Allie shook her head. "She just said, 'They've found me.'"

"So Abaddon himself could still be in Vancouver," Mortimer said slowly. "He might just be sending crews out, first after Stella and the boy, and now after Allie and the boy."

Lucian shook his head firmly. "He will want the boy too much. He would not wait behind in Vancouver and depend on clumsy new turns to find him."

"But why would Abaddon want Liam so badly?" Tricia asked with confusion.

"He wants to create another Leonius," Lucian said with grim certainty. "He spent his entire life playing puppet master first to Leonius and then to his son. With them gone . . ." Lucian's mouth firmed out. "This would be a perfect opportunity for him. The chance to get his hands on another child to corrupt and twist into a third Leonius."

"But both Leonius and his son were no-fangers," Sam pointed out. "That's why they were crazy. Liam is an immortal. He won't be insane like Leo and his father and likely to do the things they were willing and even eager to do under Abaddon's tutelage."

"What is a no-fanger?" Allie asked with confusion, but might as well have saved her breath. No one answered her; instead, Lucian responded to Sam's comment.

"You do not think that if Abaddon got his hands on Liam young enough he could twist the boy's mind?" Lucian asked dryly. "From what we have heard, Stella was a perfectly normal young woman, yet look at how she changed after her encounter with him."

"Yes, but that was like a temporary madness from the turn," Sam argued. "And Liam is already immortal."

"It was not being turned that drove Stella to do the things she did," Magnus said quietly. "It was the manner of the turn. The way their captors waited until the need for blood forced her and her husband awake and then tossed in bloodied victims to be rent apart."

"Yes, but Liam is already an immortal," she repeated. "He could not do that to him."

"Not as part of a turn," Magnus agreed. "But he could just lock him up without blood for days or weeks, wait until he is in desperate need and mad with blood lust, and then throw in victims who have been cut up so they reek of it." He paused briefly and then shrugged. "Combine that with a few other tricks and treats and you would either have another Leonius, or the boy would end up dead and Abaddon would look for another victim to try to turn into his next Leonius."

Lucian grunted in agreement and then turned back to Allie. "Did any of the rogues you have spotted the last four years fit Stella's description of Abaddon?"

Allie scowled at him briefly, still wanting to know what a no-fanger was, and just what they were talking about; but knowing she wasn't going to get any answers just now, she finally shook her head. "Stella said he looked like an accountant, unremarkable. Not one of the vampires I've seen has looked like an accountant. They've been shabby-looking, with grungy clothes, and either bald, or with hair overlong or just plain long. Even so, they've all been gorgeous, not unremarkable."

"Gorgeous?" Sam asked with surprise, and then glanced around as she commented, "I would think he'd concentrate more on size and strength than good looks."

"Abaddon prefers men," Lucian announced.

"Oh." Sam sat back.

"One of the men at the apartment last night might have fit Stella's description," Magnus said thoughtfully, and when everyone turned to look at him, he continued. "While the rest of the men piled out of the vehicles to approach the building, there was a man who remained in the passenger seat of the van and watched. He was unremarkable in looks, but better kept than the others. His hair was short and his clothes clean."

Lucian stood abruptly, nearly knocking his chair over in his haste. Turning to Mortimer, he growled, "Time to get Allie and Liam out of here and down to Port Henry."

"Should I send extra Enforcers?" Mortimer asked.

Lucian considered the question briefly, but then shook his head. "We need all hands here to search for Abaddon. He does not get away again." His gaze shifted to Tricia. "I want you and Teddy at the house." When she nodded, he continued. "And I will call Victor and have him and DJ step back into the game for this. With the four of you and Magnus and Tybo there too, Allie and Liam should be safe enough."

"Should I call Basha and Marcus now, then?" Mortimer asked, standing as well.

Lucian shook his head. "I will."

There was a moment of silence as he left the room, pulling out his cell phone as he went, and then Mortimer stood too. "Harper's pilot is down at the garage with Anders. I'll call down and tell him to ready the helicopter to go."

"I guess I should get our Go bags." Allie pushed her chair back from the table and stood. Everyone else stood up as well, but she ignored them and headed out of the kitchen. She considered going into the living room to fetch Liam first, but then decided to leave him to play. She could fetch him on the way back to the kitchen.

Allie didn't make it halfway up the stairs before she had to stop. Her heart was thumping away at a rapid tattoo that she didn't just feel in her chest, but her neck and arms too. It was more than a bit alarming, as were the sudden shakes that attacked her. Stopping on the steps, Allie tightened her tingling fingers on the rail and closed her eyes against the spots suddenly exploding in her vision. She barely heard Magnus's concerned voice over the sound of her own heartbeat before her legs suddenly went out beneath her.

"Well?"

Magnus glanced up at Lucian's impatient question as the man strode into the room, followed by Mortimer. They were in the bedroom Allie had slept in last night. He'd scooped her up as she'd fainted and carried her up here, barking over his shoulder at Mortimer to call and find out when Dani would get there. Unfortunately, it had turned out that Dani had been stopped on her way out of the hospital by another emergency. It had held her up, but only briefly this time. She'd been done and on the way when Mortimer had called. She'd arrived just minutes after Allie had fainted and was now finishing examining her.

"She is pale, clammy, breathing rapidly, and suffering from tachycardia. Rapid heartbeat," Dani added as she recalled she was speaking to laymen. "She needs a blood transfusion."

Lucian scowled at her for her trouble. "We suspected she needed a blood transfusion. In fact, Mortimer told you that, or should have, when he spoke to you."

"He did," she admitted.

"So? How long will that take?"

Dani peered back at Allie and then sighed. "I need to do some tests, Lucian. A blood count, blood typing and crossing . . ." She shook her head. "I need to take her to the hospital."

"No," Lucian said at once.

"No?" Dani turned grimly on the man in full doctor mode.

"She would not be safe in a hospital here," Magnus explained before Lucian could bark at the woman. He knew that was the main concern. If Abaddon got his hands on Allie . . . Magnus didn't even want to think about that. Losing his life mate before he even got to claim her would be . . . He didn't want to think about that either.

"You'll just have to arrange a guard for her at the hospital, then," Dani said firmly. "Because she needs—"

"Abaddon is after her and the boy," Lucian interrupted abruptly, and Magnus wasn't surprised when Dani paled. When last in Canada he had heard the tale of how Abaddon's previous pet, Leonius Livius, had kidnapped Dani and her younger sister and the horrors that had ensued. She, more than anyone, would understand the danger Abaddon posed.

Dani turned to peer at Allie briefly, and then straightened her shoulders and began digging around in the black bag she'd brought with her. "I'm going to take a couple of blood samples. One of your men will have to deliver it to the Argeneau labs for testing. I'll give her a sedative and travel to Port Henry with Allie so that I can monitor her on the way there, and be there to give her a transfusion when they call with the results."

"Is a sedative necessary?" Magnus asked with concern.

"Travel is stressful. Hell, this whole situation is stressful," Dani added grimly. "Her heart can't take much more stress right now. It's already under pressure trying to get blood where it needs to go when it has little to work with. Once we give her a transfusion she should be fine, but until then she is better off asleep." Pausing in gathering vials and needles, she glanced to Lucian and asked, "They'll be able to get the blood I need in Port Henry? Their blood bank has all blood types?"

"Yes."

Nodding, she turned back to her bag. "Then we should be able to leave in a few minutes. But someone needs to call Decker and explain what's happening. And I'll have to call my office so they can cancel my appointments for the next couple of days."

"The next couple of days?" Sam asked with surprise as Mortimer pulled out his phone and began to punch in numbers. "Surely a transfusion doesn't take that long?"

"No," Dani admitted. "A transfusion only takes a couple hours. Four, tops. But she'll need to be monitored for at least twenty-four hours afterward to be sure she isn't having adverse reactions, and I presume Lucian won't allow her to be hospitalized in Port Henry either?" she asked, looking toward the man.

"No," Lucian said at once.

"Then I will need to monitor her," Dani said on a sigh.

"Oh," Sam said with a frown, and then glanced to her husband as he began to speak into his phone.

Mortimer was short and sweet. "Abaddon's in town. Dani's flying down to Port Henry with his latest target to look after her. If you want to join them, you had best get your ass here now."

Apparently, Decker didn't waste time asking questions, because after a pause and a grunt, Mortimer put his phone away and announced, "He was already on his way here to start his shift. He'll be here in ten."

"Is there enough room on the helicopter for everyone?" Magnus asked before anyone could say something else. The number of people making this trip was growing by the minute. They were now at eight by his count, and in his experience, most helicopters could only handle six passengers and the pilot. Of course, there were larger helicopters too, but he wasn't sure how large Harper's helicopter was.

Clucking with irritation, Lucian turned to Mortimer. "How quickly can we get a plane here?"

"I'll call and find out," Mortimer assured him, heading for the door.

"Tell them it is a top priority," Lucian called after him.

"I did not know there was an airport in Port Henry," Magnus commented as Lucian turned back.

"A small municipal one about four miles east of town," Lucian said. "Teddy and Victor will have to arrange ground transportation to the bed and breakfast from there. Speaking of which, I had best go call them and inform them of the change of plans."

Magnus watched him leave, then turned back to see Dani inserting a needle with a tube holder on the end into Allie's arm. She popped a vial into the tube holder and then asked, "What does Abaddon want with this woman?"

"It is really her son he wants, I think," Magnus admitted as he watched blood fill the vial. "Although he might take Allie to tend to the boy."

"Why does he want the boy?" Dani asked, switching out the now almost full vial for an empty one.

"We believe he wants to turn little Liam into another Leonius," Sam answered.

Dani gaped over her shoulder at them with dismay. "That sweet little boy I saw downstairs with Teddy?"

When they both nodded silently, her mouth tightened and she turned back to what she was doing with a muttered, "Another Leonius. God help us."

"Lucian's call sure put the fire under the women's feet. Elvi and Mabel have been rushing around like chickens with their heads cut off trying to ready everything."

Magnus tore his gaze from where Allie lay across his lap and looked at the man driving the police SUV that he, Allie, Dani, and Decker were in. Teddy Brunswick, police chief of Port Henry and Katricia's husband, had been waiting at the airport when their plane landed. Victor Argeneau had been with him and was transporting Teddy Jr., Liam, Katricia, and Tybo in a second SUV, one that was unmarked.

"Are there enough beds for everyone?" Dani asked with concern.

"Oh, yes," Teddy assured them. "It'll be a bit crowded, but they worked out a way to fit everyone in nicely. Fortunately, they let the bed and breakfast bit slide when they had the babies. They were kept hopping with the newborns, and between that and the restaurant they were too tired and busy to keep up with guests too," the man explained, and Magnus knew it was for his benefit. From the talk on the plane, he was aware that Dani and Decker visited

Port Henry a couple of times a year at least, so probably knew all this.

"The girls are just getting to an age where Elvi and Mabel could probably manage guests again," Teddy continued. "But they aren't sure they want to be bothered."

"Constantly having guests in the house would be a big intrusion on their family lives," Magnus commented, brushing a tress of long light brown hair away from Allie's face.

"Exactly," Teddy agreed. "Elvi and Mabel didn't mind so much when it was just the two of them. They made it their lives, I guess. But now that they're both married and have kids . . ." He shrugged, and then added, "It's not like they need the money. The restaurant is always crazy busy. And, of course, Victor and DJ both have money of their own."

"How do DJ and Mabel like living in their own house?" Decker asked as Dani took Allie's pulse.

"Love it," Teddy assured them.

It was Decker who turned in his seat to explain. "Mabel and Elvi lived in Casey Cottage together when DJ and Victor met them, and the two couples lived there for a time after, but then the house behind Elvi's came up for sale and DJ and Mabel bought it."

"What a mess that was," Teddy said with amusement. "They liked the position of it, being so close to Casey Cottage, but not the house itself. Did a big renovation. Gutted it from the studs out, knocked down walls here and there to make it more open concept, and refitted it all real nice. Then they took down the fence between the two properties. The backyards are just one big shared green space now and they're all happy as can be."

"That sounds nice." Dani released Allie's wrist with a satisfied nod and sat back in her seat.

"And real convenient in this situation too," Teddy assured her. "The teams that guard Miss Chambers and her son at night will be sleeping at Mabel and DJ's house during the day, and the day guards can sleep there at night. A good thing too since there are so many of you. Harper, Drina, and Stephanie are here as well," he informed them. "When he heard so many were coming, Harper suggested that perhaps he should take the girls back to Toronto, but Lucian said no. Drina's a good Enforcer, and Stephanie's been training as one. He wanted them to stay just in case Abaddon managed to track Miss Chambers and her son here."

"Is that likely?" Dani asked with concern. "Did Abaddon know she was at the Enforcer house? And even if he did, we flew down here. He can hardly track a plane. Can he?"

Decker's voice was low and soothing as he assured her. "Lucian would hardly send Allie and Liam to Port Henry if he thought Abaddon could track them here. Not with all the immortal children presently living in the area. He is just being cautious."

"Yes, sir. Better to be safe than sorry," Teddy put in, and then added reassuringly, "I'm certain Lucian will track down Abaddon in Toronto. Meanwhile, we all get to enjoy a nice little visit down here. Kind of a family reunion for Stephanie, really, what with everyone she considers family being here at the same time for a change."

"Yes," Dani murmured, but Magnus noticed that she still looked worried. He got the feeling, though, that she was worried for Allie and not herself.

Frowning, he peered down at her still face. Even asleep, she looked exhausted and wrung out. Magnus suspected nothing short of a transfusion would fix that, and hoped there was word from the lab when they reached the house.

"Here we are," Teddy announced suddenly, and turned off the road onto a cement driveway.

There wasn't much to see when Magnus looked up. The road was blocked from view on one side of them by a line of evergreen bushes; a garage was in front of them, and a high wooden fence ran along their other side from the corner of the garage to back behind them and out of his line of vision.

"Right," Teddy said as he shut off the engine. "Dani, why don't you and Mr. Bjarnesen take Miss Chambers inside and out of the cold while Decker and I see to the luggage . . . such as it is," he added dryly as he opened his door and got out.

Magnus smiled faintly at the police chief's comment as he undid his seat belt. There wasn't much luggage to bother with. Just his suitcase and Allie's two backpacks that she called Go bags. Tybo, Decker, and Dani hadn't had time to pack anything and planned to shop tomorrow for necessities to see them through for a couple of days. So he wasn't surprised that the two men had the baggage in hand and the back of the SUV closed before he'd even finished getting Allie out of the SUV. Very aware that Allie was mortal, Magnus had moved slowly and carefully to ensure he didn't bang her head, arms, or legs into anything as he maneuvered cautiously out of the vehicle.

The second SUV, an unmarked one, was pulling in as Dani led them to a gate in the fence. As he paused to wait for her to open it, Magnus noted that Teddy and Decker were stopping to wait for the others. He briefly considered waiting as well so that Liam could see that his mother was all right. The boy had been anxious at being separated from her on landing, but it was extremely cold, and Allie was already in a weakened condition. He decided the less time they spent in the cold, the better, and quickly followed Dani through the gate when she held it open for him.

A short sidewalk led to a large deck that started halfway along the back of the house and wrapped around the side. Magnus wasn't terribly surprised when Liam and Teddy Jr. caught up to them as they mounted the steps to the deck. The boys didn't say anything; they merely fell into step on either side of him, Liam's anxious gaze shifting between his mother and where he was going as they crossed the deck.

Magnus had just opened his mouth to assure the lad that his mother would be fine when the sound of a door opening drew his attention.

"Come in, come in. Out of the cold," a pretty blonde

greeted them, smiling in welcome as she held the door open.

"Oh, Mabel, hello," Dani sighed, pausing briefly to hug the woman before leading the way past her and into the house.

Magnus nodded in greeting as he led the two boys inside, and then found himself entering a kitchen with an L-shaped counter that he followed Dani around to make room for the others now trooping into the house. A dining area was situated past the kitchen, separated only by the counter, and Dani led himself and the boys to stand next to the table before stopping, and turning back to look Allie over briefly.

"How long until the sedative wears off?" Magnus asked.

"Not for hours," Dani assured him. "Which is fine—she needs the rest."

He nodded in agreement and then the sound of creaking wood caught his ear. They were standing almost under a large archway into a spacious entry with double doors on one end and a curving staircase at the other. The creaking was someone descending the wooden staircase, he realized as a redhead hurried down to join them.

"Dani, love." The newcomer enfolded Dani in a warm and welcoming embrace, rocking her slightly from side to side. "It's been too long, dear."

"Only since last summer, Elvi," Dani protested as she hugged her back.

"As I said, too long." The woman Magnus now knew must be Elvi Argeneau smiled at him over

Dani's shoulder, and then pulled back to tell Dani, "Steph should be down in a minute. She has been excited ever since she heard you were coming."

"Oh, I—" Dani began, and then paused as a squeal drew their attention to a young woman bounding down the stairs at speed. She was almost a carbon copy of Dani except that her blond hair was up in a ponytail. Dani's sister, Stephanie, was Magnus's guess, and he watched with interest as she rushed to them and threw her arms around the doctor with another happy squeal.

"Dani, Dani, Dani! I was so happy when they said you were coming too." Stephanie pulled back to eye her in question as she added, "But I can't believe you were willing to take time off work to do it. You never do that."

"Well, Allie needed help, and it meant getting to spend some time with you, so . . ." Dani shrugged and then kissed the young woman on the cheek. "It's good to see you, sis."

"Good to see you too," Stephanie chirped, and then glanced around, her expression becoming concerned as it landed on Allie. Releasing Dani, she crossed to peer down at her, murmuring, "This is her?"

"Allison Chambers," Dani said quietly before Magnus could respond. Moving to join them, she added, "She's had a rough time of it the last couple of days and needs a blood transfusion."

"She's had a rough time of it for most of her life," Stephanie said, her voice somewhat distracted and her eyes pulsing with a glow that brightened and then darkened before brightening again. "But she's given up everything for . . ." Pausing, she turned and stared past Magnus and then smiled and breathed, "Liam."

Magnus turned to see the boy standing a couple of steps back with Teddy, watching them with interest, and then Teddy nudged Liam and said, "That's Stephy. She's weird sometimes, but cool. You'll like her."

"Yep, that's me. Weird but cool Stephy," Stephanie chuckled, the glow fading from her eyes as she stepped forward and offered her hand to Allie's son. "A pleasure to meet you, Liam. Your mom is going to be fine. My sister will make her well, Magnus will make her like us, and you'll never again have to worry about losing her. The two of you won't have to run anymore either. It's all going to work out."

"Promise?" Liam asked, his expression serious.

"Cross my heart," Stephanie assured him. "I may be weird, but I'm never wrong."

"Weird's okay," he assured her, accepting her hand and shaking it. "Mom says she's weird too. I like weird."

"Well, now that that's settled," Elvi said lightly. "Magnus, Liam, I'm Elvi Argeneau. Welcome to my home."

Liam stepped forward and offered his hand, saying politely, "Hello, ma'am. Thank you for having us."

"You're more than welcome," Elvi assured him, and then asked, "Would you like to see the room where you and your mom will be staying? That way we could tuck her in and let her rest."

"Yes, please, ma'am," Liam said softly. "Mrs. Tricia says Mom needs her rest."

"That she does," Elvi said solemnly, and took his hand, then smiled at Magnus and gestured for him to follow before turning to lead Liam to the stairs, saying, "Your mom's done a fine job with you, young man. You're very polite."

"Thank you, Mrs. Elvi."

"You're welcome," Elvi said, and then called out, "Teddy, are you coming too? The girls are watching movies in the upper porch and you can take Liam there after he sees where he's going to sleep and where his mom will be."

"Can I, Mom?" Teddy asked, and Magnus paused at the bottom of the steps to wait.

"Yes. But be good and not too much noise while Liam's mom is sleeping," Tricia said firmly.

"Okay," Teddy called, barely waiting for her words to finish before rushing past Magnus to latch on to Elvi's free hand as she walked up the stairs. It was exactly what Magnus had expected and why he'd paused. So the boy could get past him on the stairs. As he now followed the trio, Elvi announced, "Liam, you and your mother are going to be staying in the tower bedroom."

"You have a tower?" Liam asked with interest.

"Yes, and that's where you're staying."

"Where am I staying?" Teddy asked.

"In the blue room next door to Liam's so you can find each other easy in the morning," Elvi answered promptly.

Magnus smiled faintly as the boys began to chatter excitedly, and then glanced to the side. The stairs curved around on themselves and he was now parallel to the archway, though above it. His gaze landed on Stephanie, who stood in the arch watching him as Dani followed him upstairs. Her eyes were pulsing with that glow again, and he stared at them silently and then turned his face forward again, aware that she wasn't really seeing him at all. She was seeing into him. He'd encountered an Edentate like Stephanie before. A no-fanger who hadn't come out of the turn insane, but one with a special gift like Stephanie's, and it *had* been a gift . . . and a curse. He hoped Stephanie did better under its burden.

Eight

...

with the ...
and then ...
...

"Nonsense. You have been awake for more than thirty-six hours, Dani. You need to sleep. I can sit with Allison. I used to be a nurse in my day and remember the drill with transfusions. I'll keep an eye out for any symptoms that there is a problem and record her pulse, blood pressure, temperature, and respiratory rate . . ." There was the sound of paper fluttering and the woman with the slightly husky voice queried, "Hourly?"

"It isn't usually checked that often in the hospital by this point," a softer voice acknowledged, sounding weary. "But we aren't in a hospital so I've been watching her a little more closely than usual."

"Of course," the husky voice said with understanding.

Allie frowned slightly, wondering what TV show Liam was watching. It sounded like a medical drama, but he was more a cartoons kind of kid. Actually, she thought now, they didn't have a TV anymore. She hadn't been able to afford one of those for a while, so he must be watching something on the computer. She was silently running through the list of movies and TV shows she'd downloaded on the computer in search of which one he could be watching now when the soft voice said, "I'll just examine her one more time and then I'll go lie down for a bit."

In the next moment, Allie felt a cool hand on her forehead. Startled, she was about to open her eyes to see who was touching her when it was done for her. At least, one eyelid was pulled up gently.

Squawking in surprise as she found herself staring up at a petite blonde she didn't recognize, Allie tried to raise her arm to knock the woman's hand away, but her arm wouldn't move. It was restrained somehow.

"You're awake," the blonde said with surprise, and then assured her, "No, Allie. You aren't restrained. I mean, your one arm is, but only to keep you from knocking out the IV."

Allie opened her mouth to speak, and then grimaced at the pasty feel in her mouth. She'd obviously been sleeping on her back with her mouth open for a while. That was the only time she experienced this disgusting taste in her mouth, and her throat was dry so she'd probably been snoring as well.

"Leonora, could you fetch some water for Allie, please," the blonde said, glancing across the bed.

Allie shifted her eyes to see an attractive woman with black hair hurrying from the room. Once the door closed, she peered warily at the blonde again.

"She'll be right back," the woman said reassuringly. "She just—"

The blonde fell silent and they both looked toward the door when it opened. Allie felt relief slide through her when Magnus entered. She couldn't have said why. He was a virtual stranger to her. Still, she was relieved.

"It is good to see you awake," Magnus said, moving to the bedside.

"I'm afraid she was a bit alarmed when she woke to two strangers in the room with her," Dani admitted quietly.

"I knew I should have stayed," Magnus said with a frown as he sat down on the edge of the bed and took her hand reassuringly.

"You'd been here all night," Dani pointed out. "I pretty much had to threaten you to get you to go feed." Smiling wryly, she added, "It just figures she'd wake up five minutes after you left."

Allie's eyes widened at the news that he'd sat at her bedside for so long, and then the door opened again and the black-haired woman returned, carrying the promised glass of water.

Dani unstrapped her arm and Magnus helped her sit up. He then took the glass from Leonora, and asked Allie if she could hold it. When she nodded, he held it out to her. Allie smiled at him crookedly as she took the glass.

They all watched her drink, which made her feel ridiculously self-conscious. But she felt better after a couple of sips and lowered the glass with a sigh, then looked around the room she was in. It was different than the last room where she'd woken up. This one was a pale yellow with a unicorn border along the top of the wall, and dolls lined up on the fireplace mantel. A little girl's room.

"This is Sunita's room," Dani said with a faint smile as she followed where her attention had gone. "Elvi's daughter."

"Tricia mentioned her," Allie said quietly, grimacing when speaking hurt her throat a bit. "I must have been snoring up a storm or something. My throat hurts."

When amused grins were her only answer, she knew she had been and felt her face heat up with embarrassment. She also found she now had trouble meeting Magnus's gaze. Clearing her throat, she said, "So we must be in Port Harry."

"It's Port Henry," Dani corrected gently.

"Oh." She peered at the woman with curiosity. "Why don't I remember the helicopter flight here?"

"You fainted at the Enforcer house," Dani reminded her. "I arrived minutes later and examined you. You weren't in very good shape. You were low on blood and suffering tachycardia. You needed a transfusion, but I had to get some test results first so took some blood samples and sent them to the lab, then gave you a sedative to keep you calm and stable for the trip."

"So I was low on blood and you took more?" she asked with amusement. "You must be Dr. Dani."

The blonde smiled wryly. "It sounds counterintuitive, I know. But I needed your blood typed and matched," she explained, and then added, "And yes, I'm Dr. Dani Argeneau Pimms."

When the petit blonde held out her hand, Allie shifted the glass she'd been holding in both hands to one and shook the woman's hand. "Thank you. I'm guessing since I'm feeling better that you gave me the transfusion?"

"Yes. Now we're just watching to be sure there are no adverse reactions. You'll need to be monitored for twenty-four hours."

Allie's eyebrows rose. "I had no idea blood transfusions took so long."

"Took so long?" Dani looked confused. "It only took a couple of hours."

Now it was Allie's turn to look confused. "Sorry, I thought I heard . . ." She glanced to the dark-haired woman. "Leonora?"

"Yes." The woman smiled at her brightly. "Hello."

"Hello," Allie murmured, and then said, "As I woke up I thought I heard you say Dani had been up for thirty-six hours?"

"Oh," Dani said with understanding. "Yes. Well, I have, but that's not down to you. You only fainted yesterday after lunch. Lucian wanted you moved here at once, so I came with you so that I could oversee the transfusion once we got the test results back and knew what blood type to use. He was able to get a plane quickly, and we landed at a little after two in the afternoon. The lab had the test results shortly after that, but you just happen to have golden blood, which is extremely rare and hard to get ahold of. In fact, I didn't think they'd be able to find any. I should have known better. Never underestimate the abilities of Argeneau Enterprises," she added with a wry smile, and then shrugged. "They found a donor, convinced them to give blood, and flew it straight here. It arrived at five o'clock this morning and I started the transfusion at once."

Allie stared at her blankly for a moment and then said, "I'm pretty sure I have red blood, not golden. At least, it's been red every time I've cut myself and bled."

Dani laughed at her words and shook her head. "Sorry. Golden blood is what they call a blood type that is Rh null. It's—" She shook her head. "Let's just say it's rare. In fact, there are only something like forty-three people known to have it in the world. Well, and now you." Pausing, she frowned and shook her head. "I'm surprised you aren't on record. They keep track of people with Rh null blood because it's so precious." Tilting her head, she eyed her silently for a moment, and then said, "You had no idea, did you?" And then her eyes widened and she said, "You've never had a blood test? Ever?"

Allie narrowed her eyes. "You're reading my mind."

"Sorry, yes, but—"

"How could you have lived your whole life without having a blood test?" Magnus asked, interrupting Dani. "I understood mortals had those frequently."

Allie grimaced at the question, and then admitted, "My parents were devout Followers of Christ."

There was a moment of silence and then Leonora said, "I don't understand."

"Followers of Christ is a . . . religion that doesn't believe in medical intervention," Dani said quietly. "I had no idea there were any in Canada, though. I thought they were based in the States."

Allie shrugged. "I don't know. My father was from the States originally. My mother was Canadian and born Catholic, but converted when she met and married him. He was pretty fanatical about religion. He was also maniacally controlling. It made for an interesting childhood," she added dryly. "I've had nothing to do with him or his religion since I was sixteen."

"So, you're not a Follower of Christ?" Dani asked, looking worried.

"No," Allie said firmly. That answer made relief wash across Dani's face and Allie supposed the woman had feared she'd gone against her religion by treating her.

"And yet you've still never had a blood test?" she asked. "Not once since you were sixteen?"

"I've never been to a doctor. Never needed to," she added. "I seem to have a healthy constitution. I don't catch colds, or the flu. I've never been injured or hospitalized . . . until I fainted and hit my head in the blood bank," she added, and then paused and frowned. "I wonder if they took blood while I was unconscious."

"Probably not for a head injury," Dani said quietly.

There was silence for a minute and then Allie cleared her throat and asked, "Where is my son?"

"He's downstairs," Leonora said reassuringly. "He wanted to come up right away when he heard you were awake, but Elvi told him he had to finish his breakfast first. I think she was trying to give you a few minutes to wake up before you were surrounded with children."

"If Liam comes up, Teddy, Sunny, and Gracie will no doubt follow," Dani assured her with amusement.

"I know Sunny is someone named Elvi's daughter, but who is Gracie?" Allie asked with confusion.

"She is Mabel and DJ's daughter, who are good friends of Elvi and Victor's, as well as Tricia and Teddy Sr.'s," Magnus explained solemnly. "Teddy, Elvi, and Mabel grew up together and wanted their children to do the same so set out to have babies around the same time. The three kids were born weeks apart about four years ago."

"Liam's age," Allie murmured.

"Yes." Leonora grinned. "The four have become quite chummy since his arrival. Thick as thieves."

"Oh." Allie smiled faintly at the thought of Liam having friends. It would be something new for him. She was glad something good had come out of all this. Clearing her throat, she asked, "So, I've had the transfusion and everything is fine?"

"So far so good. I need to continue to monitor you over the next twenty-four hours, but problems usually pop up early on so I think everything is good."

"Does that mean I can get out of bed?" she asked.

Dani looked surprised. "If you want to."

"I want to," Allie assured her. "I need to pee." The words left her lips before she thought about them . . .

and the fact that Magnus was sitting there. Flushing with embarrassment, she avoided looking at him and grimaced.

Dani smiled with amusement, but quickly removed the rope that had been tied around Allie's left wrist to keep her from moving it and knocking out her IV.

The moment she was done, Allie pulled the blanket and sheet covering her aside, not even thinking about what she was or wasn't wearing until she saw the black jeans and blouse she still wore. Relieved that she hadn't been undressed, Allie got cautiously to her feet, noting that the rope from her wrist had been tied around the bed frame under the mattress. She didn't comment, but let Dani take her arm to lead her to the bathroom.

"Do you need help?" Dani asked as they stopped in the room.

"No. Thank you, though," Allie murmured, and much to her relief Dani headed out of the room at once.

"Shout if you need help," Dani said as she closed the door.

Allie mumbled an agreement, but knew she wouldn't need help. She felt surprisingly good. Better than she had in weeks. Certainly better than she had the last time she was awake. Her breath wasn't coming in pants from the small exertion of walking, and the cold clammy feel she'd been suffering was gone. She felt pretty much back to normal, or as normal as she had been in a long time. She still wasn't as strong as she'd been when she was first handed Liam and found herself on the run, but then she hadn't worked out for a long time, so probably wasn't as strong as she used to be, Allie thought as she took care of her business in the bathroom.

Allie peered at herself in the mirror as she washed her hands afterward and grimaced at the sight she made. She was still a bit pale, but at least the blue tinge around her lips was gone. In that way, at least, she looked better than she had in weeks. But it was the first time she'd seen the white bandages around her head. It wasn't an attractive look, especially now with her light brown hair a tangled mess where it stuck out from under it.

"I need a brush," she muttered, and reached up to run her fingers through her hair to work out the worst of the tangles, only to pause and sniff at herself with a grimace. "I need a shower."

"Allie? Are you all right? Did you say something?"

Sighing, she let her hands drop and turned to open the door, blinking in surprise when she found both Dani and Magnus standing there, concern on their faces.

"I'm fine," she assured them with a crooked smile. "Except I need a shower and change of clothes."

"Oh." Dani frowned.

Suspecting she was going to say that wasn't a good idea, Allie added, "I stink."

"Oh." The doctor sighed and then nodded reluctantly. "All right, then. But maybe I should stay in the room with you in case you—"

"No," Allie said firmly. "Really, I feel fine, Doctor. All I need is my bag."

"Dani. Call me Dani," the blonde said, and turned as if to go get Allie's bag, but Magnus had already gone and picked it up from where it sat next to the bed. He returned quickly to hand it over.

"Thank you," Allie murmured, and backed into the room. "I won't be long."

"Shout if you feel faint or—"

"Yes, Doctor," Allie said with amusement as she closed the door. Shaking her head, she set the bag on the sink counter and reached into the tub to turn on the shower. Then she paused to peer at the bandage in the mirror. After a hesitation, she quickly unwrapped it and then turned her head and tilted it slightly to get a look at her head wound. It didn't look too bad, Allie decided. She could wash her hair if she was careful and avoided the spot. Dani probably wouldn't be happy, but Dani wasn't the one with greasy, tangled hair.

The shower felt awesome. Allie stood under the beating water for several minutes, just letting it pound down over her shoulders and back before looking around for the soap. A grin lifted her lips when she saw it was small, pink, and shaped like a unicorn. Sunita apparently really liked unicorns.

She washed her body quickly and then went slower and more carefully with her hair. Once done, Allie quickly dried herself and then opened her Go bag and pulled out the jeans, T-shirt, and underwear she kept it in. They were a little wrinkled, but clean. She dressed, ran her fingers gently through her hair to get out the worst of the tangles, and then bit her lips to give them a little more color. She wished she had some lipstick or something, but that was in her purse and she had no idea where that was. Probably back at the apartment, Allie thought with a frown. She hadn't taken it with her on her "rob-the-blood-bank" caper, and hadn't had a chance to grab it when she got back from the hospital. She also hadn't got a chance to grab her computer. Fortunately, she wasn't working on any projects right now so that wasn't such a big deal, and if she was lucky and they caught Abaddon, she could eventually go back to the apartment and get all the things left behind.

That thought made her feel a little better as she gathered her dirty clothes and opened the door.

"Mom!"

Allie froze, prepared herself for Liam's jumping like a monkey trick. Fortunately, he kept his feet on the ground and merely threw himself against her legs and hugged her tightly.

"You're awake."

"Yes." Smiling faintly, Allie reached down with her free hand and caressed his head, noting that he was wearing the clean clothes from his Go bag too. Someone had looked after him while she was unconscious. She was grateful for that.

"Are you feeling better?" Liam asked, tipping his head back to look up at her.

"Yes, thank you. Much better," she assured him.

"Good." He gave her another hard squeeze and then backed up and gestured toward the door before announcing, "These are my friends. You met Teddy."

Allie looked to where Liam was gesturing and smiled at the boy as she nodded. "Yes. Hello, Teddy."

"Hello, Mrs. Liam's mom," he said politely.

Allie's smile widened at the title. She didn't correct him about the Mrs. part, but simply said, "Call me Allie, sweetheart."

"Thank you, ma'am," he murmured.

"And that's Sunny and Gracie," Liam continued with his introductions.

Allie shifted her attention to the two little girls standing just behind Teddy Jr. and felt her mouth stretch wide. They were such adorable little girls, one with red hair laying in soft, flyaway waves around her face, the other with blond hair pulled back into a ponytail. Both girls smiled shyly back.

"Mrs. Elvi told us to go watch cartoons for a bit so we aren't under her feet while she cleans the table," Liam announced solemnly. "But I'll stay with you if you want."

Allie shifted her gaze back to her son and caressed his cheek affectionately. "That's all right, sweetie, you go ahead and have fun."

"Thank you, Mom." Liam gave her legs another squeeze and then whirled away to hurry to the door with a happy, "Love you."

"Love you too, baby," she called as the foursome rushed out of the room.

"Did you want to get back in bed?" Dani asked, moving to her side to gently flip her hair around and look at her head wound.

Allie remained still for her, but her eyes shifted to

look at the bed. She found herself reluctant to return to it, though. Actually, she was hungry, she realized now.

"It's healing nicely. We can leave the bandage off," Dani decided, her hands falling away. Stepping back, she smiled wryly and added, "And of course you're hungry. I should have expected that. You haven't eaten since noon yesterday."

"Would you like me to go below and fetch you something to eat?" Leonora offered at once.

"I'd really rather go below myself," Allie admitted, although she wasn't positive she knew what "go below" was. Presumably it meant going downstairs, though, and not that she had to descend into hell to get food.

Leonora grinned suddenly, but then asked Dani, "It should be all right for her to go down and sit at the dining room table to eat, don't you think? She appears to be feeling well enough for it."

Dani nodded slowly, but warned, "Just don't overdo it. You're no doubt feeling better, and are probably fine, but I'd just rather you took it easy. At least until we're positive there are no adverse reactions to the transfusion."

"I'll be careful," Allie assured her.

"Good. I just don't want you to wear yourself out. The transfusion replaced some of the blood you lost and you aren't critical anymore, but you're still probably a pint low and need to be careful until your body builds it back up."

Allie nodded solemnly. "I will."

"Okay, then." Dani turned to Leonora. "I'm heading

to bed. Call me if there is any problem. Anything at all."

"Certainly," Leonora said solemnly. "Sleep well."

"Thank you," Dani murmured, and smiled at Allie again before slipping from the room.

"Well, let's head downstairs and find you something to eat, then, shall we?" Leonora suggested brightly.

Nodding, Allie followed her out of the room and into a hall. She was very aware that Magnus was behind her, bringing up the rear, but tried not to think about that and asked, "Where are the kids watching TV?"

"In the porch off Elvi and Victor's room," Magnus answered from behind her, and then added, "It is heated."

"Heated, insulated, and furnished," Leonora added as they started down a curving staircase. "The children actually slept out there last night. They were watching movies and decided they wanted a pajama party out there. Since it meant Liam wouldn't witness your blood transfusion and possibly worry even more about you, the adults all decided it was a good idea and gave permission so they sacked out in sleeping bags. Although, being children, I doubt they got much sleep."

Allie nodded, but asked, "Do you live here too, Leonora?"

"Oh, no, dear. I have a house across the street where my Alessandro and I live."

"Alessandro?" Allie queried with curiosity, wondering about the woman. Leonora looked young, but then she'd noticed that all of them looked to be between twenty-five or thirty years old. This woman spoke as if she was older, though.

"Alessandro is my husband," Leonora explained, and then added, "And I was eighty-four when I met him, found out I was his life mate, and allowed him to turn me. That was several years ago now," she admitted wryly. "But I don't feel a day over sixteen. At least, not on the inside," she added wryly, and then glanced over her shoulder with concern. "Are you managing all right? Do you need to stop and rest?"

"No. I'm fine," Allie assured her, and it was true—she felt fine. Going down the stairs wasn't tiring her at all. But she hadn't forgotten what had happened the last time she'd mounted stairs. She'd have to remember to take it slow when she came back up.

"Good idea . . . at least until you're sure you can manage them well enough," Leonora said brightly as if Allie had argued the subject aloud. It reminded her that these people could read her thoughts. Except Magnus. He couldn't, she recalled, and wondered if that was why she felt so much more comfortable and safe with him.

"Well, you're up."

Allie looked past Leonora to see a redhead with a pretty face and big eyes waiting at the bottom of the stairs.

"You're looking much better than you did when you arrived, dear," the woman said with a wide smile that Allie automatically responded to with one of her own.

"Allie, this is Elvi Argeneau," Magnus announced as they reached the bottom of the steps and paused in front of her.

"And I'm Mabel," a pretty blonde announced coming around the corner to join them. In tight jeans and a clingy T-shirt, she had a killer figure that made Allie feel like a boobless wonder in comparison.

Allie peered from one woman to the other and then to Magnus and finally Leonora. "You all look to be in your mid- to late twenties. But I know Leonora is in her nineties."

The blonde and redhead exchanged a wry glance, and then Elvi turned back and announced, "We're all older than you, love. Well, except for our Stephy and the children."

"But we aren't as old as our mates," Mabel added with satisfaction. "They're ancient old men."

"Oy!" A man with dark hair and a friendly face came around the corner and slipped his arms around the blonde. Hugging her from behind, he kissed her neck and said, "I may be an ancient old man, but I'm *your* ancient old man."

"This is Mabel's husband, DJ," Elvi announced, smiling at the couple, and then she turned back to Allie to explain, "The nanos are the reason we all look so young. They're programmed to keep us at our peak condition, and that would be between twenty-five and thirty for humans."

"Nanos," Allie murmured. It wasn't the first mention of the word, and her curiosity about it returned at once.

"I can hear the questions mounting in your poor mind," Elvi said with amusement. "Why don't you sit yourself down at the table. We'll put some food together for you and then answer all those things you want to ask."

"That would be nice. Thank you." Allie followed when the trio turned and led the way into a large dining room that, along with a kitchen area, ran the length of the house. An L-shaped counter divided the two sections, but did nothing to make it seem smaller. It was positively huge and had a large fireplace against the far wall that looked Victorian. But then, so did the foot-high molding and the trifold doors that sat open between the dining room and the entry she'd just passed through.

"Who wants coffee?" a tall, good-looking man asked from the kitchen as he fetched coffee cups off an open shelf on the wall next to a door that looked to lead outside.

"Victor Argeneau, Elvi's life mate," Magnus murmured by her ear, and Allie smiled faintly and nodded.

"Magnus? Coffee?" Victor asked, glancing their way.

"Not for me. I like the taste, but caffeine agitates me," Magnus said with a shrug.

"You're in luck, then, it's decaf," Victor announced. "Caffeinated coffee winds me up too."

"In that case, coffee sounds good," Magnus decided, and glanced at Allie in question even as Victor did.

"I'll have one too, please," she said as Magnus led her to the dining room table.

"What do you feel like eating, Allie?" Elvi asked,

moving around the kitchen counter to join her husband. "Something to build up your blood would be best, I suppose. How about some scrambled eggs and toast?"

"Just some toast would be fine," Allie said at once. "I don't want to put you to any trouble."

"Nonsense, scrambled eggs are easy enough to make, and there's lots of hash browns and bacon left from the breakfast I made the kids. I'll toss them in along with onions and cheese and make you an omelet, shall I?"

Allie stared at her blankly, not wanting to put her to the effort, but her mouth was watering at the thought of an omelet.

"An omelet, it is, then," Elvi said with amusement, obviously reading her mind.

"I'll do the toast," Mabel offered, moving to grab a bag of bread from a wood bread box as Elvi opened the refrigerator to retrieve the fixings for the omelet.

"Then I guess I'll help Magnus and Leonora answer those questions I hear buzzing around in your head," DJ decided, leaving Mabel's side to join Allie, Magnus, and Leonora at the table.

There was a moment of silence once he'd join them. Allie supposed they were waiting for her to start asking her questions, but she had so many she didn't know where to start and then she glanced at the people in the kitchen and then those at the table and wondered where Tricia was.

"Tricia and Teddy are working today," DJ answered

as if she'd asked the question out loud. "They'll be back around dinnertime."

"Oh." She smiled at him slightly, and then cleared her throat and asked the first question she came up with. "I was told you aren't vampires, but immortals. What is the difference?"

"Vampires are fictional dead and soulless creatures that sprung up from a curse. While immortals are merely scientifically enhanced humans," Magnus answered promptly. "We are not dead and soulless. We are alive and well and still have souls."

"Scientifically enhanced humans?" Allie asked, arching an eyebrow. "Like *The Bionic Woman* enhanced, or . . ." She couldn't think of another example to use.

"No," he said with a smile. "Enhanced as in we have bioengineered nanos flowing through our bloodstream that are programmed to keep us at our peak condition."

Allie stared at him blankly, not really seeing a connection between the human peak condition and fangs or a need for blood.

"The nanos are blood based," DJ said, obviously picking up on her thoughts. "They use blood to propel themselves as well as make repairs, and to generate more nanos when need be."

"Make repairs?" she asked with interest.

"Yes," Magnus said. "When the nanos were created, the intent was that they would repair injuries and fight illnesses without the need for surgery or chemical aid."

"So, break a leg or get stabbed and these nanos would fix it?" she asked.

Magnus nodded. "The nanos rush to the injury, rapidly replicating themselves to the number they need for the job at hand, stop the bleeding, and repair the wound or broken bone."

"Okay," she said slowly. "So where do the fangs and glowy eyes come in?"

"From laziness," Leonora said with amusement, and then added, "God bless them."

DJ grinned at the woman and it was Magnus who again explained. "The scientists who created the nanos chose to take a shortcut when it came to programming. Rather than develop separate programs for each individual ailment or injury a human might suffer, they decided to program them with a map of the male and female body at their peak condition and the instruction to ensure their host was at that peak condition and then self-destruct once it was achieved."

"To be fair to our scientists," DJ said now, "there are a hell of a lot of injuries and illnesses a human can experience. So creating just the one program probably seemed expedient at the time."

"Yes," Allie agreed. "But I still don't understand how that ended with you guys having fangs and sucking blood."

"It didn't in the beginning," DJ assured her. "At first, well, of course, with the nanos using blood to make repairs and propel themselves, it was expected that blood transfusions might be needed for the more extensive injuries or illnesses, and the patients were given those transfusions accordingly."

"But the tests provided some surprises," Magnus said, picking up the explanations again. "The first was that the nanos saw the effects of age as an injury or illness, something that needed repair. And because we reach our peak at somewhere between twenty-five and thirty depending on the person's physiology, the nanos reversed the physical age of any host older than that, returning them back to that peak stage."

"The fountain of youth," Allie murmured.

"Yes. It must have seemed like that at the time," Magnus agreed.

"What were the other surprises?" she asked.

"The nanos did not self-destruct and leave the body as expected," he answered solemnly.

Allie wasn't really surprised to hear this. Everyone she'd encountered seemed perfectly healthy, yet had the silver sheen to their eyes that she could only guess came from the nanos they carried inside them, so she simply asked, "Why?"

"Because the nanos did not ever consider their work done," Magnus said. "If they had been programmed to simply do one thing like repair a specific wound, or remove cancer, they would have finished their job and self-destructed, but they were programmed to keep the body at its peak. Unfortunately, or perhaps fortunately, the body is constantly taking on damage, even if only minute. Inhaling pollutants, damage from the sun, and the simple passage of time cause damage in the body that the nanos feel they have to repair. They don't see their work as ever done, so do not self-destruct."

"Okay," Allie said slowly. She found this fascinating, even wonderful in a way, but still didn't understand how this life-saving advancement had ended up with them having fangs. "But where do the fangs and stuff come in? I mean, peak isn't the crazy strong Stella was when she was tossing me about like a doll, or the speed she could manage. That's freaky speed and strength, not peak human abilities."

Magnus grimaced, but answered, "Right. Well, as I said, the necessity for extra blood to make the needed repairs and such was expected, and patients given the nanos as treatment were also given blood transfusions to make up for that. However, because the nanos didn't self-destruct but continued to work in the body, the need for extra blood continued as well."

"You see, the nanos use more blood than the average body can produce," Leonora explained.

"Yes." Magnus nodded. "It was a problem, but not insurmountable at the time. The scientists simply gave the patients daily blood transfusions to make up for that."

He paused then, and Allie stared at him expectantly. Nothing he'd said had seemed to her to explain the fangs.

It was Leonora who said, "The nanos were developed in Atlantis several millennium ago."

Allie's head shot around at that, her eyes wide. "What?"

Leonora shrugged. "Surely you've heard the tales of Atlantis? It existed ages ago, and was a scientifically advanced culture that was destroyed by earthquakes and an erupting volcano or something?"

"Well, yes, I've heard of it," Allie admitted. "But—"

"They aren't just tales," Leonora assured her. "The stories are true. Atlantis did exist. It was apparently isolated and well advanced compared to the rest of the world, and these nanos were one of their scientific advancements. Which was all good and fine until Atlantis fell and sank into the ocean. The only survivors were the Atlanteans with the nanos inside them. They crawled out of the rubble, or swam out of the ocean, to find themselves left with a world that was much less advanced than their home country had been." She grimaced and said, "We're talking seriously less advanced. Mud huts and wiping your bottom with bits of leaf if they wiped their behinds at all," she added with a grimace, and then shrugged. "There were no more blood transfusions for them."

"The Atlanteans started to die from lack of blood," DJ said now, and explained, "When the nanos got low on blood in the veins, they migrated to the organs and such to mine it and some of them did die, basically from lack of blood. A terribly, painful way to go," he added grimly.

"But in others," Magnus said, "the nanos forced what they saw as a necessary evolution to get what they needed to fulfill their programming and keep their host at their peak condition."

"The fangs," Allie said on a sigh.

Magnus nodded. "They gave them fangs, added speed and strength, night vision, and the ability to read and even control the minds of other humans so that they could get the blood they needed for the nanos to do their work and keep them in their peak condition."

"Forever young and healthy," Allie said with a shake of the head, and sat back in her seat, then glanced around with a start when a plate appeared in front of her.

"Here you are," Elvi said as she set the plate down. "Eat up. You have to build up your blood and get your strength back to chase after that sweet little boy of yours. He needs his mother strong and healthy."

"Thank you," Allie murmured, and then repeated the words when Victor arrived with a tray of mugs full of coffee and set one before her first.

"You are welcome," Victor said with a smile, and then removed cream and sugar from the tray to set in front of her and announced to the table at large, "I did not know how everyone took their coffee, so just brought the fixings for each of you to do it yourself."

Allie reached for the sugar, inhaling the scents wafting up from her plate as she did, and nearly swooned with pleasure.

"Wow, this smells good, Elvi," she murmured as she fixed her coffee.

"I thought so too," she admitted on a laugh as she headed back around the kitchen counter. "So I ended up making a big bowl of it so everyone can have some."

"And I made loads of toast," Mabel announced,

approaching now with a stack of plates topped with silverware. "Who wants a plate?"

Allie wasn't surprised when everyone decided they were hungry. The smell coming from her plate was mouthwatering and she couldn't wait to dig in. But good manners made her wait politely until everyone had plates and silverware, and the food was on the table. However, the moment the last person was seated and the food was being passed around, Allie dug in.

It was as good as it smelled and she was starved, so it was several moments before more questions began to filter into her mind. Allie was halfway through her meal before she asked, "So Stella was somehow given these nanos?"

There was a moment of silence as everyone glanced up from their plates, and then Magnus swallowed the food in his mouth and nodded. "Yes. Abaddon would have given both her and her husband some of his blood to transfer the nanos."

"And Liam got them from Stella while in the womb?" she queried.

"Yes," he said solemnly.

Allie nodded and took another bite of food, but her mind was churning things over, and after swallowing, she asked, "So he'll never look older than twenty-five or so once he grows up?"

"No. Physically, his aging will stop at around that age," Elvi said this time. "As will Sunny, Gracie, and Teddy."

Allie nodded, but asked, "But you all weren't born immortals?" When the others stared at her blankly, she explained, "I mean, Leonora said she was eighty-four when she was turned. So she wasn't born immortal. Were the rest of you turned too, or . . . ?"

"Mabel, Leonora, and I were all mortal by birth and turned some years ago," Elvi said, spooning some sugar into her coffee and stirring it briefly. Setting down the spoon, she added, "But Victor and DJ as well as Leonora's husband, Alessandro, were born immortals."

Allie accepted that and then turned to Magnus with curiosity.

Before she could ask, he said, "I was born mortal."

Her eyes widened slightly at this news. For some reason she would have guessed that he was born immortal like the other men. Allie wasn't sure why.

"Oh, *Madre de Dio*, something smells so delicious."

Everyone at the table turned to peer at the man who had entered the house. Dark haired like Leonora, the man quickly shed his coat and boots and moved to join them, heading straight for Leonora.

"Ah, *Gioia*, it must be you that smells so good, *sì*?" he murmured, bending to kiss her.

"I think *Gioia* means 'joy,'" Elvi explained quietly when Allie looked confused at the man using the wrong name. "A term of endearment."

"Oh," Allie whispered, and then glanced back to the couple as the kiss ended and Leonora laughed.

"No. It's not me that smells so good." Raising a hand to run it affectionately over his cheek, she murmured, "It's the omelet. I think there's some left. Did you want some?"

"*Sì*," he said abruptly, straightening. "I am a poor hungry man whose wife abandoned him to go play with her friends."

Leonora snorted. "Nonsense, Alessandro. You and Edward were playing that video game and didn't even notice when I left."

Alessandro grinned. "*Sì*. The game is good. Etienne, he has done it again. But I did notice you left, and missed you at once."

"Victor's brother, Etienne, creates video games," Elvi explained to Allie. "He has a new one coming out soon and sent a couple of beta copies to Victor to be tested. Alessandro and Edward were kind enough to offer to try it out too."

"Oh," Allie said with a smile, and then froze when Alessandro's attention settled on her and he smiled widely.

"You must be the Allison my wife came to help with, *sì*?" he said, moving around the table to take her hand.

"Oh, well . . ." Her gaze shot to Leonora. "Yes, I guess I must be."

"*Bella*. Welcome to Port Henry," Alessandro said, pressing a kiss to her hand. "But you are too pale. You must eat, *sì*? Or my wife, she will worry. So *mangia, mangia*." He released her hand and then disappeared around the counter, returning a moment later with a plate and fork to claim the seat next to Leonora.

Allie glanced around the table then, taking in everyone there and realizing quite suddenly that she'd spent the last four years running from vampires, and yet for the second time in as many days found herself sitting at a table with a large group of them as if it were the most natural thing in the world.

"Immortals, dear," Elvi corrected as if she'd spoken aloud. "Now eat. Alessandro is right. You need to rebuild your strength."

Allie flushed and turned her attention back to her food, concentrating on the taste and texture in an effort to silence the thoughts in her head. It was extremely discomfiting to have people reading your thoughts all the time. It made her want to get as far away from them as possible, which was a shame, because they all seemed rather nice.

Nine

"Time to take your pulse and temperature."

Allie had just finished her last bite of omelet when Leonora made that announcement and stood to move around the table to her side.

"Pulse, temperature, blood pressure, and respiratory rate," Leonora listed off, producing a thermometer from her skirt pocket. Removing it from its plastic case, she gave it a couple of shakes, and then popped it in Allie's mouth before taking her wrist in hand. "Just relax and breathe through your nose."

Allie watched as the others stood to clear the table, her gaze traveling from one person to another. They were all healthy-looking, but she couldn't help but notice that the women were curvy with a bit of meat on them. Not overweight or anything, but not the stick-thin twiggy figures so popular in the magazines. She thought that was interesting. Apparently, peak condition was not anorexic.

"Good," Leonora pronounced, releasing her wrist. "I need to go fetch the blood pressure cuff from your room. You just keep the thermometer in until I get back."

Allie nodded in response, but the woman was already rushing away. She watched her go and then simply sat there, waiting. The conversation in the kitchen behind her was just a murmur of sound until she heard her name mentioned, and then she tuned into it.

"Allie might need to go shopping for necessities. Dani wasn't sure, but said she had to and thought Allie might as well."

"I am not sure either," Magnus admitted. "She had two bags with her when we took her and Liam from the apartment, but I am not sure what is in them. She might need to go shopping."

"The backpacks?" Elvi asked, and snorted slightly. "There can't be much in there. She probably does need a good shopping excursion."

"I don't think Dani wanted her exerting herself, though," Mabel put in. "It's probably better if they just relax around here today."

"You're probably right," Elvi agreed, and then said, "Well, if you want to be alone to talk, Magnus, you could take her into the salon for a little privacy."

Allie was just wondering what they thought the two of them needed to talk about when Elvi added, "I'm sure she still has a lot of questions, and she might feel more comfortable asking you without the rest of us around. I think our being able to read her mind makes her uncomfortable."

She heard Magnus grunt in response and then Leonora was back, the blood pressure cuff in one hand and a clipboard in the other.

"This thing reads your pulse as well as your blood pressure, but I like to count it out myself just to double-check," she announced as she set the clipboard on the table and strapped the cuff around Allie's upper arm. "Now, let's just see if it gets the same reading on your pulse as I did."

Leonora pushed the button on the blood pressure machine twice, and as the cuff began to swell and tighten around Allie's arm, she took the thermometer from her mouth and read it.

"How is it?" Allie asked with curiosity. She felt fine, but it would be nice to have verification.

"Good," Leonora announced, and picked up the clipboard to enter the temperature.

They both fell silent then as the cuff stopped swelling and the machine began to beep. A moment later, numbers popped up on the readout and Leonora quickly entered those on her clipboard too.

"Look at that. The same pulse rate as I got," she said with satisfaction. "I haven't lost my touch."

Allie smiled faintly at the proud words and then sat still as Leonora set the clipboard aside and quickly removed the cuff.

"The numbers are all good," Leonora assured her as she set the portable blood pressure apparatus on the table next to the clipboard. "No need to bother Dani."

"Good," Allie said wryly, and then glanced past her to Magnus when he appeared with two cups of coffee in hand.

"I thought we might go into the salon and talk, if you like," he suggested.

Allie nodded and stood to follow him out of the dining room.

The salon was a room across the entry from the dining room. She had no idea where it got its name. It just looked like a little living room to her, but she settled on the couch and accepted one of the coffees with a murmured, "Thank you," then watched Magnus close the double doors, sealing them off from the others.

Magnus turned back to the room after closing the door and then hesitated before moving to sit on the couch on the far end from Allie. He would have liked to sit closer, but didn't want to make her uncomfortable. Aware that she was watching him, he sipped at his coffee, and simply waited. He expected her to ask why he couldn't read her and was trying to come up with an explanation without mentioning life mates, something he was sure she wasn't ready for, when she suddenly asked, "How were you turned?"

Magnus was so startled by the question that for a minute he was speechless. It was the last question he'd expected.

"Was it like Stella? A rogue attacking and turning you?"

"No," he said firmly, and then felt a wry smile creep over his face before he admitted, "Actually, I was turned accidentally, like Elvi."

"Elvi was turned accidentally?" she asked with surprise, and then admitted, "I just assumed she was turned by her husband, like Leonora said she was turned by her Alessandro." The admission had barely left her lips before she frowned and asked, "How do you get turned accidentally?"

Magnus's smile widened at her disgruntled expression. "For Elvi, it was in a bus accident. The bus landed on its side and apparently a wounded immortal was seated on the opposite side and ended up hanging from his seat belt above her, bleeding into her open mouth while she was unconscious."

"Oh," Allie breathed, her eyes wide. "So, the blood just has to get into the person. Even swallowed? It doesn't have to be injected into their veins?" Before he could respond, she added, "Stella didn't know how she was turned. She couldn't remember."

"I am not surprised," he said quietly. "The turn is often quite traumatic. It isn't uncommon for turnees to come out after the turn short of memories."

She nodded, but asked, "So is that how you were turned too? An accident where blood dripped into your mouth?"

"No." Magnus grimaced. "I actually did it to myself without meaning to, or even realizing I was doing it."

"How does that happen?" she asked, sounding half amused and half disbelieving.

Magnus smiled wryly at the question, and then

took a moment to figure out where to start his explanation. Finally, he decided the beginning was probably best. "I was born in 779 A.D. in what is now called Denmark."

Allie's eyes went round as saucers and her jaw dropped at this news.

Magnus grinned at her expression, then leaned forward, placed a finger under her chin, and pushed it up, closing her mouth. "You will catch flies."

"It's winter. No flies," she muttered, and then shook her head and asked with disbelief, "Are you telling me you're a Viking?"

Magnus blinked in surprise. He'd expected her amazement to be about his age, not his nationality. "We were not called Vikings back then. Or ever. We called ourselves Ostmen. We *went* 'a'viking,' which basically translated to overseas expeditions or raids. But it could be exploring too. And we usually did that in the summer between planting our fields and harvesting them."

"Oh. Okay," she said. "But you were a Viking."

He nodded rather than trying to clear that up again. She looked far too enthralled with the knowledge that he was what people now referred to as Vikings. If she liked the word that much, she could call him Viking rather than Norseman or Ostman.

"I can picture you as a Viking," she said suddenly, and then pursed her lips and added, "Well, except that you should have long blond hair instead of short dark hair."

"Aye, the lasses in my day preferred their men blond

too," he said with amusement, and then realized his speech had slipped into his old accent and cleared his throat before adding, "At least, the blond part. My hair was long then."

"Really?"

"Really what?" he asked mildly. "That the women preferred blonds or that my hair was long?"

"The blond part," she said with a faint smile.

"Yes. In fact, most of us poor men unfortunate enough to have been born with dark hair used a strong soap with a lot of lye in it to bleach our hair. Some used it on their beards as well," he informed her. "Handily enough, aside from lightening our hair, it killed lice, so that was our excuse for using it, but the truth was it attracted the ladies."

"Hmm," Allie muttered, looking a bit disgruntled, and then she assured him, "Well, dark-haired men are better-looking anyway in my opinion."

"You just finished saying I should have long blond hair," he pointed out on a disbelieving laugh.

"Well, yes, because that fits the image of a Viking better. But I wouldn't want you to actually *be* blond now. It wouldn't suit you."

Magnus smiled crookedly at the claim, and then noted the appreciative way her eyes were sliding over his features and damned near blushed. Something he hadn't done since he was a lad, if then.

"Anyway," he said to change the subject, "my family had a prosperous farm. I grew up there, learning to farm and fight, but in the summer of 793, I ran off to go a'viking."

"Why?" she asked at once. "Was it rebellion or to escape cruel parents or something?"

"No. My parents were good people," he assured her, and then admitted, "In truth, it was because of a female. I had a fancy for our neighbor's daughter, but—"

"Wait a minute," Allie interrupted him sharply. "You said you were born in 779."

"Yes."

"Then you were only fourteen when you went a'viking?" she asked with disbelief.

Magnus grinned at her expression. "We lived much shorter lives and grew up much quicker back then."

"But fourteen?" she asked.

"Lots of boys my age were already married and having children by then," he told her. "And all of us were pretty much married by fifteen."

Allie stared at him with something like horror for a minute, and then shook her head and prompted him with, "So you were fourteen and fancied your neighbor's daughter."

"Yes," Magnus said, but paused briefly before continuing. "I wanted to take her to wife, but she said I was too poor." He smiled wryly at the memory. It had stung at the time. His pride, mostly. Shrugging the memory away, he said, "A friend of mine had gone a'viking the summer before and come back with many fine treasures."

"So you ran off to go a'viking in the hopes you'd be similarly lucky, and could come back and win your lady love," she suggested dryly.

"Yes," he said, unembarrassed. It had been the way of it back then.

"I'm guessing things didn't turn out quite the way you planned, though?" Allie asked, her voice gentler.

"No," Magnus admitted solemnly. "We landed on-shore a little more than three days after setting sail, and attacked a monastery."

"A monastery?" she squawked with dismay.

"They had the finest treasures," he said helplessly. "And at that time were unguarded. Besides, we were pagans. We held no truck with their God." Magnus waited and when she just stared at him wide-eyed, he continued his tale. "It was my first raid. I had been in battle before, mostly local quarrels, but this . . ." He shook his head. "I had never seen anything like it. They were men of God, not warriors. They just stood there praying while we slaughtered them, and the survivors went like sheep when we rounded them up to take away for slaving.

"Once it was done, the men broke open the wine casks in the church to 'celebrate our victory.' At least, that was what they called it, though in truth I think it was to drink away our shame. That was what it was for me anyway. This had not been a fair fight, not even a battle, but a slaughter." He shook his head with remembered self-disgust. "I drank hard with the others, but late in the night I staggered outside to relieve myself of some of that wine I'd consumed. I had just finished watering a bush when I heard odd sounds coming from beyond the bushes. I put myself away and stumbled over to see what was what and came across one of my comrades, Erik, being choked by a stranger with the bodies of at least three of our comrades already dead on the ground around them."

Magnus paused briefly before continuing. "I should have shouted an alarm to bring the others, but Erik and I had been friends since childhood. He was the one to suggest I go a'viking to make the coin I needed to win my bride. I did not think, I simply ran forward trying to help." Grimacing, he admitted, "Unfortunately, with the battle over and drink in my belly, I was foolish enough to leave my long sword in the church. I had no weapon to hand, so I grabbed the stranger by the nearest arm and tried to pull his hand away from Erik's neck, but the bugger was mighty strong. I tried punching him, but that had no effect at all, so I did the only thing I could think of—I leapt on his back and bit into his neck. Not some little nip either," he assured her. "I full on latched my teeth into his throat, and dug in, ignoring the blood that squirted into my mouth. Swallowing it to keep from choking, but not letting go, and in fact tearing at his skin and making him bleed more because he was not letting go of Erik."

"He was an immortal," Allie breathed with realization.

Magnus nodded slowly. "Yes. The stranger was an immortal. And I accidentally turned myself."

"Did he know?" she asked at once. "The immortal? Did he know that you'd turned yourself?"

Magnus paused to consider that. It was something he'd wondered often over the centuries, but after a moment he shook his head. "He may have, but I suspect not. In battle, you do not feel pain like you should. Sometimes you do not feel it at all until after the worst of the fray is over and your adrenaline slows, and from what I know of immortals, he would have been well healed by then." Magnus shook his head again. "No. I do not think he knew. I think he walked away that night thinking he killed me along with the others."

"What do you mean?" she asked with dismay. "What did he do?"

"Well, after he finally finished wringing the life out of Erik, he dropped him, reached back to grab me by the scuff of the neck, and yanked me over his head like a wee pup. Once he had me dangling in front of him, he pulled a knife from his belt and gutted me, then dropped me and walked away, leaving me for dead."

"Oh, my God," Allie breathed, her eyes dropping to his stomach and Magnus had the sudden, ridiculous urge to suck in his gut, sit up straight, and flex his pecs. Not that he really had a gut to suck in, but still, he had the urge to do so.

"But you weren't dead," she said, shifting her gaze back up to his face.

"No. Apparently, I had taken in enough nano-filled blood that the turn was starting before he finished killing Erik. That being the case, the nanos would have rushed straight to the wound in my stomach the moment it happened, stopped the bleeding, and closed it as quickly as possible before doing anything else."

"It's a good thing you bit him, then," Allie pointed out.

"Yes. Well, I did not know any of that at the time,"

he pointed out, and continued. "I woke up on the ground the next morning, lying among the bodies of my dead comrades. There were more than had been there when I was stabbed the night before. I stumbled back through the bushes and into the monastery and . . ." Magnus shook his head as he remembered the scene. The stone floors and walls that had been splattered with the blood of the priests when last he saw them were now painted with even more blood, and the bodies of his comrades lay everywhere. They had not survived their celebrations. Finally, he simply said, "Everyone was dead. We hadn't been that large a party—only three boats, sixty men. But every one of them lay dead in and around the monastery. In truth, I half believed that I was dead too."

"What?" she asked with surprise. "Why?"

Magnus listed off the reasons one after the other. "The wound I clearly recalled receiving was no longer in evidence, neither were the other small injuries I had sustained that day. And even my scars were somehow gone, yet my body was wracked with agony. I clearly recalled that the eyes of the man I had bitten had glowed." He shook his head, and smiled wryly. "I now realize he had been an immortal, but knew nothing about them then, and worried he might have been the Christian God, or embodied by Him, and that I too was dead and in that hell the Christians carped on about. That it was a punishment for taking part in the raid on his church, and killing his priests. That I was now cursed to walk the earth as the dead for my sins."

"What did you do?" she asked, unconsciously shifting closer on the couch.

"What could I do?" he asked helplessly. "I could not sail any of the ships on my own, and the bodies were already starting to stink." He grimaced at the memory, and then said, "And I was not really sure I was dead and cursed, so I started to walk inland in search of aid. However, I was alone, unarmed, and hurting, so avoided the trails and riding paths to evade the enemy. But I was in a bad way. I walked for a day and night at least, although I do not remember much of it. At some point I collapsed in a copse where I was eventually found by a farmer. He apparently recognized that I was different and delivered me to Alodia Kenric."

"Who was that?" Allie asked at once.

"She is a very old immortal, and head of the Kenric clan of immortals."

Allie blinked, and then said with disbelief, "Very old? Are you kidding me? You were born in 779. How much older could she be for you to consider her very old?"

"I am not sure," he admitted slowly. "Even back then you simply did not ask a lady her age. But I would guess she was probably born in B.C."

"B.C.? Like before Christ B.C.?" she asked with amazement.

"It is not as rare as you would think, Allie," he said soothingly, and then informed her, "Victor was born in the second or third century B.C., and Lucian was born a good twelve or thirteen hundred years before that."

Allie blinked twice at this news, somehow seemed

to file it away somewhere in her mind where it was less troubling, and then shook her head and said, "Fine. Alodia was old. And immortal. And you were delivered to her. What happened?"

"She got me the blood I needed to complete the turn and—"

"Got you mortals to bite, you mean," she interrupted him, and then pointed out, "There were no blood banks back then."

"No, there were no blood banks," he agreed mildly. "She must have brought me people to feed on through the turn and probably controlled me to prevent my harming them."

"You don't remember?" she asked, and Magnus shook his head.

"I do not remember biting anyone, or even the turn, really, other than bad nightmares," he admitted. When she merely nodded with a grim expression, he continued. "I eventually woke up feeling rather amazing, but wondering where I was. Alodia came to me shortly after and explained about my being found and brought to her. She explained what I was now and offered to mentor me."

"Mentor?" Allie's eyes narrowed. "What exactly did that entail?"

"She basically adopted me into her family and taught me how to survive as an immortal. How to hunt. How best to avoid detection, etc."

"Oh. Right, you were only fourteen," Allie said now, relaxing a little. "Of course, she adopted you."

Magnus didn't remind her that he had been considered a man at that age, and that many of his friends had been married with a child or two under their belt by then. He merely nodded solemnly. "Family is important to immortals. They understand that it can make the difference between an immortal going rogue or not, so clans often adopt stray immortals when they come across them."

She tilted her head. "Is she still alive?"

"Yes." He hesitated and then admitted, "One of her natural sons, Edward, lives here in Port Henry. You will probably meet him in the next day or two."

"How old is he?" she asked at once.

"I believe he was born in 1004," Magnus said slowly, double-checking the date in his head. "Yes . . . 1004."

"Oh." She nodded. "Well, I'm sure it will be nice for you to see each other."

"Maybe," he said dubiously.

Allie's eyebrows rose. "Maybe?"

Magnus grimaced. "Edward was not my favorite of her sons. He was a bit of a prick growing up. Alodia spoiled him rotten," he explained. "Made him think a lot of himself. But I hear he has mellowed and become almost human since meeting his life mate, so it may be all right."

"Life mate." Allie latched on to the word like a dog on a bone. "Leonora said something about being turned after she met Alessandro and found out she was his life mate, and you called Victor Elvi's life mate," she pointed out. "What is it? Is it just the word immortals use for their mates? Or does it have some deeper meaning?"

Magnus was trying to decide how to answer her when a tap sounded on the door and it opened. He turned with relief to see Leonora's head poke in.

"It's been an hour. I need to take Allie's vitals again," she said apologetically.

"Oh." Magnus stood abruptly, beaming at the woman for her timely arrival. "Of course. Come in. I shall just take our coffee cups away while you do."

"Oh, I didn't mean to chase you off," Leonora protested as he bent to scoop up both his and Allie's cups. "This should only take a minute or two."

"And so will this," he said lightly as he walked toward her with the cups in hand. "Go ahead. I shall be right back."

Leonora peered at him with curiosity, and then her expression turned more focused and he knew she was trying to read his mind. He paused then, just feet from her, curious to see if she could. Normally, an immortal as young as Leonora wouldn't be able to read him because he was so much older than her, but immortals who had just found their life mates were supposed to be easy to read for the first year after finding them and he was curious to see if that was the case. It would be more proof that Allie was indeed his—

"Oh. I see."

Magnus blinked his thoughts away at those barely breathed words, and smiled at Leonora again. She could read him.

"Take your time," he said lightly as he eased past her to slip out of the room.

"Well, he couldn't seem to get out of here quick enough," Allie said with disgruntlement as soon as the door closed behind Magnus.

"Men do dislike anything to do with doctors and such," Leonora said with amusement as she crossed to her side with the clipboard and blood pressure cuff in hand. She set both down on the coffee table in front of the couch, and then produced the thermometer from her pocket.

"I had just asked him about life mates before you came in," Allie admitted. "I've heard the word used a couple of times and wondered if it just means 'mate' to immortals, or is something special."

"Oh, life mates are definitely something special," Leonora assured her.

"Why?" Allie asked at once.

"Because immortals mate for life," Leonora said simply, and then popped the thermometer in Allie's mouth. "That isn't to say that if their life mate dies they won't ever find another one. But while the first life mate lives, they will be devoted to her or him and never stray. For immortals, having a life mate really means until death parts them."

Allie's eyebrows rose at this news as Leonora took her wrist in hand. In this day and age when half the marriages failed, and the young weren't even bothering to marry much anymore, mating for life seemed a rare and unusual thing. She wanted to ask why that was the case, but couldn't with the thermometer in her mouth, so thought the question in her head, actually hoping, for a change, that Leonora would read her mind.

Apparently, she was too busy taking her pulse, however, because she didn't suddenly spit out the answer.

Sighing inwardly, Allie resigned herself to waiting until the thermometer was out of her mouth to ask her questions.

"You're trying to think of a way to avoid explaining life mates to Allie and admitting she's yours until you can woo her a bit."

Magnus glanced up and around from the cup he was rinsing and stared at Stephanie. He wasn't surprised to find her staring back, her eyes glowing and then fading and then glowing again as she peered at him.

"It won't work," Stephanie said when he remained silent and simply waited. "She is already attracted to you and feels unaccountably safe with you, but she won't trust that or allow it to develop into love. She's afraid of love after what it did to her sister and mother."

Magnus was startled at the mention of a sister, but held his tongue again. He knew it was better not to interrupt.

"Stephen's abandoning Stella and making her flee on her own has not helped either. Allie will not be wooed. She is afraid of what love can do to her, so is afraid to love."

Setting down the cup he'd been rinsing, Magnus turned off the tap and dried his hands on the dish towel as he turned to face the young woman.

"Except the boy. She has given up everything for him," Stephanie said slowly. "She does love Liam . . . and would do anything for him." She paused briefly, and then nodded. "She'll come to trust and love you in time if you can keep her close, but you'll have to use the boy to do that."

Movement to the side drew his gaze to the table. Elvi, Victor, DJ, Mabel, and Alessandro all still sat there and every one of them was watching Stephanie with concern. But the movement he'd noted was the arrival of another couple, who now hesitated in the archway between the dining room and the entry, their attention locked on Stephanie with equal concern. Drina and Harpernus Stoyan. Magnus had met Drina on several occasions, and had known Harper for centuries. He knew they had taken Stephanie into their hearts and home as a teenager, sharing her care with Elvi and Victor while Dani and Decker had hunted for Leonius Livius, the monster who had turned both sisters. They were all family to the young woman now, filling the holes left by losing contact with her birth family.

"Oh, stop looking so worried. I was just giving Magnus some pointers to help him claim his life mate," Stephanie said suddenly, sounding half amused and half annoyed.

Magnus turned to her again, unsurprised to see that

the pulsing glow was gone from her eyes. They were simply a pretty green again and she looked as normal as any other young woman.

"Thank you," he said solemnly.

"No problem," she said lightly, and started to turn away, but then paused and swung back to warn, "Don't let her see the passion life mates enjoy until she agrees to be your life mate and turns."

"Why?" Magnus asked with surprise.

"Because she would run," Stephanie said abruptly and with certainty. "Once she has promised to be your life mate and taken the vows, she will keep that promise, but if you let her experience life mate passion before she does . . ." She shook her head. "It would scare her silly. She would take Liam with her and flee. If that happens, she will be dead within a matter of hours, and Liam will be left to Abaddon's mercies."

Turning abruptly away, Stephanie moved around the counter and through the dining room, murmuring, "I have a headache. I'm going back up to bed to lie down for a while."

Everyone remained still and silent as they listened to her mount the stairs, and remained that way until they heard a door close and the muffled sound of her mounting the stairs to the attic rooms. Only then did they lower their gazes to exchange worried glances.

"She has the sight," Magnus said quietly.

"No," Elvi said tightly. "She just can't shut out the thoughts of everyone around her. Immortal or mortal, our thoughts bombard her constantly unless she's in her room. Harper fitted it out special with several dif-

ferent linings to help block our thoughts and it seems
to work. But it means she spends a lot of time alone,
which is worrisome."

Magnus hesitated, but then decided to let it go.
He was quite sure Stephanie had the sight, that she
could see the possible futures of those around her.
But these people were already worried about the
young woman and he didn't want to add to it. Turning back to the sink, he finished rinsing the coffee
cups, but his mind was on what Stephanie had said.
If he showed Allie the passion life mates enjoyed,
she would run . . . apparently to her death. Unless
he got her to promise to be his life mate first. And
wooing would not work. He needed to use her love
for Liam to do that.

But how? Magnus wondered over that briefly as
he finished washing and then drying the coffee cups.
By the time he'd returned them to the open shelf on
the wall, he'd decided he needed to get away to think
for a bit and come up with a plan. Hanging the dish
towel over the oven handle where he'd got it from, he
glanced to the people now talking quietly at the table
and announced, "I need to nip out and pick up a few
things. Is there a vehicle I could use?"

Ten

"Mom? Do you have a seven?"

Allie looked over the cards in her hand and then smiled evilly. "Go fish."

"Ahhh," Liam complained, and reached out to take a card. Once he had it and was placing it in with the cards fanned out in his small hand, Allie glanced at Sunita. The pretty little girl had red hair and huge eyes like her mother, but her eye color was the same blue as her father's.

"Your turn, Sunny," she said with an encouraging smile.

The girl beamed back and then turned to the pretty little blonde at her side. "Gracie, do you have a king?"

Gracie wrinkled her nose and clucked her tongue with irritation as she handed over a king faceup for all to see.

Sunny took it with a grin and then looked at Teddy Jr. "Teddy, do you have a king?"

"Go fish," he said with glee, and Allie chuckled as Sunny scowled at the boy and reached for a card.

"Your turn, Gracie," Allie said then as her gaze wandered to the clock on the dining room wall. She and the children were seated at the table playing cards while the other adults were off performing various tasks. Elvi had gone to buy groceries, something she hadn't had a chance to do before she'd suddenly found herself flooded with extra people in her home. Mabel had gone to check on things at a Mexican restaurant named Bella Black's that Allie had been told the two women owned. Stephanie was resting up in her room, and Drina, Harper, Alessandro, Leonora, DJ, and Victor were all in the large living room in the back corner of the house discussing "some matters to do with logistics." At least, that's what they'd said when they'd left her playing cards with the children and slipped away.

Magnus, though, was apparently shopping or something. That's what Allie had been told when she and Leonora had come out of the salon after the other woman had finished taking her vitals. But that was hours ago and he still wasn't back. Not that she was worried, she assured herself. She hardly knew the man, but for some reason she did feel more comfortable when he was around.

"I have to pee."

Allie blinked her thoughts away and glanced to Liam at that announcement.

"Okay. Do you know where the bathroom is?" she asked.

"Yes," he said at once with a slight blush.

"Don't worry," Teddy said as Liam slid off his chair. "I'll watch your cards and make sure the girls don't cheat."

"We wouldn't cheat," Sunita protested at once.

Teddy grinned at her annoyance, but merely shrugged and said, "Well, now you can't because I'm watching."

"Boys," Gracie muttered, and gave a long-suffering sigh before setting her own cards facedown on the table and announcing, "I have to go too."

"All right," Allie said mildly. "Go ahead. I'll watch your cards."

"And mine, please," Sunita said, slipping from her own seat. "I'm going with her."

"Oh, boy," Teddy said with some exasperation as the two girls ran up the curving staircase, presumably to use one of the upper bathrooms. "Why do girls always go to the bathroom together?"

"Maybe they both have to go," Allie suggested mildly.

"Maybe," he allowed, and then sighed with resignation and set his own cards down. "'Cause now I have to go too."

Allie chuckled as she watched him hurry away from the table, and then set her own cards down and sat back in her seat, her eyes sliding again to the clock. It was a little after noon. Magnus had been gone for a couple of hours.

"He's fine."

Allie glanced around with a start at those words and found herself peering at a young blonde she hadn't yet met. All the immortals she'd met so far looked to be around twenty-five or thirty, but this woman looked a little younger. She would have said somewhere between eighteen and twenty-one. Leonora had given her a rundown of everyone in the house as she'd taken her temperature and blood pressure the last time. It had helped to pass the time, she supposed. But now she peered at the blonde and ran through the names and circumstances Leonora had given her and guessed, "Stephanie?"

Nodding, the blonde moved around the counter into the kitchen and opened the refrigerator door to peer in at the contents. "Magnus is fine. He needed a few things and wanted time to think. He'll be back."

"Oh," Allie murmured. She didn't bother to ask how the girl had known what she was worrying about. Everyone here could read her mind. Except for the kids, of course.

"So far."

"What?" Allie asked uncertainly.

"I said, so far. So far, the kids can't read and control you," she explained, retrieving juice from the fridge and pouring herself a glass. "That will change in another year or so."

"So I gather," Allie said unhappily, her mind turning to that worry. She kept a lot from Liam. She didn't want him living in fear, so she kept their troubles to herself. He had no idea why they had to move so often.

But she wouldn't be able to keep it from him once he could read her mind.

Stephanie snorted, drawing Allie's attention back to the young woman as she put the juice away and picked up her glass. "That's the least of your worries."

"Is it?" Allie asked warily.

Stephanie nodded and said solemnly, "You should be more concerned about when he starts being able to control you."

"Liam?" Allie asked, her eyes widening, and then she shook her head. "He wouldn't—"

"He's a child," Stephanie said with a shrug. "They make bad choices all the time. It's why they need parents."

"And he has one. Me," Allie said firmly. "I'll teach him that it's wrong to control people and read their minds."

"You can't teach him it's wrong to read minds," Stephanie said firmly. "The nanos gave us that skill for a reason. Survival. He needs to know if the people he encounters are a threat."

"But I'm not a threat. I'm his mother. He shouldn't read me."

"But he will," she said with certainty. "And he'll control you too. He won't be able to help himself."

Allie took a deep breath and shook her head. He wouldn't. He loved her.

"Of course he loves you," Stephanie said with amusement. "But that won't stop him from . . ." She hesitated a moment, and then said, "Think about when you were a child. Your mother used to make cherry pie every Sunday."

Allie blinked in surprise at the words. Leonora had mentioned that Stephanie had a "gift." That where the others could only read the things you were thinking about, Stephanie seemed to be able to read everything in a person's head. They were all open books to her, and this seemed proof to Allie. She hadn't been thinking about it—in fact, she hadn't thought about it for years—but her mother *had* made cherry pie every Sunday. To please her father. He'd loved cherry pie.

"And you loved it too," Stephanie said as if she'd spoken aloud. "But you were never allowed more than one piece. Not even the next day if there was pie left, because it was your father's. You and your sister each got one very small slice apiece on Sunday, but your father ate the rest over the next couple of days in front of you and you two weren't allowed to have any more."

Stephanie took a drink of juice before continuing. "Now, imagine you could have controlled your parents. Imagine you could have put it in their minds that you should be allowed another piece of that pie. It wouldn't hurt anyone. Your father was getting a belly anyway, and it would probably be good if he cut back." She arched one eyebrow. "Tell me you wouldn't have controlled them and made sure you had a second piece of pie."

Allie looked away from the young woman. She wished she could say she wouldn't have, but she had really liked cherry pie.

"Or say your mother was making liver for dinner. You and your sister always hated liver. But they made you sit at the table until you ate every last bite of what was put on your plate, didn't they?"

Allie nodded slowly and glanced back to her, amazed the woman could pull these things from her mind.

"Now, imagine you could have made your mother decide to make spaghetti for you and your sister instead. And you could put it in your father's head that it was okay if you and your sister had spaghetti instead of the liver." She let her think about that for a minute, and then said, "That's how it would start. Just a food he wanted, or candy you didn't think he should have. Nothing big or important. But it would move on from there to things Liam wanted to do that you didn't approve of, or places he wanted to go and so on, until you were just a puppet, unable to stop him from doing whatever he wanted. Hell, not even aware that you didn't want him to do these things in the end."

Allie stared at her with mounting dismay. If what Stephanie was saying was true . . . She couldn't be an effective mother to Liam if he could just take control of her when he chose. He was a good boy, but even a saint would find it difficult not to abuse that kind of power.

"And then it wouldn't take long for others to realize what was happening. They'd decide that Liam should be taken from you and given to an immortal couple, so that he could be raised properly."

"What? No!" Allie said with dismay.

"And then they'd wipe your mind so you had no memory of Liam, or immortals or anything."

"No," she said, standing abruptly. "I won't allow that. He's my son."

"You couldn't stop it," Stephanie said solemnly, and then added, "The only way to prevent it is to become immortal yourself."

Allie froze. "To be . . ."

"Turned," Stephanie said, and then pointed out, "If you were immortal, Liam wouldn't be able to control you. There'd be no reason to take him away from you then."

Allie stared at her blankly. She'd never considered becoming immortal. It just hadn't occurred to her as a possibility. Truthfully, she wasn't sure she wanted to consider it now. Immortal? A vampire?

Stephanie shrugged. "I guess you have to decide how much you love Liam. Do you want to remain in his life?" she asked. "Because the only way to do that is to turn."

Allie stared at her silently for a moment, and then sagged back into her seat in defeat. She did love Liam. She might not have given birth to him, but he *was* her son. She couldn't lose him. Running a hand wearily through her hair, she asked, "How do I become immortal?"

"Someone has to agree to turn you," Stephanie said simply.

Allie bit her lip, and then asked, "Would you—?"

"Oh, no," she said firmly, and then added, "Trust me, you wouldn't want me to. I'm Edentate, not immortal."

She had no idea what that meant, but simply asked, "Do you think someone else would, then? Someone who was immortal?"

"Unfortunately, immortals are only allowed to turn one mortal in a lifetime . . . and they tend to save that for a life mate."

"Life mate," Allie muttered with frustration. "Everyone keeps throwing that word out, but I have no idea what it means other than that they're a mate for life. I presume there's more to it than that?"

"Much more," Stephanie agreed. "Life mates can't read or control each other. They can sit in a room together and not worry that their mind is being read, or that they'll hear a hurtful stray thought from their partner's mind, because they just can't. A life mate is an oasis of peace in a very noisy and stressful world."

"I see," Allie said slowly.

"No, you don't, because you have no idea what I'm talking about," Stephanie assured her wearily, and then suddenly narrowed her eyes. "But you could."

"I could what?" Allie asked warily when Stephanie started walking toward her.

"See what it means to be without a life mate. The noise you have to constantly block out."

"Oh, I don't think—" Allie stood up, but that was as far as she got. Stephanie was immediately before her, reaching for her head. The moment the young woman's fingers touched either side of her temple, Allie's mind exploded with chatter. Liam's hope that he never had to leave this place and the friends he'd made. He was so happy and Mom wasn't so scared here. Teddy's thinking that he liked his new friend, and it would be nice not to be the only boy all the time. Sunita's thought that with all the people here it was like Christmas. Gracie hoped she got to stay over again tonight; it was fun. Leonora was concerned that she might get distracted with the talk they were having and miss taking Allie's vitals. Perhaps she should set a timer on her watch. Alessandro was disgruntled that Leonora had taken on the duty to keep an eye on Allie; he wanted to take his wife home and make love to her. Drina was concerned for Stephanie, and what they could do to make things easier for her. Harper was struggling with concern for both Drina and Stephanie, worry over the girl, but anxiety at how crushed Drina would be if things went wrong and they lost Stephanie to madness. DJ was wondering if Mabel would make it home before lunch, or stay at the restaurant all day. Victor was thinking he should have offered to help Elvi with the shopping, but he'd felt he should stay in case there was trouble. Dani was feeling guilt even in sleep, that there might have been some way she could have better protected her sister and kept her from being kidnapped and turned. Decker was worrying about the guilt he knew his wife suffered. Tybo was hungry and wondering if he got up to get something to eat, he'd be able to sleep again after. He needed to be up all night to play babysitter. Someone named Michael was considering retiring from the fire department, taking the job in security in London, Ontario, and moving his family there. Things hadn't been the same since he and his wife had tried to kill Elvi. Someone named Karen was eyeing her dirty windows and debating whether to wash them today or—

Stephanie took her hands away and Allie staggered as silence reigned in her head.

"That is life around other mortals and immortals," Stephanie said quietly. "An unending barrage of thoughts and feelings if the others aren't constantly guarding their thoughts. This . . ." She paused and glanced around as silence fell over them, and then turned back and said, "That silence is life with a life mate. No noise to block out, no chatter. You can enjoy this in the company of another rather than having to be alone to avoid people's thoughts."

Allie frowned. "So if I was turned I'd hear all that . . . noise all the time?"

"No," Stephanie assured her with a sigh. "You wouldn't hear people's thoughts at all at first. But eventually you'd start to pick it up. However, it would never be as bad as what I just showed you. Apparently, I'm especially sensitive. You'd just pick up stray thoughts here and there if people weren't guarding their thoughts. And you'd learn to guard your own so everyone wasn't hearing your thoughts all the time either. But having to constantly guard your thoughts can be wearing. It makes having a life mate very special. You can let your guard down around them. You can find that quiet while in their company, and not have to be alone to get it."

"I see," Allie murmured, and thought she really did this time. Stephanie had only held her head for a few seconds. All those thoughts had bombarded her at once like shouts from a crowd. Or several televisions blaring around her at the same time, each one on a different channel. No wonder everyone worried that Stephanie would go mad. But even just a fraction of that kind of noise would get irritating quickly. She could see how immortals would prefer being alone. She supposed it did make a life mate special. No one wanted to be alone all the time, but if there was one person you could relax around, they would be like a lifeline.

"But Elvi and Leonora already have life mates," Allie said suddenly, her mind returning to her own problems and the need to turn to keep Liam. "They didn't turn Victor and Alessandro, did they?"

"No, they didn't. And yes, they each still have their one turn," she agreed. "But what if Victor or Alessandro die? Would you damn Elvi or Leonora to spending the next thousand years or so alone so that you could be turned?"

Allie frowned and lowered her head, struggling with her answer. She didn't want to curse Elvi or Leonora to being alone if their mate died, but she didn't want to lose Liam either.

"Fortunately for you, you're a possible life mate for someone here," Stephanie announced, regaining her attention.

"What?" she asked with surprise, her head lifting again. When Stephanie simply nodded, not willing to repeat herself, Allie hesitated and then asked, "You said possible life mate. What does that mean? Am I or aren't I?"

"It means you are, if you accept it and agree to be this immortal's life mate. If you can't accept it, then you were just a possible life mate and the immortal in question will have to hope to encounter another who will be more agreeable."

"What about him?" Allie asked, and then added, "It is a him, right?"

Stephanie nodded.

"Well, what if he doesn't want me to be his life mate?" she asked. "Does he have a choice?"

"Of course he does," she said with amusement. "But I'm quite sure he'd be willing to accept you as a life mate and turn you."

"Oh." Allie stared at her nonplussed, and then said, "But I don't want to be a life mate, I just want . . ."

"To be turned?" Stephanie suggested dryly. "And you think it's fair to ask someone to turn you when you aren't willing to be their life mate? That they should resign themselves to living the rest of their very long life alone just to help you?" Stephanie shook her head and said solemnly, "Perhaps you should think about how much you want to remain Liam's mother. And what you're willing to do to get that. Because, frankly, I'd rather see Liam raised by Elvi and Victor, or one of the other couples, then see you damn someone to spending eternity alone."

Turning on her heel, Stephanie left the room, taking her juice with her.

Allie dropped back into her chair as she listened to the young woman mount the stairs, but her mind was going over what Stephanie had said. Liam would soon be able to read and control her. She'd like to think she could teach him not to do either, but it was asking a lot of a child to resist a temptation that adults would have trouble resisting. Just look at how Tybo had taken control of her in the pizza joint when she hadn't immediately fallen in with their plans. He'd said and probably believed he'd done it for her own good, to save her and Liam, but the truth was he hadn't even really tried to convince her that they meant her and her son no harm and were trying to help. Not at that point anyway.

No. Liam wouldn't be able to resist using his abilities against her, and she couldn't be a proper mother to him as a mortal once he gained those abilities. But he was her son. She loved him more than anyone or anything in her life. She'd basically given up her career for him, or as good as, accepting fewer and fewer jobs for fear the vampires had been tracking her somehow through her work or emails. There hadn't seemed to be any other explanation. The last job she'd taken was more than four months ago, just before she'd been forced to flee their last home and run to Toronto. And she'd spotted the immortal in the grocery store just days after she'd started emailing back and forth with the new client. Allie hadn't contacted them again since reaching Toronto, however, so the only way Abaddon could have traced her there was through her job at the blood bank.

Sighing, she turned to face the table and crossed her arms on the wooden surface. She would have to become immortal to keep her son. If she did that, and if the Enforcers managed to find and catch Abaddon, she could go back to designing websites and build a good life for herself and Liam here in Port Henry. But if what Stephanie said was true, there was only likely to be one person who would be willing to turn her, and he would want her to agree to be his life mate in exchange for turning her. What did that entail exactly? Companionship, maybe? An end to having to be alone? She could manage that . . . if he was nice, and if Liam liked him.

That thought brought her to the subject of who this immortal might be who thought he was a possible life mate. The answer seemed obvious now that she allowed herself to look at it. Stephanie had said life mates were special because they couldn't read or control each other. There was only one person she knew of who fit that description. Everyone else she'd encountered had been reading her repeatedly since waking in the Enforcer house. Everyone but— "Magnus."

"Yes?"

Allie swung around abruptly, her wide eyes landing on Magnus as he pushed the kitchen door closed behind him. She's been so distracted with her thoughts that she hadn't heard him enter. But there he stood, big as life, his hair wind tossed, his cheeks ruddy from the wind and cold outside, and his arms weighed down with several bulging bags marked Walmart.

"Allie?" he asked, eyebrows raised. "You said my name. Did you want something?"

"Yes. No. I was just—" Waving one hand vaguely, she stood and moved around the counter into the kitchen to take some of the bags from him. "It looks like you've been busy."

"Yes. Well, I was not sure what you and Liam might need," he admitted as he bent to remove his boots. "So I got a variety of things. Toothbrushes, shampoo, some clothes. Though I wasn't sure about sizes," he admitted as he straightened again. "So I got several different sizes of each item. I can return the ones that do not . . ." He paused abruptly and tilted his head to take in her expression. "What is it?"

"You went shopping for Liam and me?" she asked, her wide eyes moving from the bags to him and back.

"Well, I know you have those Go bags, but they did not appear to have a lot in them. I thought perhaps you might need a few things, so . . ." He shrugged, looking suddenly uncomfortable. "But maybe I was wrong and you did not need anything."

"No. I mean, yes, the bags don't have much in them. Just essentials, really—a change of clothes, maps, some power bars, water, a blanket, and a first aid kit . . ." She shrugged, not bothering to mention the other items.

"Oh. Good. Then this stuff might be useful," he said, offering her a smile. "It would have been easier if I could have taken you with me, but you were supposed to take it easy, and with Leonora checking your vitals every hour . . ." He shrugged, but then added, "If I have forgotten anything or there is something else you wanted, we can probably go shopping tomorrow."

Allie managed a smile. "I'm sure this is fine. Thank

you." Turning, she walked to the counter to set down the bags, asking, "How much do I owe you?" and then immediately frowned as she recalled that her purse was back in the apartment they'd fled. Not that there was much money in it. She really was damned near broke. There was an emergency stash of a couple hundred dollars in one of the Go bags, and maybe as much in her purse back in Toronto, but her bank account was empty. Four years on the run had eaten up her savings and investments.

"Nothing," Magnus answered as he set the rest of the bags down next to the ones she'd taken from him. Shrugging out of his coat, he moved into a small room off the other end of the kitchen, adding, "You did not ask me to buy these things. They are a gift."

Allie followed him, but paused in the doorway to peer around. It was a small vestibule with cupboards, a coat closet, and a door leading out into what she could see was an attached garage.

Closing the closet door, Magnus turned and stopped when he saw her standing in the doorway. He peered at her silently for a minute and then asked with concern, "Is something wrong? Did something happen while I was gone? You seem off, and—"

"No. I'm fine. I just . . ." Waving a hand, she grimaced and admitted, "I'm not used to gifts. I guess I feel guilty for accepting them." It was true, but wasn't really why she probably seemed off to him. Her mind was still fixated on her need to become an immortal and his being the one person likely to be willing to turn her.

"You have nothing to feel guilty about," he said firmly.

"Yes, well—" Much to her relief, chatter erupted in the kitchen then and she was able to drop the subject. Turning, Allie stepped back into the kitchen to see that not only had the children returned from their bathroom break, but Elvi and Mabel were coming in from outside, their arms laden with grocery bags.

"Elvi's been shopping," Mabel announced dryly when she spotted Allie hurrying toward them. "Fortunately for her, I pulled in right behind her and was able to help her drag them in."

"Be careful, kids. Don't drop anything," Allie warned as her son and the other children started relieving the women of bags. The moment the children were out of the way, Allie reached for a couple of bags and then turned to set them on the counter, only to stop when she saw the Walmart bags still there.

"Liam, we need to get these bags out of the way and up to our room," she said, setting the bags she held on the counter next to the sink.

"What are they?" Liam asked, handing her the bags he'd taken to set down as well.

"I'm not sure," Allie admitted as she led him back to start grabbing the Walmart bags. As she handed Liam a couple of the lighter bags, she added, "They're some things Magnus bought us, so say thank you."

"Thank— Oh, wow! Is this for me?"

Allie glanced over to see that the bags she'd handed Liam were now on the floor and he was holding up a brand-new navy blue winter coat with red and white stripes across the chest and matching navy blue insulated pants. The boy was staring at the coat and pants like they were the most beautiful things he'd ever seen. She looked at Magnus, surprised to see that he appeared uncomfortable.

"Yes," Magnus said, and then cleared his throat and added, "Well, Victor mentioned maybe taking you kids out tobogganing after lunch, and I thought you might need something a little warmer than that jacket you were wearing when we—" His words ended on a startled *oomph* when Liam dropped the coat and pants and launched himself at the man, leaping up to catch him around the neck like a monkey.

"Thank you, Magnus!" Liam shouted excitedly, hugging the man as he caught him before he could fall.

"You are more than welcome," Magnus murmured, hugging the boy briefly back before setting him down. "Now, why do you not go hang that up while I help your mother carry the bags upstairs?"

"Show him where the coat closet is, Sunita," Elvi instructed as she began to set down the rest of the bags she carried.

Sunita, Grace, and Teddy rushed Liam off to the vestibule with the closet, chattering excitedly now about going tobogganing.

"Thank you," Allie said quietly, meeting Magnus's gaze, and then she turned away and headed for the stairs with the bags she'd grabbed. She was aware that Magnus was following with the remainder of the bags, but her mind was distracted with what Stephanie had said. He was probably the only one who was likely to be willing to turn her, and she needed to be turned to continue to be Liam's mom.

But what would he expect in return? What did being a life mate entail? She had no idea how to broach the subject with him. Or if she even should. How was this kind of thing usually done? She had no idea.

"Where are we putting this stuff?" Magnus asked as he followed her into the room. "Did you want to set the bags on the bed and sort through them now so you can see if there is anything you need that I did not consider?"

"Yes, that's fine." Allie set her own bags there even as he did. She then opened the first bag and started to retrieve the items inside, very aware that Magnus was hesitating to leave.

"I was not sure which shampoo you would like but that one smelled pretty. If you prefer a different kind, I can return it and get another."

Allie glanced to him with confusion, and then followed his gaze to the bottle of shampoo in her hand and realized she'd been staring blindly at it for a couple of minutes. Shaking her head, she turned and set it on the dresser. "No. It's fine. Thank you. I just—" Whirling back, she blurted, "You can't read me because we're possible life mates."

Eleven

Magnus stared at Allie for a moment, and then turned to close the bedroom door. It would seem they were going to have the conversation he'd been agonizing over during the last two hours as he'd shopped. He'd worried about how to broach the subject, along with where and when, but it looked like it was happening now and here.

Taking a deep breath, he faced her and opened his mouth to begin the speech he'd come up with on his shopping trip, only to close it again as she asked, "That's true, isn't it?"

He nodded.

"Stephanie said Liam will be able to read and control me in the next year or so. She said that he'd use that against me. Not on purpose," she added quickly in the boy's defense. "But he wouldn't be able to resist controlling me if he wanted something bad enough, and then it would become just what he did."

"More than likely," Magnus agreed, sorry to have to say so, but it was true. He suspected there wasn't a child alive who could resist using such an ability.

Allie glanced down at the bags on the bed. "She said once the others realized this was happening, he'd be taken away from me. Because I couldn't be an effective mother."

Magnus hesitated and then said, "It would be no reflection on you, but immortal children need parents who can—"

"I don't want to lose my son," Allie interrupted in a voice so quiet he might have missed it if his hearing wasn't enhanced.

Magnus hesitated, unsure what to say.

"But you could turn me, couldn't you? Then Liam couldn't read or control me and I wouldn't lose him."

"I could," he allowed slowly, beginning to worry that she would ask him to do just that, no strings attached. If she did, he wasn't sure he wouldn't agree. Stephanie had said he had to use the boy to get her to agree to be his life mate, but it just seemed so heartless. She was his life mate—how could he deny her?

"But you'd want me to be your life mate."

Her words didn't sound accusing or resentful, and that fact alone almost had him sagging with relief, but he held himself straight and merely nodded.

"What does that mean?" she asked. "What would you expect of me?"

Everything, he thought, but knew that would scare the hell out of her and that he had to go slowly here. "I would expect you to promise to be my life mate. I would turn you. We would marry and I would help you raise Liam."

"And then?" she prompted when he paused.

Magnus hesitated, and then said, "That depends on whether Lucian and his men catch Abaddon. If they do, and you wish to stay in Canada, I would give up my position with the UK Enforcers and we could purchase a home for us either here in Port Henry or somewhere else, hopefully near immortals who have children so that Liam would have playmates."

After a hesitation, he continued. "If, however, Abaddon gets away, then I suggest we should probably move to my home in the UK where you and Liam would both be safer. We could, of course, look for a new home there, somewhere near other immortal children of his age. I am sure there must be some."

"If Abaddon gets away?" Allie asked with a frown. It seemed obvious she hadn't even considered the possibility that the Enforcers would fail. "Surely they will catch him?"

"Abaddon has escaped before," he told her. "The first time was over two thousand and seven hundred years ago and the last was just a few years back."

"He's been around for that long?" Allie asked with dismay.

Magnus nodded.

Allie looked horrified, but then shook her head.

"That wasn't what I meant by— What would you expect of *me* after we married and you turned me?" she asked point-blank. "I don't love you."

Magnus managed not to react to those words, though he found them surprisingly painful. He knew he shouldn't. While he might have accepted her as his life mate and had started developing feelings for her that had grown as he'd listened to her tale about her friendship with Stella and how she'd come to be Liam's mother, she hardly knew anything about him other than how he was turned. And she was mortal. The fact that they were life mates wouldn't mean as much to her.

Magnus was trying to decide what he could say that wouldn't scare the hell out of her when she apparently grew impatient and said, "I barely know you. I don't think I could— I mean, when people marry they're expected to—"

"I would not expect anything from you that you were not ready to give," he said when she faltered again, and tried not to feel guilty about the relief that washed over her face. Magnus meant what he said, but he also knew it was meaningless because they were life mates. Life mates were known to have incredible, explosive sex that was so mind-blowing and overwhelming that they passed out at the end of it. They were also said to be insatiable and unable to resist each other once they experienced it. He was counting on that and would have liked to test it now, but Stephanie had warned him not to let Allie experience the passion before he got her promise. So he kept his distance and simply waited.

"I need to think about this," Allie said finally. "And talk to Liam. It affects him too."

"Of course," Magnus agreed solemnly, and turned to open the door. "Let me know what you decide." He'd barely finished the last word before he had the door closed between them.

Magnus started down the stairs, shaking his head over the fact that he'd agonized over how to bring this all up while he was shopping, and then had returned to find that Stephanie had done all the heavy lifting for him. She'd scared Allie with the knowledge that Liam would control her and she would lose her son. Which was true and what he thought would hold the most sway with her. She loved Liam. Allie would probably marry the devil himself to keep the boy. Magnus was quite sure she'd agree to be his life mate and turn. He just hoped she didn't take too long to tell him so, because he couldn't risk touching her in any way and having the life mate passion explode between them until she gave her promise and they were married. Hell, he couldn't even sleep near her until then for fear of their having shared dreams. That was another symptom of life mates: shared sex dreams that were apparently powerful. He wasn't doing anything that might scare her off until he had her promise and was sure she wouldn't run.

Which meant he needed to find somewhere to sleep tonight that was far enough away they couldn't have the shared dreams, he thought with a frown, and wondered how far away Teddy and Katricia's house was.

Allie stared at the closed door, her mind in a state of chaos. Part of her wanted to grab Liam and flee. But aside from the fact that she was broke and without a vehicle, she suspected it would be harder to hide from the Enforcers than it had been hiding from Abaddon. And that had been impossible, she thought grimly. She'd spent the last four years running, not hiding. Abaddon and his people had found her every time she'd stopped running and it was just pure good luck that she'd managed to evade them this long.

A life on the run wasn't good for Liam.

Neither would his being raised by a mother he could read and control. What kind of person would he grow up to be without parental guidance? Because that's what it amounted to. He would end up circumventing her authority when he chose until she was altogether ineffectual.

Becoming immortal seemed to be the only way she could keep her son and raise him. Something she wanted desperately. And not just because of the promise she'd made to Stella. Allie loved that little boy with every fiber of her being.

The simple answer was to promise to be a life mate to Magnus and allow him to turn her. Liam could never control her then and she would never lose him. But it added a third person to the dynamics. They would be a family. She would lose some of the control she was used to holding and control was important to Allie. She had promised herself at sixteen that she would never be dependent on a man like her mother. She would never give up control of her life and have to bow to a man's wishes. Now she was faced with a situation that forced her to consider doing just that.

Allie didn't miss the irony in the situation. Her mother had willingly given up control completely to her father, and that had ended with her losing her daughter, Allie's sister, Jilly. Now Allie was contemplating giving up at least part of her own control to keep her son.

Sighing, Allie opened the nearest bag and began pulling out items, surprised to find Magnus had thought of everything in his shopping. There were two toothbrushes, toothpaste, deodorant, a hairbrush, shampoo, and conditioner. There was a lovely and expensively packaged perfume that she'd never heard of but quite liked, a wallet and purse, and even clothes for both her and Liam. Each item of clothing came in different sizes, one of which was right, but the best thing about them was that she liked his taste in clothes. The man had similar taste to her, she realized as she pulled out a hip-length black parka with a soft faux-fur lining and trim around the hood.

It was lovely, and looked warm, which was much appreciated. Her own coat was probably still at the blood bank. She'd taken it off while she'd been gathering blood and it hadn't been around when she'd woken up in the hospital.

The sound of the door opening drew her head around to see Liam rushing in wearing his snowsuit and new boots and carrying another shopping bag.

"Elvi said to bring this up. You forgot it," he announced, rushing to the bed to add it to the pile. He started to turn away then, no doubt to rush out again, but paused as his gaze landed on a T-shirt with several comic book characters on it. "Wow! Is that for me?"

"Yes. Magnus bought it for you," Allie said, and smiled faintly when he picked up the T-shirt to get a better look at the characters on it.

"Cool. Can I wear it now?" he asked excitedly.

Allie shook her head. "No. But we'll give you a bath tonight and you can wear it tomorrow."

"Ah, but it's so cool," he protested, scowling at her with annoyance at the refusal, and she wondered if he would have controlled her and made her let him wear it now if he could.

Allie pushed the thought aside, and asked, "Why do you have your coat and pants on? It's too hot to wear it inside."

"Oh." He glanced down at himself with surprise, apparently having forgot what he had on. "Magnus is taking us out to finish making our snowman while the moms make lunch."

"Is he?" she asked with surprise.

"Yeah. We started it yesterday after he put you to bed. Dani wanted us out of the bedroom so he took us outside. But he was worried my coat wasn't warm enough, so we had to come back in. But that's okay," he assured her. "Magnus showed us fun games to play inside."

Allie blinked at this news, and then asked, "What games?"

"Alligator island and hoot owl. They were fun."

"What is alligator island?" she asked with curiosity.

"Magnus used Elvi's colored tape to make these squares on the floor that were supposed to be islands and we had to jump from one to the other without falling in or the alligators would get us." Liam started to laugh at the memory. "He fell in more than any of us."

"Did he?" she asked faintly, and then cleared her throat and asked, "And the owl game?"

"It's a board game Sunny has. We had to get the owls back to their nest before the sun came up. It was fun too, but Magnus could only watch. It's only for four players," he explained.

"So you like Magnus?" she asked.

"Oh, yeah, he's nice. And fun. And he didn't even yell when Sunny and Gracie started to get all girly and whiny. Girls." Liam rolled his eyes at the memory. "Can I go outside now? They'll all be waiting."

"Yes," Allie murmured, and then as he reached the door, she said, "Liam?"

"Yeah?" He turned back with his hand on the doorknob.

She hesitated briefly, and then asked, "Do you wish you had a father?"

The question made him pause and remove his hand from the doorknob. He actually seemed to consider it seriously. She could almost see his four-year-old mind working, and then he said, "If he was nice like Magnus, yeah. It would be nice to have a dad like everyone else. And then you wouldn't have to worry so much about the bad people getting us. I bet Magnus could beat them up."

They were both silent for a minute and then Teddy

burst into the room. "Hurry up, Liam. We're waiting for you. We won't get the snowman done before lunch if you don't come now."

"I'm coming," he said at once, and then glanced uncertainly to Allie.

"Go," she said, waving him off, but then shouted, "No running in the house!" when she heard their little feet hammering down the stairs.

"Sorry!" Liam shouted, and was echoed by Teddy as their footsteps slowed to a jog.

Shaking her head, Allie peered down at the bed, Liam's words echoing in her head.

It would be nice to have a dad like everyone else. And then you wouldn't have to worry so much about the bad people getting us. I bet Magnus could beat them up.

She'd done her best to keep her worries and fears from Liam, and still he knew about the bad people. He'd apparently told Tricia about them at the Enforcer house, and had brought them up again just now. But she had never mentioned the reason they kept moving. She had never told him about the bad people. How did he know about them?

The only obvious answer was that he was already picking up on her thoughts. Allie frowned as she wondered how much of her thoughts he was reading. And how long it had been happening? She worried over that as she returned to sorting the clothes, choosing what would fit and refolding the ones that were the wrong size to place them back in the bags for return.

Allie didn't think Liam could have picked up much

or for long. He had only just turned four. He probably didn't even understand the threat the bad people represented. At least, she hoped not. But even knowing that bad people were after them must have been scary for him. Especially when he'd woken up alone in the apartment the night she'd gone to the blood bank. He must have been terrified to find her missing. He'd probably worried that the bad people had got her.

"God, I'm a horrible parent," Allie breathed, dropping to sit on the side of the bed. Stella had counted on her to keep him safe and happy. How happy could he have been knowing bad people were chasing them? And the difference in him now . . . He'd always been quiet and well behaved. She'd just thought that was his nature. It wasn't like she had a lot of experience with children to judge from. But now, seeing how noisy and happy he was here, she wondered if his previous behavior was more a result of worry and fear than personality.

Liam said he wanted a dad like the other children had. Of course he did. She should have expected that. And he liked Magnus. Which was probably good because an arrangement with Magnus was the only way he was likely to get a dad. She worked from home and really didn't get out much, so it wasn't likely she'd meet anyone and start a normal relationship. Not that she really wanted a normal relationship anyway. That way lay pain and betrayal. Just look at how things had turned out for her mother and Stella.

Sighing, Allie glanced around for someplace to

pack away the clothes they would keep, but the drawers were all full of Sunita's clothes. It reminded her that this was another temporary stop, not really a home. Standing, she packed the clothes they would keep back in the bags they'd come in and set them on the floor next to the bed, then grabbed up the bags that held the clothes to be returned, and headed for the door. She'd set them aside for Magnus to return and see what she could do to help make lunch. And then, after lunch, she supposed she'd have to talk to Magnus and agree to be his life mate. There was no sense dragging it out.

"Magnus is very good with the children. Patient. He'll make a good father."

Allie tore her gaze away from where Magnus was flying down the hill on a toboggan with Liam before him, in a race against a second toboggan holding Teddy Jr. and Alessandro, and glanced to Elvi at that comment. She'd never got her chance to talk to Magnus. Lunch had been ready by the time she got downstairs, and the minute it was over and the mess cleared up, they'd piled the kids in the cars and driven here to what Elvi called Cider Hills. It was an apple farm on a hill where guests were allowed to toboggan before or after visiting the restaurant, which served hot apple cider, sandwiches, and various apple desserts. There were also jugs of cider and various packaged apple desserts that could then be purchased to take home as well. Allie had never seen anything like it, but she thought this place was wonderful. The kids were having a ball, and it was nice to stand here with the women sipping a warm apple cider while watching the children have fun.

"Yes," she agreed quietly, offering Elvi a crooked smile before turning her gaze back to the boys. The two toboggans had reached the bottom of the hill now and they were all laughing as they climbed off and began to slog back up the hill, the boys leading the way and Magnus and Alessandro following, dragging the sleds behind them. Now, Victor and DJ were at the top of the hill, about to push off their own sleds side by side, each with their daughter before them.

"This is a wonderful place to raise children," Elvi said suddenly. "I hope you'll consider moving here once this mess is over. I think Teddy Jr. would like having a little buddy to hang out with other than the girls. They love Teddy," she added. "But sometimes I think it's a bit overwhelming for him."

Allie smiled at the thought, and nodded. "It does seem idyllic, and I'd like to be able to make a home here for Liam. I think he'd love it. He certainly seems to enjoy having friends. But I gather it depends on whether they catch Abaddon."

"Abaddon," Elvi sighed the name. "We thought Leonius was bad until we found out Abaddon was his puppet master." She shook her head. "I guess we'll have to hope they catch him."

"Yeah," Mabel muttered, and then turned to peer

at Allie and asked point-blank, "So are you going to agree to be Magnus's life mate or not?"

"Mabel," Elvi said with dismay.

"Oh, don't try to say you aren't wondering too," Mabel said with exasperation. "The suspense is killing me."

Allie smiled wryly at the women, not terribly surprised they knew about that. Rather than answer, she said, "Well, you can read my mind. What do you think?"

"That's the problem," Mabel admitted. "Your mind's all confused on the subject. One minute you're thinking yes, the next you're shying away from it. Tell us what you're afraid of and maybe we can help."

Allie's smile faded at the words. "I— It would be— Really, I don't think I have a choice. I don't want to lose Liam."

"Oh, honey," Mabel said with gentle sympathy. "You make becoming Magnus's life mate sound like a trip to the dentist. Believe me, being life mates is wonderful."

"Is it?" she asked, almost desperate to know what it would entail.

"Yes," Mabel assured her. "Those nanos know their business. If they've hooked you up, then you and Magnus will suit each other like salsa and cheese on tacos."

Allie smiled faintly at the analogy, reminded that Elvi and Mabel owned and ran a Mexican restaurant. But she asked, "You think the nanos decide on life mates?"

Mabel shrugged. "What else? They're why we can

read minds, so it just stands to reason they're why we can't read our life mates. And trust me, they're never wrong. If Magnus can't read or control you, you're the one for him. And he'll be the one for you."

"How?" she asked at once.

"Well . . ." Mabel glanced to Elvi.

"You'll have similar tastes," the redhead said, "and similar values. None of us seem to argue much. That's not to say never, but they aren't serious arguments. Mostly it's a case of irritation on the part of the women when the men get too protective, or the other way around."

"And even then you make up pretty quick," Mabel put in.

"Yes." Elvi fell silent for a minute, and then said, "It's hard to explain, but they really do seem like your other half. A soul mate, I guess." She frowned briefly and then admitted, "I was married as a mortal. My husband died long before I met Victor," she added quickly, apparently concerned that Allie might think she'd tossed him over for the immortal. "I was happy with him. I thought we had a good marriage, but really it couldn't compare to what I have with Victor. He's my best friend, my confidant, and my rock. I know he would give his life for me, and I would do the same for him. They're a true partner. It makes you . . . I don't know, confident, of course, but at peace too. You know you can always count on your mate."

"But why?"

"Because a life mate is the most important thing in the world to an immortal," Magnus said quietly, and

Allie glanced around to find he had joined them and now stood behind her. Taking her arm, he turned her and asked solemnly, "Will you be my life mate, Allie?"

She stared at him silently for a minute, Elvi's words replaying in her mind. Best friend and confident, a true partner you could always count on. It sounded nice. It would be nice not to always have to carry the burden alone. Not that Liam was a burden, but keeping him safe, making money, raising him right, always being the bad guy and having to say no . . . He was reaching the age where he would need to be home-schooled soon too, another chore she'd be tasked with. It would be nice to have a partner to lean on.

"Yes," she breathed so softly a mortal wouldn't have heard her, but he did. They all did, and Allie found herself being hugged and congratulated by first Elvi and then Mabel as they assured her she wouldn't be sorry. Allie wasn't sure they were right, she was already half regretting it, but knew that was her fear talking.

"—and we'll hold the wedding dinner at the restaurant."

Allie's thoughts fled as she caught the end of Elvi's words. She tuned back in fully to hear Mabel add, "We'll close it to customers, of course, so we can have a private celebration."

"Wait. What?" Allie asked, glancing around with confusion.

"The wedding dinner," Elvi explained. "We'll hold it for you at the restaurant after the ceremony at the courthouse."

"The courthouse?" she asked blankly.

"Yes, dear," Elvi said, and then frowned. "Oh, did you want a big wedding? We didn't think you had a large family and would want one, but you can always do the big wedding deal later and just do the court- house and dinner now."

"Now?" she asked with alarm.

"Well, not right this minute," Mabel said with amusement. "We have to go back to the house and call the courthouse and see how quickly it can be arranged."

"That's a good idea," Elvi said, and then turned to call out, "Victor, round up the kids. We have to go home and arrange a wedding. Allie's agreed to be Magnus's life mate."

"Really?" Liam squealed, rushing to them from where he and Teddy had been watching Victor and DJ lead the girls back up the hill. Expression excited, he stopped in front of Allie and Magnus, looking from one to the other as he asked, "Does that mean you're getting married and Magnus will be my dad?"

"Yes," Magnus said when Allie remained silent, her expression stunned. Taking Liam's hand in his, he slid his other around Allie's back and urged her toward the parking lot where the vehicles were, saying, "We better get your mom home. She'll want to figure out what to wear."

"Oh, my God," Allie breathed, but allowed herself to be led.

Twelve

"You're not eating, Allie. Do you need something? More sour cream, maybe?"

Allie raised her head at Tricia's question, stared at her briefly, and then lowered her gaze to the chimichangas on her plate. Apparently, she'd requested them. She didn't remember. But then everything from Cider Hill to their arrival here was a blur. She had a vague recollection of the women fussing over her at the house—ushering her into the shower and out, and then dressing her in the gown she was wearing, a pretty pale blue lace dress that flared out at the waist and reached her knees. She had no idea where it had come from but thought Elvi had loaned it to her.

The next clear memory she had was of standing in the courthouse next to Magnus in the charcoal suit he was still wearing, and stammering the words, "I d-do."

Now they were at Mabel and Elvi's restaurant, Bella

Black's, for her wedding dinner. She was married. The words were a whisper in her head when it should have been a scream. Dear God, she was *married*. And it had all happened so fast. One minute she'd been standing on the hill watching the kids tobogganing and the next she'd been rushed off to the courthouse to marry Magnus.

How had it all happened so fast? That was a question that just kept running through her head. Well, she knew *how* it had happened, but didn't understand why, or if it had been the right thing to do. At the moment, it felt like she'd got caught up in a tornado on that hill and then been dumped here in the restaurant, storm tossed, bewildered, and married.

"Allie? Are you all right?" Tricia eyed her with concern and then her gaze slid past her and a smile curved her lips. "Oh, look. Teddy was able to get away and join us, after all."

Allie dutifully turned her head and stared at the tall, dark-haired man moving confidently toward them from the entrance to the kitchens. He'd obviously parked behind the restaurant and used the back door as they had done, she thought as he made his way through the empty tables. As Mabel had mentioned, they'd closed the restaurant to their normal customers so that it was just the immortals present. There were more of them than Allie had expected. Aside from Elvi and her husband, Victor, Mabel and DJ, Leonora and Alessandro, Dani and Decker, Magnus and Tybo, and Tricia as well as the four children, Stephanie had come too, along with a couple named Drina and Harper that she'd introduced as "part of my family too."

"Teddy looks worried," Magnus commented next to her, and Allie silently agreed. Port Henry's chief of police had concern written all over his face and, she realized, wasn't moving with confidence so much as urgency.

"I'll see what's wrong." Tricia slid out of her seat and hurried to meet her husband.

The people around the table, which was really several small tables pushed together so everyone could sit together, fell silent as they watched Teddy and Tricia talk. If Teddy looked worried, Tricia looked positively alarmed by whatever her husband told her. She also turned abruptly and made her way back to the table at a quick clip.

"We have to go," she announced the moment she reached them. She also took Allie's arm to urge her to her feet.

"Why?" Allie asked with surprise.

"What is happening?" Magnus asked at the same time. But he was already standing and taking Allie's other arm even as he reached for Liam, who had been sitting beside him with Teddy Jr. on his other side.

"You know how I said this is a small town and strangers would be noticed?" Tricia asked. "Well, two vans, two pickups, and a couple cars are circling the downtown, all packed full of what Teddy suspects are rogues."

"Christ," Tybo muttered from behind Allie. Everyone

was on their feet now and moving up to surround them as Tybo asked, "What's the plan?"

"There are too many to take on with the children and civilians around," Teddy said abruptly. "I suggest we head back to the house and call Lucian. See what he wants to do."

"We're going back out through the kitchen to the parking lot," Tricia announced, and Allie glanced anxiously toward Liam. Magnus immediately lifted the boy into his arms. Settling him on his hip where Allie could see him, he then caught her hand again and Allie offered him a grateful smile.

"Wait at the back door for me to give you the go-ahead," Teddy instructed. "I want to make sure they're still on Main Street. I don't want you rushing out the back just as they cut down the side street to turn around or something."

Tricia nodded, and gestured for Tybo to lead the way. She then followed closely, pulling Allie along.

The kitchen was hot and bright white, a sharp contrast to the restaurant's colorful dining area. It was also occupied by the cooking staff, who all turned startled gazes their way when they entered, and then stepped back out of the way as they moved through the cramped space.

"Wait at the door for my okay," Tricia reminded them, releasing Allie and stopping at the beaded curtain that hid the kitchen from the diners.

Tybo glanced back and immediately took Allie's arm, keeping her close behind him as he continued to the back door. Pausing there, he put his free hand on the handle and then turned to look back toward the beaded curtain.

Heart beating rapidly, Allie turned to look back too, but there were so many people crowded up behind them that she couldn't see anything but the stressed smile Elvi offered her.

"It will be fine," the other woman said reassuringly.

"Fine, my ass," Mabel said, not bothering to hide her worry. "Teddy's in a panic and he never panics."

"There must be a lot of the buggers," DJ said grimly.

"Two or three per pickup, four to six per car, and two to twelve or more in each van if there are people in the back," Victor calculated. "There could be anywhere from sixteen to forty or more people in the six vehicles."

"Stella said Abaddon had thirty or forty people that he'd turned when she was with them," Allie told them anxiously, and then added, "But that was four years ago. There could be more now."

"And we have what?" DJ glanced around. "Five hunters?"

"Hello," Drina said with annoyance. "I think you're forgetting that Katricia and I are hunters too."

"And Stephanie's a hunter in training," Elvi said proudly.

"And I used to be a mercenary," Harper said with dignity. "I can handle myself."

"I was a soldier and can handle myself too," Teddy said firmly as he and Katricia hurried to join them. "Time to go, people. Tybo, check to be sure the coast is clear and then we move quickly."

Allie turned back as Tybo opened the door, waited

as he peered around, and then Tybo started forward, pulling her, Magnus, and Liam behind him in a chain. Elvi, Victor, and Sunita made up the next link in the chain, the pair ushering their daughter between them, with Mabel, DJ, and Gracie following doing the same. Teddy, Katricia, and Teddy Jr. were the last link with Stephanie, Drina, and Harper moving to one side of the group while Dani and Decker took the other, flanking the families.

They moved swiftly and silently, the groups breaking up to go to different vehicles.

Allie had no idea who rode where except that Tybo, Decker, Dani, and Stephanie joined them in their SUV, Tybo taking the wheel and Decker in the front passenger seat. Magnus ushered her into the back seat, set Liam in her lap, and then climbed in beside her even as Dani slid in on her other side, while Stephanie opened the back door and climbed into the cargo area.

The last door had closed and Tybo was starting the engine when his phone rang. He pulled it out at once and then listened briefly. Grunting approval a moment later, he dropped the phone back in his suit jacket and announced, "Teddy wants us to stick together and avoid the main road. Back roads only. He's going to lead the way."

Both Magnus and Decker grunted in what Allie guessed was approval as Tybo put the vehicle in gear and steered up behind the police SUV moving toward the exit to the road. A tense silence then filled the vehicle as Teddy led them away from the restaurant. Allie didn't relax until they were following the police cruiser into the driveway at Casey Cottage several moments later. Apparently, she was the only one who had thought they were safe now, however. At least, that was the conclusion she came to when Magnus took her arm in a firm grip, but didn't immediately open the door, instead waiting until Decker and Tybo turned in the front to peer back at them.

"How do you want to do this?" Decker asked.

"Everyone exits on the driver's side," Magnus said without hesitation. "Stephanie, you will have to climb over the seat to come out my door. I want a tight group till we are in the house."

It was definitely a tight group. Allie and Liam were surrounded and herded into the house at a quick march. She didn't even realize the others were on their heels until they got inside and the kitchen filled as they entered. There were several moments of chaos as coats and boots were shed and put away, and then Elvi suggested the children should go watch a movie in the living room. Everyone then helped gather pop and chips for the children and get them settled in front of a movie with their goodies. But the moment the adults were alone and the living room door was closed, Magnus turned to Tricia's husband and asked, "Are you sure they were immortals, Teddy?"

"As sure as I'm standing here," Teddy Brunswick said firmly. "I turned onto Main Street just as they were passing. My headlights reflected off their eyes. Caught my attention, so I took the next side street, backtracked on the next road over, got in front of them, and pulled up to the corner to get a good look at them as they passed to be sure they weren't Enforcers Lucian might have sent down."

"I'm guessing they were not?" Magnus said grimly.

Teddy shook his head. "Not any I've met. They all had long hair and were slovenly. A couple had bloodstains on their clothes."

"Rogues," Tybo said grimly. "And it has to be Abaddon and his people. They must have tracked Allie here."

"Yes. But how?" Magnus asked, and everyone turned to look at her.

Allie stiffened as she found herself the focus of so many eyes.

"At the Enforcer house we decided they must have been tracking her car somehow, but that is back at the apartment in Toronto," Magnus pointed out, holding out his hand to her.

Allie found herself moving to his side without even thinking about it, an unconscious bid to escape being the center of attention. It didn't really do that, but she still felt better having him next to her, his hand closing warm over hers.

"Obviously, it wasn't the car," Tybo said with a frown, and then shook his head. "But the only things they brought here with them were the clothes they were wearing and the Go bags."

"I'll get the bags," Drina said, and hurried out of the room to jog upstairs.

"There's nothing in them that anyone could trace or follow," Allie said with a frown. "I packed them. All they have is protein bars, a first aid kit, a blanket, some money, and bottled water."

"It is best to check," Magnus said gently. "They could have slipped a tracker into one of the bags when they were at the apartment, or at an earlier point when they caught up to you."

Allie didn't think that was likely, but kept her opinion to herself and simply waited with the others. Drina was back quickly, both bags in hand, and they all moved to the table to go over the contents. It made Allie glad that she'd already removed and put on the underwear she'd had in her bag as she watched them paw through the items on the table. But it was also depressing as hell to think that those were her only possessions other than the black jeans and blouse she'd been wearing when she'd first encountered these people, and the jeans and T-shirt she'd put on after her shower that morning.

Had it only been that morning? she wondered suddenly. It felt like days had passed since she'd woken up from the transfusion. So much had happened . . . Or perhaps it wasn't really that a lot had happened, as that one particularly huge thing had happened and she was now married.

"There's nothing here that they could have tracked," Drina said with obvious frustration as they finished examining everything on the table, including the bags themselves.

Allie wanted to say, *I told you so,* but bit back the words.

"The necklace."

Allie turned to look at Stephanie when she murmured that, and found the young woman staring at her chest, her eyes pulsing with that eerie glow she'd witnessed earlier. Lowering her head, Allie followed the young woman's gaze to Stella's winged heart. She'd put it back on before coming downstairs that morning, and had kept it on for the wedding. It had come out of her dress at some point and now lay gleaming under the light from the dining room chandelier.

"May I see it, please?" Magnus asked.

"Yes, but it can't be the necklace," she protested as she lifted the necklace off over her head. Pausing then, she said, "Please be careful with it. Stella wanted Liam to have it to remember her by."

"Of course," he said solemnly, and then surprised her by kissing her forehead gently before taking the necklace she was holding out.

Biting her lip, she watched him turn it over in his hand and then carefully open it. They were all silent as he peered at the picture inside, and then Allie had to clench her hands to keep from protesting when he ran one finger over the silver frame that ran around inside the heart, on top of the photo.

"I need tweezers," Magnus murmured, glancing up.

"On it," Victor said, and slipped from the room.

When Magnus then moved to the table where the light was better, Allie followed, ready to rip the necklace away from him if he did anything that might damage the locket.

"Here you go." Victor was back, holding out tweezers, and Allie was again amazed at the speed these immortals could manage.

"Thank you." Magnus accepted the tweezers and used them to remove the thin silver frame he'd been poking at earlier. He did it so quickly Allie didn't get a chance to protest, but she was scowling as he set it on the table and then used the tweezers to gently pluck out the picture.

Her frown died at once, replaced with confusion as she noted the small black circle inside. It was smaller than a quarter, and not much thicker than one. "What is that?"

"A tracker," Tybo said grimly.

"It is how they kept finding you," Magnus added as he now used the tweezers to remove it from the locket and set it on the table.

"But how did it get in there?" Allie asked with dismay, staring at the little black disc, and then she glanced to Decker with surprise when he snatched up the disc and moved over to Dani.

"What are you doing? Just break it," Teddy demanded. "Put it on the ground and stomp on it, or flush it down the toilet or something."

"That may not be a good idea," Magnus pointed out. "We might be able to use it to lure Abaddon into a trap."

"That's true," Tricia said with a frown. "But we can't keep it in the house. What if it's still sending the signal? It will lead Abaddon and the others straight here. You can't put the children in jeopardy that way."

Allie couldn't agree more, but her attention was on Dani and Decker as the pair whispered back and forth. They only spoke briefly before Decker nodded and announced, "We'll take it with us and drive back to Toronto."

"What?" Elvi asked with concern. "But they'll follow you."

Decker nodded. "That's the idea. Dani has to get back and we were planning to head home in the morning anyway. But if we leave tonight, we can take the tracker with us and lead Abaddon and the others away from here. It will keep the children safe," he pointed out, and then he added, "And we might be able to lead them into a trap if Lucian can set one up before we hit Toronto."

"I'm sure he can," Tybo said, pulling out his phone and heading for the entry. "I'll call him now and tell him what's happening."

Allie watched him go and then turned her concerned gaze back as Elvi asked, "But what if they run you off the road or something before you reach Toronto and this trap?"

"They aren't likely to do that. We have the necklace. They'll think Liam and Allie are in the vehicle."

"I hate to say this," Teddy began in a grim voice. "But if you're going . . ."

"Go quickly?" Decker suggested with amusement when Teddy hesitated to say it after all.

The police chief nodded apologetically. "The longer you stay, the more chance there is that they'll find, surround, and attack the house before you can lead them away."

"Right. Well, on the bright side, we didn't have time to grab anything to bring with us, so we don't need to pack. Now." Decker glanced around the people in the room. "We flew here. What vehicle do we take?"

"My SUV," Victor said at once, pulling keys from his pocket and offering them. "It's in the garage. They won't see who gets in if they are already outside, and the windows are tinted so they won't know who's inside."

"I guess we are going to have to move some vehicles, then," Magnus said, walking toward the pantry, presumably to get his coat.

"There's no need," Victor said, catching his arm to stop him, and then explained, "We added a second vehicle door on the side of the garage shortly after Elvi and I married." When Magnus turned with surprise, he shrugged. "We were still running the bed and breakfast then, and it got to be a pain in the ass having to make people move their vehicles every time we wanted to go somewhere. The garage was big enough, so it was just easier to put in a second door and short driveway, and start parking facing the road rather than the driveway."

"Well, then, I guess we'd best go," Decker said.

There was an immediate convergence of people, as everyone moved forward for hugs and to admonish them to be careful.

Allie wanted to thank Dani for everything she'd done for her, but felt her family had more right to say goodbye, so she stood back. But then Dani pushed through the throng and took her hands.

"Thank you," Allie said at once. "For everything."

"You're more than welcome," Dani assured her, and then looked at Magnus and said firmly, "Turn her. Now. The minute we leave."

"Oh, no," Mabel said, joining them. "It's their wedding night, Dani. He can't turn her tonight."

"Do you want what happened to me to happen to her?" Dani turned on the other woman, anger vibrating through her. "I thought I was safe in the care of the En-forcers too, and then Leonius kidnapped me and turned me. A no-fanger turned me, Mabel. And now I'll never be able to have children or—" Pausing abruptly, she took a deep breath and closed her eyes as if fighting for control.

Allie watched her with concern. She had no idea what a no-fanger was, or why Dani couldn't have chil-dren. She'd thought the doctor was an immortal like the others. Before she could ask, Mabel gently pointed out, "Abaddon's immortal, not a no-fanger, Dani. He couldn't do that to Allie."

Eyes flashing open, Dani glared at the other woman. "No. You're right . . . All he can do is kill her," she said harshly, and then turned to glare at Magnus again. "Turn her."

"He'll turn me," Allie said before Magnus could re-spond. "We're life mates now."

Dani didn't even take her eyes off of Magnus to look at her, but stared past her at him and insisted, "Tonight."

"Tonight," Magnus agreed on a sigh.

"Good," Dani said, relaxing. Finally looking at Allie again then, she smiled and hugged her. "Congratula-tions. I hope you two are very happy."

"Thank you," Allie murmured, hugging her back. "Stay safe."

"We will," Dani said, and then released her and turned to slip back through the crowd to Decker's side. Expression solemn, he took her hand and then turned to lead her out to the garage.

Allie watched them go, but her mind was on the

subject of no-fangers. Sam had mentioned them first, back at the Enforcer house. She'd wondered about it then, but they had been under Lucian's "no questions until after" order and by the time "after" had come, she'd forgotten.

"Allie? You are very quiet. Are you all right?" Magnus asked with concern, clasping her shoulders and urging her to lean back against him.

Before her back could touch his chest, she turned and managed a smile. "I'm fine. I was just wondering what a no-fanger is."

He hesitated briefly, but then said, "An immortal without fangs."

"Oh." She considered that briefly, and then asked, "Is that such a bad thing? Your people don't bite people anymore anyway. You drink bagged blood. And why would that stop her from having children?"

Magnus paused briefly as if considering his answer, and then explained, "No-fangers are the result of different nanos than immortals. It was an early batch that were tested, but proved problematic. While it worked well in a third of the patients, a third died and another third went insane. That was enough to make them halt testing with those nanos and go back to the drawing board. They eventually came up with a new batch of nanos, the ones that immortals have. After the fall of Atlantis, those of our kind with the second batch of nanos gained fangs, but the patients who had received the first batch did not. We called them 'Edentates' if they were sane and 'no-fanger' if they were insane to differentiate the two," he explained. "As for Dani having children, technically she could, but she does not wish to risk having a no-fanger child."

"Oh," Allie said quietly, glancing toward the people crowded into the pantry, watching Dani and Decker leave. Apparently, someone was holding the door between the pantry and garage open. She could smell a faint whiff of exhaust and hear the hum of the automated garage door being raised. Glancing back to him, she asked, "So are you really going to turn me now?"

He peered down at her solemnly. "Do you want me to?"

Allie nodded at once. There seemed little reason to delay. This is why she agreed to be his life mate.

Magnus was silent for a minute, and then nodded slowly. "All right. Then once everyone comes back from seeing Dani and Decker off, I shall inform them of your decision and we will start the preparations."

"Preparations?" Allie asked with surprise. "What preparations?"

"Mom!"

Allie turned her head as Liam came rushing into the room with Teddy and Gracie on his heels. "The movie stopped playing. Can you come fix it?"

"Oh." She hesitated. Elvi had found a movie on Netflix for the kids when they'd taken them pop and chips. If it had stopped working, the modem probably needed rebooting or something. She glanced back to Magnus, but then sighed and moved toward her son. Explanations would have to wait.

Thirteen

"Why is Leonora setting up an IV?" Allie asked with concern as Magnus led her into her room at Casey Cottage. It had taken her longer than she'd expected to fix the Netflix problem. And of course the minute she was done, the kids needed bathroom breaks and more to drink and she'd had to pause the movie she'd just got going. She'd then had to wait there until they were all set again before unpausing it for them. By the time all that was done, Allie had come out to find Magnus waiting to lead her here to perform the turn.

Allie had been surprised to hear the turn would be done in her room. She hadn't really considered where she would be turned, but supposed because it was a medical procedure she'd had a vague thought of a hospital or a clinic now that Dani was gone. Which was ridiculous, Allie realized now. Immortals would hardly want their existence known. But then, apparently, there were a lot of things she hadn't considered. Like: "Why are they attaching chains to the bed?"

"The IV is to give you blood during the turn," Magnus explained.

Crossing the room to join them by the door, Elvi added, "Leonora will also use it to administer the drugs Dani left for you."

"Drugs?" Allie asked with distraction as she watched Alessandro finish attaching a length of chain to the top end of the bed on this side and then move down to attach another at the foot of the bed. The comforter had been stripped from the bed and a length of what looked to her to be clear plastic sheeting had been laid over the remaining bed linens. Katricia was now opening an old fitted sheet to put over the linens and plastic sheeting.

"The drugs help ease the turn a bit," Elvi explained.

"Uh-huh," Allie muttered, hardly hearing the explanation as she watched Alessandro finish with the chain at the bottom of the bed on this side, and then carry two more lengths around to the other side. "But why is Alessandro attaching chains to the bed?"

Elvi turned to watch Alessandro too, and said, "Well, we used to have to run the chains under the bed, but after Tiny's turn, Victor got special reinforced bed frames so we didn't have to worry about them snapping and now we can just attach them to the frame itself. Of course, we haven't had anyone turn here since he did that." Shaking her head, she turned back with a wry smile. "Isn't that the way of it? Have something happen several times, and then once you're prepared for it, these things never occur. Or at least not for years, since it's about to happen again."

Allie had no idea who Tiny was, but didn't really care in that moment either. She was more concerned with: "Why do we need chains, though?"

"Rope wouldn't hold up against immortal strength," Elvi pointed out, and then patted her arm. "It will be fine."

"Why don't we get you on the bed," Magnus suggested, trying to urge her forward by the hold he had on her arm.

Allie dug her heels in, resisting. "Not until someone explains what the chains are for. They aren't necessary. I'm doing this of my own free will."

"Yes, of course you are," Elvi said at once. "We wouldn't do it otherwise. It's against immortal law to turn someone unwillingly."

"Yes, but the point is, since I'm willing, you don't need to chain me down."

"Oh, goodness, no!" Elvi said at once. "We know that. The chains aren't to keep you here. They're to . . . help you."

"Help me what?" she asked with a frown.

When Elvi hesitated and then turned to Magnus expectantly, he grimaced and merely said, "It will keep you from rolling off the bed or . . . anything," he ended lamely.

"You're going to chain me to the bed to keep me from rolling off of it?" she asked dubiously, and then demanded, "What aren't you telling me?"

"Probably a lot," Magnus admitted on a sigh.

"Right-o," Mabel said brightly as she sailed into the room. "The kids have been shifted up to Stephanie's room to watch the movie on her TV. The soundproofing and double walls should prevent their hearing and being alarmed by the screaming. Now, what can I help with in here?"

"Screaming?" Allie asked with dismay.

"Oh, Mabel," Elvi groaned with despair.

"What?" Mabel glanced over the threesome, her eyebrows rising slightly. "Haven't you told her what to expect yet?"

"No!" Elvi barked. "We were trying not to upset her."

"Oh." The blonde bit her lip briefly, but then released it and scowled instead. "Well, that's nonsense. The girl has a right to know what she's signing up for here."

"She knows what she's signing up for, Mabel," Elvi said with exasperation. "She's about to become an immortal. But I see no reason to upset her with the horror stories of the turn when she won't remember most of it afterward anyway."

Oh." Mabel blinked, and then grimaced and admitted, "I suppose you're right. I don't remember much of my turn. I mean, I remember the nightmares and have a vague recollection of terrible agony. But I have absolutely no recall of attacking you or any of the other things I did."

"So," Allie said when both women fell silent, "I'm guessing from the mention of screaming and terrible agony that this is going to be incredibly painful." She didn't wait for a response, but continued. "And the chains aren't really to help me at all, but to keep me from attacking any of you?"

"No, no. The chains are meant to protect you too," Mabel said at once. "They'll keep you from trying to claw out your own eyeballs, or rip open your stomach in an effort to stop the pain."

"Mabel!" Elvi gasped with dismay.

"What?" the blonde asked with exasperation. "We have the chains. She won't be able to do that, but she needs to know we're looking out for her if we want her to place herself in our hands for this." Turning to Allie, she added, "We really do know what we're doing, dear. I promise everything will be fine."

Allie stared at her wide-eyed. Now that Mabel had mentioned it, she was recalling a discussion back at the Enforcer house that had included some nasty descriptions of the turn. How could she have forgotten that, she thought, and then turned to Magnus. "This is going to be bad, isn't it?"

Magnus hesitated, but then sighed and nodded reluctantly. "It is not going to be pleasant."

"Birth never is," Mabel said at once, and when Allie turned a startled gaze her way, she shrugged. "Well, this is like a rebirth. You're going to go through a period of pain and suffering and come out immortal born."

Allie blinked at the description, and then snapped bitterly, "Yes, except in birth, it's the mother who suffers and Magnus is the mother of my rebirth, but he isn't going to suffer anything at all."

"Oh, he'll suffer some," Mabel assured her with amusement. "As for the other, do you really believe it's only the mother who suffers in birth? Do you think it was pleasant for Liam to be born? I don't imagine being squeezed and pummeled by his mother's contracting muscles was fun, and at the very least he probably had a pounding headache from having his head squeezed in a vise. But the end result for him was life. Here, the nanos will invade your body, fixing anything that needs repair, and it will feel like acid pouring through your body, but the end result will be your life as an immortal. It *will* be worth it."

Allie was still staring at the woman, her words running through her head, when Magnus took her hand, regaining her attention.

"If you want to wait, I completely understand," he said gently. "It is our wedding night, after all."

"God, no!" Allie snatched her hand away at the very thought, and headed for the bed. "I'm not putting it off and then freaking out over what's coming for however long we delay. Let's get it done."

"All set," Tricia said, straightening from tucking the last corner under the mattress as Allie reached the bed.

Allie smiled at her weakly, glad the other woman was there. Elvi and Mabel were lovely, but Tricia was the first female immortal she'd met when she encountered these people. She also kind of reminded her of Stella, though they were polar opposites in looks. Allie liked her, and thought they could be friends. Turning, she started to sit on the bed, but then stopped and straightened again as she caught sight of the dress she was wearing.

"Should I maybe change into something else?" she asked uncertainly, running a hand over the soft blue lace. "I wouldn't want this dress to get damaged or—"

"Oh, good Lord, yes." Elvi turned and hurried for the door. "I'll grab something else for you to wear."

"I have my jeans I could change into," Allie called after her, but the woman was already gone.

"You don't want to ruin your clothes, dear," Mabel said when Allie started to move away from the bed to grab the jeans and T-shirt she'd folded neatly and set on the dresser. "Anything you wear will be ruined in the turn. Elvi will fetch you something old and ready for the rag bin."

"How will they be ruined?" Allie asked with confusion as she paused. "I'm not going to hulk out or something, am I?"

"No, nothing like that," Magnus assured her quickly. "But the nanos will be removing a lot of toxins and . . ."

"Gunk," Mabel put in when Magnus seemed unsure how to describe it. "The nanos remove everything nasty from your body, break it down, and push it out through your pores. At least, that's what it seemed like to me. I woke up feeling like I'd been dunked in a vat of slimy grease. And the stink . . . Woo-ee." She grimaced and shuttered at the memory. "You can wash it off your body with enough scrubbing, but nothing gets the stink out of cloth. Which is why Katricia put the plastic sheeting and an old bedsheet on the bed.

It saves having to toss and replace the mattress later. We'll just toss the plastic and the old sheet."

"Oh," Allie said nonplussed.

"Here you are." Elvi returned, carrying a white cotton nightgown. "This is something I haven't worn since before I was turned. My old granny gown," she said wryly, and held it out. "I won't be sorry to see it go. The only reason it wasn't sent off to the Salvation Army ages ago was that I thought I should keep it in case a situation like this came up. And it has," she ended brightly.

"Thank you," Allie murmured, accepting the gown and heading for the bathroom. She didn't dally. She didn't want the opportunity to think or worry, so Allie stripped off the lovely blue dress, hung it carefully from a hook on the door, and then slid the granny gown on over her panties and bra. She knew it meant her underwear would most likely need to be tossed after the turn, but she wasn't getting chained to that bed pantiless and risking flashing the room if she was thrashing about during the turn.

Finished, Allie reached for the doorknob to exit, but then stopped as Stella's locket moved against her skin. She'd forgotten all about it. But it wasn't a good idea to wear it during the turn. Lifting it off over her head, she set it on the bathroom counter and then reached for the doorknob again.

Everyone gave Allie reassuring smiles when she walked back out in the voluminous white gown, but it didn't hide their anxiety. It seemed obvious she wasn't the only one worried about what was to come. Pushing that thought down to join the other worries trying to overwhelm her, Allie climbed onto the bed, laid on her back, and spread her arms and legs out toward the sides.

"Go ahead. Chain me up and let's get this party started," she said with more bravado than real courage. God, she was scared.

"Are you sure?" Magnus asked with a frown. "We can leave the chains off until the turn actually starts if you wish."

Allie didn't miss the dismay that crossed Elvi's face at those words and shook her head firmly. "Go on. Chain me down and let's go. The sooner we start, the sooner it'll be done."

Alessandro and Leonora moved to the chains at the foot of the bed, while Magnus and Tricia chained her wrists. Tricia did it standing, but Magnus settled on the side of the bed to do up his and she swallowed and avoided looking at him while he worked.

Once they were done, Allie tugged on her arms and legs, managing a brave smile when she couldn't move them at all. They'd trussed her up good. "Okay," she said, and then paused to clear her throat when her voice came out a squeak. Much to her relief it sounded almost normal when she tried again. "Okay, so . . . Now what?" Allie peered uncertainly around the group that had now gathered around the bed. They looked like devil worshippers at a virginal sacrifice. Her gaze landed last on Magnus, who still sat next to her, and she asked, "I suppose Leonora uses a needle to withdraw your blood and give it to me?"

"No, honey," Mabel said when everyone else remained silent. "He has to give you his blood himself. Needles don't work with this."

"What?" she asked with disbelief. "Then how is he going to—" The words died abruptly and her jaw dropped in shock when Magnus suddenly raised his arm, allowed his fangs to slide out, and then ripped into his wrist with a violence that was both startling and really quite disgusting, she thought with dismay as he lowered his arm and she saw the blood smearing his face. Then she saw the damage he'd done to his wrist. He hadn't just sunk his teeth in and bit, he'd torn his wrist open and blood was squirting out like a geyser as he turned it toward her.

Her mouth hanging open in shock came in handy. Magnus was able to place his wrist quickly across her open mouth so the blood gushed in. But Allie just laid there for a heartbeat, gaping at him over his arm, and then she struggled to raise her hands to force it away, but they, of course, were chained.

"Swallow," Magnus instructed.

If looks could kill, Magnus would have been incinerated on the spot, but that didn't happen. Allie had to swallow to keep from choking on the thick fluid pouring into her mouth and hitting the back of her throat. It was disgusting—warm, salty, with a hint of rusty metal—and she wanted nothing more than to spit it out, but didn't have that option with his arm across her mouth. They stayed like that for what seemed to Allie to be a long time, but she knew that was a function of the unpleasantness of the situation.

Stuck there glaring at him as she swallowed his blood, Allie came up with quite a few inventive words she wanted to call him once her mouth was free. She never got the chance to use them. When he finally removed his wrist, she'd barely opened her mouth to spit out some of those invectives when a large clawed talon ripped across her stomach. At least, that's what it felt like. A great winged dragon had clawed her stomach open and the wizard riding it had poured acid into the gaping hole.

Gasping in pain, she tried to curl up to protect her stomach, but, chained down as she was, could only lift her head. Allie saw that she wasn't injured, but that wasn't what the pain was telling her. And then that pain intensified a thousandfold and Allie began to shriek.

"Well . . . That was different." Katricia's comment filled the silence left when Allie passed out after nearly an hour of thrashing and screaming.

Magnus glanced at the woman in question. "How so?"

"It usually starts in the head. You see the metallic glitter in their eyes, or . . ." She shrugged. "But with Allie it seemed to be her stomach."

"Yeah," Mabel said with amazement. "Her stomach was jumping like one of Sigourney Weaver's *Alien* babies was about to burst out of it."

"It must be where she needed the most work," Magnus said, glancing at her stomach now. He'd kept his gaze on her face until then. She'd looked at him with such anger and betrayal when he'd forced his wrist to her mouth . . .

"Probably ulcers from all her worry," Elvi said solemnly. "Tybo said she was running and hiding from Abaddon for years. That must have been stressful."

There were grunts of agreement from everyone around the bed and then they were all silent again until Mabel shifted restlessly, and asked, "How long do you think she'll be unconscious before the pain wakes her up again and—"

Her question died abruptly as Allie's eyes shot open and she began to shriek again.

It was going to be a long night, Magnus thought grimly as he watched Allie, helpless to do anything to end her agony. He'd take it for her if he could. She was his life mate. His wife . . . and this was their wedding night. Every prospective bride and groom no doubt hoped their wedding night would be unforgettable, and his certainly would be . . . Just not in the way one would expect.

I woke up feeling like I'd been dunked in a vat of slimy grease. And the stink . . . Woo-ee.

Those words ran through Allie's head as she woke up. Probably because they described perfectly what she was experiencing. The first thing she became aware of, even before she opened her eyes, was the smell surrounding her. Wrinkling her nose, she opened her eyes and shifted restlessly on the bed, grimacing when her legs slid together with a squelching sound and a slimy feel.

Lifting her head, she looked down her body, noting that the chains were gone. So was the IV stand. She didn't see any of the gear they'd set up for her. The nightgown was still on her, though, and she was on the same old sheet Katricia had put on the bed, but both the gown and sheet were now soaked with liquid the same color as the ear wax she'd once removed from the infected ear of a dog she'd had as a child.

Oh, God, the smell was unbearable, Allie thought with disgust, and shifted her attention to the room. At first, she thought she was alone, and then her gaze landed on a chair that had been set next to the bed. Magnus sat slumped in it, eyes closed and mouth open, sound asleep. Allie stared at him for a minute, wondering how long he'd been there, but then she couldn't stand her own smell anymore and sat up on the bed. Much to her amazement, she managed the move without any difficulty at all. She wasn't experiencing any weakness, or pain. No aftereffects at all from the turn. In fact, other than the slimy feel and smell, she felt pretty great.

That fact made Allie curious about how she was different now, and she raised a hand to poke at her teeth with her fingers. It was a bit of a disappointment when her teeth didn't feel any different than they had. There were no pointy incisors or anything. She supposed she shouldn't be surprised. Liam's teeth looked normal until he got hungry, or when he was feeding.

She supposed that meant she'd get them too when she was hungry.

Another odiferous cloud of stink wafted up to her nose, turning her stomach, and Allie lost interest in anything but getting rid of the aroma presently enshrouding her. Sliding off the bed, she moved quickly to the bathroom door, a little startled when she moved at double speed like a film in fast-forward. Pausing at the bathroom door, she glanced back to be sure Magnus was still sleeping, and then slid into the room and quietly closed the door.

Allie turned on the shower and then stripped off the ruined nightgown, bra, and panties. She then stood there, shifting from one bare foot to the other as she waited for the water to be warm enough to use. In the end, she stepped into the bath and pulled the curtain closed before the temperature was really where she wanted it, but it was good enough.

Grabbing up the unicorn soap, Allie quickly started to clean herself, but her hair was slimy too, and swung down into her face as she bent to clean her legs, so she gave up on that for now and switched her attention to her hair. She washed it using Sunita's shampoo, something that had a friendly-looking monster on the front and smelled of coconut, apple, and some other fruit that Allie couldn't name at the moment. There was no conditioner, and she had to wash her hair three times to completely rid it of the other smell, but after the third shampoo and rinse she pressed her nose into a handful of the wet hair and sighed with relief and pleasure. She smelled like a tropical fruit salad, and she liked it.

Chuckling to herself, Allie reached again for the unicorn bar soap, noticing this time that it too had a coconut smell to it. But instead of apple, here the coconut was mixed with citrus. Still a tropical fruit salad, though, she thought, and grinned as she cleaned herself everywhere, twice. Lathering and scrubbing to remove any hint of the previous odor that had clung to her.

Allie was much happier when she was done. She felt clean and . . . a little hungry actually, now that that awful smell wasn't turning her stomach, she thought as she turned off the taps, wrung out her hair, and then stepped out on the bath mat. She was just looking around for the towel she'd used that morning when the door opened. Turning to look over her shoulder in surprise, she stared at Magnus, who had frozen with the door half-open.

Eyes wide, he stared at her standing there naked and then gave his head a shake, cleared his throat, and muttered, "Sorry. I woke up and you were gone."

As explanations went, Allie supposed that was as good as any. She expected him to back out and close the door then, but he seemed rooted to the spot, his eyes locked on her naked back and behind and swimming all over both. Knowing he was seeing the scars there, she was embarrassed for about three seconds, and then his scent hit her and Allie's embarrassment was pushed aside by something else. Nothing could have stopped her from turning and following that delicious scent to stand in front of him. But even she was shocked when she slid her hands up his chest, clasped the collars of his shirt, and used them to pull his head down toward her until she could nuzzle his neck and inhale that lovely aroma that had her stomach quivering with excitement.

After a brief start of surprise, Magnus relaxed and let his own hands slide up to clasp her waist on either side. He turned his head to nuzzle her hair and chuckled softly. "You smell like a fruit salad. Good enough to eat."

Allie released the breath she'd been savoring and breathed in again, squirming against him as her nose was filled with his spicy bouquet. The movement rubbed her breasts over his chest, sending tingles of excitement running through her, and she gasped breathlessly, "You smell good enough to eat too. Like steak."

She was vaguely aware of Magnus stiffening at that description, but was too desperate to breathe in more of his scent to pay it much attention. Burying her nose in his neck, she inhaled deeply and squirmed again with pleasure, sending another burst of excitement shooting through her.

Magnus groaned as if he were the one experiencing that excitement and clasped her behind, urging her lower body against him as well.

Allie gasped as her excitement ratcheted up several notches and then sighed as his scent filled her lungs. "Yes. Magnus," she moaned, nuzzling closer still. "Please. I need you. Let me—" She licked his throat, desperate to see if he tasted as good as he smelled and moaned again as his salty goodness exploded on her tongue. She was so close to what she wanted. If she could just— Allie felt an odd shifting sensation in her mouth and opened it, but in the next moment, Magnus had used his hold on her waist to spin her in his arms so her back was to him. Catching her wrists in his hands, he then whirled them both to face the mirror.

"That's what I was afraid of," he said on a sigh, peering at their reflection. "Honey. You need blood."

Allie stared at their reflection. She saw the fangs poking out from between her lips, but his arms were around her and she was surrounded by his smell. All she could think was that she wanted to rub herself all over his body until his smell was all over her, and then she wanted to lick every inch of him and she wanted to sink her teeth into him and—

Groaning with frustration because she couldn't do any of that with him holding her as he was, Allie pressed her bottom back and rubbed against the hardness she could feel there, sending another bolt of excitement through her own body. "Magnus. Please."

Cursing, he stepped back, released the hold he had on one wrist, and used the hold he had on the other to drag her behind him as he opened the bathroom door and headed out.

Allie's gaze landed on the bed as they crossed the room and she was surprised to see that the stained bedsheet and plastic had been stripped away, leaving just the sheet set that they had protected. She assumed

Magnus had done it until he muttered, "Leonora must have stripped the bed. Her arrival is what woke me and made me come check on you."

Allie didn't comment, but couldn't help thinking it was a relief not to have the stained sheets there stinking up the room.

"Here."

Allie glanced around with a start when he stopped and urged her to sit on the bed, and then watched as he bent over in front of her to open a cooler. Her gaze traced the curve of his behind as he did, and she found herself licking her lips and wondering if it was as firm as it looked and if a little nip at it would answer the question. Before she could do it, though, he straightened and turned with two bags of blood in hand.

Allie peered at them with curiosity, but they had no smell at all, and then her nose quivered as his scent drifted to her again, this time more earthy. She didn't even think, just followed the scent to his groin and pressed her face to it as she inhaled.

Fourteen

Magnus had turned toward Allie and then paused to

Magnus had turned toward Allie and then paused to
hold an inner debate over whether two bags would be
enough or he should grab two more when Allie suddenly pressed her face to his crotch. He damned near
squawked in surprise and dropped the bags he held,
but managed to avoid both reactions and simply gaped
at her. She started out poking him with her nose and
sniffing him like a dog, and then she inhaled deeply
and held the breath as she turned her head and rubbed
her cheek over the bulge like a cat marking something
with their scent.

Even more shocking to him was the fact that even
those ridiculous gestures had him hardening further
in his dress pants. Or perhaps that was understandable, he thought in the next moment as her hands
slid up his legs to clasp his butt cheeks and urge him
closer. The woman was his life mate, after all . . .

and naked . . . and God, she had beautiful breasts, he thought faintly, and let one of the bags fall to the bed so that he could reach for one of the enticing globes. The first brush of his fingertips over the excited nipple brought a moan from Allie even as it sent shocks of excitement through him. Magnus couldn't resist palming the breast and squeezing eagerly.

The action made them both gasp, and then Allie turned her face and nipped at the bulge in his pants, recalling him to the issue here. She didn't really want him. She was confusing the hunger for blood for sexual hunger, if she was even capable of thinking at this moment. He suspected she was just following her body's urgings and it was sending her after what she wanted, but she was inexperienced and had no clue what she wanted or how to get it.

His thoughts were sent flying when she brought one hand around to squeeze his bulge, sending a jolt of need shooting through him . . . and probably herself, he realized as she squirmed on the bed and licked his bulge.

"Right," he said firmly, and caught her chin to force her face up. "Open your mouth."

Much to his surprise, while she appeared confused at the order, she did obey. The moment she did, he popped the bag he still held onto her fangs, and then knelt in front of her to hold it there so she didn't pull it away.

He didn't speak then, but simply watched her, his eyes first focused on her face as she stared at him over the bag, and then his gaze lowered, following its own course down to her breasts. One nipple was just inches from his face. It was also erect and seemed to harden even further as he peered at it. That made his mouth water and he unconsciously licked his lips.

Magnus didn't think he was the one to move, but it suddenly swayed closer and brushed against his lips. He didn't even think, he just opened his mouth, and when it pressed inside he suckled the eager nipple, clasping it with his lips and rasping it with his tongue. Magnus was vaguely aware of Allie moaning and her hands gliding around his head to urge him on, but he was experiencing the pleasure he was giving her and that muffled everything else. He had heard of the shared pleasure life mates enjoyed, but this was the first time he'd experienced it . . . and it was glorious. Every suckle, nip, and lap sent shivers of pleasure and excitement through him, urging him on to do more.

Releasing the first nipple, he turned his head to claim the other and gave it the same treatment while fondling and teasing the first with his fingers. But it wasn't enough and he released the now nearly empty bag so that he could urge her legs open and shift between them to get closer. He let his hands slide up the inside of her legs then, and sucked hard on her nipple as both her and, in accordance, his body grew feverish with need and anticipation. And then his fingers brushed over her heat and he nearly bit her nipple when a jolt of excitement shot through him.

Letting her nipple slip from his mouth to keep from hurting her, he glanced up to see how much blood was left in the bag. There wasn't much—another moment and they could remove it—so he slid his fingers over her more firmly and they both groaned at the pleasure that sent rolling over them.

In the end, it was Allie who tore the bag away. She also lowered her head, and urged his head up toward her with the fingers tangled in his hair. Accepting the invitation, he kissed her, his mouth hungry and demanding as he continued to caress her. Allie kissed him back just as hungrily, her body shifting into his caresses, and her arms tightening to pull him closer.

Growling into her mouth, Magnus reached down with his free hand to undo his pants. The expensive cloth slid off of him at once and he caught one of Allie's arms and urged her to her feet even as he stood so that he wouldn't have to stop kissing and caressing her. He felt her hands pushing at his boxer briefs, and then his erection burst free and he felt one delicate hand close around him. Magnus nearly lost it right there as their combined excitement exploded between them. He knew Allie was in the same place because they were sharing that pleasure.

Determined to consummate the wedding before their excitement overwhelmed them, he stopped caressing her, but continued to kiss her as he urged her backward and onto the bed. Catching her around the waist then, he lifted her slightly and took her with him to the center of the bed before easing to rest on top of her.

Magnus broke the kiss then and Allie moaned in protest. But he nuzzled her ear and growled, "Spread your legs."

Allie did, and then gasped and clutched at his arms when he rubbed himself against her. They were both so excited he didn't dare do that a second time, however, but instead repositioned himself a little and thrust into her.

Magnus half expected it would be more than either of them could take and they'd scream in pleasure, orgasm, and faint as life mates were said to do during life mate sex. Instead, his excitement was interrupted by a sudden sharp pain and shock. He froze at once, struggling briefly with disbelief and the sudden death of excitement, and then, still buried deep inside her, raised himself a little to peer down. "Allie? Were you a vir—?"

She slapped her hand over his mouth, silencing him, and then groaned with what he could only guess was something like embarrassment, before mumbling, "Jeez, how many girls told me in college they didn't even feel anything the first time? Liars," she added bitterly.

Sighing, Magnus started to withdraw, but Allie dug her nails into his arms in a panic. "Wait! What are you doing?"

He hesitated, and then said uncertainly, "I thought you would wish to stop."

"Yes, but no," she said at once.

Magnus peered at her uncertainly. "Which is it? Yes, or no?"

"I don't know," she admitted unhappily, and then bit her lip briefly before blurting, "What if you pull out and it heals? Am I going to have this pain every time?"

Magnus found it heartening that she was considering having sex with him again. He knew that she'd

married him planning on avoiding the marital bed and
he'd let her believe that was a possibility because he'd
counted on the life mate thing to change her mind for
her. But the pain he'd just experienced through her
had rather killed the pleasure and he wouldn't have
been surprised if she'd shied away from the marital
bed after it, at least for a while. But now she'd raised a
new concern and asked a question he couldn't answer.
He'd never bedded an immortal virgin before. In fact,
he hadn't expected her to be one at her age. Not in
this era of free love and whatnot. Or perhaps that was
ancient history now, but he knew that women today
didn't have to marry and took lovers as they liked.
He'd just assumed that she was experienced.

"Magnus?" Allie asked impatiently when he was silent too long. "Will it heal?"

"I do not know," he admitted apologetically. "I have
never taken a virgin to my bed before."

"What?" she asked with disbelief. "You're like a ba-
zillion years old and have probably bedded a gazillion
women, yet you've never slept with a virgin before?"

He ignored the insult about his age, and said, "Not an
immortal virgin. Besides, I have not bedded a gazillion
women. In fact, I have not indulged in sexual activities
since just before the Battle of Maldon in 991."

Allie stared at him blankly for a moment, and then
asked, "Are you kidding?"

"No," Magnus assured her quietly. "Immortals often tire of food and sex at some time between the ages
of one hundred and two hundred. I lost my interest in
food twenty or thirty years before, but held on to my

interest in sex until I was 212 . . . although it had waned quite a bit before it died out altogether," he admitted.

She narrowed her eyes, and said, "But I've seen you eat. And what was this, then? Because you seemed pretty interested when—"

"Life mates change all that," he explained patiently. "They reawaken an immortal's passions, both for food and for lovemaking. They reawaken interest in everything. It is another reason why they are so valued and cherished." He paused briefly, and then added, "The shared pleasure simply adds to it."

"Shared pleasure?" she asked uncertainly.

Magnus hesitated, but then asked, "When you were sitting on the side of the bed and touched me, did you not experience my pleasure as your own?" He already knew the answer, but was still a little relieved when she nodded.

Realization and amazement growing on her face, she asked, "So when you were touching me . . . ?"

"I felt your pleasure," he said quietly, his previously flagging passion reawakening and stretching within him at the memory. He'd begun to lose his erection the moment the pain had struck, but now he was hardening inside her again.

"Something's happening," she said uncertainly. "Are you moving?"

"No," he said at once, but didn't explain, and instead said, "Allie, we cannot remain like this indefinitely. And I cannot answer your question about the healing. Do you wish me to go fetch Katricia or Drina so that you may ask one of them?"

"God, no!" she gasped at once, and then bit her lip briefly before saying, "Maybe if we just stay like this for a little bit the nanos will heal me around you and not completely rebuild my hymen."

He thought that was a ridiculous idea, and was becoming uncomfortable lying there, chatting as if at tea, so teased, "Or maybe they will heal you to my member."

"What?" she squawked with horror.

Magnus was immediately sorry he'd said that and tried to reassure her. "I am sure that will not happen. I was just—"

"Oh!"

Both of them turned their heads to stare at Katricia, who had opened the door and started in, but was now backing out of the room.

"Sorry. I didn't know. I was just checking— I'll go—"

"No! Wait!" Allie cried, her fingers tightening around Magnus's arms.

Katricia paused midturn away from them, but kept her eyes pointed at the door and the side of her face to them as she waited.

Allie hesitated, but then sighed and asked, "Will the nanos heal my hymen?"

In her surprise, Katricia started to turn toward them, but caught herself at the last moment and asked carefully, "Allie, are you saying you were a virgin before . . . ?"

"Yes," she admitted with disgust. "And now I need to know if it's going to heal and I'm going to have this pain every time, or if there is something I can do to prevent that?"

Katricia blew her breath out on a sigh, and shook her head. "I'm sorry. I didn't even consider . . . I should have talked to you first."

"Talked to me about what?" Allie asked, staring at the woman.

"The nanos won't repair a hymen on a mortal who is turned after it's been ruptured and healed. But I'm afraid that, yes, they will repair it if it is ruptured while you are immortal unless the man remains inside you for an extended time. Then they will heal around him and not close the gap."

They were all silent for a moment, and then Allie asked, "Why do they not heal it on a mortal during the turn if it was ruptured before she turned?"

"Good question," Katricia said wryly. "We think that the original programming didn't include the hymen. Or possibly labeled it as optional because some would have it but some would not, so the nanos only repair it when it originally exists in their host and is ruptured. They immediately set out to repair what they see as a wound. But that's not necessary on a mortal who was turned after losing her hymen and it has already healed."

"But they won't heal me to Magnus, will they?"

That startled a laugh out of Katricia. "No, of course not. Oh, God, wouldn't that be a fix?"

Allie turned to scowl at Magnus, and it was he who asked, "How long must we remain joined to ensure she heals around me?"

"No one's really sure," Katricia admitted slowly. "I mean, it's different for different women. We all have varying healing speeds depending on how much blood we have available in our system and what's going on." She paused briefly and then added, "I have heard of women who waited only ten minutes and were fine, and others who waited twenty and yet the healing wasn't done and it grew back." Smiling wryly, she confessed, "Breaching mine was so painful I waited half an hour my first time just to be sure I didn't have to go through it again."

"I waited half an hour too," Drina announced from somewhere beyond Katricia. "And I'd suggest that for you, Allie. The nanos will heal it right away because it is a bleeding wound, but might be slow about it because they are spread out so thin taking care of the other repairs they're still tending."

Magnus felt Allie stiffen at the sound of Drina's voice and wasn't surprised. Neither of them had realized the other woman was in the hall as well.

"I thought I was done turning?" she whispered now to him.

Magnus shook his head. "The majority of it is done, the more painful stuff. But the nanos will be working to finish off less crucial fixes or changes for the next while, perhaps weeks. You'll need to take in extra blood while that's happening."

"Oh," she said unhappily.

"I agree with Drina," Katricia said, reminding them of their presence. "I'd go with half an hour to be safe."

"Okay," Allie said unhappily, and then added, "Thank you."

"Anytime," Katricia said lightly, and then said more seriously, "Really, Allie. I'm sure you will have a lot of questions as you adjust to being immortal, and I'm happy to help. Just ask and I'll do my best to answer."

"That goes for me too," Drina called.

"Thank you, guys," Allie said sincerely. "I appreciate that."

"Okay, then. Have fun," Katricia said as she closed the door.

The last comment had been said in a wry tone that suggested it wasn't likely. Magnus understood that thoroughly. He had to remain inside Allie for half an hour. Well, perhaps only twenty-five minutes now, but he wasn't sure how long he'd been in her already so would say thirty rather than risk having to do this again. The point was, however, he needed to maintain his erection to remain in her. If it shrank too much it would slide out no matter what he did, so they had to keep him at least mildly excited. But if he got too excited and passion overwhelmed them . . . well, an orgasm would certainly put an end to the exercise. So, it was going to be a terrible balancing act.

"Something's happening again," Allie said anxiously.

Her words drew his attention from his thoughts to the realization that he was losing his erection again. Sighing, he laid his forehead on hers and said, "I am shrinking."

"Well, don't do that!" she exclaimed with dismay. "You have to stay in me for half an hour."

Magnus released a helpless chuckle and raised his head. "I am aware of that, but ordering me not to lose my erection is not going to . . ." His words died as she suddenly shifted beneath him, thrusting her hips up to press herself tighter to him, probably in an effort to make sure he didn't slip out. Fortunately, it had the added benefit of restirring some excitement in him and he felt himself hardening again.

"What can we do to keep you . . . interested?" she asked now, and then added, "But not too excited."

She understood the situation and didn't need it explained to her. That was good at least, Magnus decided, and was considering her question and the best way to approach the problem when she suddenly knocked his legs out from under him with one of her own and then turned him onto his back, coming up on top of him. She then sat up, only to raise an arm to cover her breasts from his view.

"Don't look," Allie ordered, and he raised disbelieving eyes to her face.

"You have gone shy?" he asked with surprise. "Now? After prancing around naked in front of me for—"

"I wasn't prancing," she said with a roll of the eyes. "And I'm a virgin. Or I was," she added with a grimace. "Of course I'm shy."

"Forgive me," he murmured with amusement, raising his hands to her upper arms and running them lightly up and down her skin. "But you did not appear shy in the bathroom."

"No." She shivered slightly at his light caress, but then wrinkled her nose. "I don't even know who that woman was. I was just desperate to . . ."

When she paused, looking confused, he said gently, "It was blood lust."

Allie's eyes widened slightly, and she peered at him with surprise. "Really? Because it felt like . . ."

"Desire?" he suggested gently. "Blood lust can be easily mistaken for desire at first, I am told."

"Oh. So, I was actually hungry for blood not sex." She considered that briefly and then nodded. "Yeah. That makes sense. I mean, you smelled like a big juicy steak when you came into the bathroom. But after that bag of blood . . ." She inhaled briefly and then nodded. "Not as hungry. You still smell good, but more like meat loaf than a steak. Steak I'd crawl around naked for. Meat loaf." She shrugged. "Not so much."

"Meat loaf?" he asked with dismay. Magnus had heard the mated men he worked with complain about meat loaf meals. According to his comrades, they were all right, but simply couldn't compare to steak.

Allie leaned down to pat his arm sympathetically, leaving only the one arm to cover her breasts, and then straightened again and contemplated him with a frown and again asked, "So, how do we keep you excited, but not too excited?"

Magnus was considering the question when she said, "In porns, the men seem to get turned on when the women play with their breasts and stuff."

"You watch porn?" he asked with disbelief.

"I'm a thirty-four-year-old virgin who works on the computer. What do you think?" she asked dryly, and then raised her eyebrows. "So, do you want me to caress my breasts or something?"

The question the first time had startled him. This

time he imagined her doing that and immediately began to swell inside her again.

"I'll take that as a yes," Allie said dryly and, after a hesitation, moved her arms to the sides until her hands covered her breasts. He didn't even get a peek of nipple, but it didn't seem to matter and he watched, fascinated, as she began to knead and squeeze her own flesh. But it was when she squeezed her breasts close together and let her head tip back, her mouth opening and her tongue running across her upper lip, that he felt his cock jump in her.

Growling softly, Magnus sat up at once to cover her mouth with his own and thrust his tongue out to rasp over hers. The change of position shifted her slightly in his lap, moving her on top of him and sending another jolt of excitement shooting through them both, and Allie kissed him eagerly back. She released her breasts then and slid her arms around his shoulders to hold him close as his tongue thrust into her. It pressed her breasts closer to his chest, and he felt her excitement as his chest hairs fanned over the sensitive nipples. In the next moment, he slid his hands between them to urge her back a bit so that he could cover her breasts and squeeze and knead them as she had been doing.

They both groaned at the excitement that sent through them, and then Magnus began to pluck at her hard nipples with his thumbs and fingers, tugging and twisting lightly as he thrust his tongue into her mouth with increasing demand. When she then raised and lowered herself on his shaft, he gasped with pleasure and released her breasts to catch her hips and urge her on before he realized what they were doing and how close to the fire they were dancing.

Tightening his hold on her hips then, Magnus made her stop and muttered, "Too much."

"Yes," she gasped, but couldn't seem to help herself and tried to move again. The hell of it was, he wanted her to. But he also didn't want to hurt her again the next time they made love. Cursing, Magnus wrapped his arms around her and dropped back on the bed, taking her with him. Then he tightened his hold on her, preventing her from moving again.

They lay like that for a moment, both breathing heavily until the throbbing in his erection eased a bit, and then he asked the first question to pop into his head. "Why are you still a virgin?"

Allie stiffened in his arms and he was guessing the question washed away a lot of her desire, because his own quite suddenly receded like a wave pulling back from the shore. Finally, she shrugged against him, and muttered, "I don't know. I guess I never met anyone I was interested in sleeping with."

They were both silent for a minute, and then she said, "That's not true. I guess . . . while I was interested a time or two, I was afraid."

"Of sex?" he asked uncertainly.

"No. Of getting involved with someone," she admitted quietly.

He considered that briefly, thinking that while it was causing them difficulties right now, he was actually quite pleased that he was her first lover. And her last. At least as long as he lived. She would not be interested in sex with anyone else so long as they both lived. However, he didn't like the idea that she'd spent her life in fear of relationships. That would certainly affect them, so he asked, "Why?"

Allie was silent so long he began to think she would not answer, but then she sighed and said, "I had a weird childhood. I told you my father was raised a Follower of Christ."

"Yes," he acknowledged, though he wasn't sure what that meant. He'd thought it was a cult, and knew they didn't believe in medical intervention, but that was about where his knowledge of the subject ended.

"Well, I don't know if he still followed all their tenets or made up some of his own after he left the US, moved to Canada, and married my mother, but life with him was . . . difficult," she ended solemnly, and recalling the scars on her back he suspected that was something of an understatement.

"We were raised on a farm that was . . . well, it was practically *Little House on the Prairie*," she said dryly, and then raised her head slightly to look at him. "Seriously. We had no electricity, and a hand pump faucet on the kitchen sink was how we got water. We used to drag this big tub into the middle of the kitchen once a week and we had to pump and boil water for a bath." She dropped down to lie on his chest again with a sigh, and then admitted, "It was all I knew, so it was fine at the time."

"But?" he prompted when she fell silent again.

Allie didn't respond at first, but then said, "We were homeschooled, and weren't supposed to make friends of children on nearby farms lest they—as my father put it—corrupted us."

Magnus felt her begin to move a finger over his chest, circling his nipple in a wide arc before she admitted, "But I did make a friend."

"How?" he asked at once.

Allie shrugged. "There was a copse of woods at the back of our property. My father used to send me out there to collect smaller branches and whatnot for starting fires for the cookstove and for heat when the weather turned cold. One day when I was about ten, I was sent out and I heard children laughing. I was curious so I followed the sound to the back of the copse, and there were these kids back there, playing. Their farm backed onto ours. Half the copse belonged to their farm and they were playing hide-and-seek in the woods."

She flicked his nipple, sending a ping of excitement through him that roused his fading erection, and then continued, "When they saw me they gave up their game and came running. They were nice, and invited me to play. I knew I wasn't supposed to, but they were laughing and . . ." She shrugged. "I played with them.

"After that, every time I was sent out to get wood, I'd look for them. Sometimes they were there and sometimes they weren't, but if they were, we played together. There were four of them, all brothers and sisters. The youngest was Bethany. She was my age, and we became good friends. We had a blast in those woods," she said, and he could hear the smile in her voice.

"And your parents never knew?" Magnus asked.

"No. We didn't play that long. Not like hours or

anything, maybe one hour. And the kids always helped me gather wood afterward so I wouldn't get in trouble." She shrugged against his chest. "Anyway, I don't remember how it happened, but one day I ended up following them back to their house. I remember it was summer and hot, so probably we went in search of drinks. But what I got was an eye-opening," she said dryly. "Their farmhouse looked a lot like ours on the outside, an old Victorian house. But the inside had been completely renovated. It was like a palace to me, and a marvel too. They had *air-conditioning*, and running water, and lights that turned on by electricity instead of oil lanterns. And they had television, and radio and computers." She gave a short laugh. "I thought it was heaven."

Magnus smiled faintly at the claim, not surprised by it.

"I think you're shrinking again," Allie said suddenly.

Magnus frowned as he realized it was true. He'd got so invested in her story that his desire had fizzled out and he was now at dire risk of slipping out of her.

"What do we do to—" Her words ended on a surprised gasp as he urged her to sit up on him and reached down between them to caress her just above where they were joined. He saw her eyes widen and her head drop back on a moan, just before her pleasure hit him, and he squeezed his own eyes closed.

God, she felt so good, and what he was doing was sending wave after wave of mounting pleasure and excitement through him too that immediately revived his faltering erection. He found that circling motions worked best, running his thumb lightly around the nub that was the center of her excitement, just brushing the edges at first. But then Allie began to move on him, riding him in search of the satisfaction she sensed waited for her, and he had to stop caressing her to catch her hips and stop her from pushing them over the edge.

"Tell me . . . what happened . . . with your new friends," he got out between gritted teeth, and then took a couple of deep breaths before asking, "Did your father find out?"

Panting, Allie lowered her head to peer at him blankly. She didn't immediately cover her breasts this time, however. Progress, he thought, and then she swallowed and gave her head a small shake as if to clear it.

"No," she said finally. "He was too busy working on the farm to pay me much attention when I was sent for wood. We all worked hard. Everything was made from scratch, even our clothes."

Magnus relaxed a little, relieved that she had the sense to give them a break.

"A couple of years passed with me keeping my friends secret, and then when I was twelve, a whole week passed where none of them showed up in the copse. I'd only been to their house a time or two and never went there without them, but I was worried so made my way through their field to the house and knocked. Her brother Brandon answered and said Bethany was sick, but would be happy to see me, so I went into her room to visit with her. That's when I found out about doctors," she said solemnly. "Her appendix had burst. I had no idea what that was, but she'd ended up in the hospital where the doctors had apparently removed her appendix. I guess the whole family had spent a great deal of time at the hospital with her, which was why her sister and brothers hadn't come to the copse to tell me what was happening. She'd only got home that day and was supposed to take it easy for a while. So for the next week or so we spent all our visits at their house. We watched TV or movies or played on the computer. I *really* loved the computer," she said with a grin.

Magnus wasn't surprised. She made her living designing websites on a computer.

"After that, we spent a lot more time in their house. We were getting older and playing hide-and-seek didn't appeal to any of us anymore," she explained. "In truth, I think they only continued to go to the copse for so long to make Bethany and me happy," Allie admitted, and then added, "And maybe because her brother Brandon liked me." Grinning, she confessed, "I liked him too. He was the most handsome boy I'd ever seen. Of course, he and his brother were pretty much the only boys I'd ever seen," she acknowledged with a wry twist of her lips. "But anyway, he gave me my first kiss at thirteen, and was my first make-out partner."

Magnus stiffened, jealousy gathering on the edges of his consciousness.

"I was fourteen when their father had a heart attack and died. Bethany and Brandon's mother immediately sold the farm and moved the kids to the city." She grimaced at the memory. "It all seemed to happen terribly fast. They were there and then they were gone and I was left heartbroken. I'd lost my friend and the boy I loved just like that."

"And your parents never even knew they were a part of your life?" he asked, finding that hard to believe.

"I think my mother suspected something was going on. Sometimes she got this look . . . and one time when I was out too long she came to find me. She must have heard us laughing and chattering before one of the boys spotted her. But when they hid and I hurried to meet her, she didn't say anything. She just helped me gather sticks and led me home." Sighing, she shrugged. "But they found out about it when I was sixteen."

"How?" he asked with surprise. If her friends had moved two years prior to that, how could her parents possibly find out she used to have friends?

"I told them," she admitted grimly, and then explained. "I had a little sister. Jilly. She was seven years younger than me so always remained at the farm when I went to the woods, but when I was sixteen she became ill. We'd had colds, fevers, and flus before, but this was different. She was in terrible pain and so sick," Allie said with remembered anguish.

"What did she have?" Magnus asked with concern, running his hands over her arms in an effort to soothe her.

"I don't know. They wouldn't take her to the doctor to find out," she said with frustration. "I thought maybe they didn't know about doctors and how they could help. I guess I was incredibly naïve," she admitted with a sigh. "But that's why I told them about my friend Bethany and her appendicitis. I thought if they realized doctors could help Jilly, they'd take her to see one."

"But they refused?" he guessed quietly.

Allie nodded. "I think Mother wanted to. She kept giving Father this pleading look as I talked. But he wouldn't even consider it. Illness was a trial given to us by God, a punishment for our sins. We had to have faith in Him and pray for forgiveness and healing. That was the only thing that could save her, he said, and then he beat me for my sin in disobeying him, telling me the whole time that Jilly's illness was because I had sinned and allowed those heathen children to corrupt me."

"You did not believe him, did you?" Magnus asked with concern.

"I was a very young, very unsophisticated girl for sixteen," she told him solemnly. "And yes, I might have believed him, but as she bathed the welts on my back, my bum, and the back of my legs from his beating, Mother told me—"

"The scars," he interrupted solemnly, recalling how the sight had shocked him when he'd seen them covering her back, bottom, and upper legs. The memory of them now told him how violent and vicious her father's beating had been.

"Yes. Pretty, aren't they? A constant reminder of the father I loathed," she said bitterly, and then closed her eyes and lowered her head with something like shame. "I knew you'd seen them when you came into the bathroom. You seemed transfixed by how ugly they were. I suppose you're sorry you married me now."

"No," he said with amazement. "They were a surprise, yes. But they would never have made me not take you as my life mate or I should not have married you." When she shook her head in disbelief, he admitted, "I saw them before we married, Allie."

Her eyes blinked open with surprise at that. "What? When?"

"When we got here, Dani and Elvi were going to change you into one of Elvi's nightgowns so you would rest more comfortably. I left so they could do it, but returned to find they'd stripped you but had stopped there. You were lying on your stomach, the scars visible."

"But they didn't change me," she said with confusion and agitation.

"No." He ran a hand down her arm soothingly. "The scars made them worry you would be uncomfortable with the knowledge that anyone had seen them. When I returned, they were debating continuing to change you, or putting you back in your clothes. But Stephanie told them you would not be happy to know anyone had seen them, so they redressed you in your clothes."

"Oh," she breathed unhappily, her eyes closing in shame again.

Magnus hated that she was ashamed of something like that. Scars were a result of life for mortals. Every mortal had them. Some were just worse than others. She was no longer mortal, however, and he said gently, "They are gone, Allie."

Allie stiffened, her eyes shooting open to search his face, and then she turned her head as if to try to see if what he said was true. But, of course, she couldn't see her own back no matter how she tried. Realizing this, Magnus sat up again and began to scoot toward the foot of the bed, taking her with him. The movement caused friction between them, and sent shafts of pleasure through them both, reawakening his once again flagging erection. Magnus could only think that was a good thing, but ground his teeth against it, determined she should see her back, and not wanting to have to stop until he got there.

Pausing once he reached the end of the bed and sat with his feet on the ground, he wrapped one arm around her to help keep her in place and then stood, ordering, "Wrap your legs around me."

Allie did as instructed and they both groaned as he started to walk. Fortunately, the dresser was only a few steps away. If he'd had to carry her like that to the bathroom, Magnus had no doubt they would not have made it. The pleasure would have overwhelmed them, leaving them passed out on the carpet halfway to the bathroom door.

Setting her behind on the dresser, Magnus pressed himself deeper into her, fighting the urge to withdraw and push in again, and said through gritted teeth, "Look."

Fifteen

It took Allie a moment to look. Not because she didn't want to see, but because her body was presently humming with desire, and she really wanted to claw his ass and urge him to finish this torture. Dear God, the ups and downs of trying to keep him erect inside her without pushing past the point of no return was like a roller coaster ride.

Sighing, she rested her forehead briefly on his chest as she took a couple of deep breaths, and then raised her head and turned to peer at their reflection in the mirror.

Allie's eyes widened at the expanse of pure, unblemished skin she saw. The scars she'd carried for nearly twenty years were gone. At least her outer scars, she thought, and stared at herself, and then her gaze slid to Magnus. He had done this for her. His turning her had removed the marks she'd hidden for all these years.

Turning abruptly, she leaned up and kissed him, the action raising her slightly on his shaft. Magnus groaned in response and kissed her back, his mouth hard and almost rough. Allie liked it. It turned her on, and she scraped her nails across his scalp, pressed closer against his chest, and sucked hard on his tongue as she shifted her hips, urging him to move. Much to her relief, Magnus thrust into her hard, closing the space she'd made, and they gasped into each other's mouths at the pleasure that brought them. But then Magnus broke their kiss and caught her hips to hold her still.

"Christ, woman," he muttered, leaning his forehead against hers, and then he turned it slightly from side to side. "We cannot."

Allie didn't say anything, she just clung to him and tried to catch her breath.

After a moment, he cleared his throat and prompted, "What did your mother tell you as she cleaned your wounds?"

Allie sighed, and forced herself to relax her hold on him. After a moment, she was able to pick up where she'd left off. "Mother knew about doctors and all the wonders I'd seen at Bethany's. She was raised Catholic, and lived that life before she met and fell in love with my father. She said that when I was old enough I should leave and seek that life too. But for now, my father was in charge and his belief in God was strict and hard, but beautiful and pure. He'd assured her that Jilly would get better if they prayed hard enough and she believed him. God surely wouldn't take such a precious little girl from us."

Allie closed her eyes. "Jilly died two days later. By then I was feverish and terribly sick."

"Your wounds were infected?" Magnus asked, pulling back slightly.

Allie raised her head and nodded. "My back."

He ran one hand soothingly over her back now, and she smiled faintly before continuing.

"Mother was beside herself with grief and hysteria over both my infection and Jilly's death. She shrieked that father had lied—God had taken her baby, and He was going to take me too." She grimaced and leaned her head against him again. "I really was very sick. Even I thought I was going to die."

"And that's when she took you to the doctor," Magnus guessed, the words a rumble that she could feel in his chest.

Allie shook her head against him. "That's when she hung herself."

"What?" He pulled back and she raised her head to see the shock on his face as he asked, "She left you to die and killed herself?"

Allie nodded. Normally when she thought about this, she became angry and emotional. This time, however, she wasn't feeling much at all and merely said, "My fever was crazy high when she came to me, but I remember it very clearly. She told me she loved my father more than life itself, and even at that point, with one child dead and one dying, couldn't bring herself to betray him and seek medical help. But she also couldn't live with the fact that her doing nothing had killed my sister and was most likely going to kill me. So she was going to take her own life. If I died, she and Jilly would be waiting to greet me when God took me home."

"I thought she was Catholic," Magnus growled with disgust. "Suicide is a mortal sin according to the Catholic church."

Shrugging, Allie said wearily, "At that point, I think she was just crazy. The whole time she was telling me all of that, she was patting my shoulder and smiling as if what she was saying was perfectly normal and should be good news because I'd have her and Jilly to greet me when I died. Then she just got up and left my room. I tried to follow, but the effort caused me terrible pain and I passed out without even managing to get out of bed."

Allie was silent for a minute, and then continued. "When I woke up, my father was there placing cold cloths over my forehead. He told me mother had 'lost her faith in our God' and hung herself. It was just the two of us now. We'd have to live right and pray for her soul and that of Jilly's."

She paused briefly, wondering where the usual anger was. Allie hadn't spoken of this often. In fact, aside from Bethany's mom and the police, Stella was the only other person she'd told about her past, but she'd felt rage and anger and grief every time she'd told the story before this. Now she just felt sad as she thought about the family she'd had. They'd been so screwed up.

Shaking her head, Allie said, "I didn't die. My fever broke, and my father nursed me back to health. We never spoke again about Jilly or my mother, other than his telling me he buried both in a very old little graveyard at the back of the property. It was illegal, but so was refusing to seek medical help for children, so I doubt he cared." She shrugged. "It took a couple of weeks for me to get my strength back, but once I thought I could manage it, I packed a bag and left. I just walked out of the house and kept walking."

"Where did you go?" Magnus asked, and she could hear the concern in his voice.

"To Bethany's family," Allie said with a faint smile. "She'd given me her new address before they moved and I found it eventually with the help of a farmer who picked me up on the edge of the city and gave me a ride the rest of the way into town and to their house. To say they were shocked to see me would be a bit of an understatement," she added with amusement. "They were all very nice, but Bethany had changed. The country girl was gone, she was all city now and I could tell she didn't know what to do with me. There were a house full of teenagers there, some kind of party, and she was just embarrassed by me in my homespun clothes. As for Brandon, he just acted like he didn't even know me. But Mrs. Wilson sat me down and made me tell her everything. Then she drove me to the police station and made me tell them."

"Was your father arrested?" Magnus asked.

"He would have been. They mentioned criminal negligent homicide in regards to my sister, and something about burying their bodies on the farm, but I can't remember what the charge was." She took a moment to try to remember, but then shrugged. "It doesn't matter. He wasn't there when they went out to the farm. But they dug up Jilly and my mother and took them in for autopsies to strengthen the charges against my father. He, however, was long gone," she added, and then explained, "I saw him in the field as I headed out, and I know he saw me. He stopped working and straightened and just watched me go. I think he probably realized I'd tell someone what had happened and they'd come for him, so he packed up his truck and left."

"Do you know where he went?" Magnus asked.

"I have no idea, and don't care," Allie said with a shrug.

Magnus hesitated, and then asked, "And what about you? What happened to you then?"

"I was put into the system and placed with a foster family. They helped me get a social insurance number and stuff." She gave a laugh. "I was born at home and my birth was never registered so I had to prove I existed and was a Canadian, but they helped me with that."

"And school?" he asked.

Allie grimaced, but she'd been honest up to now, so continued with that honesty. "My foster mother took me for testing to see where I should be placed in school. Fortunately, my mother was apparently a good teacher and my homeschooling turned out to be up to snuff. They put me in grade eleven with my peers, but I was a freak and didn't really fit in."

"You are not a freak," he said at once, sounding upset.

Grinning, Allie leaned back and eyed him with disbelief before assuring him, "I am definitely a freak." When he started to shake his head, she pointed out, "I'm an introvert, a computer geek, the mortal mother of a vampire, and almost half an hour ago I was a virgin at thirty-four. That's a freak," she assured him, and then added, "But I'm okay with that. We can't all be Mrs. Brady. Besides, you guys are vampires, and that makes you all freaks too, so I'm in good company."

"You just called me a freak," he said with a combination of amusement and disbelief.

"Yes. I did," she said unapologetically, and then shifted against him, sending another wave of passion through them both. "What are you going to do about it, mister?"

Magnus's hands tightened on her hips to keep her from moving, and he growled, "Don't tempt me. A half hour has not passed yet. Finish telling me about your life."

Allie met his gaze briefly and then nodded and said bluntly, "I was socially inept and uncomfortable around other people, so I avoided them as much as possible. It gained me a reputation as a weirdo at school, but for the most part the other kids left me alone. I graduated and got a job as a janitor in an office building, working nights. It gave me enough money to live off and some extra to take computer courses at college. I made a few friends there, but not close ones.

Mostly I worked, either at my janitorial job or on web design. Eventually my web design business did well enough that I could quit the night job. And then it did well enough that I was able to buy my own home." She shrugged. "And that's where I was when I met Stella. Working. Living. Alone."

They were both silent for a moment, Allie because she had nothing else to say, and Magnus . . . Well, he appeared to be thinking, and some pretty serious thoughts, Allie decided as she took in his solemn expression and faraway gaze. Probably wondering how he had ended up with such a misfit for a life mate, she thought wryly, and then his eyes focused on her again and he said, "Look at your back."

Allie raised her eyebrows, but then turned her head to peer at their reflection in the mirror again. She knew the scars were gone, had already seen that, and yet the sight of her unmarred back struck her anew. Dear God, there wasn't even a slight dimple to hint that the scars had ever been there. Her back was as pure and untouched as a newborn baby's. The thought made her recall Mabel's words.

Well, this is like a rebirth. You're going to go through a period of pain and suffering and come out immortal born.

"Immortal born," she murmured.

"Yes." Magnus met her gaze in their reflection. "You are immortal born. The nanos have removed the scars from your old life." She saw his eyes drop to her, and then he caught her chin and turned her face so she would look at him as he said solemnly,

"This is a new life for you, Allie. A new beginning. You do not have to carry any of the past with you if you do not want to. You can be Mrs. Brady or a freak as you wish." He paused briefly, letting that sink in, and then said, "And you are not alone anymore. I am not like the others in your past. I will never harm you as your father did. I will not turn from you like Bethany and her brother. I will not abandon you as your mother and Stella did. You are my life mate, and my life. I will spend however long I live cherishing you, adoring you, and keeping you safe and happy, because your very existence makes me happy."

Allie was staring at him wide-eyed, his words still rolling through her head, when he suddenly stepped back. Her thoughts immediately scattered as he slid out of her, and she gasped in alarm and tried to pull him back, but he simply caught her hand and tugged her off the dresser, then led her to the bed.

"Magnus," she groaned unhappily. "Now I'm going to heal and—"

"The half hour is up," he interrupted gently as he paused next to the bed and turned toward her.

"Oh," she said with surprise, and then glanced at the bed and back before asking uncertainly, "What are we doing?"

"I'm going to show you some of that cherishing now," he said, his voice a deep rumble that sent shivers through her as he lowered his head to kiss her.

Allie kissed him back and let her arms creep up around his neck as he began to run his hands over her back and sides. She tried to move closer then, but his hands slid between them, preventing it so that he could caress her breasts, and she eased her hold and moaned into his mouth in response, and then gasped when he tweaked her nipples.

Breaking their kiss then, he nuzzled her ear and murmured, "Put one knee on the bed."

The request confused her, but she did it, realizing why he'd wanted her to when his hand slid between her now open legs and found her core.

"Oh," she gasped, and clutched at his shoulders as he began to caress her, his fingers moving in tantalizing circles that soon had her pressing forward into the caress and moaning with need. When his mouth found hers again, Allie kissed him eagerly, almost desperately, and reached down to cover his hand, urging him on. Even so she was caught by surprise when his finger suddenly shifted and thrust into her in concert with his tongue thrusting into her mouth.

Her cry of pleasure was echoed by his, but both were muffled by the kiss they shared, and then he eased his finger out and broke the kiss. Breathing heavily, he urged her onto the bed, and came down on top of her, but then raised himself up slightly to look at her.

When Allie merely stared back uncertainly, he smiled.

"You are beautiful."

Flushing, she shook her head, quite sure she probably wasn't at that moment, but he nodded solemnly.

"You are," he insisted, shifting onto one arm beside her so that he could run his hand up and down her side as he looked her over. "Your lips are swollen from my kisses, your cheeks flushed, and your eyes are molten silver right now with desire."

That startled her and her eyes widened. "Really?"

She hadn't looked at her eyes in the mirror. Not in the bathroom, and not on the dresser. She'd been busy looking at other things and now wondered what her eyes looked like.

"Really," he assured her. "It tells me you want me as much as I want you."

Allie felt her face heat up and knew she was blushing, but didn't deny it.

"But I want to taste you this time if that is all right with you?" His hand drifted down and slid between her legs again, leaving her in no doubt about what he meant.

The very idea of experiencing that left Allie a mass of confusion. She'd read books that suggested it was awesome, but the idea of being open to him that way—Her thoughts died abruptly as he suddenly shifted away, moving down her body and urging her legs apart so that he could rest between them.

Allie clenched her hands, and bit her lip as he positioned himself, but then he raised his head to meet her gaze and her heart stopped when she saw that his eyes were glowing pure silver.

Magnus stayed like that briefly, though she felt his fingers glide over her, spreading her for him, and then he lowered his head and she felt the first rasp of his tongue over her heated flesh.

Allie cried out, her eyes slamming shut and her body jerking. And then she tangled her fingers in the sheet and held on for dear life, her hips lifting off the bed and moving to his rhythm as he finally drove them both over the edge they'd danced so close to repeatedly this past half hour.

The explosion when it came was much more powerful than Allie could have imagined, sending her almost into a seizure that left lights exploding behind her eyes and her whole body shaking before darkness swept in to claim her.

Allie woke up to find herself cuddled against Magnus's side, her head resting on his chest and his hand moving soothingly up and down her arm. For a moment, she just lay still, enjoying the caress, but then she sighed, and said, "Sorry."

Magnus's hand stilled at once and then he asked, "For what?"

"I fainted again," she pointed out with a grimace. "I guess my blood levels are still a little low. Dani said they would be."

She felt him relax and his hand started to slide up and down her arm again.

"Yes, you fainted," Magnus agreed, and she could hear the smile in his voice. "But that was not a result of your blood levels. It is because we are life mates. I lost consciousness too."

Allie pushed herself up on one arm to stare at him with disbelief. "What?"

"For life mates, the shared experience of lovemaking is so overwhelming that both members usually lose consciousness on completion," he explained, and then added, "At least, for the first year or so."

She considered that briefly, and then asked, "Why only for a year or so? Does it get boring after that or something?"

"No," he assured her. "It is just that it takes that long for our bodies to adjust to the intensity of the experience."

"Oh." Allie nodded. She could see that. It *had* been pretty intense, she thought, recalling his glowing eyes staring up at her as he— Blinking, she rolled away from him, nearly tumbling off the bed before she caught herself and gained her feet.

"What is it?" Magnus asked with concern, and she heard the rustle of the sheets as he followed.

She didn't answer, but hurried to the dresser to look at herself in the large mirror over it.

"Damn," Allie breathed as she saw herself.

Her hair was a tumbled mass of waves around her face, that sexy just-rolled-out-of-bed look that no application of hairspray and curling iron had ever managed to achieve for her, and the blond streaks in her light brown hair were more obvious for some reason. She shifted her attention to her face then, noting the complete lack of anything resembling acne scars, which she used to have a few of. Now her skin was completely unblemished and the pores were so tiny they were nonexistent.

Her eyes were different too. The hazel was now greener, the brown having been pushed to the outer edge so that it acted almost like eyeliner for the iris. She didn't see any silver, though, Allie noted with disappointment.

"Is something wrong?" Magnus asked, appearing behind her in the mirror.

Allie smiled wryly, and admitted, "I wanted to see the silver in my eyes, but they aren't silver anymore."

He looked surprised, but then slid his arms around her waist and drew her back against his chest. Pressing a kiss to the top of her head, he said, "We can bring the silver out if you like."

Allie peered at their reflection, her gaze sliding over his wide shoulders, and the muscled arms wrapped around her under breasts that were fuller and perkier than they used to be, and she nodded. "Let's make them glow."

Magnus chuckled, but caught her hands when she reached back to touch him. "I will make them glow. You watch. I would not wish you to miss it again."

Releasing her hands then, he glided his own up her arms and then around to cover her breasts. Her hands moved up to cover his when he began to knead the tender flesh, urging her more firmly against his chest. She watched their reflection, finding the sight of his body framing hers and his hands on her incredibly erotic. But then he bent to kiss her neck and her head tilted to the side, her eyes closing as she shivered and moaned at the combined caresses.

"Open your eyes," Magnus whispered, and nipped at her neck.

Groaning, Allie forced her eyes open, her breath

becoming a shallow pant as she watched him tug and tweak at her nipples, sending wave after wave of pleasure through her.

Moaning his name, she pressed her bottom back into him, squirming against the growing hardness there, and then watched with mounting anticipation when one of his hands dropped away from a breast to slide down her stomach and glide between her legs.

Allie gasped and arched against him, her breasts thrusting out and bottom pressing more firmly back into him as he added this new caress.

"God," Magnus growled by her ear as he caressed her. "You are so hot and wet. I want to be inside you."

"Yes," Allie gasped, grinding herself back into him. "Please."

Magnus hesitated, but then stopped caressing her to catch her by the hips and lift her until she was on her tiptoes, although he was taking most of her weight. His back forced her to bend forward slightly over the dresser, and she felt his erection bump against her, and then he shifted and it began to slide in. He entered her so slowly Allie thought she might gnash her teeth. She wanted to push back into him, but his hands at her hips prevented that and she couldn't do anything to speed up the process.

"No pain," Magnus breathed with relief by her ear when he was finally all the way in.

Only then did Allie understand why he had been going so carefully. He'd wanted to be sure the half hour of waiting with him inside her had worked, and her hymen hadn't healed back to its original status.

The man had been looking out for her, and she hadn't even thought of it. He was— Allie's thoughts died as his hands shifted, one sliding under her stomach to hold her up at the height he needed, while the other slid between her legs again. Now he was lodged inside her, filling her to capacity, but he was staying still and caressing her instead. Hands clenching on the dresser top, Allie gasped and squirmed on him, her inner muscles clenching and adding to the excitement for both of them until she couldn't take it anymore.

"Magnus, please," she gasped, reaching back to claw at his leg and behind, anything she could reach to make him move. "I want—"

"Look at your eyes," he growled, caressing her more firmly.

Allie glanced at the mirror. Silver had poured in to mingle with the green and brown of her eyes. But it wasn't solid silver as his had been last night, and then Magnus began to move, withdrawing partway and thrusting back into her even as he continued to caress her. Allie cried out and bucked against him, her gaze never leaving the mirror. She watched the silver flood her eyes, was amazed at how alien she looked, and then Allie didn't care anymore and lowered her head as she concentrated on meeting him thrust for thrust, helping him drive them toward that high precipice and the sweet oblivion that waited beyond it.

Sixteen

Allie woke up on top of Magnus. She didn't realize it at first. She opened her eyes, confused as to where she was when she found herself staring at the front of a drawer. Turning her head, she followed it up to another and another and then spotted the top edge of the mirror above it. That was when she realized she was lying in front of the dresser.

With that mystery solved, Allie immediately became aware that she was lying on something not flat and really quite uncomfortable. Grimacing, she rolled to the side and immediately slid off of her previous perch onto the hardwood floor. Shifting to her knees, she turned to look at what she'd been lying on, eyes widening when she found herself staring at an unconscious Magnus. She'd been lying on top of him.

Memory rushed in then to tell her what had happened. Or at least what she'd been doing before she'd lost consciousness. Obviously they'd passed out and ended up on the bedroom floor, Magnus taking the brunt of the fall.

Allie eyed him with concern now, worried he'd hit his head as they fell, but there was no blood and a brief examination of his head didn't reveal any bumps. Of course, he might have hit his head and already healed, she thought as she scrambled to her feet.

Allie paused once upright, not wanting to leave him alone there on the floor, but not wanting to stand there naked while she waited for him to wake up either. Spotting his dress shirt on the floor beside the bed, she walked over and scooped it up to put on. It smelled like him, and she paused to inhale the heady scent before doing up the buttons.

Turning back toward the dresser then, Allie stopped when she saw herself. His shirt was big on her, the tails reaching almost to her knees. Despite that, she didn't think she looked too bad. Kind of sexy, really, she decided with a grin, and then moved back to Magnus. Settling on the floor with her back to the dresser, she lifted his head and then slid to the side until her thigh was under it and then she let it lower to rest on her leg.

As she waited for him to wake up, Allie examined this man that was now her husband. It was still an alien thought to her. Husband. She'd never thought she'd marry, and suspected that if her life hadn't taken this path, she never would have. She certainly couldn't imagine doing the things she had with Magnus with any other man. Actually, she was surprised she had with him. That hadn't been part of her plan when she'd agreed to marry him. But things rarely went to plan in life. That was one thing Allie had definitely learned the last four years as she'd run from Abaddon and his crew. She'd also learned it was often easier if you didn't make plans for the future, because you never knew when a vampire might pop up to ruin them. It was just easier to roll with the punches and work with what you had. Now she had a son and a husband. A family.

She'd have to work with that, Allie told herself. She could do it. She'd be open to him until he gave her reason not to be, and hope for the best.

"That is a serious expression. What are you thinking?"

Allie glanced down at Magnus's face to see that his eyes were open and focused on her. She managed a smile, but rather than answer his question asked, "Why do you speak so . . ." She hesitated, unsure of the proper term, and finally said, "You don't use contractions."

"Alodia taught me English and she spoke most properly and without contractions. Most old immortals do," he said, and then sat up and got to his feet.

"Lucian talked like you," Allie murmured, getting up as well. "But you said Victor was old, and his speech is more modern."

"You can thank Stephanie for that. She has spent years working on getting him, DJ, Harper, and Drina to use contractions. She claimed their speech made them sound old."

"It does," Allie said with amusement. "It kind of makes it obvious that you're somehow different too."

Magnus's eyes widened at that claim, and then he frowned and said, "Then I shall endeavor to change my speech pattern."

"I'll help if you like," she offered.

"I like," Magnus said with a smile, and then bent to press a kiss to her forehead. Straightening again, he asked, "Are you hungry?"

"I could eat," Allie admitted, and then grimaced. "And since you're smelling like steak again, I probably need more than just food."

"Of course. I should have . . ." Shaking his head, Magnus left her by the dresser and strode around the bed to the cooler next to it. He bent to open it, and then slammed it closed and snatched up his dress pants.

"We are out of blood. But we can get that along with the food," Magnus announced as he pulled on his pants. He did them up quickly, and then moved back around the bed and caught her hand in passing on the way to the door.

The upper hall was dark and silent, but the lights were on downstairs and enough of it reached the stairwell that descending the stairs was no problem. Victor was in the dining room, peering out the front window. He glanced around at their arrival and smiled faintly, but then turned his gaze out the window again. Allie was relieved. She knew Magnus's shirt covered her decently, but still felt uncomfortable wandering around in it.

"There's plenty of food in the fridge if you want it," Victor said, still looking out the window.

"That is what I was hoping," Magnus admitted as he led Allie around the counter into the kitchen area. Releasing her then, he opened the refrigerator and retrieved two bags of blood. He handed her one, but when she peered down at it with bewilderment, unsure what to do with it when her fangs weren't out, he moved closer and set the other bag on the counter behind her. Much to her surprise, he then caught her by the waist and pulled her against him as he lowered his head to nuzzle her ear.

Allie bit her lip and leaned into him at the caress, a little distracted by the knowledge that Victor was just twenty feet away staring out the window, and then Magnus nipped at her ear and whispered, "When I get you back upstairs I'm going to lick every inch of you, from your toes to . . ." One of his hands slid between her legs and rubbed her gently there and Allie gasped as shock and pleasure ripped through her. Distracted by the excitement he'd stirred and the awareness that Victor was just across the room, Allie didn't notice the shifting in her mouth as her fangs dropped until Magnus stepped back, snatched away the bag she held, and popped it to her fangs.

As she stared at him wide-eyed, he placed her hand gently over the bag, and then winked at her and turned away to open the refrigerator again.

"When the girls checked on you earlier, did they mention that the trap worked?" Victor asked.

Allie glanced toward him with surprise and then back to Magnus as he stilled and then glanced over his shoulder to ask, "They caught Abaddon?"

"They think so," Victor said. "They got all six vehicles and caught thirty-six rogues in all. One of the men has short hair and fits the general description of Abaddon, but Basha and Marcus are the only people still living who have actually seen the bastard and can identify him for sure."

"And?" Magnus asked, straightening and turning now to look at the man.

Victor shook his head. "Lucian and Mortimer still haven't been able to get ahold of them." He ran a hand wearily around his neck, and admitted, "We're starting to worry that they ran into something in California that they couldn't handle."

Allie's eyes widened slightly at this news. She recalled the couple being mentioned when she was at the Enforcer house. Lucian had seemed to think it was important that they be in on the search. Now she knew why. They were the only people who could identify Abaddon. But this was the first she'd heard that they hadn't been able to contact the couple.

"I thought they were checking out a rumored sighting of Abaddon in California," Magnus said now, reclaiming her attention as he grabbed a tray that rested on the counter and moved back to the refrigerator.

"Yes," Victor agreed. "Obviously that was wrong if he's here. But it doesn't mean there wasn't a different rogue nest there that they stumbled into."

Magnus stood with his hand on the fridge door as he considered that, but then shook his head. "I met Basha the last time I was here, and I have known Marcus for centuries. They can handle themselves."

"We both know sometimes that isn't enough," Victor said quietly.

Neither man spoke for a minute, and then Victor turned to look out the window again. "Anyway, until we have verification that Abaddon is among the immortals they got, we're still on the alert."

"Right." Magnus opened the refrigerator door to poke around at the contents. Allie frowned from one man to the other and then, looking down at the bag at her mouth, saw that it was empty and tore it from her fangs. "Can't you just ask the other rogues if it's him? Or better yet, read their minds? It sounds like they're all new turns, so should be easy for you to read."

Her question made both men turn to peer at her as if her question surprised them. She couldn't tell if they'd just forgotten she was there, or the idea really hadn't occurred to them. But then Victor said, "There's no one to ask. They're all dead."

When Allie gaped at him at this news, Magnus explained, "Rogues are rarely taken alive. Knowing they will be judged and executed, they usually fight to the death to escape."

Allie turned to look at him, and then back to Victor. "So Lucian wants Basha to look at the bodies?"

"Something like that," Victor muttered, and looked back out the window in what she suspected was a bid to avoid her gaze.

"Here."

Allie turned and found several bags of blood pushed into her arms. "You carry those and I'll bring the food."

She arched an eyebrow, not at all fooled. Allie knew he was trying to get her out of there to prevent her asking what Victor had meant by "something like that." But she let him get away with it for now and trailed him back up to her room. Or was it their room now? She wasn't sure.

Magnus urged her to sit on the bed, helped her bring on her fangs, and then popped another bag onto her fangs before moving away to put the rest of the blood in the cooler. Once that was done, he grabbed the tray he'd set on the dresser when they entered and carried it back to join her on the bed.

"We have cold fried chicken, cheese, bottled water, and a couple of bananas," he announced as he settled cross-legged in front of her with the tray between them. "And your bag is empty."

Allie tugged the bag from her fangs, and handed it over when he held out his hand.

Magnus tossed it on top of the cooler next to the bed and then turned back to survey the food he'd gathered, muttering, "Hopefully you like something here."

"I like it all," she assured him, reaching for a drumstick and a napkin from the small stack he'd also included. "Thank you."

They were silent when they first started to eat, but then Allie said, "So, you know all about me. Now it's your turn."

Magnus was silent as he finished chewing and swallowed the food in his mouth, but then he asked, "What would you like to know?"

"What you've been doing the last twelve hundred

years," Allie said dryly, and then asked, "Did you go home after you were finished turning and learning how to survive as an immortal?"

Magnus shook his head. "No. That was not possible."

"Why?" she asked at once. "You were only fourteen, so the nanos wouldn't have changed you that much. I mean, it's not like they had turned you from an old man into a young stud."

He smiled at her words, but said, "Age is not the only thing they change. I had been in battles and had scars. Those, of course, were gone and that certainly would have been noticed. Aside from that, however, the whole village knew I had gone a'viking with Erik and the others. Their first question would have been to ask after the fate of the other men and I could not explain that."

"Right," Allie said slowly. "So you don't know how your family fared after you left?"

"Actually, I do," he admitted. "While I did not go back right away, I did visit my village twenty years later."

"Did anyone recognize you?" she asked at once.

Magnus shook his head. "I did not actually talk to anyone. A stranger would have been noted and confronted, so I approached at night and more or less skulked around spying on everyone to learn what I wanted to know."

"By that you mean reading minds and such?" she suggested, and when he nodded unapologetically, she asked, "And what did you learn?"

"My parents were both still alive but very old. My

sister had married and ran the farm with her husband, while my parents looked after her children. They all seemed content."

"And the girl you wanted to marry?" Allie asked. "The one you went raiding to win?"

"Ah." He smiled wryly. "It turns out I made a lucky escape there. A friend of mine had been more successful with his viking efforts. He sailed out with a different group just days after we left, but they made it back alive. He returned with enough gold to convince her to marry him . . . and came to regret it."

"Why?" Allie demanded.

"Because it turned out that Sassa was as rotten inside as she was beautiful on the outside," he said with a grimace.

"That was her name? Sassa?"

Magnus nodded. "From what I read from their minds, while he had done his best to make her happy, nothing would. She, on the other hand, delighted in making him miserable." He grimaced. "My old friend was by that time resolved to simply drinking himself to death so he need not deal with her further." Smiling wryly, he added, "As I said, I made a lucky escape."

Allie nodded silently, but was oddly pleased that his young love had turned out to be such a disappointment. She didn't look too closely at why, though. "So, what did you do then?"

"I was a warrior for Kenric and had been since Alodia finished teaching me about what I was now and how to survive. One of the tasks I was given had taken me to a town close to my old village, which is

why I stopped in. Once my task was done I returned
to Kenric."

Allie smiled faintly. She could imagine him as a
warrior of old, swinging a long sword or battle-axe.
He had that kind of body with his wide shoulders
and strong arms. "How long were you a warrior at
Kenric?"

"About two hundred years," he answered, dropping
the chicken wing he'd picked clean, and choosing a
thigh next. "By that time, I had moved up the ranks to
be her first in command over the men and had been in
that position for more than a century."

"Then why did you leave? And wasn't that dangerous?" she asked before he could answer the first
question. "Not being a warrior—that, of course, is
dangerous. But I mean remaining in one place so long.
None of you age. Didn't it raise questions by the mortals around you?"

"Alodia had several properties across England. We
never stayed in one for more than a decade before
moving to another. And fifty or sixty years would pass
before we returned to a previous keep. By then most of
the mortals we had known had died, and the few who
remained were old, often blind, or too decrepit to get
around." He shrugged. "We rarely had trouble."

Allie nodded, and wondered if that was how all immortals avoided detection, by moving every decade.
Before she could ask, though, he answered her first
question.

"And I left because I grew weary of battle and wished
to return to my roots."

"You became a Viking again?" she asked with interest.

Magnus smiled crookedly and shook his head. "I am sorry to disappoint you, but no. My roots were farming. I grew up on a farm," he reminded her. "That Viking expedition was a one-time thing."

"Oh, right." She shrugged at her mistake. "So you gave up fighting for farming."

He nodded. "It was nice for a time. My father had taught me well and I was a successful farmer. But eventually I tired of that too, and decided to travel around. I tried various things along the way."

"Like what?" she asked with curiosity.

Magnus considered her question briefly, and then said, "Blacksmith, stonemason, carpenter . . . I seemed to most enjoy doing things with my hands, creating things," he explained. "Eventually I decided I should like my own castle, but I needed a lot of coin for that. And land, of course, which only the king could bestow on you. So I became a mercenary to earn the coin."

"And controlled a king to get the land?" she suggested.

"No. I might have, but it was not necessary in the end," he said with a grin. "I was a very successful mercenary. Most immortals are. We are strong, fast, and hard to kill, after all."

Allie nodded, but said, "Which makes me wonder how Basha could identify Abaddon among the dead rogues when the only way I know that one can be killed is by fire."

Magnus blinked, and then smiled wryly. "I knew you would revisit that subject eventually."

"Hmm," she murmured, and then arched an eyebrow. "So? Is there a way to kill your kind without fire?"

"Beheading," he said solemnly. "An immortal can survive it if the head is placed back on the body quickly for the nanos to heal, but if not . . ." He shrugged.

"So Basha will be expected to inspect the beheaded bodies?" she asked, grimacing at the thought of thirty-six bodies laid out with their heads severed.

"The bodies will have been burned," he assured her. "But the heads will have been kept for identification purposes unless ID was found on their bodies. Enforcers try to keep track of mortals who are turned by rogues in case their disappearance causes problems in the future."

"Oh, God, poor Basha," Allie said with disgust at the thought of being expected to look over a bunch of detached heads. It sounded like a horror story to her. Although she supposed it was no worse than having to look them over with the bodies lying nearby. Still . . . Shaking her head to remove the images now playing through her mind, she said, "Fine. Thank you for telling me the truth. Now finish telling me about your efforts to get a castle."

"I will always tell you the truth," Magnus assured her solemnly, and then took a sip of water before saying, "Successful as we were, it was not long before I had the coin I needed to build my castle, but I needed to be granted land to put it on. Fortunately, the Battle of Agincourt was one of the last contracts I took."

"Oh, I know about that one," Allie said, excited to recognize a part of his history. "The Battle of Agincourt happened in 1415."

Magnus smiled and nodded. "Yes. The history books recorded a great deal of that endeavor. What they did not record was that an attempt was made on Henry's life the night before the Battle of Agincourt."

"Really?" Allie asked with interest, and then demanded, "Tell me."

Magnus chuckled, but complied. "One of the mercenaries was actually a French spy. He had traveled with us, eaten with us, and even fought at our side. He had everyone fooled."

"Except you," she guessed. "You must have read his mind and realized his intent."

"I did," he acknowledged.

Her eyes widened. "Oh, my God. You knew and didn't say anything. You just bided your time and waited until he made his attempt and then stepped in to save the king at the last minute."

Magnus grinned. "You know me so well already."

Allie shook her head at the claim. "And I imagine the king was so grateful he granted you land."

"And a title and even coin," he assured her. "He was most grateful."

"Oh, my God, Magnus," she said on a laugh. "I can't decide if that was incredibly brilliant or somewhat evil."

"What was evil about it?" he asked, looking offended. "I did save his life. I earned that land. Certainly more than if I had just controlled Henry and made him give me the land and title of baron. And if I had not been there, the assassin probably would have succeeded. Everyone liked the man. No one suspected him of a thing. Even me until I read his thoughts."

"All right, it wasn't evil. Just a brilliant use of the situation," Allie decided.

Magnus grunted, but still looked out of sorts about the evil bit. In fact, he reminded her of Liam when the boy got sulky.

Biting her lip to keep from laughing, she quickly put the remaining food back on the tray, set it on the dresser, and then climbed back on the bed and crawled to sit sideways in his lap.

"So," she said, smiling at his startled expression as she snaked one hand around his waist and allowed the other to play over his chest. "You're a baron with his own castle."

"That turns you on, does it?" he murmured, running a hand up her outer leg.

Allie shook her head. "Your cleverness does. Castles are drafty old buildings. Besides, it's probably a pile of rubble now."

"Our castle is not a pile of rubble," he assured her as his hand drifted up under his shirt to skim its way up her side.

Allie pulled back to peer at him with surprise. "Our castle?"

"We are life mates," he said solemnly. "What's mine is yours . . . Baroness," he added with a grin.

She stared at him for a moment, enthralled at the

idea of having a title, but then frowned and said, "But I have nothing to offer you in return."

His hand had just reached the underside of her breast, but he withdrew it now to clasp her cheek and assured her, "You have everything. You *are* everything. You and Liam are far more valuable than the pile of rocks that make our castle. With the two of you there it will finally be a home. Anywhere we live will be a home with the two of you in it, and that is something I have yearned for, for more than a thousand years."

"Home," Allie whispered, surprised to find her eyes growing moist. But his words had touched her, and what he offered sounded so lovely. Home. She'd left her childhood home beaten and broken, had bought a town house, but it had never really felt like home. Although it had got close with Stella and Liam there to fill it with laughter and caring. But then Stella had died and she'd been forced to flee to save Liam.

Allie had spent the last four years dragging Liam from one temporary hidey-hole to another, always running, desperate to evade Abaddon. Now Magnus was offering her a home again. Himself. Because home wasn't a pile of bricks or boulders, it was the people in it, and she was beginning to believe this marriage had not been a mistake. That she could make a home and a life with Magnus. One she wouldn't have to flee.

Magnus kissed her nose, drawing her attention from her thoughts. Once she met his gaze, he smiled softly and said, "I know you do not love me. I know you agreed to be my life mate to keep Liam. But I want you to know that I love you. No," he said firmly when she started to protest. "You no doubt think that is impossible, that it is too soon. But I know you, Allie. I know your whole life. I love you for your rebelliousness in making friends you weren't supposed to, the strength you showed when, rather than crumble under the loss of your sister and mother, you walked away from the only home you had ever known. The determination you showed in getting through school and starting your own business. The kindness and friendship you offered to a lonely frightened woman despite the fact that she was what you thought of as a vampire. The love and courage you displayed keeping her child safe these last four years and taking him into your heart as your own son."

Brushing away the single tear that slid from her eye, he added, "And I love you for your passion, and your sass, and your sense of humor. I feel happy when I am with you."

Allie stared at him, her own thoughts in a jumble as she realized that she felt happy when with him too. She'd felt comfortable and safe with him from the start, but now she realized that she hadn't been afraid since meeting him. Not really. She'd felt anxiety when she'd learned the immortals were in town, but not the outright terror she'd previously experienced on spotting someone with eyes that reflected light. There was a lot she liked and admired about Magnus—his cleverness, his kindness and care with Liam, the thoughtfulness he'd displayed repeatedly since they'd met . . . and she certainly enjoyed his passion too. The man could make her toes curl with a look. Was it possible she was falling in love with him too? She suspected she was.

Cool air brushing across her breasts drew her back from her thoughts to see that Magnus had undone the buttons of his shirt and opened it to free her breasts to his attention. Even now his head was lowering to claim one quickly hardening nipple.

Allie didn't stop him. She wanted the distraction from thoughts that were almost more frightening to her than Abaddon was. Because love could kill you as surely as Abaddon would, but Abaddon could only take your life—love could destroy your soul.

Magnus's lips latched on to her nipple then, his tongue rasping the sensitive tip, and Allie gasped with pleasure and relief as her thoughts scattered. This was what she needed. He always seemed to know what she needed. But maybe it was time she showed him some cherishing, Allie thought, and suddenly tangled her fingers in his hair and pulled his head away.

When Magnus raised his head, surprise and question on his face, she pushed him back on the bed. Shifting to straddle his groin, Allie smiled at his startled expression and reached to undo the dress pants he still wore, saying, "My turn."

Seventeen

Allie woke up to find the bed beside her empty, but the smell of coffee redolent in the air. Confused, she looked across the bed at the bedside table. When she didn't spot a coffee there, she turned to examine the one on her side of the bed, but her gaze halted on Magnus standing by the window. His hair was wet, there was a towel wrapped around his waist, and he held a coffee in hand as he gazed down at the yard. Allie remained still for a moment, staring at him. He was a beautiful man, she thought as she watched shadows dance over his back and arm, and then she realized it was shadows cast by firelight and glanced to the fireplace, surprised to see the flames flickering there.

"The room was a bit chilly, so I built a fire."

Her eyes shifted back to Magnus to see he was glancing over his shoulder at her.

"I also brought you a coffee if you want it," he added, and then turned to rest his behind on the window ledge and just looked at her with a small smile playing about his lips.

"Why are you looking at me like that?" she asked, shifting to sit up in bed and reaching for the coffee cup on her bedside table.

"Because I like looking at you," he responded at once, and then added, "And because I cannot believe I am lucky enough to have you for a life mate and wife."

Allie stilled, her heart going all mushy in her chest, but she ignored it and said, "How do you know you're lucky? Maybe I'll be a terrible wife."

He shook his head. "If you show me half the care and concern you have given Liam, you will be the most amazing wife," he assured her solemnly.

That made her shift guiltily. She hadn't left this room or seen her son since before the turn. She hadn't even thought of him until Magnus brought him up. How many days had it been? she worried. And what must he be thinking? She was a terrible mother, Allie thought unhappily.

"He is sleeping," Magnus said gently. "The children slept up in Stephanie's room."

Allie bit her lip uncertainly. "How long has it been since we came upstairs for the turn?"

He checked the bedside clock and she followed his gaze to see that it read 6:45 A.M. "Just short of fourteen hours."

"What?" she asked with disbelief.

"We left the restaurant just after four thirty," he reminded her.

Allie nodded. They'd got to the courthouse at three in the afternoon, were married and leaving by a quarter to four, and had gone to Bella Black's for an early, celebratory dinner. That had been at Allie and Magnus's suggestion. They'd known Elvi and Mabel were insisting on closing the restaurant to other customers during the celebration, and had hoped it would be over and done in time for the restaurant to open to regular customers by five thirty or six to handle the dinner crowd. She wondered now if they'd opened it up to others after they'd left, or had kept it closed to avoid the possibility of Abaddon and his crew going in and causing trouble.

"And we started the turn just after five P.M.," Magnus continued. "Now it is nearly seven in the morning."

"I thought days had passed," she admitted. "I didn't realize the turn had gone so quickly."

"It was nearly two A.M. when I woke up and you were in the shower," he said quietly. "That is relatively quick for a turn, but as I said, it is still going on."

Allie nodded solemnly. "I guess we must not have slept as long as I'd thought between . . ." Flushing, she said, "When we passed out, I mean."

A slow smile curved his lips and he straightened and crossed to the bed. Taking her coffee cup, he set it, along with his own, on the bedside table and then bent toward her. "We did not sleep long between . . ." he murmured, and then pressed a kiss to her lips. "The kids probably will not wake up for another half an hour or better." He kissed her again. "More like an hour." His hand found her breast and began to caress her through the sheet she'd pulled with her as she sat up. "I think we could manage another short nap before they wake up."

"A nap sounds nice," she said breathlessly, letting the sheet drop as her body responded to his touch.

His other hand immediately slid beneath it to glide down between her legs and he stilled briefly. When she opened her eyes, he was smiling and said, "You are already wet for me."

"It happened the minute you got that naughty smile and started toward the bed," she admitted huskily.

"I like that," Magnus whispered against her lips, and then kissed her properly, his tongue sweeping out to invade her mouth, and his lips demanding. The minute she moaned, he urged her to lie back on the bed and started to come down on her, only to freeze and jerk the sheet back up to cover her when the door burst open.

"Mom, I'm hungry. Can we have pancakes for breakfast?" Liam asked, rushing into the room in a pair of the new pajamas Magnus had bought for him. These ones had dinosaurs on them.

Allie stared at the boy blankly, her brain slow to switch gears, and it was Magnus who answered.

"If Elvi has the fixings and it is okay with her I could probably manage pancakes."

Allie swung her gaze back to him with surprise. "You cook?"

"No," he admitted with a shrug. "But I am sure I can figure it out."

"Yeah, right," she said on a laugh. She was definitely cooking, Allie decided, and turned back to Liam, pausing briefly when she spotted Teddy Jr., Sunny, and Gracie peeking into the room from the hall. She smiled at them briefly, but then said, "Okay, Liam, go get dressed and I'll find some clothes and get dressed too, then we'll go downstairs and make pancakes."

"I don't know where my clothes are," Liam said at once.

"They are up in the room you slept in," Magnus told him. "The Walmart bags in the corner of Stephanie's room. Find something to wear and then bring the bags down here. Your mother's clothes are in the bags too."

"Okay." Liam spun away and rushed out of the room.

"Mabel did not know which bags held his clothes and which held yours and did not want to poke through them so took them all up," Magnus explained as the door closed.

"Oh." Allie nodded and then blinked as her eyes landed on the towel around his waist and she noted that it was presently imitating a tent.

"Do you think he noticed?" Magnus asked dryly, peering down at himself.

Allie burst out laughing at the question, and slid out of bed to head for the bathroom. "I'm sure he did. He rarely misses anything. I'm just surprised he didn't ask you about it." Pausing at the bathroom door, she turned back and warned, "But prepare yourself, because he'll probably ask you later, and no doubt when it will be most embarrassing. Like at the breakfast table when everyone's there."

She heard Magnus groan as she closed the bathroom door and grinned as she turned on the shower. By her guess, she had just enough time for a quick shower before Liam returned. It was going to be a cold one.

"**W**here is everybody?"

Allie looked up from the crossword puzzle she was doing at that question, and smiled at Tricia as the blonde closed the kitchen door and bent to remove her boots. "Well, let's see. Stephanie, Victor, and DJ are sleeping. They stood guard all last night, so headed to bed as soon as Tybo, Drina, and Harper got up to relieve them. Mabel and Elvi went to Mabel's house to get a few things for dinner tonight. Tybo stepped out just a minute ago to check on something and said he'd be right back. The kids are in the rec room downstairs playing hoot owl, and Magnus went shopping."

Tricia's eyebrows rose at this news. "Shopping for what?"

"I don't know. He wouldn't tell me," she said with a shrug. "He just kept smiling and saying you will see."

"Oh. I see," Tricia said with a knowing smile as she shrugged out of her coat.

Allie narrowed her eyes. "What are you thinking? Sex toys?"

A laugh burst from Tricia and she shook her head. "Why, Allie, who knew you had such a dirty mind?"

"You did," Allie said dryly as the blonde walked

over and dropped into a seat at the table. "Or you should. You've been reading my mind since we met."

"I don't remember reading any dirty thoughts before you turned," Tricia assured her with amusement. "But I can read that you're just teasing me now."

"Yeah," Allie sighed. "I was never really interested in sex before Magnus. Now I'm a raving horndog. Is that the nanos? And how long does it last?" she asked with frustration.

Tricia and Drina had said to ask them if she had questions, and she had questions. Mostly how long this torture was going to persist. All Magnus had to do was smile at her and her nipples got hard. The brush of his arm against hers made her shiver and get wet, and a kiss, even a light peck on the forehead or cheek, was enough to make her want to drag him upstairs and jump his bones. Allie knew this because the man had driven her crazy all morning before going out shopping. He'd helped her make pancakes this morning and she'd discovered the kitchen was much smaller than it seemed. They'd constantly been bumping into each other, and when they weren't, he was touching her. Innocent little touches—the sweep of his fingers down her arm, his hand at her back, brushing against her as he reached for something. She'd been in a constant state of arousal since coming downstairs, and it hadn't left when he had. She'd been sitting here pretending to do a crossword puzzle, but her mind was not on it. It was wondering how long Magnus would be, and if they could sneak upstairs for a quickie when he did return. Although quickies weren't really quick when you had to factor in the fainting spell that followed.

"Yeah, it's tough," Tricia said with a grin.

"Your sympathy is underwhelming," Allie said dryly, and another laugh slipped from the blonde.

"I'm sorry. I *am* sympathetic," she assured her. "I remember how overwhelming it was at first. But you'll adjust."

"I'll adjust?" Allie asked slowly, and then squawked, "You mean this doesn't go away?"

Tricia shook her head, her smile turning wry. "Not as far as I can tell. You just learn to deal with it better . . . or multitask."

"Multitask?" she asked with disbelief. "What can you possibly do while— I mean, you pass out at the end."

"Yeah. That can be a problem," Tricia admitted. "I was once sewing a badge on my uniform when Teddy started to . . ." Pausing, she apparently decided that was sharing just a bit much and simply said, "Anyway, I only had two stitches left, so I announced that I was going to finish while riding him." She shook her head. "Should have just put it down. Only managed one stitch and it was crooked anyway and had to be redone. Plus, when I woke up after, it was to find the needle sticking out of his eye. I'd impaled him when I passed out. Nasty," she said, shaking her head. "Fortunately, he was still unconscious. I pulled it out and he was all healed by the time he woke up. Didn't know a thing."

"Oh, my God," Allie breathed with horror, and then shook her head. "Why would you try to keep sewing?"

"Well, it was my uniform," she said as if that should

mean something, and when Allie stared at her dumbly added, "My first shift on the Port Henry police force was just two hours away. My uniform was only delivered that morning, and I had to sew the badges on before I showed up for my shift. It's not my fault Teddy decided he wanted to celebrate my first day that way."

"Yeah, but . . ." Allie shook her head helplessly. "I would never—"

"Yes, you will," Tricia assured her cheerfully. "Maybe not that, but something else. I hear Sam and Mortimer ended up trying to do it while he was driving on the highway."

"No!" Allie gasped, eyes wide.

Katricia nodded. "I guess they damned near had an accident before Mortimer pulled over . . . apparently just seconds before they passed out," she added dryly, and then shrugged. "But that shows you how little sense we all have when it comes to life mates."

Allie just stared at her with a sort of horror.

"So." Tricia clasped Allie's left hand and lifted it off the table to examine as she changed the subject. "Look at this, a married woman without a ring on her finger."

Allie peered at her bare hand and smiled wryly. "Magnus put his signet ring on me for the ceremony, but it was much too big. I gave it back to him as we left the courthouse rather than risk losing it."

"Hmm." Tricia nodded and then pursed her lips and arched her eyebrows. "Now I wonder what Magnus could be shopping for?"

Allie's eyes widened. "He went for a ring?"

"I don't know," Tricia admitted, releasing her hand. "But that would be my guess. It really bothered him that he didn't have a proper ring to give to you."

"He said that?"

"No, honey. He thought it. He's easily read right now," she explained. "It's a symptom of meeting a life mate. Even old immortals are easily read then."

"Oh," Allie murmured, peering down at her bare hand again.

"You said the kids were in the basement?" Tricia asked.

Allie nodded. "Playing the owl game."

"Well, it's good they're getting some use out of the rec room Victor insisted on putting down there," Tricia said with amusement.

"It wasn't always there?" Allie asked with surprise.

"No. The basement was concrete walls and floor before. Victor had it finished to give the kids a place to play, but they usually stay upstairs," she said, and then stood up. "I think I'll just pop down and say hi to my son. I'll be back in a minute."

"Okay." Allie smiled after her.

It seemed to her that the basement door had barely closed when Drina called, "Tricia? Is that you I hear down there?"

Rising, Allie moved out to the entry to look up at the woman standing at the top of the stairs. "She just went downstairs. She'll be right back. Is there something you need that I can get for you?"

"No. The postman is coming through the gate with a package and I was hoping she could sign for it so I don't have to leave my post," Drina explained, shifting on the spot with indecision.

"You go on and get back to your post. I can get the door," Allie assured her, and turned to walk toward it.

"No, no, no," Drina cried, rushing down the stairs as Allie reached the entry and peered out. The mailman was just closing the gate, his back to the house, when she looked out, but she could see his mail bag and the large box he was carrying. Turning to walk slowly up the sidewalk, he dug through his bag, eventually pulling out a sheaf of multicolored papers.

"Someone's got a big package coming," Allie commented as Drina reached her side.

The woman glanced out at the mailman and nodded, but then said, "Go wait in the kitchen."

Allie's eyebrows rose at the order. "Why? It's just the mailman."

"Yeah, but I don't want you by the door when I open it. Go on. The kitchen." She waved her hand in a shooing motion and Allie grimaced, but moved away.

"Fine. I'll go make coffee," she announced, starting into the dining room, but then paused and turned to look back as she heard the front door open and the rumble of a deep voice.

"Sure. I thought you guys had digital things to sign nowadays," she heard Drina say with amusement as she turned her back to the man and placed the stack of multicolored papers on the open door to have a flat surface to sign on.

Allie's gaze shifted to the mailman then and her eyes widened slightly. He looked familiar. She was trying to sort out where she'd seen him before when three things happened in quick succession. She heard a door open behind her, felt a cold draft, and heard the murmur of Mabel's and Elvi's voices as they apparently returned, a second door opened and she heard Tricia call a greeting, and then movement drew Allie's attention down to the box the mailman held and she saw that it was open and he was pulling a machete out of it.

"Drina!" she shouted in warning as he swung the machete back. She rushed forward as he started to bring it down.

"I'd just pulled out the machete when the human screamed a warning. The vampire bitch turned and saw it coming at her. She tried to duck, but I still clipped her a good one in the head."

Allie could hear the speaker, but she couldn't see anything. She was lying on a cold, damp floor on her stomach, her head turned to the side with her eyes closed and no desire to open them. Her head was pounding as if she was the one who had taken the machete to the head. In fact, Allie wasn't sure she hadn't. The last thing she remembered was running to Drina and then pain exploding in her head. Now there was blood dripping down her face, and terrible pain radiating from the back of her skull. If he hadn't hacked her in the head like he had Drina, then the man had thumped her with the handle of it hard enough to do some serious damage.

"Just a head wound?" another voice asked, this one closer to her. Standing over her, she guessed, and at first thought he was talking to her. But then the other man answered.

"Yes. I was going to cut her head off, but once the human screamed there was no chance of that happening. The bitch'll be out of commission for a while, though."

"Yes, yes. Good. But how did you end up bringing Allie instead of the boy, Stephen? It is your son we want."

Stephen. Stella's husband, Allie thought, and realized suddenly why he'd looked familiar to her when she'd first seen him there in the door. She'd looked at the picture in the locket often enough since Stella died that she was sure she would have recognized him at once if he hadn't been dressed in the mailman gear. That had thrown her off.

"Well," Stephen said, "she rushed over to try to help the vamp bitch. But her scream had raised the alarm. People were coming from every direction. There was no chance of looking for Liam, so I knocked her out, threw her over my shoulder, and ran. I thought maybe we could trade her for Liam."

"Ah. Yes. Clever," the second man complimented. "Fast thinking too."

"You think they'd trade my son for her, Abby? She's just a human."

Abby, Allie thought grimly. So she was in the presence of not just Liam's father, but of the man who had turned Stella so violently and made her into a monster.

If only temporarily. Apparently, her husband hadn't been so lucky and was still in crazy town.

"Allie *was* human," Abaddon corrected. "But not anymore. She's been turned."

"Has she?" Stephen sounded truly surprised. "I didn't notice."

"Well, she has. Which means she is a life mate to someone in that house, which makes her *very* important. I have no doubt they will trade Liam for her. After all, he is not related to any of them."

"So I did the right thing?"

"Yes. You certainly did. Come now, we shall plot how to arrange a trade."

Allie heard their footsteps move away. She listened until she couldn't hear them anymore before risking taking more than the shallow breaths she'd allowed herself until now. But she didn't move. She wasn't sure she could. God, her head hurt. Shouldn't the nanos be fixing that?

Forcing herself to calm down, she concentrated on her breaths rather than the pain. Or tried to. Unfortunately, her mind was turning to what Abaddon had said about the others being willing to trade Liam for her.

"No." The word slid out in a soft whisper of denial. Surely Magnus wouldn't trade Liam to get her back? Hand her son over to these madmen and let them twist him into another Leonius? She didn't want that. And Stella certainly hadn't. She'd killed herself to prevent that happening. And Allie would too, without a single regret.

Well, that wasn't completely true. She already had

a regret. Allie wished that when Magnus had told her he loved her, she'd done more than sit there staring at him with fear rolling through her. She wished she'd had the courage to admit that she thought she might be falling in love with him too. She could have given him that at least. But she hadn't realized that she might not get the chance later. She supposed that meant she'd learned another of life's lessons today. Always tell people how you feel about them. Don't withhold it out of fear. You never knew if you'd get another chance.

Well, this was bullshit, Allie thought suddenly. She would get the chance. She wasn't dying here, and she wasn't lying around waiting for them to try to get Magnus to give them Liam in exchange for her. She wasn't chained down and her captors had left her alone. She was getting up and getting out of here.

"Now," Allie muttered aloud when her body didn't immediately start moving. Clenching her teeth, she shifted first one hand and then the other closer to her body, and then started to push herself upward. She managed to lift her upper body perhaps an inch off the ground before the pain in her head increased from agony to shattering.

Allie wasn't conscious when she hit the floor again.

Magnus was whistling happily to himself, his gaze repeatedly sliding to the pale blue jeweler's bag with the bow tied to the handle on the passenger seat. He was pretty pleased with himself. He'd got exactly what he'd envisioned when he'd set out to find Allie's rings, both an engagement ring and a wedding band. Of course, he'd had to drive into London to find it, and it might not be the right size. But the salesman had assured him they could alter the size to fit later.

Now he just had to hope Allie liked it, Magnus thought, and felt a flutter of anxiety push in to join the pleased feeling. He wanted her to like it and she'd seemed to like the clothes he'd chosen her, so he hoped their taste in rings would match up too, but jewelry could be such a personal thing. Maybe he should have waited until he could have taken her with him.

"She will like it," he reassured himself, but was still oddly nervous about presenting it to her. Maybe he should do something special. Take her to dinner, or—

His thoughts fled as he approached Casey Cottage and saw Teddy's SUV in the driveway. The lights were flashing and the door was wide open. Hands clenching on the steering wheel, Magnus hit the gas, sending Mabel's car shooting the last twenty feet up the street and squealing into the driveway. He was out of the car the minute it stopped, rushing inside, leaving the door open as Teddy had, the pale blue bag forgotten on the passenger seat.

Eighteen

The main floor of the house appeared empty when Magnus rushed in, but he could hear the murmur of voices from upstairs. Hurrying around the kitchen counter, he headed for the stairs, his feet stumbling to a halt when he spotted the blood splattered on the front door and the pool of it on the entry floor.

Desperate to find Allie and assure himself she was all right, Magnus turned and ran up the steps. The door to Allie's room was wide open, showing that it was empty. His footsteps slowed a bit as relief coursed through him. She hadn't been hurt, then. It was someone else, he thought, and then a surly voice barked, "She saved my life, Harper. If she hadn't screamed out that warning I wouldn't have my head. We have to get her back."

"I know, honey. And we will. But you have to let them give you more blood so you'll heal. You took a terrible wound." Harper's voice drifted down the hall to him, sounding as anxious and upset as Magnus had been feeling just moments ago. Turning that way, he headed down the hall to see what he could do to help . . . and get a look at Allie. He'd feel better once he could actually see her and know for sure that she hadn't been injured.

"No. We have to go look for her. I'm an Enforcer. I have to find her. She saved my life."

"Honey, I'll go look for her. I promise. But you have to stay here and let them give you more blood."

"No. She saved my life. I have to—"

"No, she didn't, Drina honey," Mabel said now, obviously trying to help calm her. "She maybe saved you getting a more serious wound, but immortals can survive a beheading if the head is replaced quickly enough. You know that. So just take your blood and leave finding her to the men. You need to—"

"Not always. Sometimes it doesn't work," Drina muttered, and then, voice rising to a shout, she told them, "It wouldn't have worked on me!" and then almost in a whimper, "I need to find her, Harper. She saved my life."

Magnus reached the doorway as she said that, and stared at Drina with shock. The woman was seated on the side of the bed, hunched over, holding her head and rocking slightly. If he hadn't recognized her voice, he wouldn't know who she was by looking at her. Drina was covered with blood from the gaping wound on her head, almost to her waist, and the deep red stain was spreading even as he watched.

"I'll go look for her. But you have to let them give you more blood, Drina," Harper said pleadingly. When she shook her head and tried to stand, he grasped her shoulders and held her down, but finally lost it and barked, "Jesus, woman! There's a gaping wound in your head. Stop being so bloody stubborn and let them give you blood."

Drina raised her head, her eyes a mix of silver and bloodred. He suspected she was about to argue again, but then she spotted him and, instead, moaned, "Magnus."

The room went silent as all eyes turned to him, and Magnus asked with concern, "What the hell happened?"

"The mailman took her. I'm sorry," Drina moaned. "I told her to go in the kitchen. But she saved my life and he took her."

"Took who?" Magnus asked, fear creeping up his back as he glanced around at the pitying looks he was getting from the people in the room. "Where's Allison?"

"The mailman took Allie," Elvi said quietly, moving to his side. "I'm sorry. We tried to stop him, but he slid the machete through the handles of the double front doors and we couldn't get out that way. By the time we ran out the back door and around, they were gone."

"What?" he asked with confusion and disbelief. "Why would the mailman take her?"

"Actually, it wasn't the mailman," Tybo explained. "He's dead in a van down the street. We think it was

Abaddon or one of his men wearing the dead mail-man's uniform. He came to the door with the mailbag and box. He looked like a mailman. Drina went to sign for the package and . . ." His gaze slid to Drina. "It sounds like he was going to cut off her head, but Allie shouted a warning and Drina ducked."

Magnus's eyes shifted back to the gaping wound on Drina's head. It was a bad wound, but would heal.

"Unfortunately," Tybo continued, "aside from shout-ing, Allie rushed forward, we think to help Drina, but he hit her over the head with the butt of the machete, tossed her over his shoulder, and fled."

"But he stuck the machete through the door handles so you could not follow," Magnus muttered what Elvi had said.

Everyone in the room nodded and Magnus stared at them with bewilderment, and then burst out furiously, "Well, why the hell are you all standing here, then? We need to be out looking for her."

"We were going to do that, but have no idea where to start," Victor said quietly. "He could have taken her next door, or all the way to London. We don't have the manpower to search that big an area door to door."

"Well, we cannot just stand here doing nothing," he growled with outrage.

"Lucian is on the way right now with Basha and Marcus," Victor told him. "He thinks she can narrow the search. And we expect Abaddon to call soon too. It's not Allie he wants. It's Liam."

"We think he'll call offering to make a trade," Tybo explained. "Liam for Allie."

"Yes. He will do that," Magnus breathed, feeling a little hope creep in to join the fear clutching at his chest. Abaddon wouldn't kill Allie. He'd try to use her for a trade.

"In the meantime, we're trying to get Drina to take blood so she can heal," Elvi put in now. "But she's determined to go find Allie and won't let us give her blood."

Magnus frowned and glanced to the woman. "Chain her down and make her take the blood."

"We're not chaining her down," Harper growled. "We just need to talk some sense into her. She—"

"You cannot reason with her, Harper—she's in shock, and probably has brain damage to boot," Magnus snapped impatiently. "And if you do not chain her down, eventually she is going to try to get up again, fall over, and you are going to be scraping her brain off the floor and trying to put it back in her head. So chain her down, put an IV in her, start pouring blood down her throat as well, and open another bag to pour over the wound. She needs all the blood she can get and quickly or she is going to lose that baby she is carrying."

Paling, Harper turned back to the bed and barked, "Where are the chains?"

"I'll get them," Victor said, slipping from the room.

Knowing they were kept in the linen closet in the hall, Magnus wasn't surprised when the man was back quickly. Victor handed one length of chain to Harper, but gave Magnus and DJ each one too, then took the other and they moved out around the bed.

Drina didn't lie down nicely for them to chain her. She fought like a wildcat, screaming that she had to find Allie the whole while. Magnus was right there with her. He wanted to be out looking for her too, and was fighting himself not to flee the house and jump in the car to do it. The only thing that kept him there was the hope that Basha really might be able to narrow down the search, and the possibility that Abaddon would call and possibly say something to give away his whereabouts. It was hard, though.

The moment they got Drina in chains, the women rushed forward, Katricia setting up an IV, Mabel popping a blood bag to Drina's open, screaming mouth, and Elvi kneeling at the top of the bed, slowly pouring the contents of another bag over Drina's head wound.

"How did you know?" Harper asked, concern clouding his face as he watched the women work.

"Because she said Allie saved her life, and she would have died if he had cut off her head," Magnus said grimly. "I only know of a couple of cases where an immortal was beheaded and did not heal when the head was replaced quickly, and both of them were women who were pregnant."

"Why would that make a difference?" Elvi asked, glancing up briefly from what she was doing.

When Magnus sighed wearily, and ran a hand through his hair, it was Katricia who explained. "The Argeneau scientists aren't positive, but they think when the mothers were beheaded, the nanos automatically turned to the baby as a viable replacement host and moved into it to try to keep it alive."

"Abandoning the mother," Elvi murmured.

"Like rats from a sinking ship," Mabel said with disgust.

"Drina didn't tell me she was pregnant," Katricia said now with a frown.

"I didn't know either," Elvi admitted.

"She didn't want anyone knowing until we got past the fourth month," Harper said quietly. "She wanted to be sure she wouldn't lose the baby."

"Will she lose it?" Mabel asked.

No one had an answer.

Finished with the IV, Katricia stepped back, peered down at Drina, and commented, "Allie really did save her life, then."

"Most likely," Magnus agreed, and thought now he just had to save hers.

Allie woke abruptly and opened her eyes before she stopped to think. It didn't increase her pain much, but then she was already hurting pretty good. Not as bad as the last time she'd woken, though, and supposed she had Abaddon to thank for that. The bastard had forced blood on her the last time she'd regained consciousness. Knowing it wouldn't be bagged blood, she'd tried to refuse, but he'd simply forced her mouth open and poured mug after mug of the tinny liquid down her throat. It had still been warm.

Not wanting to think about that or where the blood had probably come from, Allie lay still for a moment, waiting to see if the pain in her head would increase. It didn't, and remained a constant, dull throb that was at least bearable. Actually, it had eased enough that she was now aware of other aches and pains. Her back and hip, for instance, Allie noted, and shifted to her side, drawing her legs up almost into a fetal position in an effort to ease her discomfort.

"There you are." Abaddon's cheerful voice was not what she'd hoped to wake up to, but there it was, coming from somewhere behind her but moving closer. "When you stopped screaming I knew you would wake soon."

Allie didn't comment. She simply waited.

"Now that you are awake again and feeling a bit better, we really need to speak."

He could speak all he wanted. It didn't mean she had to answer, Allie thought grimly.

"First, I should thank you for raising the boy for us."

That made her stiffen. She hadn't raised Liam for these two monsters.

"I fear I am not good with babies," Abaddon continued in a chatty voice. "But then, really, all they do is cry, scream, shit, and stink up the place. It bewilders me why so many mortals and immortals are enthralled with them."

The screech of what sounded like metal on concrete accompanied the appearance of a chair in front of her. Allie ground her teeth against the brief increase of pain in her head that the sound caused and raised her eyes to look at her tormentor as he settled himself in the chair.

Abaddon was just as Stella described. He looked utterly average. An accountant in a jogging suit, she thought grimly, and then glanced to the man who appeared behind him. Stella's husband, Stephen, looked a lot like his photo, and at the same time, nothing like it at all. It was the same face, the dark hair cut in the same preppy style, but the eyes were different. In the photo, his eyes had almost sparkled with happiness, now they were bleak and empty. Of course, his clothes were different too; instead of the wedding tuxedo, he was wearing the mailman's uniform, but while it had been clean when he'd come to the door of Casey Cottage, now there were several bloodstains adorning it.

Stella would weep to see him like this, Allie thought, and shifted her attention back to Abaddon. They stared at each other silently for a moment, and then she asked, "If you dislike children so much why did you tell Stella how to keep from losing her baby?"

"You misunderstand. While I dislike babies, I do like children," he assured her, and then turned to Stephen. "Help her sit up, my love. I will get a crick in my neck staring down at her like this."

Allie started to try to sit up herself to avoid his touching her, but she'd barely shifted her hands to push herself up when Stephen was at her side. Grabbing her by the upper arm, he raised her to a sitting position, and then dragged her back several feet until she felt the wall at her back. Releasing her then, Stephen returned to his position a little behind and to the side of Abaddon.

Like a good little slave, Allie thought bitterly as she struggled with the pain the movement had raised in her head. Much to her surprise, Abaddon didn't start talking at once, but waited until the worst of the pain had left her and she released a little sigh.

"As I was saying, I do like children," he assured her. "They are so eager to please . . . and easily molded too. That is the best part about them."

"Right," Allie said wearily. "So you told Stella about the baby, let her escape, and . . . ?"

"Kept an eye on her, and gave her a little scare once in a while to send her scurrying."

"Why?" she asked at once.

"Because it entertained me," he said with amusement. "Watching her run, thinking she could escape me . . ."

"But she couldn't because you had put a tracking device in her necklace," Allie said grimly, and then shifted her gaze to Stephen. "Or was that you?"

Stephen scowled at her irritably, but didn't bother responding.

Allie shifted her attention back to Abaddon. "So you always planned to reclaim Liam?"

"Yes."

"In the meantime, you had your men pop up once in a while to scare her into running again."

Abaddon nodded, a small smile playing about his lips. "Which they continued to do with you after she killed herself."

Allie stared at him, thinking of how useless Stella's sacrifice had been, and then thinking of herself and all the money she'd wasted running, all the fear and anxiety she'd experienced . . . because he'd wanted to what? Fuck with her head? See her run? It made anger writhe inside of her like snakes in a basket. It made her want to hurt him back, and she said, "Lucian set up a trap and caught your men. They're all dead."

"That was expected," he said with a shrug of indifference. "They were just pawns. Sacrificed so that the security at the house would ease and give us a chance to snatch Liam away."

"Which failed," she pointed out, and saw irritation flicker over Abaddon's face. When he didn't say anything, she asked, "How did you know Liam and I were still at the house when the tracker left?"

"Stephen and I happened to be looking through the garage window when Dani and Decker got in the car. You and Liam were not with them."

"You were already at the house?" she asked with dismay.

"We tracked you to the house that very first night and had been watching it ever since," he said with a faint smile. "But the security there was too tight to take the boy. So, I had the men ride up and down Main Street while you were in the restaurant in the hopes of spooking the Argeneaus into taking you away. Whether they drove back to Toronto, or flew, they'd have to leave the house by car and the plan was to run your vehicle off the road and grab Liam. But when I saw Dani and Decker leaving and the tracker moving away on the tracking app on my phone, I knew it was a trap. I ordered the men to follow."

"And sent them to their deaths," Allie said quietly.

"They were pawns," he repeated. "Pawns are meant to be sacrificed."

"And what is Stephen?" Allie asked. "Just another pawn? I bet he doesn't even know he's an immortal, not a vampire."

"He does know. I told him everything," Abaddon assured her firmly. "I have been honest with him from the moment he agreed to be my life mate."

Allie gaped at the man, and then turned to Stephen and asked with disbelief. "Seriously? You tossed over Stella for this asshole?"

"He's my life mate," Stephen said simply.

"You were a *possible* life mate," Allie corrected. "That's what they told me. I was a possible life mate and could refuse."

"But you did not refuse, did you?" Abaddon pointed out. "Which brings me to my question. Who is your life mate?"

"Why?" Allie asked warily.

"Because your life mate is the one we will contact to arrange the trade. He is the one who will be most willing to turn Liam over to get you back."

"No, he won't," she said with certainty.

"Our kind will die for our life mates, girl. He will think nothing of turning over a child to get you back. Especially when Liam is not his child and he would be turning him over to his father, who I will explain merely wants to raise him." Abaddon nodded firmly. "And when I then tell him what will happen to you if he does not turn the boy over . . . Well . . ." He shrugged.

Allie swallowed, some of her certainty slipping away. Magnus might give up Liam to save her if he thought Liam wouldn't be harmed. He might convince himself that they could get Liam back once he had her safely away from Abaddon.

"Which one is it?" Abaddon asked now. "Tybo or Magnus?"

"Who says it is one of them?" Allie asked.

"I say, because I know the others are all mated," he growled impatiently. "Now, which one is it?"

Instead of answering, Allie asked, "Why haven't you read it from my mind? Can't you read me?"

"You were in too much pain when I tried earlier," he said with irritation, and then his eyes narrowed. "But the pain is not as bad now."

His eyes shifted to her forehead and narrowed. Knowing he was trying to read her, Allie did the only thing she could think to do. She slammed her head back into the wall. Pain burst through her skull like fireworks, shooting out to every corner of her brain, bright white and hot, then black. She wasn't conscious to hear Abaddon's curses, or feel his kick before he stormed out of the room.

Nineteen

"We'll find her. We'll get her back."

Magnus grimaced at Tybo's words as the man dropped into a chair at the dining room table with him. He was the third person who'd come to give him that reassurance in the hour since he'd left the room where Drina was being treated. He wasn't reassured.

What he was, was terrified. He couldn't lose Allie. She was . . . everything.

"Magnus?"

Lifting his head, he peered at the boy approaching the table, and had no doubt his expression was probably as blank as his thoughts at that moment. He hadn't once thought of Liam since learning Allie was missing, he realized. He was the boy's father now, but he hadn't even thought to ask where the boy was, or if he knew what was happening.

"Where's Mom?" Liam asked, pausing beside him,

a troubled expression on his face as he rotated a small toy car in his hands. "Teddy thinks the bad men got her. Did they?"

"Why would Teddy think that?" Magnus asked to stall for time to figure out how to answer.

"Because of all the screaming," he said solemnly. "And when we came to see what was happening, they sent us away, but we saw the blood. And Drina kept yelling that she had to go save Mom."

Well, that pretty much nixed his being able to offer a comforting lie, Magnus thought grimly. Sliding his chair back from the table, he scooped the boy up onto his lap, but delayed answering again by asking, "Did the other kids put you up to asking?"

"Uh-huh." Liam nodded solemnly, his gaze on the toy car he held, and then he glanced up and added, "But I wanted to know anyway."

"I imagine you did," Magnus murmured.

"She's my mom," he pointed out.

"Yes, she is."

"Did the bad men take her?"

Magnus closed his eyes briefly, and then nodded. "Yes, son. They took her."

Liam lowered his head for a moment and then looked up and said, "But you're going to get her back, right?"

"I am going to try my hardest," Magnus assured him.

Liam considered that, and then nodded and asked, "Are you my dad now?"

Magnus opened his mouth, closed it, and then said tentatively, "I should like to be, if that is okay with you?"

"Okay," he said solemnly. "But you have to get Mom back first. Families have a mom *and* a dad, and I've always wanted a family. My whole life."

"So have I," Magnus said quietly.

Nodding again, Liam slipped off his lap and headed back to the living room. Apparently, the conversation was over, Magnus thought wryly, and then glanced toward the door to the deck when it burst open to allow wind, snowflakes, and Lucian Argeneau in. He was followed quickly by his niece, Basha, and her husband, Marcus Notte.

Magnus was on his feet at once, but paused when Lucian met his gaze and raised his eyebrows in question.

"Has he made contact yet?" Lucian asked abruptly as he toed off his boots.

Magnus shook his head.

"Right." Expression grim, Lucian undid his coat as he moved around the kitchen counter, but didn't remove it. "Where the hell is everyone?"

"Victor, Teddy, Katricia, and DJ are upstairs watching the four sides of the house for anyone approaching, and Harper, Elvi, Mabel, and Stephanie are with Drina," Tybo answered at once.

"Well, get them down here," Lucian barked.

Tybo hesitated, but then said, "Shouldn't someone stay on guard? In case—"

"In case what?" Lucian asked grimly. "The horse is already out of the barn."

"But the pony is in the living room," Magnus pointed out sharply, and when Lucian looked at him blankly added, "Liam. We still need to protect him. They could come back."

"They will not come back. They think they have a bargaining chip to get him without risking a return visit," Lucian said with certainty, and then looked at Tybo. "Go on. Get everyone down here."

Tybo turned at once to rush upstairs.

Giving a grunt of satisfaction, Lucian turned back to Magnus. "You know Marcus, and have met Basha."

Magnus gave Marcus a nod of greeting, but asked Basha, "Can you really narrow down where he might have taken her?" It was his only hope now, unless they got a call.

"Maybe," she said, and turned to Marcus. The man immediately pulled a large, folded map from inside his coat and unfolded it on the table to reveal the streets of Port Henry.

Basha stepped up beside her husband and opened her mouth to speak, but Lucian forestalled her by saying, "Wait until the others get here or you will just have to repeat yourself. Magnus does not know Port Henry. We need Teddy, Elvi, or Mabel for this."

Basha nodded, but gave Magnus an apologetic look.

"Basha!" Elvi cried, rushing into the room with Victor, Mabel, and Katricia on her heels. The woman hurried to Basha to embrace her. "Thank goodness you're all right. We were worried when they couldn't get ahold of you."

"Sorry. We ran into a nest of rogues in California. My phone was destroyed and we have no idea what happened to Marcus's," Basha explained, looking somewhat uncomfortable as she hugged Elvi back. Magnus knew Marcus had been taking Basha around to meet her family members to let her get reacquainted. Marcus had told him that she was having a bit of a struggle adjusting to having family again. It showed right now. She seemed happy to see Elvi, but wasn't yet comfortable with displays of affection. She would adjust, he knew.

"Are you sure it's a good idea for all of us to be down here, Lucian?" Teddy barked as he led DJ into the room.

"Yes, I— What the hell are you doing out of bed?" Lucian interrupted himself to ask as he caught sight of Drina entering the room with Harper and Tybo.

"I am healed," Drina said, glaring at him mulishly. "Now let's get this going. We have to get Allie back."

Lucian scowled at her, but then turned to Basha and gestured for her to go ahead.

"Right." Basha returned to the table and the map of Port Henry as the group spread out around the table. "Abaddon has shown a preference for old abandoned buildings in the past."

"He still might," Magnus murmured. "Stella told Allie she was kept in an old abandoned building."

"He kept us in one too, when he tried to kill us," Marcus announced.

Basha's mouth tightened, but she said, "Obviously Abaddon prefers that kind of dwelling for some reason, and will have taken Allie someplace like that. So we need someone who can mark out all the abandoned buildings in Port Henry. We'll search those first, and move farther out if he isn't in one of them." Peering at Teddy, she said, "Lucian thought you could help with that part."

Teddy stepped up to stand across the table from her and peered over the map, then placed his finger on a spot nearly in the center. "There's an old abandoned print house here. It's been empty for decades."

"That's right downtown," Basha said, shaking her head. "He likes to make his victims scream and wouldn't want nosy neighbors."

Nodding, Teddy looked over the map again, his finger slowly moving from spot to spot, but finally, he stepped back. "There are several empty houses since the truck plant shut down, but all of them have neighbors."

"Truck plant?" Basha asked with interest.

"That's on the outskirts of town," Elvi pointed out, moving closer to the map now. "The property is huge with a parking lot that spreads out from both sides of the building. One side was for workers to park, the other for the finished vehicles. They could park hundreds of vehicles in those parking lots. No one would hear screaming coming from there."

"Yeah, but that place is a wreck," Teddy said with a frown. "They don't even bother with security to protect the building anymore. They're planning on tearing it down soon."

"Perfect," Basha said succinctly. "Any other places like that in or around Port Henry?"

When the only answer she got were shaking heads, she straightened. "Well, I don't like to put all my eggs in one basket, but I suggest we search the plant first. If we don't find anything, we'll have to go farther afield."

"You shouldn't have done that. You really pissed off Abby."

Those were the first words Allie heard as she woke up. Blinking her eyes open, she ignored her pounding head and scowled at Stephen when she saw him standing just inside the door of her prison. Not bothering to respond to his words, she glanced around the room instead, getting the lay of the land. Something she hadn't really had the chance to do earlier.

The room wasn't very big, office-sized, maybe. And it was dark, the only light coming from the lantern Stephen was holding and the bit that was creeping through the open metal double doors. The floor was a concrete slab covered with so much dirt one could have been forgiven for thinking the floor itself was dirt.

Allie finally shifted her attention back to Stephen and said, "I'm glad Stella's not alive to see what you're up to."

"I'm just trying to get my son back," Stephen snapped.

"So that Abaddon can twist his poor little mind and turn him into a monster like he is?" she asked sharply. "He's your son. Don't you care about him at all?"

"Of course I care," he said irritably. "That's why I want him. We're going to raise him together. We'll be a family."

"A family of rogues," Allie said grimly. "Abaddon *has* told you that there are laws about biting mortals, hasn't he? That you're supposed to feed off bagged blood, and if you bite mortals you're considered rogue and executed?"

Stephen looked away with a frown and muttered, "Abby's smart. They won't catch us."

"Right," Allie snorted.

They were both silent for a moment and then Stephen asked, "Why did she do it?"

Allie peered at him silently for a moment and then said, "You mean why did Stella kill herself?"

He nodded silently, unhappiness wreathing his face.

"To save Liam," she told him. "She was hoping you'd think both she and Liam died in the fire and I could raise him. Give him a normal childhood."

"He's not a normal child," Stephen said at once.

"He is," she assured him. "If you've been watching us in Port Henry you must have seen him playing outside with the other kids, building snowmen, making snow angels, tobogganing."

"I saw the tobogganing," he acknowledged reluctantly. "He seemed . . . happy."

"He *is* happy," she assured him. "He drinks bagged blood, but otherwise he's as normal as you were as a boy. He has friends, he plays, he even had a sleepover with the other kids. His life can be normal with me," she said pleadingly. "What will it be like if you and Abaddon get him?"

Stephen shook his head, his expression a combination of anger and upset. "You're asking me to choose between my son and my life mate." Meeting her gaze, he said helplessly, "I can't do that."

"You already have," Allie said wearily. "Stella sacrificed herself for Liam, but you're sacrificing Liam for Abaddon." Shaking her head, she muttered, "At least, my mother killed herself rather than make the choice. You're just going to stand by and watch Abaddon ruin your son and, of course, reap the benefits of hot life mate sex while he does."

"Shut up," Stephen snapped, his hand clenching on the lantern. "I doubt you could choose either were you in my position."

"I would never sacrifice Liam for—" Allie cut herself off at the last moment before saying Magnus's name, and then began to frown as she stared at Stephen. He was almost holding his breath in anticipation. And then she recalled the conversation she'd heard when she first woke up. The man she'd heard telling Abaddon what had happened at the house hadn't sounded anything like the tortured man in front of her now. There had been no guilt at what he'd done, just frustration that he hadn't succeeded in beheading Drina, and a certain disgust every time he'd referred to Allie as the human. As if her status as a human made her less somehow.

Stephen was playing her, Allie realized with amazement. This whole conversation was an effort to get her to reveal her life mate's name.

"So did the turn drive you insane and ruin you? Or have you always been this nasty shit underneath and managed to hide it from Stella?" she asked suddenly.

The tortured expression slipped from his face at

once, and Stephen smiled wryly. "I almost had you. You almost gave up his name."

"Yes," she agreed, but suddenly just felt tired. For a bit there Allie had hoped she might convince him to let Liam go. But that wasn't going to happen, she acknowledged, and then raised her head, unable to resist asking, "Do you even care that you drove Stella to kill herself? Did you ever love her?"

"Stella was weak," he said with disgust. "Abaddon made us immortal. Gods. But she couldn't handle it. She wanted to play house and raise babies when there is so much more out there for us now."

"Like killing and torturing mortals," she suggested grimly.

"Don't knock it until you've tried it," Stephen said with a grin.

"Thanks. I think I'll give it a miss," Allie said dryly.

"That's because you don't know what it is you're missing," he assured her. "It's one hell of a rush to hold a puny mortal's life in your hands. To listen to them plead for mercy, and let them hope you might let them live or even escape, only to rip out their throat and watch all that hope fade from their eyes along with their life." He shivered delicately and then admitted, "I like it. I like their screams and weeping, and I like their warm blood rushing over my lips and tongue." His smile widened. "Almost as much as I liked letting Stella think I still cared and that we'd have a life together someday. But I most liked watching her scamper away every time we spooked her, thinking she could get away when there was no way she could." He laughed. "God, what a rush."

"Thank God Stella never saw this side of you," Allie said solemnly, and meant it. She was quite sure that Stella would have been crushed to see how far into madness Stephen had sunk. How cruel he had become. It made her wonder if the cruelty hadn't always been there, merely hidden behind a thin veneer of humanity.

A shuffling sound caught her ear then and Allie turned toward the door as Abaddon entered the room.

"Sorry, Abby," Stephen said with a shrug. "I almost had her giving up the name. Not sure what gave me away, but . . ." He shrugged again.

"Never mind, my love. She will tell us when she is hungry enough. That, or we shall just call the house and ask for Allie's life mate," Abaddon said, and then paused, realization dawning on his face.

Stephen burst out laughing. "I didn't think of it either until you said it."

Abaddon clucked with exasperation and shook his head as he headed out of the room. "Well, better late than never. Come, we shall make the call at once."

Stephen followed with the lantern. This time he pulled the doors closed behind him, leaving her in darkness, and she heard the rattle and clatter of chains being pulled across metal. They were locking her in. Metal doors and a chain would probably work, she thought grimly.

Allie sat still for a moment, hoping her eyes would adjust to the darkness, but apparently even immortal eyes couldn't see in a complete absence of light. After a moment, she gave up and crawled to her feet. The pain in her head increased a bit with movement, but wasn't killer. She could handle it, Allie told herself, and took a deep breath before moving cautiously forward in the direction of the door with her hands outstretched. It seemed to take forever to cross the room, but eventually her hand bumped into cold metal. Allie paused and ran her hands over the door until she found the inner handles. She gave them a testing tug, not expecting the chain to snap or anything, so wasn't disappointed when nothing happened.

Releasing her breath, Allie then felt along the door to the wall on the left and followed that to the corner. Once there, she followed this new wall, walking what she thought might be several feet before stopping and beginning to tap on it.

One of the boys who had been in the foster home Allie had lived in for two years had told her a story about another foster kid named Bobby. Bobby had been a runaway artist, fleeing every foster home he was put in, only to be caught and returned or taken to a new one. Desperate to keep him from running again, one of his families had locked him in a room in the basement with no windows. But Bobby was a clever boy who wasn't going to be kept where he didn't want to be. He'd used a jackknife to cut a hole in both pieces of drywall between his room and the next, crawled through, and escaped yet again.

Allie didn't have a jackknife, but she had immortal strength. The tapping was to try to figure out, or at least make an educated guess, as to where the wall studs were. When she thought she knew where to punch without hitting one, she made a fist, pulled her hand back, and then kicked the wall instead. Allie wasn't a great fan of pain, and really she was suffering enough of it already. While her headache wasn't as bad this last time she'd woken up, the pain was now spreading out to the rest of her body. An acidy, biting pain that she suspected might be the nanos either making their need for blood known, or actively looking for it themselves in her organs.

Unsurprisingly, her foot went right through the drywall. It would have even when she was mortal. Smiling to herself with satisfaction, Allie bent and felt around for the edges of the hole, and began to tear off the drywall. She hadn't tried this on the wall to the hall because she had no idea where Stephen and Abaddon were holed up in the building, or if they had a direct view of the hallway. She didn't want to risk breaking out straight into the hall and being seen and stopped. And since Abaddon had turned right as he left the room, she'd chosen the left wall. There was less worry that way that they might hear her making her escape and come to investigate. It would also give her at least a bit of a head start if she was spotted and had to run.

Finished with the inner layer of drywall, Allie hesitated about the outer. Noise was her concern. She hadn't worried so much with the first layer because the outer layer would muffle it. That wouldn't be the case here, though. After a moment, rather than kick, she pressed her hand against the drywall and simply pressed firmly and kept pressing until the drywall cracked and her hand went through. Allie was quite sure she couldn't have done that with mortal strength, but who knew?

Working quickly and quietly, she started to peel the drywall away, pulling it into the room with her, and had soon made a hole big enough for her to climb through sideways.

Much to her relief, there was light in this room. It was coming through the open door to the hall, and there wasn't much of it, but it was enough for her immortal eyes to show her what they could do. This room was not empty; there were boxes, filing cabinets, and chairs strewn around like land mines and Allie moved slowly, careful not to hit or kick anything that would give her away. When she reached the door, she hesitated, and then eased her head forward to look to the right. What she saw was a hallway with loads of doors, several of them closed. A door at the end of the hall, though, was wide open and that was where the light was coming from. From what she could see, the room was full of candles and lanterns. It was actually kind of romantic-looking. But she didn't see Abaddon or Stephen.

Biting her lip, Allie glanced the other way, and immediately spotted a door with a sign that hung at an odd angle. It had a squiggly line on it meant to represent stairs, and was only halfway down the hall from where she was. But it was a long hall, and the distance she had to cross seemed miles when Stephen or Abaddon might come out in the hall, or just look out at any moment.

"Right. Courage, Allie," she whispered to herself. She took one more look to the right to be sure it was safe to go, and then moved quickly out of the room and along the hall. She was nearly to the door when she heard Stephen shout in warning behind her. Allie didn't even look around; she simply burst into a run, charging the stairwell door at speed. She'd forgotten that she had more strength and speed now, but was reminded of it when she crashed through the door so hard and fast that the door hit the wall with a loud crash that seemed to echo through the building. Allie took the stairs so fast she was amazed she didn't trip and fall, but when she reached the next level and spotted the door, she crashed through that one as well and found herself in a small area with a closed door on her right and an open arch on her left. Spying a long, large room with nothing but columns and broken windows, Allie instinctively swung left and charged in.

"Did you hear that?" Tybo asked in a hushed voice.

"Yes," Magnus growled, his gaze sliding over the far end of the room where the muffled crash had seemed to come from. They were searching the abandoned factory. Elvi, Mabel, and Stephanie had stayed behind at Casey Cottage to guard the children, but everyone else had come. They'd parked their vehicles in the driveway of a farmhouse across the highway and approached on foot to avoid their arrival being detected. Once at the building, they'd split up into groups of two or three and spread out to start their search. Magnus and Tybo had teamed up and gone left, moving quickly through huge cavernous rooms with nothing but large columns with peeling paint, some yellow, some green.

"It came from that direction," Tybo said, gesturing to an arch at the end of the room. "Maybe from the next room."

Magnus nodded and started forward, wishing he'd brought his sword with him from England, but he hadn't expected to need it on a trip to romance a possible life mate. Fortunately, Lucian had brought a selection of weapons with him from Toronto, and Magnus had found a short sword among the collection that he liked. He pulled it out of its scabbard now. There had been a kill order out on Abaddon for a long time. Magnus knew Basha was eager to carry it out as repayment for the centuries of torment she'd suffered at the rogue's hands. If Allie was well, Magnus would be happy to stand back and let Basha take the man's head. But if Abaddon had harmed a hair on Allie's head . . . all bets were off.

He and Tybo hadn't crossed a third of the distance to the end of this room when a second crash sounded. This one wasn't muffled, though. It was loud and still echoing through the building when a figure came shooting from the open arch at the end of the room, running at immortal speed.

Magnus had just recognized that it was Allie when a second crash sounded and another figure came charging after her. Cursing, he burst into a run.

Allie knew Stephen wasn't far behind her. She could tell by the sound of his footsteps that he was closing the distance, and desperately put on a burst of speed as she raced down the open area between two rows of columns that seemed to stretch on forever. But she also started to look for the nearest exit. She'd jump through a window if necessary. She had to get away and return to the house before Magnus made a choice she might not be able to forgive.

A shout caught her ear and drew her attention to a figure rushing toward her on the right. She instinctively veered left, and then recognized Magnus's voice as he shouted her name. Without even thinking, she switched direction, pulling on the last bit of strength she had to put on a burst of more speed as she felt Stephen's hand brush down her back, grabbing at her.

Magnus wasn't expecting that and wasn't prepared for it when she crashed into him, sending them both slamming to the ground. She heard the skitter of something heavy sliding across the concrete floor, and then was thrown violently away to the side. Grunting as she hit the ground and rolled, Allie threw out a hand to catch herself, and turned to look back, just in time to see Stephen bring down his machete. Magnus tried to roll out of the way, but the blade caught him in the shoulder, bringing a grunt of pain from him.

It would have hit her had Magnus not tossed her aside, Allie realized, and then spotted another machete, or perhaps a sword, just inches away from her right hand. Snatching it up, she launched herself to her feet as Stephen pulled his machete free. She was vaguely aware of someone else rushing toward them, but when Stephen raised his machete in preparation of another blow on Magnus, Allie reacted instinctively. Shrieking, "No!" she rushed forward and swung at his throat like it was a baseball and she held a bat. Unwilling to have to witness what was about to happen, she then closed her eyes just before the blade made contact. Allie felt it, though, and knew she'd hit her mark. She also heard a wet thud followed by another as the man fell.

Opening her eyes, she sought out Magnus, relief coursing through her when she saw he was getting to his feet. He was alive, but injured, his arm hanging at an odd angle.

"Are you all right?" Magnus asked with concern when she hurried to him.

"Me?" Allie asked with amazement. "You're bleeding."

"I am fine," he assured her, his gaze sliding over her bloody face and then up to her head wound. "You are hurt."

Allie opened her mouth to assure him she'd be fine, but then stiffened at the sound of the rusty hinges of the stairwell door squealing as it was opened in the room beyond this one. She hadn't noticed it making noise when she'd crashed through it, but perhaps it had opened too quickly then to squeal.

"That'll be Abaddon," she whispered anxiously, and then a loud anguished roar echoed through the cavernous room.

Swallowing, Allie tightened her grip on the sword she held and spun around to face the rogue.

Abaddon stood frozen just feet away, horror and despair on his face as he stared down at Stephen, she saw, and then noticed Lucian Argeneau and a couple she didn't know coming through the arch and approaching the rogue from behind. While Allie had never seen the couple before, the woman had the same white-blond hair and silver blue eyes as Lucian. A relative was her guess and she wondered if this was the couple everyone had been worried about. Basha and Marcus.

"You killed my life mate," Abaddon growled, drawing Allie's attention again. His eyes were glowing pure silver with emotion as he glared at her, and his fangs were even now sliding down out of his upper jaw, she saw with fascination, and then felt Magnus catch her arm and draw her back against him.

She noticed movement out of the corner of her eye and looked around to see Tybo moving up beside her, but then the woman's cold voice pierced the silence. "Couldn't have happened to a nicer guy, eh, Abby?"

Allie swung her gaze back to the man in time to see him spin around to face the newcomers. The men had stopped walking, leaving the woman to continue forward alone, and she was hefting a sword like the one Allie was holding.

"Basha!" The man spat the word even as the blonde swung her sword. The blade sliced clean through his neck, sending his head tumbling to the floor. His body remained upright for a moment, blood spurting from the open wound, and then dropped heavily to the ground.

"Ewww," Allie said with disgust, whirling toward Magnus and burying her head in the uninjured side of his chest.

There was a moment of silence, and then Tybo gave a disbelieving laugh. "Ewww? You just did the same thing to his buddy over there not two minutes ago."

"Yeah, but I didn't look when I did it," Allie muttered, easing back from Magnus a little, afraid she might cause him pain.

"What?" Tybo squawked with disbelief, even as Magnus peered down at her with shock.

Lifting her head, she turned to frown at the Enforcer and explained, "I closed my eyes."

"You closed your eyes while cutting off a man's head?" Tybo asked with horror.

"Well, I didn't want to see his head come off," she said defensively.

Tybo stared at her for a moment, and then turned his gaze to Magnus. "Magnus, buddy . . . *she closed her eyes*. I mean, who does that while wielding a sword?"

"My wife apparently," Magnus said mildly.

Allie sighed with relief when she saw the grin pulling at his lips and pushing away his pained expression. He would be okay.

Raising his hand, Magnus brushed it lightly down her cheek and added, "Is she not magnificent?"

Allie smiled in surprise, and then reached up to cover his hand, her expression becoming solemn. "Magnus, I promised myself I'd tell you this if I survived today, so . . ." Pausing, she took a deep breath, and then blurted, "I think I might be falling in love with you."

Magnus stilled, his smile replaced with an expression of wonder. "You do?"

"Yes. I'm quite certain I do," she said, and then wanting to be honest, admitted, "Well, seventy-five percent certain anyway . . . Or maybe sixty-five."

"Your certainty is decreasing by the minute," he pointed out dryly as Tybo started to chuckle.

Allie frowned, and then sighed with frustration and said, "Well, I've never been in love before. How do I know this isn't just lust, combined with liking and respect?"

"Actually," Magnus said gently. "I believe that might be the very definition of love."

"No," she said, shaking her head, and then, "Really?"

"It is, and you are," Lucian said dryly. "Now can we clean up this mess and get out of here? I have a wife and children at home that I would like to see before the sun rises."

When Allie turned to scowl at the man, he looked her over more closely and then shifted his gaze to Magnus and grimaced. "On second thought, Magnus, take your woman to the van. You both need blood. We can handle this."

"Allie! Oh, thank God they found you! I've been so worried."

Allie shifted to the side to look past Lucian at that cry, a smile of relief curving her lips when she saw Drina rushing toward them with Harper, Teddy, and Tricia on her heels. You couldn't tell by looking at her that she'd had the top of her head sliced off by a machete a couple of hours earlier. The woman looked as good as new if a little pale.

"Yes, yes, we found her," Lucian said impatiently as Drina and Tricia reached Allie and hugged her one after the other, murmuring over her head wound. "Now she and Magnus need blood, and so do you, Drina. You are still healing and pale. Harper, take the three of them to the van, give them blood, and drive them home. The rest of us can take care of this."

"There are live mortals in the basement," Allie heard Teddy say as Harper began to usher her, Drina, and Magnus away. "They're locked in a room someone had written Livestock on with a marker," he added dryly. "Some are in bad shape. They'll need tending and their memories wiped."

"Victor, DJ, and I will tend to them," Lucian decided. "The rest of you drag what is left of Abaddon and Liam's father out behind the building and burn them."

"I am so relieved we found you before anything horrible happened. Well, more horrible than that head wound you have," Drina said, drawing her attention. Concern cresting her face now, Drina added, "My God, your head must hurt."

"Not as bad as it did," Allie assured her. "And I'm glad to see you too. You were in pretty bad shape when Stephen carried me off." She grimaced at the memory. Drina's wound would have been a death blow on a mortal.

"You saved my life," Drina said solemnly. "He was

aiming for my neck when your shout made me turn and duck. If you had not done that I would have lost my head. I would have died."

Allie shook her head. "Only if your head wasn't returned to your neck quickly, and Tricia or someone would have done that right away."

"No, Allie. I am pregnant," Drina said solemnly, and assured her, "You saved my life."

"Pregnant?" Allie asked with surprise, and then pulled free of the hand Magnus had on her arm to stop and hug the woman. "Congratulations. Do you know if it's a boy or a girl?"

"Not yet," Drina said with a small smile as they pulled apart and continued to walk, heading for a set of double doors that were hanging half off their hinges. Allie could see a parking lot and the night sky through the opening.

"Allie, you are swaying on your feet. Are you all right?" Harper asked with concern as they neared the doors.

"I'm fine," Allie assured him, but frowned as she realized she *was* swaying a bit. She was also leaning heavily on the hold Magnus had on her arm, and she realized that now that the panic was over, her adrenaline was waning and apparently taking her strength with it.

"I am going to run ahead and get the van," Harper announced, starting to move a little more quickly. "Wait for me at the doors and I shall come and collect you."

The moment they murmured their agreement, he burst into a run that quickly carried him out of the building and out of sight.

"Harper and I have always split our time between Toronto, Italy, and Port Henry," Drina murmured as they paused at the open doors of the building and looked out. "But now that we're going to have a child, we have decided to buy a house in Port Henry and spend most of our time here."

"Oh, that'll be great," Allie said with a smile, leaning against the door frame to take her weight off of Magnus. "The baby will have kids to play with and you'll have Elvi, Mabel, and Tricia."

"Yes." Drina smiled, and then asked, "What about you two? Abaddon is gone now. You could settle here too."

"Oh." Allie glanced uncertainly to Magnus. She wanted to say hell yeah, she was staying in Port Henry. She'd love that. Both for herself and Liam. But where she lived wasn't just her decision anymore . . . a rather annoying realization for someone who had been independent for her entire adult life.

"Liam seems very happy here," Magnus murmured, pressing a hand to his wound. "And I think it would be nice for him to grow up with friends."

"Yes, but would you be happy here? What about your castle?" Allie asked with concern, and not just for where he wanted to live. Magnus was trying not to show that he was in pain, but she would guess he was suffering as much as she was, and she was suffering pretty badly now that the excitement was over. Enough that while she wasn't looking forward to the pain of healing, she would take it to get to the after healing.

"We could always use the castle as a vacation home,"

he said. "As I told you, my love. I will be happy wherever you and Liam are. Wherever the two of you are is home. Which reminds me," he muttered, and pulled out his phone. "I promised him I would call the minute we got you back."

Allie's eyes widened and then a smile began to pull at her lips as he punched in the number to the house and spoke briefly to Stephanie before asking for Liam. Magnus put the call on speakerphone as they waited for Stephanie to fetch Liam and they both smiled when his young voice greeted them with, "Did you find her?"

"Yes. We found her," Magnus assured him. "And we are on our way back."

"Yes!" Liam shouted, and then, "I knew you'd save her. Now we can be a family, Dad."

Allie felt her heart stutter when Liam called Magnus that. It was so unexpected . . . and sweet.

"We *are* a family now," Magnus said firmly, and then smiled wryly at her and admitted, "But I fear I did not save your mother so much as she saved herself . . . and me."

"But Magnus saved me first," Allie said at once, not willing to let him diminish what he'd done. The man had pushed her out of the way of the machete, knowing it would leave him unprotected from the coming blow.

"That's what families do," Liam said solemnly. "They save each other."

"Yes, they do," Allie said quietly, and decided she

must have brain damage from that blow to her head, because tears were welling up in her eyes.

"I love you, Mom."

"I love you too, son," Allie said softly, and then cleared her throat and added, "You go on and play with your friends. We should be home soon."

"Okay," Liam said at once. "Can we have pizza when you get back? Teddy says pizza is awesome. Why have we never had pizza?"

Because we didn't have money for things like that by the time you were old enough to eat it, Allie thought, but Magnus said, "We can have pizza. Tell Stephanie to order enough for everyone and we will celebrate that you and your mother are free of the bad men and never have to move again."

"Really?" Liam squealed. "You smoked them?"

"Smoked them?" Allie whispered with disbelief.

Where had her son heard words like that? she wondered as Magnus said, "Well, actually, Basha smoked one."

"Yeah, Teddy says Basha is badass."

Allie's jaw dropped at that. Liam had never sworn before in his life. She reached for the phone, ready to give him hell and threaten to wash his mouth out with soap, but Magnus turned so she couldn't take it and said, "Yes, well, so is your mother, son, because she smoked the other one."

"Really?" Liam sounded shocked, and Allie scowled. First cussing, and now thinking her helpless. Who had kept him alive for the last four years?

Well, as it turned out Liam wasn't in any physical danger, really, but he'd certainly been in danger of—

"Yes, really," Magnus said, distracting her. "But I suggest you drop the word *badass* from your vocabulary until you are older, or we are going to have to have a serious talk. Understand?"

"Yes, sir, Dad," Liam said at once.

"Good boy," Magnus said warmly. "Now, say goodbye to your mother and give the phone back to Stephanie."

"Bye, Mom," Liam said

He must have immediately handed the phone to Stephanie because she heard a rustling sound and then Stephanie's slightly muffled voice saying, "Go ahead. I'll be there in a minute."

Allie didn't listen to Magnus's conversation with Stephanie. Mostly she just stared at him, thoughts chugging slowly through her head. Magnus had played the heavy with Liam about his choice of language, sparing her from being the bad guy for a change. But he'd also done it well in her opinion, being firm but following it with love. And she hadn't been lying to Liam. Magnus *had* saved her life when he'd pushed her away as Stephen was about to have at her with the machete. She had no doubt he had been aiming to take her head. But Magnus had saved her from that, and had done so despite the fact that it had put him at risk and seen him terribly wounded. And the man was willing to give up his castle and use it as a vacation spot to live here in Port Henry to make her and Liam happy.

Added to the constant thoughtfulness he'd already shown her, as well as the passion he gave her, Magnus Bjarnesen was really something special. His love was nothing like the versions of love that she'd experienced growing up. He would never stand by and watch her die. She was quite sure he would fight for her with his last dying breath. And Allie thought she might do the same for him. He was a man worthy of that kind of love . . . and she was now one hundred percent certain she did love him. Because just looking at him right now was making her heart hurt and filling her with a longing to take him in her arms and simply hold him and never let go.

"Allie?" Drina said quietly.

"Hmm?" Allie turned to smile at her, promising herself she would tell Magnus that she definitely did love him later, when they were alone.

"I've been thinking," Drina said, her hand moving to her stomach. "If I haven't lost this baby . . ."

"Yes?" Allie asked when she hesitated.

"Well, you know Elvi, Mabel, and Tricia deliberately had babies at the same time so their kids could be friends, right?"

"Did they?" Allie asked, but wasn't really surprised. It actually sounded kind of smart to her.

"Yes, they did," Drina assured her. "And, well, I've been thinking," she began, and Allie listened to her plan with mounting interest.

Epilogue

"Time to wake up, sleepyhead. Your surprise baby shower is in thirty minutes."

Allie groaned in protest at having to get up, but then smiled when she felt Magnus's chest against her back and his arm slip around her very large waist. Yawning sleepily, she covered his hand on her belly with her own, and muttered, "It's hardly a secret. Drina figured it out weeks ago and told the rest of us."

"Yes, but you, Leonora, Dawn, and Drina will all act surprised to keep from upsetting Mabel and Elvi, who have worked very hard to arrange this surprise combined baby shower for the four of you."

"Yes, we will," she agreed, snuggling back against his groin and wiggling her bottom.

"None of that, wife. We don't have time for any of that nonsense today," he reprimanded, removing his hand and rolling away from her to get out of bed.

"Meanie," she accused, sitting up to scowl at him as he pulled on his jeans. "You know, I'm pretty sure withholding conjugal rights is illegal. Or should be."

Magnus chuckled at the claim, and reminded her, "We just woke up from a postcoital bout of unconsciousness."

"Postcoital bout of unconsciousness," Allie echoed with amusement. "God, you turn me on when you talk all highfalutin' like that."

"Everything turns you on," he countered with a grin as he did up his jeans.

"Everything about you does," she agreed, unembarrassed.

"Hmm." Crawling halfway onto the bed again, he gave her a hard, thorough kiss, and then broke it to lean his forehead against hers and admitted, "Everything about you turns me on too."

Allie snorted at that. "I'm bloated, tired all the time, have swollen ankles, and a big fat belly."

"I love your big fat belly," he assured her, running one hand over her extended stomach. "It's holding our child while it develops and grows."

Allie smiled softly and covered his hand. "Have I told you I love you yet today?"

"Only three or four times," he said with a soft smile. "I was beginning to worry that you might be tiring of me."

"Never," she assured him, and then bit her lip and leaned back to peer at him. "I've been thinking of names for the baby."

"So have I," he said solemnly, sitting on the side of

the bed and taking her hand in his. Before she could say anything else, he asked, "How do you feel about Stella if it's a girl?"

Allie's eyes widened. "Really?"

Magnus nodded solemnly. "I think it would be fitting to name our daughter after the woman who gave us our son, and helped bring us together."

"Yes," Allie breathed, tears filling her eyes. "I'd like that. In fact, I was about to suggest it myself."

"Perfect. Then it's settled," he said, kissing her hand. Releasing her then, Magnus stood and grabbed his shirt to pull it on as well.

"But what if it's a boy?" Allie asked, slipping out of bed now to find her own clothes.

Magnus paused in the act of doing up his shirt, and then shrugged. "I picked our daughter's name. You get to choose for our son if we have one."

Allie was silent a moment as she dressed, but as she did up the light summer dress she'd donned, she said, "Then I think I would like Erik."

When Magnus turned to her with surprise, she pointed out, "He was your friend, and if he hadn't convinced you to go a'viking, you never would have been turned and I never would have met you."

Magnus nodded solemnly and walked over to slip his arms around her. "Then Erik, it is."

Allie smiled, but then asked anxiously, "Are you sorry we're having a child right away like this?"

"No, of course not. As I said when you told me about Drina's plan the night we killed Abaddon, I have *always* wanted a family."

"Yes. But I've been worrying that you just agreed to make me happy. Most newly married couples want a little time to enjoy each other before—"

"Allie, my love," he interrupted. "We have hundreds of years to enjoy each other. Besides, with Drina, Leonora, and Edward's Dawn all having babies too, our child will be as lucky as their brother, and have friends and playmates to grow up with. That is a rare and wonderful thing."

Allie relaxed, and then rose up on her tiptoes to kiss him lightly on the chin, "*You* are rare and wonderful, Magnus. I love you."

"Allie, I have lived more than twelve hundred years and can tell you without any doubt at all that you are the most rare and wonderful find in this world." He kissed her softly on the lips and then took her hand to lead her to the door to the hall, adding, "And I have lived everywhere in this world."

"Everywhere?" she asked with interest. Magnus had told her some of his history, but he had a *lot* of history. Twelve hundred years' worth, and they were both too easily distracted by each other and ended up making love before he could tell more than one story. Fortunately, they had a long future in front of them; she'd hear it all eventually.

"Everywhere," Magnus assured her now, and then added wryly, "But never did I imagine I would end up living in Baby Central and so happily."

Allie burst out laughing at that comment. She always found it amusing that the men had taken to calling Port Henry Baby Central, and was still smiling over the name as Magnus ushered her out of the house. Pausing on the back deck of their new home, she glanced over the large backyard. It was actually the combined backyards of Casey Cottage, Mabel and DJ's house, and now Allie and Magnus's own home beside Casey Cottage as well as the house backing theirs.

The minute Magnus had heard that Elvi's neighbor was considering moving his family to the city and selling their house here in Port Henry, he'd walked next door and made a very generous offer. Shortly after, Harper and Drina had bought the house next to Mabel and DJ's.

It all felt perfect to Allie, and as she stood there she pondered how funny life could be. She had never imagined she would marry, and her life had never been easy before coming to Port Henry, and yet here she was not just married, but happily, and with those bad times nothing more than a memory. Oh, she wasn't foolish enough to think that hard times wouldn't come again. That was part of life. But she knew they would pass, and she could survive them so long as she had Magnus at her side. In truth, their love was really the most rare and wonderful find in this world, and she thanked God for it every day.

The clang of a screen door drew her gaze to Elvi and Victor's house and Allie smiled when she saw Liam rush to the deck railing to wave at them.

"There you are," he said, sounding excited and impatient all at once. "Elvi sent me to get you. Us kids want to play alligator island and Elvi says Dad has to make the tape islands for us."

"All right," Magnus said easily, taking Allie's hand as they started across the yard to the deck. "Tell her we're coming."

Liam nodded happily and whirled to rush back into Casey Cottage.

The moment the door closed, Magnus squeezed her hand and asked, "Have I told you that I love you and our son yet today?"

Allie's smile widened. "Only three or four times. I was beginning to worry you were tiring of us."

"Never," he assured her as he released her hand to wrap his arm around her instead, and Allie leaned into his chest, believing him.

ABOUT GOLLANCZ

Gollancz is the oldest SF publishing imprint in the world. Since being founded in 1927 Gollancz has continued to publish a focused selection of bestselling and award-winning authors. The front-list includes **Ben Aaronovitch**, **Joe Abercrombie**, **Charlaine Harris**, **Joanne Harris**, **Joe Hill**, **Alastair Reynolds**, **Patrick Rothfuss**, **Nalini Singh** and **Brandon Sanderson**.

As one of the largest Science Fiction and Fantasy imprints in the UK it is no surprise we have one of the most extensive backlists in the world. Find high-quality SF on Gateway written by such authors as **Philip K. Dick**, **Ursula Le Guin**, **Connie Willis**, **Sir Arthur C. Clarke**, **Pat Cadigan**, **Michael Moorcock** and **George R.R. Martin**.

We also have a strand of publishing in translation, which includes French, Polish and Russian authors. Gollancz is home to more award-winning authors than any other imprint, with names including **Aliette de Bodard**, **M. John Harrison**, **Paul McAuley**, **Sarah Pinborough**, **Pierre Pevel**, **Justina Robson** and many more.

The SF Gateway
More than 3,000 classic, rare and previously out-of-print SF novels at your fingertips.
www.sfgateway.com

The Gollancz Blog
Bringing you news from our worlds to yours. Stories, interviews, articles and exclusive extracts just for you!
www.gollancz.co.uk

GOLLANCZ
LONDON